RAVENTOWER & MERRIWEATHER

3: MISSING

By

LAZETTE GIFFORD

Raventower & Merriweather 3: Missing
A Conspiracy of Authors Publication
www.aconspiracyofauthors.com
Copyright © 2020, Lazette Gifford
ISBN: 978-1-936507-92-4

Cover Art: Copyright © 2020, Lazette Gifford

First Print Edition, February 2020

Dedicated to Russ who is the best friend a person could ever have and who has never stopped believing I can do this writing and publishing thing.

Thank you.

TABLE OF CONTENTS

CHAPTER ONE

Something howled through Mica's nightmare, a loud wail that rose and fell and returned once more to send a shiver through him. Something wrong, and he didn't even know what to do to fix it this time. Did he hear the whisper of a lost god? Of his dead father, freed from the clock where he'd stored his soul for so long? Were they coming for him, all the dead he'd seen, touched -- given over to clockwork creatures? They'd stayed of their own accord, hadn't they?

The howling could be anything. The howling could be --

Mica opened his eyes.

The howling could be the wind of a fierce winter storm as it rushed past the window of his tower bedroom. Home. Safe and home in his own bed. The dawn had come, and for a moment he could pretend that all was well.

Mica turned slightly and stifled both a moan and muttered a curse. Every part of his body ached today. There were pains he could not even name, and they were persistent enough to wake him entirely on this miserable cold day. He could not fall back asleep, no matter how he pulled the blanket up higher around him or how tightly he closed his eyes against the growing gray light that filtered in around the edges of the shutters. He really needed to fix that problem.

And the wind still howled.

Mica cursed again and sat up, grabbing his night robe and pulling it tight around him, hoping to block some of the breezes that leaked in around the window. The steam heat worked, at least. When he'd first returned to Raventower, ice was apt to form anywhere but the kitchen during winter.

Today Mica could go and take a shower with water heated by the steam system that heated the room. He could go down to the kitchen and find out what wondrous things Ada had made for his homecoming. He didn't have to go out into the cold.

Merriweather would be there. She had, he suspected, already gotten up and gone down to check things out. That got him moving out of the bed, feet on the nice, though cold, carpet. He pushed aside the shutter just enough to see what he had expected; snow fell in a white sheet that blocked the view of even the courtyard below. Ice had cracked as he moved the outer covering with a slight bell-like sound. It all would have been pretty if it hadn't been so cold.

A good day to be home.

Mica didn't take long to shower, avoided trying to count bruises and cuts, and dressed in warm clothing. The battle with the Atrians was at least over for the moment. Maybe even for the entire winter -- that thought put him in a better mood. By the time he'd done dressing, Mica had gotten used to some of the pains and thought he could present himself as something less than an invalid limping along and cursing the world.

As he had expected, Merriweather's door stood open and her room was empty. He tried not to be embarrassed. She was, after all, a soldier, and used to early hours. He was a clockwork scientist with a dubious link to the realities of daily life.

Mica stopped at the stairwell and looked up and down. One flight led up to his workshop, a place he'd missed dearly of late. He almost went there, just to tinker around for a little while - but the idea of breakfast drew him downstairs instead, one limping step after another while he tried not to moan where anyone might hear him.

The lower of the old tower's floors smelled of everything he had hoped: exotic spices, baked goods, fruits, and herbs. Ada had the food ready almost before he sat down. The older woman smiled brightly at his arrival. Merriweather already sat at the table, her fingers wrapped around a cup of tea, and the others were there as well -- Nyle, Roe, and Fern, plus Gran and even Shipley. Bear, the huge, long-haired dog, stretched out atop of the steps leading down to the kitchen and kept well away from the heat of the hearth today. He probably thought longingly about romping in the snow.

They had an excellent breakfast, all of them pleased. No one spoke about any type of work, except that Ada and Gram talked about cooking more food. Neither Mica nor his friends could not see the wreckage of the city from here which meant they could avoid the memory of the war for a little while longer. Mica appreciated the break from the constant feel of disaster lurking nearby. They couldn't even see or hear the winter storm, although sometimes the hearth gave a little huff of sound as a bit of wind found its long way down the chimney.

Reality came back to them before the meal was finished. The knocker pounded. Nyle waved the others to stay seated and went up the steps toward the main floor and the big door. Merriweather looked likely to follow him but changed her mind.

"We have an entire company of soldiers out there," she said when Mica looked her way, curious at her sudden trust. "Nothing bad is going to get through to knock on the door."

A cold breeze blew past and a moment later the door closed again. Nyle came back with an envelope and dropped it in front of Mica by his teacup. "Looks like it is from your brother."

"Yes," Mica agreed, studying the seal with some trepidation. *Official.* Not even something come by one of Mica's clockwork ravens, though then that might not have been possible in this weather. It had looked like a major storm.

The last thing Mica wanted to face this morning was some official missive from General Gregorian Raventower.

"You might as well read it," Merriweather said with a sigh -- so he wasn't the only one with feelings of distrust toward the inoffensive beige paper and blue wax seal.

He broke the seal and pulled the paper open.

The King has a job he would like you and Merriweather to do for him.

"Damn." Mica read it over again as though the words might change. Then he passed the paper to Merriweather who took the paper with two fingers as though she feared the note would bite.

"This can't be good," she mumbled after she'd read the words. "I should hate to think that King Abertus believes we're actually competent because of the last few days."

That won a slight laugh from Mica and grins from the others. He wanted to pass this off as just a minor problem, and something they need not worry too much about -- no. Gregorian wouldn't have sent that note today, and especially in this weather, if it were a minor problem. Gregorian knew what hell Mica and Merriweather had gone through already. This had to mean something dire.

Gregorian did not order them to come to the palace immediately, but the implication that they should hurry was there in those sparse words. The King wanted their help and the King did not deal with minor matters.

When Mica looked at Merriweather, he would tell that she felt the same way. He nibbled at his toast and marmalade, barely noting the taste. Was this something more with the war?

They had barely gotten past the battle with Atria, but that didn't mean the enemy had entirely given up. Though, with their god gone -- if not destroyed -- they might have trouble getting the drive they needed for another try at an invasion.

"I'll arrange for our escort," Merriweather said as she stood, though with obvious reluctance. "I'll come back in and have more tea before we leave. Finish this fine food."

"Oh, but do you have to go in such bad weather?" Ada said with a shake of her head.

"We're asked to the palace," Mica said. He tried not to sound annoyed and depressed. "This has to be something important. Gregorian wouldn't have sent for us in this weather otherwise."

Gregorian didn't say why they were wanted which was another worrisome piece to this note. Mica took up the paper and read it over again as though he might have missed something in the single line. He hadn't, so he put the note away in his vest.

Roe and Nyle got up and went on about their business, Roe even daring a hand on Mica's shoulder when he started past. "It's good to have you back, my lord. Whatever this new trouble is, do be careful. Things aren't altogether settled."

"We'll be careful," Mica promised and smiled.

Damn, he just wanted to stay home.

Mica felt the cold brush of air as Merriweather opened the door and stepped outside as the cold rushed into this warm haven. Even Bear moved out of the draft. They would be taking horses in this weather, Mica supposed, and not a lovely comfy carriage where he could stretch out a bit and cover up in blankets. They would also have the guard. He thought about taking Kandris, his magnificent clockwork horse, but the metal would be cold as ice in this weather, even though the cold would not affect the animal.

Ada fussed over him as she always did and managed to

lighten his mood. Merriweather came back, trailing some snow after her even though she left her cloak at the door.

"They'll be ready." She sat down and nodded her thanks to Fern who poured her warm tea. "It's going to be a cold ride, but the guard tells me they've heard of no serious trouble in the city."

"Good." Mica sat up straighter, ready to put on a show for the others. He would not go out there looking sullen and bad tempered.

This was only a ride through town and talk to the King and Gregorian. They'd dealt with misplaced gods and haunted statues. He had become the High Priest of Torger -- or maybe he was the high priest of Seldon, since that was the God's current incarnation, and someone he had already considered a friend all this life before he had learned the truth.

What could the King want with him now?

Merriweather stood. Mica sighed and did the same, knowing it was time to face the storm. Maybe the weather would be too daunting, and they'd have to turn back? He could hope for that answer and a delay in facing more trouble. Mica still hadn't gotten up to his workshop, and as they headed out of the kitchen, he looked upward with a sigh of regret. Tippet would be up there, still waiting for him. He thought Fern kept the little clockwork dog company when he wasn't around, though. Ada had hinted at it in the past.

Mica and Merriweather pulled on winter boots, long hooded cloaks, and wrapped themselves in scarves and donned gloves. He gave one last wave to the others who had come to watch, and then followed Merriweather out into the white world beyond the door.

The wind howled around them.

"I suppose we really have to go, don't we?" Mica asked as they carefully headed for the horses that the soldiers held ready at the bottom of the stairs.

"I would be glad to go alone and come back, my lord," Merriweather said, all proper guard again.

"What? Go off and get into some trouble without me?"

"You can't have it both ways," she reminded him.

He was already swinging up into the saddle and trying not to moan at the movement. Maybe the cold would be a bit of a blessing if he lost the feeling of aches and pains.

"I suppose you are going to be the voice of logic, right?" he said.

"One of us has to be."

Two of the soldiers looked away with sudden coughing fits. Merriweather grinned slightly at Mica, and he wondered if the others realized how much she enjoyed the word games they played. It was a pleasure to talk to her. Mica had never been one of those fools who thought women were lesser beings, though he did have trouble connecting with them too often -- but then he had the same problem with men, he supposed. They were no more interested in making clockwork butterflies than the women had been. Gregorian's wife had tried to find him a bride. Someday he would have to ask her just what she had thought when she presented some of those women to him. It certainly wasn't anything to do with anything approaching intelligent conversation.

As they started away, Mica looked back at Raventower itself, the old battered building still standing tall over the craggy cliffs that led down to the sea. The wind blew from north to south, and ice and snow had covered this side of the vast building. He could see one of the windows to his workshop, the shutters pulled tight and ice plastering it. The room would have been cold and drafty even with the fireplace going, he supposed. He had looked forward to a few days there, working with clockwork butterflies and maybe even talking to Merriweather about their distant wedding. Nothing more serious than that bit of fun.

Soldiers still camped in the courtyard. He wondered how long until Gregorian called the watchdogs off -- though maybe he was wise. They had beaten back the Atrians, but they had tried to kill Mica more than once. There might still be soldiers or assassins hiding in the ruins. That made going out into the storm even less appealing.

The resident soldiers were camped in tents placed near fizzling fires. If the weather got any worse, they knew enough to move into the tower for the duration, so he didn't feel too guilty about seeing them huddled in blankets and sipping from steaming cups. Half a dozen of the men already sat on horses, the animals stomping their feet in the growing snow and no one looking happy.

Mica only paused to look over Kandris; the clockwork horse moved away from the wall. The horse looked forlorn, having lost his partner and now relegated to staying inside the keep. Mica almost changed mounts, but a brush of his hand on the metal brought a chill even through the gloves.

"Sorry, but not until the weather is better," Mica said and patted the horse when he neared. Their live mounts were a little anxious but didn't try to bolt. Kandris glanced out the open gate and then gave a nod of understanding. Well, maybe he didn't want to go out into the cold weather either, now that Mica thought about it.

The soldiers seemed resigned to the ride, though. Probably, they thought about what would happen if they let Mica out on his own. What General Gregorian Raventower might do to them if something happened to his younger brother did not encourage the risk. Mica couldn't say he liked the constant feel of having people hanging over him, but he did understand. So did Merriweather. She was still tasked with keeping him alive and having a few extra eyes and swords probably seemed a blessing to her.

The gate opened wider with a slight grinding sound that

made Mica wince.

"I'll need to check the clockwork mechanism," he said aloud and won a nod from Merriweather and glances from the others. Mica looked back at the building as well. "And I'll need to make certain the tower didn't take any extensive damage. I should have told Nyle and Roe to start looking for cracked walls --"

"I suspect they already have looked, you know," Merriweather replied. The gate squealed closed behind them, and the steep road to the lower ground curved downward amid drifts of snow. The horses were not sure-footed here. "They are as fond of that place as you are, my lord."

"Yes, I suppose so," he replied and held his horse to one slow step at a time. He glanced at Merriweather but said nothing --

"Yes, I am fond of the place, too," she said aloud.

He grinned. "I hope that it's stood up well. It would be a shame to lose the place now."

"Yes, it would," she agreed and glanced back over her shoulder.

Mica's older brother and sister didn't care for Raventower. Lately, he had wondered if his draw to the place had to do with being a high priest and the tower having been built over the site of an old temple. Now though -- no, he thought the draw was his own. He was a Raventower, and this was the tower that had been in their family for centuries. Honoria and Gregorian had moved on to other lives, but he had never wanted more than to be part of this unique home. It probably helped that he didn't like to socialize much, and Raventower was not a place people came to stay.

They reached the bottom of the hill with nothing more than one horse bumping another and both animals getting so annoyed that the riders had to take positions as far apart as possible.

The road curved continued to curve downward from here to the fishing village that sat at the edge of the Raventower cliffs. Those buildings had taken damage that Mica could see even in the fall of snow. Men and women were out in the weather and trying to make repairs despite the storm. He needed to do something for them. They had stood with him and helped in a dark time.

Truth be told, Mica got along better with most of them than he did with any of his peers. The other lords all thought him odd. He didn't disagree, but their complaints tended to be more about the company he kept -- like fishermen -- and not that he built clockwork creatures.

Granted, neither side knew about his link to the newly dead or the fact that some of his clockwork creatures had the souls of recently deceased humans. Mica had no intention of letting those things be known.

The storm began to die down a bit, the snow lessening as the wind only came in gusts and howled very little around the ruins. The souls of the dead? That's what some might think, but Mica watched for pretty life lights instead.

Whatever battles and deaths had taken place on this stretch of road, they had happened long enough ago that the bodies had been removed and the dead souls moved on to -- wherever they went. Mica thought he might ask Seldon one day if he got up the nerve.

He bowed his head, but not so much against the cold. He didn't want to see the destruction all around them. Shadow Walk had looked oddly untouched, but it had been a slum before the war came, and it might have been difficult to note new damage amid the old ruins. He had seen smoke from a few chimneys in there though. No one would freeze with so many destroyed buildings and pieces of wood everywhere.

The scenery grew worse beyond that already blighted area. Buildings had fallen almost everywhere, though the main road had been cleared of debris. Mica knew this was not his fault, and yet he had been so intricately involved in everything that had happened that he couldn't help but feel a strong surge of responsibility. What if he had acted sooner? What if he had figured things out faster?

What if the assassins had killed him?

They rode along in silence, Merriweather alert for trouble while Mica considered all the things that might have gone wrong and hadn't, despite what he saw here. Kamere could have fallen to the Atrians. The entire country of Sedina would have been crushed, the people killed or enslaved. Argine, to the south, might have tried to help, but they'd have been too late. No one had expected the force of the attack that had been thrown against the city, despite the years of war they'd had with the Atrians.

Mica glanced out at the city once more, noting the sullen fires that were finally dying down in the storm, but also taking note of how much still stood, rather than everything that had fallen. He watched people working, even in this weather. Good people, here in this city. Kamere had suffered through disasters before, and it had always come back.

The Atrians had not won.

So, while he might have done better -- he might have done much worse, as well. That was something to remember on this miserable day. The signs of the war would disappear. Besides, the gods had been on their side -- literally on their side, though that was not something he wanted to think about right now. He didn't want to spend any more time working with those beings.

"I cannot imagine what the King might want of us, Merriweather," Mica finally admitted. The silence had become too filled with dire thoughts. They had gone wide of the temple district this time, the paths there still being cleared from what he could see.

"I hope it's not more trouble from the Atrians," Merriweather replied and glared out at the shadowed fallen walls and piles of debris, as though she might see one of the enemies at any moment. "I've seen no sign of new battles, though. Have any of the rest of you heard about any more trouble?"

"No, Captain Merriweather," the guard just ahead of her replied. He glanced around as though to even say such a thing might bring a fight down on them. Mica suspected they all felt that way, but at least Merriweather faced it head-on. "From what we have heard up at the tower, there's been very little going on at all. Scouting parties have found a few Atrians hiding in the city, but they seem to be just people who were left behind when the attack failed. I heard from the guard who came in last night that they've been no trouble. It's as though they lost all interest in why they even came here."

Now there was a fascinating insight, Mica thought. There had been considerable magic involved in the invasion. How much power did Atric have over his followers? Once they took Atric out of the equation -- one could not actually kill even part of a God, after all -- did he lose some special link to the warriors?

They had trapped Atric and he would not return. Mica had to believe that part because while Atric had been his enemy from the start, now he would be an enraged enemy and probably less sane. No, Mica did not want to think about Atric returning and wanting his temple back, which had once stood where Raventower now rose. He was only part of that old god, but powerful enough to be far too dangerous.

Mica could barely see a hint of the castle ahead of them, glad they were almost to their destination. Even that august building had taken some damage, though not as much as other parts of the city. They'd gotten lucky there, though Mica supposed some of the factory owners who had lost their buildings didn't feel the same way right now.

The castle, though, remained a sign of their power and a promise of their future. Maybe the others didn't realize the power of symbolism. Maybe they didn't look to the castle and understand that it meant Kamere and Sedina still stood, their pennants still flying.

Going there today didn't seem so bad after all. Maybe this was even a ride Mica had needed to make, to see the city and reconcile himself with all that had happened -- and to remember all the things that might have gone wrong and hadn't.

Yet.

What did the King want with them?

CHAPTER TWO

Mica began to take more note of the world, drawing his attention back. The damage appeared worse toward the shore and docks, and he didn't want to know what it was going to take to rebuild the port. The number of ships sunk in the bay would make the place dangerous for anything that sat low in the water. Ships would have to go to places like Fintail to the north, and then items would be carted down to the city from there.

Fintail was a charming little fishing village with a small, but adequate port. Soon they would have more business than they could handle. They were not going to enjoy the change.

To the other side of the road, in an area with fewer buildings and more uneven terrain, the ancients had laid out a large cemetery. Small statues and large rocks marked new graves where the disturbed ground was now frosted with snow. Mica did not look that way for long, but the impression of a vast, terraced field stayed with him.

They came across a spot where several priests and priestesses of the various temples were out clearing debris from an area where a few buildings still stood and must be harboring those who had lost homes. And there stood Honoria Raventower, Mica's older sister, helping. Well, she was directing at least. He hid his smile and pulled the hood closer to conceal his face as they rode on.

Merriweather glanced his way and stifled a laugh. "Typical."

"Her directing, or me hiding?" Mica asked.

"Both I suppose."

They reached the hill that led up to the castle, a road less steep and treacherous than the one they had taken down from Raventower. The old guard posts had been supplanted by new towers and shacks at every 500 feet, and the hill had a surrounding ditch that had not been there for long. The moved dirt still showed dark despite the falling snow, and yes - - even as he watched, a few men hauled up more soil and carted it over to a horse-drawn wagon. Mica wondered where they were dumping it.

Farther up the hillside, they found others digging up the ground and putting pikes into place, which would stop anyone on horseback from getting closer. Soldiers marched along the curtain wall that towered over them and watched out toward the sea, but Mica didn't think they could see even the shore through today's falling snow. They watched for a closer enemy, he supposed.

It was a depressing sight, making Mica realize that despite his best wishes, the war was not over.

On the other hand, a long line of people had just started down from the castle grounds where they had gone for safety. They carried a few meager belongings and small children, though several carts -- some pulled by men -- carried a few people who were clearly too weak or old to walk. Despite the weather, they appeared to be in good spirits.

They were mostly the poor, returning to their hovels and ready to rebuild what parts of their lives they could salvage. Mica would have thought they'd stay at least through the storm, though the morning spat of snow and wind seemed to have died down.

"Too early for them to leave," Merriweather mumbled to him with a shake of her head. "The King won't have kicked them out, so why are they going?"

"We know things were tense up there," Mica reminded her with a nod toward the towers and curtain walls above them. "It wouldn't take much to push that group into riots. They're smart to clear out. Except for food supplies, I imagine many of them won't be much worse than they were before the attack."

"True," she admitted. Her glance took in the road behind the castle, the one that led to better homes, protected in the castle's shadow. "No, don't say it. I already know my parents and the rest of the family are fine. The King asked for both of us to see him, so I'm not kiting off to visit them."

Mica nodded agreement, and they turned the horses to go past the first guard house. Here Mica put back his hood and so did Merriweather. Both were well known, but he had the feeling it was the sight of Captain Merriweather that got them through without question rather than the power of his title as a Lord of Kamere.

His pride was salvaged not long afterward, though.

"Lord Mica, sir!" a man called out from the line of refugees, and several others took up the call of greeting. They were all huddled in makeshift coverings made of rags and blankets, and their grim faces changed when they looked to him. People smiled, and children waved. "We're that glad to see you back, me Lord! People down in Shadow Walk ha' been worried about you!"

"And the fishing village," a woman added.

Mica and his guards stopped. The soldiers looked bothered, but Merriweather smiled. That's all he needed to see. He didn't get down -- that would be asking for trouble, but he did lean down to hear the news.

"What has happened that I should know about?" he asked.

"Oh, naught but what you've seen, I'd say," one of the men replied with a sidelong glance at the soldiers. The poor and the soldiers did not always get along, though that strain had mostly disappeared during the trouble. "The war was a vicious but short battle, weren't it, me Lord? They been held off. We don't need no more than that."

"I can't say how much damage there's been to your homes," Mica said with a glance back the way they'd ridden. "And this weather --"

"Oh, now, we've seen worse weather," the woman replied. She shifted a bag of goods on her shoulder, and a boy of about ten hung about her skirts, while another girl hovered nearby with another baby that she carried. They were all looked anxious to leave, he realized. "Why there's hardly a winter what goes by that we don't have to rebuild a good part of the Walk, you know. Heavy snows take down roofs. Two years ago, a dinner fire got out a hand and nearly took it all down -- but we be use to that and to rebuilding. The King says he'll send food when he can. That's better than what we usually get."

"And how often is the fishing village wiped out by a storm, eh?" said the man. "Best to get to it. Take care Lord Raventower, sir. Just know we're glad ta' have you back."

Several others nodded and moved on, so Mica and his guards headed up the trail again, a slow walk as people got out of the way, many of them still shouting greetings. Oh, he saw despair in many faces; they were not the happy poor, content with their world, but they wouldn't cause trouble at a time like this.

"No one asked me for anything," he said at last as they reached the final gate.

"Do they need to ask?" Merriweather replied.

Mica said nothing the rest of the way to the barbican,

though he did see Merriweather give him a pleased look or two. He didn't understand people; looking back at those who streamed out of the castle grounds, he thought about how Kamere would not be long in rebuilding. They were damaged, not destroyed, and those poor already going back to their homes were going to be the ones who did most of the labor. They were the heart of Kamere.

"We'll leave you here, Lord Raventower, Captain Merriweather," the soldier in the lead said as he pulled his horse back. The gate stood open, but a half dozen castle guard stood to the right and left, and more soldiers had taken their places in the tower overlooking the road. Nothing would get this close without being seen, though Mica worried about all the strangers who might dress like the poor and get close enough to do harm. "The castle guard will take you from this spot, and there will be other soldiers to see you back to the tower. We'll ride back now."

"Can you do me a favor?" Mica asked. The man gave him a dubious look, no doubt for the *favor* rather than an *order*. "When you get back, let Ada -- my cook -- know that the others are returning to their homes. She'll know what to do. I daresay she and Gram are probably already at work."

"I'll do that, sir," the man said and gave a proper bow, as best he could from the saddle.

Their guards rode away, moving carefully back down the road past the unfortunate poor who would go back to whatever was left of their lives. Of course, they had rebuilt before, but that didn't make this any easier.

The guards signaled he and Merriweather in, looking far more worried at having the two around.

"Do we draw trouble?" Mica asked with a glance at Merriweather.

"You really have to ask?" she said and gave a nervous glance back at the guards who were heading back to

Raventower while others moved in around them.

"I'm not sure what's normal," he admitted.

"Here's a clue, my Lord. We are not normal."

Someone laughed.

The guards got them through the iron gate, and into the King's world. Mica noted some damage to a couple of the outer walls, but they'd stood up well. They'd had a long, lingering war with Atria, though there had been few times it had broken out into a major battle, let alone something as vicious as the attack they'd just beaten back. Even so, they'd made certain of their defenses as best they could, and the castle was built to withstand more than a few bombardments from a couple airships. Lucky for all of them that the Atrians had such poor ships, he supposed. The design had been stolen from his own late father decades ago. They should have waited for a better model.

Just before Mica went inside the protecting outer walls, he turned back to see Raventower standing high over the landscape at the opposite end of the city. It could not compare in beauty to the Castle of the King, but he would not have traded them. Raventower was a symbol of remaining strong and protecting others, no matter what the situation or the consequences.

They rode through the twisting opening and into the castle grounds. The constant track of people in and out had turned the path and the land around it to muck and ice, the path so treacherous that the castle guard went on foot and took hold of the horses, two on each side. Merriweather frowned, but she didn't argue. Mica would have been just as glad to walk, but then they'd have been tracking everything into the building, he supposed.

The grounds were a mess, of course. Bushes where flattened by more than the snow and ice. Some of the fountains looked bathed in dirt, and he didn't think a single rose bush had survived, nor probably any of the other flowers. Mica winced as he thought about how bad this was going to look in the spring, as though that would be important when considering all the trouble that had happened.

Tents and hovels were still coming down under the work of the army, the men shouting and grunting, working hard in the cold winter air. Merriweather seemed to be especially interested in what was going on, and since others led the horses, they both had time to look at the worst of what had happened here.

"They did well here," Mica said aloud, reassuring himself as well as Merriweather. "It looks awful, but the King saved a lot of people we are desperately going to need, you know. Those were the locals who will rebuild the city, not people like you and me, Merriweather. Not the Lords and Ladies. We're going to need their good hands and strong backs if we want Kamere to be anything like it was before."

"True, my lord," Merriweather agreed and looked around with a nod this time. "Everything could have been much worse."

Mica didn't say the other thing he feared -- that the war was far from over yet. He didn't need to since everyone, including Merriweather, were still looking for trouble. They had beaten the enemy back, although even without Atric, the demigod who tried to lead them to victory, Mica feared that they would still be vicious. He feared they would return, and soon.

Should he turn all his life to that possibility? Live every day expecting the war to return? For how long? Oh, it would be a while as the Atrians regrouped. The people of Sedina would be fools to just pretend everything was over. Nevertheless, Mica would start looking toward a more peaceful future, especially since they had already beaten back the army led by a demigod. He was almost certain they'd only face humans after this.

Mica felt a little better for that thought.

They reached a spot where the tents and huts piled up for redistribution. Good. The people of the city didn't have much for supplies out there, and even a tarp for a roof and some wood to burn might make a difference over the next few days. What other supplies did they have at the tower that might help?

"I need Nyle to start making nails out of anything he can find," Mica said. "I should have thought of that before we went the soldiers off."

"We'll be back at the tower before long, Lord Raventower," Merriweather said, all proper here in the castle and before other members of the King's Guard, to which she officially belonged. "And like Ada and Gram, I wouldn't be at all surprised to find he's already busy at the job. They're aware of what will be needed and what you'll want to be done, you know."

"Meaning they don't need me."

"Probably not for that part," she admitted. "So, let's find out if the King has something you can do to keep you busy for a while. We might even keep you out of trouble."

A couple of the guards made amused sounds at that one -- so there, again, they spread a little more humor where they passed. Mica supposed that was important too.

The guards took them to the stairs at the ornate entrance to the castle. This area had been carefully cleared of snow, ice, and mud. He had been here, not so long ago, with Merriweather in a lovely dress ... such a memory made this easier to bear because he would work harder to have such a time again.

Mica took a deep breath before he headed up the steps with Merriweather. The guards would take care of the horses -- he saw a small makeshift enclosure to the left of the building, somewhat sheltered from the wind and storm, and already holding a few other horses. From the looks of things, he and Merriweather were not the only ones at the castle today, though he didn't see anything that pointed to other lords. They usually rode with banners and carriages. Mica didn't expect to see them out in this weather.

However, the King had expected him to come despite the weather, and maybe so that he would be here without the others. Interesting thought.

Extra guards stood at the door, but they were polite as they gave proper bows and salutes. Merriweather wasn't used to her rank yet, he noted, and probably because she had spent all the time with him, rather than with other soldiers. He'd have to ask if she wanted more time at the palace --

Well, not yet. They still had work to do, and Mica was not looking for a reason to send her away. He did, however, want Merriweather to be happy, and he knew that she had been intent on her career as a king's guard.

Mica had expected to find the entrance hall mostly empty. After all, the Queen and many of the others had been sent into the backcountry for safety -- including Gregorian's wife who was the King's daughter, and their children. This was not a place for any of them, and for a moment Mica wondered what it would take to pack up all the children in the city and send them somewhere safe.

Mica lost all track of that thought as they stepped inside. The area was crowded with faces, colors, voices -- more people than he'd ever seen in this little area, and for a moment he feared he would freeze as the servants worked their way through the others and took his cloak. Merriweather stood beside him, and she touched his arm, drawing his attention. He wondered when she had figured out that he had trouble with loud, noisy situations. Had Gregorian told her? Had Seldon?

Having her at his side helped. Mica watched Merriweather

for a moment until he got better control. Then he looked around the area and found something he hadn't expected. The room seemed to be crowded with priests and priestesses, all of them in little groups, the robes for various temples congregating into splashes of color against the white and gold walls. He had the odd feeling that they couldn't decide if they were staying or going.

Mica saw a few glares from one of the groups to another, but that had been normal before the war. He found those stares both amusing and hopeful in an odd way; they showed that not everything had changed. However, he wished all those people would clear the hall, or at least let Merriweather and him through.

Then, through the crowd, came someone else -- a person Mica would rather not have run into just now. He and Mayor Corinth were not friends, and the snarl that came to the older man's face showed that nothing had changed in the last few days. The tall, lanky man had looked annoyed even before he spotted Mica, but that moment of eye contact turned the man's attitude even more sour. He'd grown a thin, scraggly beard lately. It did not hide the man's weak chin.

No easy way to avoid him in this crowd, either.

Mica had hoped that they might just step aside and pass each other without any trouble. Corinth had other ideas, though. Mica could not begin to figure out why the man wanted a confrontation, and especially in front of this crowd, which held at least a couple high priests and priestesses.

Mica sighed and prepared for the usual harassment.

Merriweather had other ideas. She stepped forward and cut between them. Merriweather's hand almost went to her side and the pistol she carried, the hand twitching in that direction. There was no doubt she recognized the man as an enemy.

"Mayor Corinth," she said with a bow of her head. Polite,

though her voice sounded cold. "We have business in the castle." The man's face grew dark, and his mouth opened. "This is not the time or place to bother with any pettiness," she added.

Well, that was not going to win Corinth over, but then nothing would, so Merriweather might as well have fun and handle this. Corinth's face had gone from dark to red, to dark again, all in a matter of a few breaths.

"You, Merriweather, don't know your place --" the man began to snarl.

"My place, Mayor, is as a Captain of the King's Guard and assigned to get Lord Raventower to a meeting -- and precisely because of people like you."

"What are you implying?" he demanded.

"I am implying that you are standing right there and stopping us from getting to where we need to be," she said and with a bit of amusement this time. "Is there something more I should consider?"

That brought a new snarl. "How dare you --"

"If you want to discuss my position and my work, do take it up with General Gregorian."

"And should I trust another damned *Raventower*?" Corinth demanded with a snarl.

Oh, now that was the wrong thing to say. Mica started to react this time, but he didn't need to make any show of defending his brother. Protests began in the servants -- that surprised him -- and spread to priests and priestesses and on to the guards. Mayor Corinth had just made a severe mistake for a career politician. Gregorian had taken command and fought off the enemy here at the city. He was the hero of the day, and everyone in the town knew it.

Corinth had wanted a jab at Mica, but he'd taken the wrong path with that one. The man continued to stand there and glare at Mica as though he'd pushed Corinth into such a stupid statement. Then the man grabbed his cloak from one of the servants, shoved the woman aside, and hurried out of the building.

"Well," Mica said. "That was far more fun than I had expected."

People made nervous sounds, but no one else slowed them on their way through the crowd. Gregorian could have all the glory and deserved it, too. What Mica and his companions had done was esoteric and not known by many. Mica had no problems with that reality. Crowds made him uneasy, and even now, he did his best to just stare at the back of Merriweather's head or at the floor as they kept moving. A rush of words had started up behind them, and the sounds curled and echoed, and tried to take his mind away from one step after another until he got to this meeting.

The crowd thinned out away from the door. Servants and guards lingered here, far less of a distraction. Mica managed to look up and around. He had hoped to see Seldon back there, but so far there had been no sign of him.

"That was a bad move on Corinth's part," Merriweather said. She stopped and looked back at the people. "What was he thinking?"

"He was too focused on me and not thinking about the other people around him. Just about me. I know he doesn't like me because I'm popular in the city, but that just seems a ridiculous reason to lose all sense."

"He's had trouble for the last two years," Merriweather said softly as they walked on. "He's messed up a few contracts, lost track of supplies -- all things that are going to go bad for him if he doesn't get matters sorted out soon. The King has been lenient so far because it wasn't anything drastic, but now, with the war, everything is important."

"Just got lazy, I assume," Mica said.

"Maybe so. How did Corinth ever get into such a position

of power? He's an idiot."

"I believe he's an excellent tax collector," Mica offered.

"Oh yes, a true sign of a good human," she mumbled.

One of the servants had come to lead them to the King. Mica saw a quick grin on the man's face before he bowed. "This way, please."

Mica had relaxed somewhat. Being inside the castle was almost like being inside the tower -- you did not really see the problems of the city beyond, at least not from the lower levels. He had spent a lot of his younger years here. The people lived in a shell, and he could appreciate that protection from both enemies and views of disaster. A quick view of the grounds might look a mess, but the snow would cover even that over for a few months.

Maybe they all needed this haven.

The servant took a turn to the right -- so they were heading for Gregorian's office and not to see the King. That was fine. Mica suspected that King Abertus was a busy man right now. Probably his brother would fill them in on what the King would like them to do.

They found relative quiet farther into the castle, though Castle Guards and a few men from the army were apt to turn up at any corner. Mica had a sudden fear that someone had died. Gregorian had sent for him before -- but no. He would not have used the King's name if that had been the case. The sudden pounding of his heart died back down before they reached the hall to General -- and Prince by marriage -- Gregorian's office door. He could face his brother calmly.

The guard who stood at the door didn't even pause to knock. He just pushed the door partly open and waved the two in. He looked bothered.

And maybe with reason. Gregorian sat at his desk, but the King was there -- without his guards -- and pacing.

Mica had never seen King Abertus pace before.

Something like a large stone settled in the pit of his stomach.

CHAPTER THREE

"Your majesty," Merriweather said with a quick, though belated, bow of her head. Mica realized that the sight of the King pacing had taken her by surprise as well. The man looked back at them and gave a single, distracted nod.

Mica mumbled the same greeting and mimicked her move, but his mind had begun tumbling again, trying to piece together anything that might be wrong -- and that amid a world where everything seemed wrong already. He glanced at Gregorian, but this time his brother said nothing at all. He looked grim. That was not good for someone who had just saved the country.

The guard pulled the door closed behind them. The room seemed too quiet, the noise of the rest of the building disappearing behind the stone and wood paneled walls.

Too hot in here, Mica realized, after the cold outside. They'd rushed through the always cool halls of the castle and now into this room with the coals burning in a sullen red glow and ash to the far side of the room.

This office would usually have soothed Mica; this was a place he knew, from the feel of the carpet beneath his boots to the lovely waterfall painting to the right where Gregorian could look at it and think calming thoughts. Behind his brother's desk was a painting of his wife and children. Despite having to sit for the painter, they had all looked happy.

That, oddly, reminded Mica that there had once been a painting of him and his brother and sister hanging there. He wondered what had happened to it.

The King paced across the room twice more without speaking. Mica and Merriweather remained by the door and Mica was willing to take that escape at any provocation. Gregorian looked their way and shook his head, but Mica could not begin to guess what that might mean. The movement of the King and the growing heat made him feel half ill, and it was only when he found some gears in his pocket, letting his fingers play over them, that he calmed again. Whatever was wrong, he would learn soon enough.

It seemed King Abertus only now took note of them, though. He stopped and looked their way with a curt nod.

"Sit down, sit down," King Abertus said and waved to the chairs by the desk. Gregorian started to stand to give the King his place, but Abertus waved him back down as well. "Stay there. I would rather not sit. I must do so too often and pretend that all is well elsewhere. At least I can stand and pace here without people coming apart."

Mica wasn't so sure of that last part, but he did take a seat as directed, and Merriweather, reluctantly, did the same. Under any other circumstances, she would not have sat with the King standing. The look on her face showed the level of discomfort she felt -- and the worry.

Mica again looked to his brother, but the General only nodded to the King, and so they waited for him to speak. He paced across the room once more, back, and again before he finally stopped at the desk, leaning one hand against it as though he needed the support.

"Kistrin is missing," he said.

"Kistrin," Merriweather said before Mica could respond. She shook her head this time, and the shock had overcome any discomfort. "Prince Kistrin, the crown Prince --"

"Yes," King Abertus said, and for a moment the true worry flickered across his face. He and the crown Prince did not always get along, but the disagreements had never been anything serious. "It's a damned mess, Merriweather. Mica. I don't know how long I can keep it secret, either. I hope you can find him."

Mica tried to remember the last time he'd seen Kistrin. The Prince, who was several years older than him, had often been gone of late, out on diplomatic missions.

"Was he with the army?" Mica dared to ask. "The air patrol? Not out in the bay --"

"No, dear gods, none of those," Abertus replied with a frantic wave of his hand as though to chase those thoughts away. "I had a hard time keeping him out of the forces, you know. Oh, he did work with Gregorian now and then, as long as it wasn't too dangerous. We had an agreement, Gregorian and I, that the Crown Prince would not march out in the lines in a battle. As a boy, Kistrin had the kind of wild imagination that would have him do so if he could have found a way into battle. No, Kistrin was not in the heat of battle during the war, though if he had been here, I might have had a hard time holding him back this time. That did not mean I didn't realize he had his uses. Kistrin has a wonderful way with words -- so I sent him on diplomatic missions. He even learned to enjoy them."

"Where did he go?" Merriweather dared to ask when it looked as though the King might start pacing once more.

"South to Argine in hopes of hiring some mercenaries to guard the southern quarter of Sedina along with the smaller ports in that area. He sent his last missive just outside the border where there was some uneasiness, but nothing unexpected. I've had no contact with him since."

"We've had no sign of Atrian invasions that far south," Gregorian added with a tap of papers on his crowded desk. "We don't think he ran into that trouble. Still, somewhere between that border and the capital, something happened."

"And there's more," Merriweather said drawing the attention of all three men. "I heard from the soldiers that there's been a growing civil war down in Argine?"

"Something like it," Gregorian agreed. The King seemed grateful to let them talk among themselves. Mica wondered how long he'd kept this secret about his son, putting the safety of the city and the country first. "It appears more likely to be trouble from the western mountain tribes and not anything widespread. They've had trouble with those tribes before, and they might have tried their hand at taking some land."

The King had begun to pace again.

"Gregorian?" Mica said, looking to his brother again. What could they possibly do to help?

Gregorian stared at some papers but did not hand them over. Mica could hear voices out in the hall and Merriweather went to the door, ready to guard them all -- but the noises went away, and the King nodded.

"That was Mayor Corinth," she said. "We passed him as we were coming in. He should have left the castle by now. What was he doing back?"

"He wants an airship specifically for the use of the city government. Admiral Rose already told him no, and I agreed," Gregorian replied. "What could he possibly want with one that he doesn't already have with the fleet camped on the city's doorstep?"

"Prestige," Merriweather replied with a glance at Mica who nodded agreement. "That's all he really cares about."

That was not a very political thing to say. Mica would not have dared it, but it seemed that Merriweather knew how the other two felt anyway. She had spent a long time in the castle, part of it serving Gregorian, and she'd probably heard how these two felt about Corinth.

"I'll deal with him later," Abertus said with a wave of his hand that Mica thought dismissed the man from more than the current discussion. Corinth was not going to be happy. Going to look for Kistrin might be far safer than staying in Kamere.

"There is not much more I can tell you," Gregorian said and pushed the papers aside. Mica only now noted that the desk and most of the room seemed to be one pile of chaos after another. While Gregorian was not as fastidious as his brother, he didn't tend toward creating messes. This was a sign of all the trouble with the Atrians that still lurked out there. "Kistrin did not go with a normal delegation. He was not, after all, going to the rulers, but rather to find mercenaries."

"Of which Argine is well-supplies," Merriweather replied. "It's a handy port, open year-round since it rarely gets bad weather."

"Kistrin didn't sail because of the war," Gregorian replied to an unasked question. "It would have been faster, but far more dangerous. He went with his four guards, and nothing extra to weigh him down, and no papers to point to his true identity. The group went in the guise of a band of merchants who had joined together to get out of Sedina. They did not even take much in coins. If they found mercenaries they could buy, Kistrin would go to some of our people in the city and get the funds. They would know him."

"So, they did nothing to draw attention," Mica said and felt another chill. I would have been better if someone knew who the Prince was, after all. Ransom was better than at least one alternative. "Who here knew about his mission."

"Only the four guards who went with him -- and it would have been odd if they stayed around with him gone," Abertus said. He sat on the edge of the desk, waved Gregorian to stay in his chair, and continued to speak. "You know them, both of you -- but especially you, Mica. Ovete, Teren, Dak, and West: they grew up with Kistrin."

Mica nodded agreement. He wouldn't believe anything bad of them.

"His mother is asking after Kistrin," the King suddenly said. "I swear that woman has a sixth sense when it comes to trouble and that boy. She is still at your country estate, Lord Raventower. I should like to keep her there for a while longer if you don't mind."

"Of course." Mica glanced at his brother. "All of them should stay there for now. Get at least some of the destruction cleared away and make their coming back to the city into a festival. Maybe in the spring."

Gregorian nodded, though he didn't look very confident that the queen and her daughter, Gregorian's wife, would stay away for much longer, no matter what the orders.

"What do you want Merriweather and me to do?" Mica finally asked.

"We want you to go to Argine," Abertus said softly. He looked more troubled now. "I would like you to go look for him, as quietly as possible."

"That doesn't seem likely with Merriweather along," Mica replied. That won a bit of a smile from the King, an amused snort from Merriweather, and Gregorian's eyebrow rose. Probably he just wasn't used to his brother making any sort of joke.

No one, especially Merriweather, denied the claim, though.

"We need someone we can trust, Mica," Gregorian said as he leaned forward on the desk. Had he really aged so much during the short war? Or did he just need sleep? "We're doing our best to keep the idea of the Prince missing a secret. He's gone off on missions before and now would be an important time for him to go out and do work for his country. However, it's not something we can hide forever. Besides, it is important we know where he is."

"Seldon --" Mica started and stopped when both King and brother shook their heads.

"I talked to him," Gregorian explained. "All I got was that it was best if the Gods keep quiet and not draw any attention right now, especially from Gods of another country. He said that fate will be our best guide, whatever that might mean. I had the feeling that maybe we'd already stepped over the line."

"I can't imagine how we could have done so," Merriweather mumbled and none of them said aloud any of the odd things they'd done lately.

"We must learn what's happened to him," the King said. He started to pace and then stopped again "He is the Crown Prince. He is my heir, and I am not young, nor is this a safe time. If something has happened to the boy, we all need to know and make arrangements."

This with a glance at Gregorian because it would be his wife who became the next heir to the throne. Kistrin hadn't married yet, though he was older than his sister who had married Gregorian and had children. Mica, who had talked to Gregorian about the Prince not marrying, knew there was a reason other than not finding the right marriage alliance. If Kistrin married and had a child, he or she would be the next heir to the throne if something happened to his grandfather and father. These were dangerous times, and a fear of putting a babe on the throne in the middle of their long war had held Kistrin in check for now.

"I know you two are resourceful," Abertus said after a shake of his head as though to dislodge all the other thoughts. "I trust you. Will you go and see what you can learn?"

Mica glanced at Merriweather; this was not the sort of thing he could agree to without her input. She frowned and seemed to be thinking about the situation before she gave a solemn nod of agreement.

"How long has he been gone?" Mica asked.

"He left twelve days ago and sent his last note five days later. I sent Kistrin right when we started seeing the Atrian fleets out at sea, and it looked as though we might have some trouble on land. I thought the mercenaries might help to keep any force from coming in through that area. Gregorian didn't think it likely -- it's a miserable stretch of land between here and Argine, after all -- but we both agreed this was the best way not to take any chances."

"And now there's trouble in Argine," Gregorian reminded them. "We have sent a company of soldiers down to reinforce the border. If Kistrin had been anywhere around, he'd have shown up there and had someone send a message home."

"How do we head that way without drawing attention?" Mica asked. "Where we go is bound to draw notice."

"Admiral Rose is taking a few airships out to the Middle Islands and maybe beyond," Gregorian replied. Mica wasn't shocked to find that his brother had things worked out already. "You are supposedly going on board with her. It's not as though you haven't flown with her in trouble before."

"True. When does Rose leave?" Mica asked.

"Tonight, though we could find a reason to hold her here until dawn --"

"No," Merriweather replied with a quick shake of her head. She had the look of someone considering all the angles of a coming battle. "Best to let her go, and we'll appear to be on the ship with her. I noted a few small craft in the port. Is there anything heading south?"

Mica searched through his papers and finally tapped one. "A coal ship, the *Grayrun*, but it's only going to Stravil. That's still some distance from the Argine capital where Kistrin was headed."

"That will do," Mica decided. "It will allow us to get there quickly and search out the area where he was last seen -- and then go on into Argine and on to Taginta along the same path he would have taken."

"We'll need a reason to book passage, though," Merriweather said with a slight frown. "And it will cost plenty, I assume."

"Not a problem," Mica replied.

"Business -- that's our cover," Merriweather added with another nod. "There are bound to be many traveling merchants on the move right now, hoping to get clear of the city before more trouble strikes. We were caught here in Kamere during the troubles, and now we're heading to Stravil and out of range of the war. From there, we head inland and south along the main road. I don't assume they would have varied from that path unless there was a good reason, and if so, we'll find it."

"Yes, I think that would work," Gregorian agreed. The King simply nodded and looked relieved. Mica didn't like to think that everything was shoved into their hands. "I don't know how disrupted things are down there. Mica, Merriweather, tell me that you will be very careful."

"We will," Merriweather said and seemed to mean those words.

"Coin --" Gregorian said and pulled a bag from his desk. "Just take it, Mica. This is mostly Argine coinage, which should help. They'll take coin from Kamere, but having local funds draws less attention. And this should get you a place on the ship."

He tossed another bag to Merriweather.

"And with that, I think we have the basics of what we need," Merriweather said and pushed the bag into her pouch. "Cloth merchants, my lord?"

"Yes, that would work best."

"Good." Merriweather stood and signaled Mica to remain. "I am going to go see about our passage and a few other details. I suggest the three of you discuss everything you can remember about the Prince's preparations, including what clothing he took and what jewels he wore. Do the same for the guards."

The three of them nodded in unison. Then Merriweather leaned down closer and looked Mica in the face. "You will not leave this palace without guards and guards on the guards. Do you understand? You will not go help friends in the fishing village or Shadow Walk. You will get done here, and then you will go home. If I hear you did anything else, there will be hell to pay, Lord Raventower."

And with that, Merriweather turned and hurried out of the room. Mica looked back at the two other men.

"I'll make certain of the guards," Gregorian said. "Because after she finished with you, she'd come after me. At least now I understand how she kept such good control of my children."

CHAPTER FOUR

Mica left the palace in the late morning, several notes stashed inside his vest, and his head swirling with all they'd discussed. The crowd around the front door had disappeared, but Gregorian had been serious about making certain he had guards. A full dozen soldiers stood just outside the castle door, and Mica knew that nothing he said would stop any of them from riding clear across the city with him and walking him straight to his own door. Mica felt like a ten-year-old who could not be trusted out on his own.

And that was unfair. Mica knew it, but the thought lingered as the guards brought up his horse, made sure he was properly seated --

"For the love of the gods, I have ridden before, you know!" he finally said as yet another guard checked his stirrup. Then he frowned. "This isn't my saddle."

"No, it isn't, Lord Raventower," the lieutenant in charge said as he finally mounted and maneuvered his horse next to Mica. "There was someone in the corral, sir. The men thought the person was at your horse, so we changed saddles, just to be safe. We made sure everything was removed from the other and put in this one. There wasn't much and nothing of importance -- unless someone already took it."

"No, nothing of importance," he agreed, and quickly curbed his temper. "Thank you."

"You are going to have to put up with us, sir," the soldier continued. "We've all served with Captain Merriweather, you see, and there is no way in hell -- begging your pardon -- that we are going to mess up on this lovely little ride."

Well, that made sense. And truthfully, Mica felt odd traveling even across the palace grounds without Merriweather beside him, let alone the journey across the city. The weather had turned worse again, and the snow had begun to pile up along the path giving just slightly better traction as long as the horses didn't go too fast. Mica was in no hurry.

He had too much to think about still. He and Merriweather would try to find the Prince. They would be leaving yet tonight. Mica would have been upset except that he remembered the King's final look to him as he apologized for sending the two of them out again so soon.

Mica had no idea how they would locate Kistrin. The notes he and Gregorian had made were hardly more than a few hints at what had happened before the Prince left the city. After that, it was all a blank piece of paper. The few notes Kistrin had sent back via the messenger service had been sent to Gregorian and not the King so even they would not draw too much attention. Merchants often worked as spies, after all, and most of them right out in the open. Besides, nothing Kistrin had sent had amounted to anything significant, except the last -- that they'd found a lot of unease closer to the border, despite on Atrian soldiers invading.

Mica suspected it all had to do with the war with the mountain tribes, and that could be very bad. He stayed silent as they rode on through the ravaged parkland of the palace grounds, out through the gate, and downward again. The guards remained alert for any trouble, and they'd do well to protect him. Mica let his mind wander just a little, wondering how they could track someone gone twelve days already. He hoped Merriweather had some good ideas --

They reached the bottom of the hill. To the right was the road that led to the townhouses, including one that belonged to Merriweather's parents. To the right was the gate that blocked the path into the city from the army camp and airfield. Mica hadn't notice on the trip up to the castle that the gate had taken some battering and was partly down. A few guards still stood there, though, and nothing was going to get through.

They still ran into trouble, and not a yard farther along the road into the city.

Mayor Corinth stepped out of the gatehouse and stalked straight at them, unsettling two of the horses. Mica realized first that the man must have been waiting for him, and second that he clearly hadn't tried to stop Merriweather or else he still wouldn't be here.

"There you are, you little bastard," Corinth shouted. Had the man been drinking? "Get off that horse. We have things to say."

"Actually, we don't," Mica replied. "Ride on, lieutenant."

The man nodded and cast one glare at the mayor.

"Coward!"

"I don't fight fools and drunkards, and I suspect you combine the worst of both. Go back to your office and count your coins. I have work to do."

"You will not ride away from me --"

"Actually, he will," the lieutenant said, cutting his horse between the man and Mica. "I believe the local guards will take you off our hands?"

"Yes, sir," one of the men said. He was young and red-faced. "He showed up and camped out with us, and honestly, we didn't know what to do with him. I had no idea what he intended."

"No harm was done. See that Corinth gets home safely."

"Yes sir, we will. Thank you."

"I'll have guards of my own soon!" Mayor Corinth shouted as they rode away.

"Prestige?" Mica said aloud as the lieutenant rode beside him. "Is that what this is all about? That I have guards?"

"Oh, that's part of it," the man agreed with one glance back. He seemed willing to talk, which Mica appreciated, though the man constantly looked anywhere but at Mica -- and that made him nervous as though assassins might be watching at every broken window and fallen wall. "Corinth is annoyed that the Raventowers have taken over."

"Taken over?" Mica repeated the words, not sure what they might mean.

"As far as I can tell, that's how he sees it, sir. I've had to travel with him a few times, so I heard more about it than maybe most. Just talk, you know, but he does go on. And yes, he does like his drink too much, too. But here's the thing...."

The man stopped speaking and looked at Mica as though weighing if he could trust him. Mica rather suspected it was not him the soldier trusted so much as Merriweather who had stood by him through all this madness.

"Here's the thing," he said again. "I think the man intended to marry the Princess, though he's at least twenty years older."

"I think the King might have had something to say about that."

"I got the impression he thought she was up for the bidding."

Mica snarled, which apparently worried the man, but then Mica lifted his hand. "Sorry. I can't imagine why the man would think such a thing, though."

"Everything is about money for him. And now, sir, you have become more popular in the town than he is as mayor. He's not happy about that, but I don't know what he expected.

I can't think of a single time he's tried to help people. Just the same, he thinks everything is aimed at him -- that even the war was staged to give the Raventowers more power."

Mica rode on, shaking his head in disbelief this time. He finally turned back to the man.

"I like to make clockwork butterflies. That is my real goal in life. Has anyone mentioned this to Corinth?"

He'd amused the others, which was good. What they said only reinforced what he'd already known about Mayor Corinth, though he hadn't realized the extent of how much the man disliked the Raventowers in general. He'd have to give that information to Gregorian because his brother saw the man more often than Mica. Mica hoped he could avoid the mayor as much as possible.

The King had hinted that when he had time, Corinth was going to be in for a change in life. If the King removed him from his post....

Maybe Mica could stay in the south for a while. The winters were better there, he'd heard. Not much snow and ice at the capital, though a lot of rain sometimes. He could stand that change, especially if it meant not dealing personally with Corinth.

Mica talked to the soldiers about the city and learned that several factories had been destroyed, two of them by bombs long after the primary battle had been over and the Atrians in retreat.

"We think there might be a dangerous group of Atrians in town still, you see," one of the men said and looked out past the temples and toward the city. "There's a reason to worry, sir. You and Captain Merriweather take chances now and then, but best to keep your eyes open and be safe right now. It won't be long before we get it all sorted out."

Mica didn't say that they wouldn't be around. Even saying they were going off with Rose seemed worrisome right now.

"The docks are going to need work," another soldier said with a wave of his hand toward the distant sea. "My brother works down there, and he says it will be a long time before they can get the bay cleared enough to rebuild. What in the name of the gods did the Atrians think they were doing? The city would have been useless to them if they'd actually won."

"I've come to suspect they never expected to win," Mica replied with a shake of his head. Snow fell from the hood of his cloak. "I think they just wanted to do as much damage as they could to make sure we suffered."

"Well then they lost that battle," the lieutenant replied. His head came up. 'We're going to make a better city."

By the time the tower came entirely into view, Mica had made a mental list of ways he could help others, even if he wasn't physically here. He did have enough funds to start things moving -- but later they were going to need others to join in with the work of rebuilding the city, the fleet, the airships ... even Mica didn't have enough funds to handle it all on his own.

He would have to talk to Gregorian and Merriweather -- when they got back. The new trouble with the Prince had to be handled before anything else.

He'd known Kistrin in the castle, of course. Not well -- Mica was a decade younger and far quieter than the flamboyant Prince. Kistrin had been a troublemaker of a teen, too, although he had rarely made the kind of trouble for others that they might have held a grudge. That might be something to investigate if this jaunt to Argine didn't turn up anything.

The snow fell in spats, and the wind kicked the flakes into the air and obscured the sight of Raventower again. Mica tried not to sigh aloud. All he'd wanted to do was go home and rest; that was not going to happen. He tried not to resent that the King trusted him with this matter. It did seem odd to Mica, in fact, that after all these years, he was suddenly trusted at all.

Honoria had led the battle with a blatant distrust of him, though even she had changed lately.

Did Mica want his old world back?

The one before Merriweather?

No.

So, Mica sat up straighter and looked around at the fallen buildings. Then he started focusing on the ones that had not been destroyed. What was done in those buildings and how could they help now? Who owned them? Could they be converted to things that were needed in the short run to make sure people survived until spring? They would not be doing much work in the city before then, so they had time to sort things out. That would give people time to work out some plans, and to rebuild on a pattern that would improve the city.

They would come out of this better.

The closer they drew to Raventower, the more people came out to greet him as he passed. Mica had the feeling that word had spread, as it often did through the poorer quarters, that he was out with the soldiers. These were mostly the poor, too. Many he knew by name.

"Daylin," he called out to one lanky man of middle age. Daylin gave a wave, and then reluctantly came closer when Mica stopped and signaled him. The man clearly didn't like the soldiers, but that happened a lot with the poor. "Daylin, you're just the man I hoped to see. Nyle is going to need help making nails. I suspect he's going to want you to give him a hand. Also, can you get people to start gathering up what little bits of metal they can find to take to him? Nothing bigger than a hand -- leave the rest for the city crews as usual. And spread the word that there will be bread and soup at the tower this afternoon. No one needs to go hungry."

The man unexpectedly stepped closer and took Mica's hand, and this despite the reactions of the soldiers.

"Thank you, me lord. We done all right by the King, you

know. But you always takes care of us. We'll do what we can for you."

Then he turned and hurried away, already shouting names and drawing people to him.

"Good man, that Daylin," Mica said as they rode on. "He'll get things organized down here in Shadow Walk, and that will spread outward. The last thing we need is for these people to worry about food and shelter right now."

Mica and the soldiers rode a few more feet in silence before the lieutenant turned to him. "Begging your pardon, my lord -- but do you really think you can keep feeding the poor?"

"I can as long as my supplies hold out," he said. The man frowned a bit. "Lieutenant, Kamere has always been top-heavy with rich. We need these poor because we have no one else to do the work. Besides, they are good people. I don't want to see a fever wipe out half of them this winter and leave us all the weaker come spring. That's when we'll start to rebuild, and there won't be anyone else around to do the hard work -- except the army. However, I suspect all of you are going to be busy enough protecting us from enemies who are going to think that we're weak enough to take now that the Atrians have worn us down."

"Yes. True." The man rode on in silence for a few more steps. "I hadn't considered that these people were more than factory workers, you know. Interchangeable with the next person in line to work the looms or shape the pottery. People who went off to their own world and we to ours when the work was done. I didn't even consider what they'd do now that my uncle's pottery factory is in ruins."

"We're going to rebuild, but it will be a while. First, we must survive the winter. Pray to the gods -- really pray -- that it is not a bad one."

All the soldiers nodded. Maybe he had changed their view of the world on this miserable ride.

He thought about Kistrin back in the days when they had both lived in the castle. He'd thought Honoria had rather liked the Prince at first, but then she'd gone off to the temple. Mica hadn't been sure if Kistrin even noticed his prim and proper sister.

The Prince had been wild in those days. Mica had twice seen his father the King send him off under guard to stay in his suite, though that never lasted for long. Kistrin had been likable, and even kind -- in a passing way -- to Mica.

There had been rumors of him sneaking out of the palace with his four guards and spending far too much time at local taverns. That had seemed scandalous and the court -- until Mica learned that King Abertus had done the same at his age. The scandal, he supposed, was just the court's way of being entertained.

Mica remembered being glad no one looked too closely at him. He'd started to go more and more into seclusion then, spending his time making clockwork creatures and reading in the archives. He was glad to leave the fame to the Prince.

Kistrin had grown up to be more outgoing, and he had taken up his role as Crown Prince rather well. People in Sedina liked him, especially since he had taken up the travels around the country that his father gladly relinquished, visiting various areas and attending local celebrations. Mica had not seen much of Kistrin in the last few years.

He hoped nothing had happened to the Prince. They needed him back -- a sign of strength, and not an irreparable loss. Jenlyn would make a fine queen, and Gregorian a good King -- or consort, depending on what they decided -- but now was not the time to make that change.

How in the name of the gods could he and Merriweather hope to find Kistrin?

They'd reached the break in the road that led to the tower or the village. A couple of fishermen were carrying nets full of fish and had just started up the curve.

"Me lord! Thought we'd bring what bits we could catch up to add to the larder, so to speak. Gram and Ada will be making food, no doubt. A little fish will help spread it out some!"

"That's most kind of you. The fish will be appreciated!"

"Oh, and your pod, sir -- it's fine down there in the shed. We keep an eye on it. No one but what you say goes near. Go ahead, go ahead. We'd just slow you down."

They rode past, and halfway up the hill, the lieutenant turned to him. "Those men could get a good amount of coin for those fish if they took them to the other side of town."

"True. And those fishermen could hoard the coin for better days. Some will. However, I'm not the only one who can see that things are going to be much worse before anything gets better. The King will do what he can, but we shouldn't have to leave it all to him."

They passed through the gate. The soldiers went to talk to the guards who were still assigned here, and Mica let them take the horse as he hurried to his home.

He noted that Merriweather's cloak was not back yet. He tried not to worry about her out there. People were starting to associate her with him, and lately that just seemed to mean trouble.

Gram and Roe had already set up a long table in the main hall, along with the battered old bowls and spoons that Mica's people had collected down through the years. This wasn't the first time they'd faced a disaster and helped. Gram, although she hadn't lived here until lately, still knew what to do.

"Fish coming up, Gram," he said with a wave toward the gate. "That should help."

"That it will, me lord. I think we should spit some out here, don't you think, Roe?"

"Yes, Gram," he agreed and already went to work.

Good people.

Mica went into the kitchen and sat down. The place smelled of food and a dozen loaves of bread already sat at one end of the table. Huge pots of stew hung over the fire, and more chopped vegetables were piled up by the bread. His people had been ready, and the sight made him smile.

Ada poured him tea, and then took the seat across from him.

"It's trouble, is it?" she said.

"I'm afraid so. Merriweather and I will have to leave. Today."

"Already?" she asked, shocked by the news.

"The King has asked us for help," he said but didn't say more. He trusted his people, of course, but he had not been given leave to spread the word to anyone at all.

"Well then, you must," she said though she didn't sound happy. "Drink your tea."

Merriweather arrived before he was halfway through the second cup.

"I have been to the dock," she said with a glance at Ada.

"She knows we're leaving. The others will have to know as well."

"True," Merriweather said and looked relieved. "I've been to the dock, and we'll board the *Grayrun* late tonight just before she sails. We'll have to ride out to the airfield first, though. I've had a trunk with some cloth delivered to the ship. I brought us some clothes to wear -- not bad clothing, but not as fine as you're used to. And I'll have to give up my uniform."

He hadn't thought of that, but it made sense.

"At least it will be warmer in the south, right?"

"A bit warmer," she agreed. "Though not on the ship as we head south. It's a coal freighter, my Lord. And not one in the best of shape, but we won't be on it for long."

"Ada, can you get the others? I'll need to tell them," Mica

said with a sigh. "We'll have to leave soon if we're going to get to Admiral Rose's ship in time."

Before long they were gathered around the table, and it was apparent Ada had broken the worst of the news to them, which he appreciated.

"Merriweather and I have been asked to go to Argine and look into some matters there," he said. "I don't know how long it will take us, but I expect all of you to carry on as though we were here. Be careful because there may still be enemies about. I don't expect the guards to leave, so put them to use helping to feed people when they arrive. Nyle, Daylin will be along with metal for nails and he'll bring a few people to help."

"Excellent, my lord," Nyle said. "I was already setting the forge up for nails. Small things, but they help in a time like this."

"I been asked by Admiral Rose ta' check around town like," Shipley suddenly said, surprising them all. "She thinks there might be some spies hiding in the ruins, and she knows I'm good at spottin' things what are out of place."

So, more people in power were starting to take note of the boy's unusual talents. In some ways, that was good, because Mica wouldn't have to worry about Shipley's future. Having the General and the Admiral both watching out for Shipley made Mica feel better.

"You will be careful," Mica said.

"Oh, yes me lord. Admiral Rose, she pointed out how me learnin' something wouldn't help her much if I didn't survive to tell her. Made sense, that did. I only said about this now because I thought you should know before you left."

"Excellent point," Merriweather said and clearly approved of the way the boy thought.

"Well, at least you got time for a good meal afore you go," Ada said. "We all might as well eat now. It's going to be a busy night."

No one argued. Mica even had a pleasant meal, all his people happy to have survived the battle and none of them asking about what Mica and Merriweather were off to do. That was King's business.

Mica spent a few hours in his workshop, mostly making little clockwork insects and dropping them in his pocket and pouch as each one was completed. Merriweather sat at her spot by the door, but she mostly read and seemed to relax more than he had seen in a long time. They opened the shutters to the window overlooking the city, but neither stared out through the glass at the ruins.

"Show," Merriweather had said when she pulled them open. "Let people look and think all is fine. You are back at your work."

"I wish --"

"I know," she said. "As do I, but I'm also worried about Kistrin. We need him back."

Mica agreed with a nod, and neither mentioned what might happen if they didn't find him -- or didn't find him alive. Mica refused to say such things aloud. He made more insects, their tiny wings attached to gears, attached to rotating flags that caught the breeze when they were tossed. Nothing fancy, and certainly nothing Mica could control. All he could do was toss them at people, but they had been good distractions in past trouble.

The ravens were in their tunnel to the roof. Mica finally stood and opened it.

"We are going south," he said to the clockwork creatures. "I can carry two of you in my pack --"

"No," Merriweather said. "You don't dare, Lord Raventower.

"Not go?" one of the Ravens said. Mica saw heads tilt and eyes glow red.

He considered arguing with Merriweather, but then he realized she was right. Anything so obviously attached to Mica Raventower would give them away and could cause a more significant problem.

"You can't go with us," he agreed. "Merriweather is right. Keep things safe here."

He closed the door and looked back at her. "This work is not going to be easy. I had counted on them. The ravens could have looked in places we don't dare. The insects I've been making --"

"Just keep them hidden. They're not noticeable like the ravens. We must be careful. You haven't been out much beyond the city, and people won't recognize you unless you give them a reason to."

"And you think being recognized would be bad."

"I think, Lord Raventower, that you draw trouble, especially with the Atrians. I think if the King had wanted any notice to this case, he would have sent Admiral Rose to Argine and maybe half the army. We need to be careful. If someone is holding him -- and I think that might be the case -- we don't want to frighten them into killing the Prince."

"You don't think he's dead."

"No. Maybe that's mostly hope, but if he had died, word would have gotten back. One of his men would have gotten clear -- they had plans for such a situation, you know. One was always designated to pull out of any fight if things went bad, and to get clear."

"But no one did, or if they did, they never made it back here."

"And that's why I think the Prince isn't dead. I suspect the guards are still with him, somewhere."

Mica wondered if he dared let that much hope work into his thoughts.

"It's time to go," she said with a sigh.

They closed the shutters, and both went downstairs, bade goodbye to the others, and headed out to gather horses and ride out to the airfield.

People were being fed in the courtyard -- not inside yet. That was set up for worse weather. A couple of guards played with some children, keeping them busy and out of trouble while their parents got the food and found places to sit. Everyone looked worn and cold, the snow still falling in light flakes, the breeze brisk and chilly.

Tonight these people did better for his help.

It made leaving a little easier.

CHAPTER FIVE

The journey across town was no more pleasant than the one earlier in the day. Everything looked dull, broken, and ruined. Another fire had broken out down toward the docks, and Mica thought he could see people pulling the building down while sparks flew. He hoped the place had been empty of people, and they had not lost more precious supplies, either.

Mica and Merriweather had guards with them, of course. This was the part where they drew all the attention they could as they headed to the airships. No one seemed very happy about the ride this afternoon, and even Merriweather didn't do much talking. That was alright. Mica had enough to think about as he considered how to track down Kistrin. Mica thought he had come up with at least something of a story they could use -- a cousin, also a traveling merchant -- had gone missing. In all this trouble, they feared the worse and were trying to track him down as they, too, headed for Argine to escape the war in Sedina. He and Merriweather would have a couple days to work out the details on the ship.

The bitter wind came off the sea, tore through his clothing and numbed Mica's face. He wished they were going to the airships for the real journey, and not off again to catch a ship at the docks. That was going to be another cold ride -- back and forth, back and forth. He hoped this part of the ruse worked.

The ride along the sea cliffs to the north of the city put them in direct line with the storm. The horses protested this time, though they kept going, keeping well back from the edges, though the road sometimes wandered too close that way. The airfield itself was a stretch of white desolation, snow and ice blowing in sheets across the even ground. Even picking out the airship was difficult in this weather.

They left their horses at the gate with the local guard. The men who had brought them his far turned back to the city and Admiral Rose's own people took them to *Flash*, the admiral's ship.

Rose must have seen them coming and met them at the ladder up to her ship. "Up, up," she said. "Too damned cold to stand out here, and I have a couple questions I need to ask before we fly."

Did she know about Kistrin and their work? If so, she never brought it up, not on her deck with others around. The questions turned out to be entirely for Merriweather who had been in the army during a battle on the Middle Islands.

"No, if any of your ships take damage, aim for the little island to the southwest, not the big islands. When I was there, it was flat, almost treeless, and nearly impossible to get to so you would have some time to set up a defense. The winds are hellish there sometimes, though. The big islands are almost all too craggy, Admiral. You'd have to get really lucky or come down on a village. Even the fields are terraced into the hills."

"Good to know," she said. "Greenwood --"

"I'll get a memo off to the other craft," he said with a nod. "Good luck, Lord Raventower, Captain Merriweather."

"Same to you," Merriweather said. She looked out the wide window and nodded. "Dusk. Time for us to take our leave."

"The weather is going to hold us up for a while," Rose said with a scowl out at the world. "But that might help you. I can send a message back to your brother under your name if we're held up."

"Yes," he said. "I'm not even certain how soon we'll sail."

Merriweather looked out at the snow spattering the window. "We need to be ready. We need somewhere to change clothes."

Admiral Rose took them to two rooms across from each other. Mica pulled on some plain pants, a nice shirt -- though not as soft as he was used to -- and a cloak that was heavy and warm. When he stepped out, he found Merriweather in a dull gray dress, the skirt divided for riding, and a light gray cloak. The outfit did not suit her at all. Her hair longer than he recalled, hung in two braids. Mica said nothing.

Admiral Rose took them to the ladder and leaned close to Mica. "Find him if you can. This could be just one disaster too many. We'll do what we can to keep it secret that you are not with us."

Mica nodded. The King, Admiral Rose, and General Gregorian often worked together, and he had not thought they would keep this secret from her.

Other workers left nearby ships as the crews prepared to embark on their long, over the ocean mission. Mica hoped Rose's assignment came to nothing more than scouting to see where the Atrians had gone. As the workers left, Mica and Merriweather gathered into the line and moved along with the others, all of them with their heads bent against the cold, cloaks pulled tight. At the gatehouse, horses waited for everyone, but no guards would ride back to the city this time. Best just to stay with the group, give over the horses at the stop just inside the city, and disappear into the shadows.

The wind off the sea helped as it howled around them, ice

forming on cloaks as the horses protested, though it seemed to him that the weather was not as bad as when they'd ridden to the airfield. No one paid much attention to the others, everyone intent on getting back to their homes. They left the horses with the others and headed toward a line of apartments where most everyone who did regular work for the airfield lived. Eventually Mica and Merriweather found the darker shadows and slipped away.

Rats moved through the streets tonight, but the animals kept their distance. The cold kept down most of the smells, except for the persistent hint of smoke in the air. Some of that came from the bonfires where many of the poorer, homeless people had gathered. They paused at a couple; it was a cold evening, and they had a good distance to go.

Colder still down on the shore. Ice hung in lines from any object where it could take hold, and the wooden walkways proved especially treacherous. The lighting grew dim and more than once Merriweather looked back over her shoulder.

"Rats," she finally said. "Far too many rats. I suspect we're being followed, though. Just a local. He's not very good at it, and I don't think he'll try anything."

"We don't look as if we have anything of worth."

"Right. That was the point. Even the cloth we'll barter with down south is already on board. We just need to get there and get off the streets."

Being bundled against the cold did help to keep them from being recognized. Mica didn't think he'd ever before gone all the way through town, day or night, and not had someone call out to him.

They'd reached the docks. There wasn't much left of the area, and most of that had been hastily nailed together. Three small ships sat there, none of them very inspiring. Merriweather led him toward a mid-sized craft half wrapped in a layer of fog which didn't entirely hide the dingy gray. The crew had expected them, and the two men who brought them aboard were quiet -- one did not want to say sullen. The *Grayrun* didn't seem to be too stable at the dock, despite that she must have a full load of coal from the way she sat low in the water. A converted sailboat, Mica realized -- the masts and sails were still in place, but they clearly had not been used in a long time. The glassed-in Captain's deck stood over the back half of the bow, a golden light already showing inside. A couple rowboats sat secured high up on the two sides of the stern and looking like folded wings.

Mica glanced at Merriweather, and she gave a slight wave of her hand, indicating the definite lack of other ships. He said nothing aloud.

The ship was not local, and that was the most important part right now. These people had no reason to recognize him. They were registered out of Stravil and heading back with some coal, having stopped here to off-load food supplies from the north, which they'd taken on without charge. That counted in their favor in Mica's estimation.

The Captain came on deck to meet them, and his men went on with the work. The Captain smelled of meat and onions ... but not of liquor which was another good sign. He was a squat little man with a weathered face and a perpetual squint -- and his hands and clothing showed that he worked with his crew, not just ordered them. Mica thought better of the craft.

"Didn't want to take no passengers, you see," he said as they trundled down into the ship and along none-to-clean passages. *Grayrun* seemed an appropriate name; the dark gray of coal dust had coated everything. "But your clerk there, she insisted. I hope you know how much she paid."

The southern accent was strong but understandable. Even in Argine they still spoke the same language, having still been part of Sedina little more than a century ago before a mutually acceptable parting of the ways that had avoided a war. When Mica made no comment, the captain stopped and gave him a look that clearly showed he didn't much trust women with money. Mica suspected Merriweather might be biting her tongue by now, but she said nothing and kept just behind Mica, all proper.

Mica pulled his cloak closer and gave a delicate little shudder. "I told Hope to spare no expense to get us out of this blighted city and back to the south, Captain -- I don't know your name."

"Captain Browton," he said with a bit of a frown. Mica was not what he had expected.

"Captain Browton," Mica repeated and gave a slight sniff, though not quite a show of disapproval. "I do not wish to be caught up in this war again. We are leaving as soon as possible."

The captain looked him over with a grunt, obviously seeing a dandy behind the cloak. That was part of the act, and Mica felt better for having pulled it off already.

A couple of the crew passed them by, letting the Captain know they were loaded and ready to move as soon as he gave the order. Better still. There was no reason to stay around at the dock and wait for trouble. Mica wanted on the way, to get this job done, and to return home --

Mica didn't want this journey to go long. He also wanted a good answer. Probably he was asking too much of the gods.

The captain glanced his way and gave a slight, disgruntled shake of his head. The man did not take Mica seriously at all, and that was the impression he had wanted to make. He didn't want the man seeking him out. When Mica glanced at Merriweather, she gave him a quick grin.

The interior looked no better the farther they went, and Mica was not really impressed -- but he might have been spoiled, having just come from Rose's *Flash*. Few ships, in the air or on the sea, could compare to the admiral's flagship. This was a working coal ship, so he started paying more attention to the crew rather than the walls, and Mica was pleased enough with them.

Oil lamps with heavy crystal covers were bolted against the walls, giving flickering light every time that the boat moved. They were just barely enough to illuminate a few feet so that it seemed as though they walked from light to darkness every few steps. Streaks of gray coal dust had spread in patterns across what had once been white walls. At one corner one of the crew had painted with the coal dust so that they found an odd, black rose growing up the wall. Well-done, given the medium.

Mica would have preferred to stay on deck as they sailed, but that was not safe. Many of the local people worked well into the night trying to clear the bay and salvaging what they could. He hadn't seen any of them out in this weather, but they might be close by, waiting for the storm to break. Mica could have been recognized by anyone, no matter what he did to try and disguise himself. Their only hope had been a to get him on a ship that was not out of the Kamere port, and so far, it had seemed to work.

Mica still hated the idea of slipping away like this, and he wondered how long Rose would keep up the ruse and be out on that patrol of hers. It was likely her fleet would return long before Mica and Merriweather could get back, but he supposed anyone would be told that they'd gone on another craft or stayed at another site -- it had happened before. Mica supposed they could say the two had remained on the islands for some reason -- some work that they could do.

Mica would have rather gone to the islands, even if they were disputed territory right now. The more he thought about this journey and what the King hoped from them, the less he liked it.

He had to hope that this did not take long. That was all.

Something squeaked, and the captain cursed. "Damn rats. We don't usually see them so much. My apologies for that, at least."

"I'm sure it's not your fault," Mica said and tried to sound sincere.

The man grunted again and shuffled forward. They passed one window, and Mica paused despite himself. They had an odd view of the city from here. He saw nothing but ruined walls and fires, some of them more than bonfires. At least not all the city was in flames, though. Raventower itself stood tall and dark against the sky to the left, though the fog seemed to pour in more quickly just then. Soon all he could see was the glow of the fires and none of the shapes. A flash of light surprised him, but then he realized it came from the opposite side of the craft. The lighthouse still worked, praise the gods on a night like this. They had shut it down during the war. Just too much of a target and one they didn't dare to lose. The caretakers lit it up with the fog rolling in.

Captain Browton took them to a narrow, stooped hall of peeling white paint. Mica thought he saw two more rats disappear into the shadows and started harboring dark thoughts again. Too bad he couldn't have brought the ravens and put them to work on it. They'd done an excellent job at the tower.

"Here," the man said and hit a door. "Not much --"

"Captain, we're ready --" someone shouted down the hall.

"Yes, yes! I'll be right there!" he shouted back, a loud voice that echoed through the ship. "Here! We eat at dawn, noon, sunset unless the weather is bad. Best if you stay in the room. The door across is the private. Not much to see anyway and since the winds are dying down, we'll be out on this tide since we have our pilot ship already. Glad you made it in time. Was thinking would have to haul your trunk back out and put it under guard on the dock."

Captain Browton shoved the door open and then stalked away. Mica and Merriweather both watched him go.

"An honest man, at least," Merriweather said. "He might have kept the money, but he'd make sure we still had our goods."

"We won't be aboard long," Mica added. He started to look in the room, but Merriweather shook her head and pushed him aside. She pulled a knife from somewhere and moved just inside the door, giving herself a moment to adjust to the dark.

"Safe," she said and pushed the door open wider. "But small. Be careful not to trip over the trunk."

Mica had moved to the door and looked across to the porthole. Fog drifted up over that little window, and he could barely see the land beyond.

Merriweather got the lamp lit by the door, and it cast golden light and harsh shadows all around them. *Small* seemed like a rather extravagant word for the room. The trunk sat squarely in the middle of the floor with two cots on either side of it. There was barely enough room to sidle by on either side.

The ship gave another little shake, and Mica grabbed at the door jamb, glancing back down the hall while Merriweather checked under the cots. Someone shouted up on deck, and he had the distinct impression the shake had not been planned or part of the undocking. Was it too late to go back up?

"No rats in here," Merriweather reported after a quick check. "Get in and close the door before we have a few join us."

Mica took a deep breath and stepped inside, pushing the door closed and throwing the bar into place, glad to see that they could seal the door from their side. The Captain bellowed orders somewhere above them, and the ship lurched to the side. Mica knew that meant a tug was preparing to pull them out of the harbor, which made sense. There couldn't be very many cleared spots between here and the open sea. It wouldn't do for another ship to hit debris and sink, adding more trouble.

The room smelled of coal, fish, and other people. Merriweather had checked the trunk.

"No one tried to take a look inside," she said. "Not that they would have found anything, but I wanted to know if we could trust them. You had better sit down. I think we're in for a rough ride."

CHAPTER SIX

The small porthole sat only ten small steps away across a plain metal floor that was devoid of even a threadbare carpet. Mica maneuvered around the trunk, Merriweather, and the cot on the right to stand beside the small window. He stared out and could see the edge of the tugboat ahead of them and heard the labored sound of its engine as it dragged the more massive ship out past the dangers in the ruined bay.

Lamp lights quivered in rowboats out in the tumultuous weather and the flickering light showed like odd fires on the water. As the ship came closer, Mica could see people on one small craft, the men hooking pieces of ruined ships and pulling them up. Those workers would have the harbor cleared before spring unless the weather turned so terrible that they had to give up the work -- and everyone badly wanted it cleared so the city could get in more supplies. The saltwater bay never entirely froze, of course, but there had been winters where everything else was covered in so much ice that ships had a hard time pushing in and out of the dock. The little craft out there doing this necessary work wouldn't stand up to a storm worse than today's weather.

Mica pulled back when they came close to another of the

boats, afraid that he might still be recognized. He hated slinking away when there was clearly work to do here at home.

"The pod could help with this," he said to Merriweather. "With clearing the bay, I mean."

"Yes. We'll have to consider that as soon as we get back."

The tugboat went past another small craft, and Mica recognized the voice of one of the fishermen, so he kept to the side of the port. Then their own ship happened to turn just enough so that he caught one last glimpse of Raventower wreathed in fog before they turned again and began heading toward the open sea.

Mica sighed and turned around to find Merriweather sitting on one of the two beds and looking around the room with a frown.

"Problem?" Mica asked as if there were not dozens of them.

Merriweather stared at him with one eyebrow raised. "You are joking, right? This is, among its other faults, a tiny room. Sit down. You're making me nervous. I fear you're going to fall on me."

"We won't be here for long," Mica reminded her as he headed toward the other cot. "A day at most, and I think this was the best way to get out of Kamere without notice."

"Yes," Merriweather agreed but didn't look any happier. Then Mica saw the way she grabbed at her skirt and shoved it around. He realized at least part of the problem was that she was not in her uniform. The dress did not suit her.

Mica sat on the cot opposite her, and the mattress sagged under him so much that he nearly fell through to the floor. Merriweather did her best not to grin, but he was the one who laughed first. He stood, pulled up the mattress, which seemed to be some old straw stuffed into burlap. Beneath were unevenly placed wooden slats. He'd just happened to find the spot between two of the pieces of wood. A little rearranging made it slightly better. At least he didn't fall through when he sat this time.

The water was not unexpectedly choppy. He had never suffered from seasickness and from Merriweather's steady look, he suspected this was not a problem for her, either. He should have thought to ask before they left the port.

However, there was another problem he had to face and one not so easily fixed. This one was related to the trouble he'd had at the palace earlier that day and other times in his life: the sounds on the *Grayrun* were too strange, and there were too many of them, from the shouts of the crew above deck to the creaks and groans of the moving craft, and even the splash of waves breaking against the ship just below the porthole. He settled with his head bowed for a while and tried to sort through everything he heard and force each ping, swish, and shout into a category, a safe place that he could explain.

Mica thought Merriweather must have understood. She sat quietly as well, though maybe she listened to the crew to get an idea of what they were doing. He hadn't thought much about being alone on this ship with no one to back them up. Granted, Merriweather was worth a dozen soldiers, but he feared that she would worry too much about the responsibility of keeping him alive.

Merriweather suddenly stood, startling him. A hand signal kept him still and silent as she went to the door and listened, carefully pulling up the bar. She yanked the door open and even leapt out into the hall but didn't go out of sight. In a moment, she came back in and pulled the door closed and sealed it again.

"I thought someone might be at the door listening, but if they were, they were gone by the time I got it open," she explained as she sat down again.

"Probably just as well. We don't want to scare the crew.

You do realize you had your knife in hand, right?"

She looked down with a little shock and then pushed the blade into a sheath hidden in the folds of her skirt. "Automatic reaction. I'll have to watch that," she admitted. "I'm too much on edge. Ah, sounds like the tug is casting off from us. We'll soon really be on our way."

"I wish the fog would clear," Mica replied with a look at the little window. "But we are moving --"

He was cut off by the bellow of the ship's horn, so loud that for a moment he thought they must be sitting right beside the thing. Then two more blasts yowled out before he could speak again.

"That's going to be annoying," Mica decided.

Merriweather nodded.

Somewhere deep in the ship, the engine clanged, banged, and finally roared to a start sending the boat leaping forward with a hard jump. Then it clanged and banged some more as the ship fought its way forward against the unrelenting sea.

"That engine is in serious need of some work," Mica said.

"Which you, being a cloth merchant, cannot do," she reminded him.

"Damn. I'll go crazy listening to that sound." The horn blared again. "And that one."

Merriweather snarled agreement. She moved slightly, moved again, and then gave up and settled on the floor, shoving the trunk toward the door.

"Neither of us is going to be comfortable," she admitted. "And with this much noise, we aren't going to get too much discussion about what to do next. I don't want to shout out our plans, even with all that noise in the background."

"I suppose, given what we've been through lately, perhaps we ought to take advantage of this situation and rest?"

"You can rest in this noise?" she asked and looked surprised.

"Not easily," Mica admitted and settled on the floor as well. "And I won't guarantee sleep, but I am still exhausted."

"I'll rest soon," she agreed. "I need to get a better feel for things still."

Maybe they were too much alike.

The ship moved, chugging and bouncing over the waves as they headed outward. The horn sounded off-key, and the captain liked to avail himself of it quite often. Before they were even fully out of the harbor, Mica had a growing headache.

Merriweather looked unhappy, but she didn't complain. Neither did Mica. After all, they didn't really have much of a choice in this, unless they had ridden horses all the way to the south. While a nice horse sounded wonderful right now, they would have drawn attention, especially close to the city. That would have ruined all the work and made it impossible for the two of them to pretend to be anything but who they really were -- and then the news would have spread quickly. At least here they were not out in the wind, snow, and cold.

Not yet.

Mica sat on the uncomfortable bed and watched the light play against the walls as they bounced and danced forward. Before long they would turn sideways to the waves, though as the last of the storm blew over, the waves shouldn't be so rough out farther from the shore over deeper water.

The more Mica thought about this journey, the more he wondered what they were supposed to do. Did the King honestly believe they could find Kistrin? Surely the man must have realized how unlikely it was that he and Merriweather would locate anything if Prince Kistrin hadn't appeared in so long. He had been about to say something like that to Merriweather, but he was stopped by the damned horn again. Maybe just as well. He didn't have to tell Merriweather the obvious, after all.

From the look on her face, Mica knew she was thinking

much the same thing anyway. Maybe she would come up with a plan still. The King was desperate -- that's what made him send the two of them on this impossible errand.

The ship took another leap and drop over the waves. Mica tried not to snarl over yet one more thing he did not control. However, the weather hadn't looked this bad to him as they were heading out not so very long ago. Granted, he'd been in a daze since the last battle with Torger. With a start, he realized how he had not really been paying much attention, just shuttling from one place to another, agreeing to odd plans, and throwing himself onto this ship and out into the sea -- all in one day.

"I am not ready for this, Merriweather," Mica admitted, and she looked at him, her head tilted slightly as her eyes focused on him. "I am not sure I can think straight, not since all this trouble with Seldon, including the knowledge that I'm his High Priest --"

"I see a big part of the problem right there," Merriweather said with a nod, surprising him. "A person should *never* be on a first name basis with a god."

And she made him laugh, just like that. She was right, of course -- that was a major part of the problem -- which included their relationship with Seldon and the trouble that they had just settled. Mica couldn't get it out of his mind, the moments seared into his soul -- including the moment when he had died.

Mica did not bring that part up since it had been Merriweather who shot him. His death had all been part of the plan, and it had worked -- but the event was better left unmentioned right now. Maybe this new job wasn't so bad after all. It forced him to look at something far more mundane than dealing with gods -- if he could get his mind to focus in that direction.

"We've been through a lot worse than hunting down a

missing person," he said aloud, and she gave a slight nod, still watching him. "That doesn't mean this will be easy -- but it's not as though we haven't done the impossible before. I don't know that we can pull this off, but here is one fact: Kistrin went somewhere, Merriweather. I don't have a clue where that might be, but I do know that you and I are tenacious --"

The horn blew again. He glared at the door. Merriweather laughed. Well, at least it was better than before, and the movement against the sea seemed less pounding now.

"Have you ever been to Argine, my -- Mica?" she asked, catching herself. That was better than he had done, and a good reminder.

"Twice when I was younger." He settled better on the cot and tried to lean against the wall, but nearly fell through again. "We --"

She held up her hand and scrambled across the floor to recheck the door.

"I swear there was someone," she said as she shoved it closed again. "This ship must be haunted."

"Oh, now there's a new idea to help us out," Mica replied. "Sit down. I'll settle beside you, and then I won't have to yell quite so loud above the engine."

Merriweather agreed and signaled him to sit first, so she could be on the side by the door. He supposed that made sense. She had her knife, after all.

He pulled his mattress from the bed and spread it out for them, along with the blanket. They shoved the trunk against the shell of his bed, and she pulled the second mattress down so that they could lean against it.

"Argine," he said, unusually aware of how close he sat beside her. "I went twice with Gregorian when he was there on diplomatic missions."

"And from the sound of it, you didn't have a joyous time."

"Gregorian had feared to leave me behind in Kamere because my *gift* had started to manifest. By the same token, he worried about me being with him in a foreign country where my behavior might cause diplomatic problems. So, rather than leaving me alone in our lovely suite with a few cogs and gears, he dragged me with him to every damned boring meeting and event that he had to attend."

Merriweather winced at that thought, which made him like her even more. They both had the same feeling toward official events, he knew -- though he hadn't minded going to the one with her. Maybe they'd try it again. Perhaps it wouldn't end with a sword fight against Merriweather's brother the next time -- though that had added a bit of spice to the evening.

Mica thought about those two trips to Argine with something akin to horror, though. Forcing Mica into that kind of public situation had been hell on him.

"I doubt Gregorian ever realized how close I came to walking away and disappearing into the city. I could have done it, too. He always misjudged my abilities."

"I don't know if misjudged is the word," Merriweather replied as she shifted position again. "Not misjudged, just not able to judge at all, and therefore he acted on the side of caution."

Mica considered those words. He had never felt as though Gregorian mistrusted him, only that he feared circumstances would cause Mica to act in a way that would be a problem. How likely was it that someone would fall over dead in his presence, though? More likely at one of the fancy gatherings rather than in the suite.

So, it was more about protecting him if a death did happen.

"Maybe so," he finally said. "After we got back from the last journey, Gregorian did begin to leave me alone more often. I don't think it was because he started getting serious about Jenlyn, either. In fact, I think the opposite is probably true; he was able to get interested in Jenlyn because he no longer felt the need to watch over me."

"Oh, good point!" Merriweather winced as the ship took two more sharp bumps.

"But you want to know about Argine, not my adventures there. Rose flew us straight to the capital. It was spring both times and what I saw of the capital -- Taginta -- was lovely. Gregorian had more trouble understanding the local accent than I did. We stayed on the castle grounds. Beyond that, I fear I saw very little at all, but I will think about it."

Bump.

"I do hope we don't have this weather all the way to Stravil," Merriweather said with a bit of a growl.

They didn't.

It got worse.

They'd napped a little during the night, but at least it was a little sleep. Mica rose with the first hint of light and used the private across the hall while Merriweather guarded -- and then he guarded for her.

Mica had expected the wispy fog to disappear with the first light of day. Instead, the fog grew denser. Gray spread everywhere around them, so thick that he suspected the crew couldn't see from one end of the ship to the other.

Then the fog gave way to a torrential rain replete with pieces of ice that hit and stuck to decking and railing. The wind grew worse, the ship tossed one way and another until they had to hold the trunk in place or risk broken bones.

"The shore here isn't good," Mica said above the pounding rain and roar of the wind. "Too rocky to dare try for the land."

Merriweather nodded understanding.

It did not take long before Captain Browton arrived at their door and Merriweather let him in. The man dripped water all around him, his hair plastered to his forehead and his clothes sticking to his skin. He wore no hat or cloak, not even in this weather -- but he probably would have lost a hat in this wind anyway.

"We have a problem, as you can no doubt tell," he said and sounded almost apologetic. "This weather is more than we looked for, you know. Things didn't look bad what we could tell in port -- but here we are. I have taken this journey a few times a year, and I know the way as best as any man -- but in this wind and with so little we can see, I don't dare go on, and we sure has hell -- begging your pardon -- don't dare the sails in a contrary and strong storm as this. I'm not certain the crew could even handle them right. Been trying to sell them off, truth be told. But ... we're going to make slowly for shore if we can even get a reading on it and put down anchor as soon as we come to any spot where it will catch. And there we'll sit out the weather."

He looked from Mica to Merriweather and back again, his mouth set, and waiting for an argument.

"That sounds most wise," Mica replied, and Merriweather gave a definite nod of agreement.

Captain Browton's eyes blinked in surprise. He must have expected some protest, but Mica wasn't stupid, and he was glad to find the Captain a wise man as well. Maybe he wasn't acting in character just now, but he didn't care. Getting to what safety they could was far more sensible than pretending to protest just for the show.

"Well, good, then. I'll send down some food. Nothing hot, you know -- not in this weather -- but we'll eat fine. Good day."

The man turned and left, and Merriweather sealed the door behind him again. She grinned as she staggered across the floor and settled down with her legs braced against the trunk to help keep it from moving again.

"I think I was out of character," Mica said.

"I don't think it matters," she said. "I just don't want the ship to sink."

The engine roared with more power -- and a few more clanks and bangs -- as the bow turned slowly to the right, moving a bit better with the storm at their stern and the waves pushing them toward the shore. They found anchorage more than an hour later, and not before at least one scrape of stone against the hull. The storm had not eased, either, but the engine powered down and now they heard only the sounds of nature around them. The crew must have mostly abandoned the deck for safer places to ride out the weather. The Captain let the horn wail one more time warning any other fool out in this weather of where they were, and then it went silent.

They waited.

CHAPTER SEVEN

"Blessed silence," Mica said after the last clang and rattle of the engine had drifted away, and even the sounds of the crew grew quiet again. The boat rocked still, sometimes with sudden viciousness. "There must be a hellish storm out there and not nearly far enough away."

Merriweather gave a grunt of agreement and stood, stretching toward the ceiling and then working her way around him to the porthole.

"If I read these waves right, it's coming our way," she said with a sigh and turned to lean against the wall. "A little journey by ship to get there faster and safer. Right. I should have known this would go badly. We should have fixed the pod and gone on it. Even in this weather, it would have been better."

"We may still have that opportunity if this storm doesn't let up. I do worry about how far we would have to swim to shore and hike back, though."

"This journey has been more than a little annoying already, and we can't have been gone more than fifty miles."

"We have quiet now, though," Mica said as he leaned back, stretching shoulders and legs.

"True. Do you know that there is a tiny breeze and a spray of water through this window? We're never going to be cold and wet without ever going up on deck."

"Here. Cover up." Mica tossed her a musty brown blanket; Merriweather sniffed and snarled but put it around her shoulders.

Neither of them looked likely to sleep soon. The two settled back on the floor and talked for a while, trying to come up with any kind of plan that might help once the ship reached land. The best idea so far had come from Merriweather, and basically revolved around the concept of never setting foot on a boat again.

A crewman brought them bread, cheese, fruit, and some dried meat, all of it reasonably fresh. The food even improved their moods. It was not Ada and Gram's cooking, but still a pleasant surprise. Mica would have liked something warm, but there was no way the cook would want a fire in this unsteady sea. There was also a bottle of good cider and a pitcher of fresh water.

Odd. Mica listened to the crew settling in, a few noises barely heard over the sound of the storm, and even that didn't seem so dire now that they had stopped and let it blow by. In fact, except for the weather, he thought they were safer than they had been for a while. One night in Raventower hardly counted.

The cabin boy came back later for the tray, and Merriweather handed it over with a polite *thank you*. The tall, narrow-eyed boy looked startled, as though she'd spoken another language. Then he muttered something that might have been polite and hurried off again.

"Can you imagine Shipley as the cook's boy?" Mica asked after the door had been closed and sealed again.

"No," she replied, surprising him. She settled back on the floor. "Once Shipley came aboard, he'd be aiming at taking over. The only way he'd be running food through the ship was if he knew it would get him something he wanted."

"A bit mercenary, you think?"

"A bit too smart to do menial work when he can see a better way to survive."

Mica grinned an agreement. It had been good to see everyone at the Tower, even for such a short time. The talk about home gave Mica a new surge of incentive to get this job done and return to the tower. He hoped he could bring Kistrin with him -- but whatever happened, he and Merriweather would return home again. He made that silent vow, and he did not even ask the gods to witness it.

"This is going to be a long day," Mica admitted. "I'm not sure I can sleep yet -- even though that would be the wisest thing for us to do right now in this relative calm in this storm of our lives."

Merriweather pulled the pouch she'd carried aboard to her side and opened it up. She pulled out a smaller bag. "I thought this might help."

Mica took the leather pouch -- heavier than he had expected. Metal? He didn't hear the clank of coins.

He untied the top and peered inside, smiling brightly at the cogs, gears, and other bits pieces. He even found a small case with some of his tools.

"You are a wonder, Merriweather," he said with such sincerity that she blushed. He didn't laugh at her reaction. "Thank you."

"I knew you didn't dare carry them," she said as she reached into the pouch and pulled out a book; a leather cover and no visible words. "I was ready to toss them at any moment if someone tried to stop or search us. I'm sorry I couldn't also bring the ravens. They could have come in the trunk since it was never opened."

"Well, I suppose I need to go out on my own at some time," he replied. "I can't always rely on them. Besides, I have you."

She laughed. Then she took a moment to pour more oil into the single light and then settled down to read. Mica pulled out a few little things and began to tinker.

Was this how life was going to be for them? Nice quiet evenings -- well, not on a ship bound for some mission for the King, but still -- the quiet and the calm. He rather liked it.

What did Merriweather read, though? Mica couldn't see anything of the words, though he glanced her way often, shifting ever so slightly. He thought she knew and adjusted the book accordingly, a little smile playing at her lips.

Did she enjoy the new lady romance novels? Was it an adventure story? A cookbook? A study in military weapons design? He didn't want to ask as he considered each one in turn. That, and having his hands busy putting together those useful little clockwork insects kept him entertained and content while they waited out the rain and wind.

Eventually, he leaned back and napped, uncomfortable though it was. He didn't mind. Merriweather sat by him. She had nodded off to sleep as well, though not before carefully closing the book. He found even that amusing today.

The crew started making more noise. They both came back awake.

"The storm has died down quite a bit," Mica noted. He checked his pocket watch and found that they'd been at anchor for about four hours.

"Sounds as though they're in the engine room," Merriweather said. She was right. He could tell by the direction of their voices, though the words were muffled. He thought there was some agitation, though. That might come just from the idea that they wanted to get moving and get to the safety of a port. The weather was better, but it was not great. Waves still dashed all the way up against the little window. If the *Grayrun* hadn't been transporting so much heavy coal, they would have bounced and tipped far more.

Mica could see water running down the wall from the porthole. Oh, this was not going to be his favorite journey at all.

But they were getting the engine ready. Clang, clang. Shouts. Clang again.

Then with a roar and tremor, the engine rumbled to life again. Mica gave a sigh of relief and leaned back as the engine caught --

And with a louder clang it died.

"That can't be good," Merriweather said with a look at the door as though she could see all the way to the engine room.

They could hear more shouts, but no more clanging and the engine did not come back to life. After a few minutes, Merriweather finally sighed and stood.

"I had better go find out what's happening," she decided and brushed at the skirt again. "Come to the door and seal up after me. I won't be long."

Mica wanted to say that he was the one who should go, and Merriweather clearly expected him to make that claim. He bowed his head instead. She went out, and he closed the door and put the bar in place. At least she wouldn't have to go out on the wet and miserable deck to reach the engine room, which had to be about midway and down at least one level.

He stayed by the door and waited -- and after a while, he thought he heard someone creeping by and listening. He was tempted to open the door and see if he could spot the person if they ran away -- but if he did that Merriweather would be mad for doing something so stupid. It was possible the person -- he could hear him breathing just the other side of the door -- knew Merriweather had gone out.

Should he try to warn her?

No. Merriweather wasn't stupid. She'd take more precautions than he would have, and she wouldn't be caught by someone prowling around the corridors. Mica could almost wish that the fool would stay and try for her. Merriweather wasn't happy. She wouldn't show any mercy.

Mica crossed the small room and looked out the portal, wondering how far they might be from land. Were they beyond the sight of the cliffs? Lost? It wouldn't be hard to get their bearings if the storm just eased a bit.

Merriweather was taking too long. Mica thought he heard her shout a couple times and he smiled -- she was mad about something, and he had the feeling that Merriweather had scolded the crew about the shape of the ship in general.

The person in the hall hurried off, and Merriweather arrived a moment later.

"Let me in," she said. Mica could hear the snarl in her voice. He pulled up the bar and held it open as she swept in, kicked the trunk once, and then turned to him. "They have some major problem with the engine ... and they have no engineer."

Mica tried to parse that line to mean anything except that the ship was out here in the middle of the sea, in bad weather -- yes, it was growing wore again -- with an obviously bad-tuned engine, and no one to even do the minor work on it.

"They sailed without an engineer?" he finally managed to ask. "With *that* engine? The thing sounded like it would fall apart the moment we started moving!"

"The engineer was on board when we sailed, for whatever good he could do, considering how bad the engine had sounded from the start," Merriweather explained. She shook her head looking more bemused rather than angry now. "He's not on board now. Someone thought they heard him yell once during the storm, and they suspect he must have gone overboard. I'd feel worse for the man if the engine that was in his keeping wasn't in such bad shape."

"Well hell." Mica looked at the porthole, judging the worsening rain, and back at her. "We can't just sit here and hope for help, Merriweather. Unless there was an assistant who can do the work?"

"I met the other crewmember from engineering," she said. "I think you better get down there and fix this."

CHAPTER EIGHT

The two of them carefully made their way down to the *Grayrun's* engine room, but Mica saw no one along the way. The area smelled of oil, coal, and seawater, though Mica could see no water on the floor or seeping through the walls. That was the only saving grace. He could see bits of smoke trailing up through the air from the heart of the huge machine bolted to the floor. Whatever had gone wrong, it had done so disastrously.

Captain Browton saw the two coming down the steps and stalked the little ways, cutting the two off from the engine.

"I don't believe this is the place for --"

"We haven't been properly introduced," Mica said meeting the man's startled look. "My name is Lord Mica Raventower."

Mica stepped past the stunned man, Merriweather at his back, and bent to look at various spots in the engine. Captain Browton followed.

"You can't possibly be -- why would Lord Raventower sneak out of the city on a ship like this?"

"I heard there were assassins," one of the crew offered. "Had some right nasty problems with them."

Merriweather looked pleased at that unexpected answer.

The man had just given the best reason for Mica to be careful when heading south. Neither of them made any comment.

"Has anyone here ever seen Lord Raventower?" the Captain asked, still giving him an incredulous glance.

"Yes, sir," one of the men said and shuffled forward, moving as though he didn't dare let his feet leave the floor. He squinted and then nodded. "Yes sir, I'd say that's him, a'right."

"Fine. You are Lord Raventower," the captain said with a sigh of frustration. "Is that supposed to make me feel better about this disaster?"

"I do have a reputation for working with engines."

The Captain stopped and stared at him, his face showing a bit more hope finally. He stepped back and gave a nod. "I would appreciate it if you would do what you could, my lord."

Mica nodded and looked around the small room. This had clearly been part of the ship's hold before it was walled off and the ship converted to steam power. Several smaller ships had done so, and like the *Grayrun*, still had sails -- for whatever good it would do them. Newer craft were almost entirely steam powered, though. The older craft were starting to disappear from the seas -- and he thought they would miss seeing the sails coming up on the horizon.

As he neared the engine, Mica dropped to his knees, peering up through the engine from different angles and trying very hard not to make disparaging sounds. He hardly heard anything that Merriweather said to the other men, though he did hear the Captain say he was going back up top to keep an eye on the storm.

After he had looked everything over, including crawling half under one section, Mica finally stood again and tried to brush the coal dust from his hands and clothing. It only smeared more.

"Well?" Merriweather asked. She was, he could tell, being purposely informal to put the men at ease.

"I'll need the engineer's tools."

"He kept them locked in his room," one of the men said.

Merriweather looked at Mica and then gave a quick nod. "You better show me his room, then," she said and went off with the man.

That she left was trust, both of the crew and of Mica.

Mica continued to poke and prod at things. He could see a good part of the problem, though. One of the large gears had cracked and come apart, and when it did, it had destroyed most of the pieces nearby.

"Is it hopeless?" someone said near him.

"No," he answered and stood up straight again. "Not easy, but not hopeless. I can't believe the engine was let go in this bad of shape, though."

"Old Ally Jack didn't let people down here to mess with his work," the young man said. He didn't have the look of a sailor and Mica had a moment of mistrust -- but surely Merriweather must have had a good answer from him. "Even I couldn't get access unless I wanted to go head-to-head with him. I'm sorry he fell into the ocean, but I'd like to have my hands on him right now to pound his head against the bulkhead a few times."

A few others made sounds of agreement.

"Who are you?" Mica asked.

"Oh, sorry. I introduced myself to your companion, but you were busy. I'm Drew Grayson. My father owns this ship and a few others. He put me on as the new pilot to find out if things were as bad as he'd heard. To be honest, they were worse in some ways, though I don't blame all of that on Captain Browton. He should have had more funds to do repair work."

"There had been complaints? About the engine?"

"No complaints, but a lot of turnover in the crew," he said. "I don't --"

A gunshot startled everyone.

"Don't worry, that's just Captain Merriweather taking her frustration out on the lock." Mica turned his attention back to the engine. "I'm going to have to pull a lot of it apart, you know. This is going to take time."

"I had that feeling," Grayson admitted.

Merriweather returned carrying a crate full of tools and set them on a bench. She began sorting them, obviously knowing the types of things Mica would need. Then the two of them went to work. Others helped for a while, but eventually, everyone wandered off, though some did check with them all through the rest of the day.

"Rats," Merriweather said with a wave of a wrench toward the far wall. "I have never seen so many rats --"

"Neither have we," Grayson said as though trying to reassure her. He had been sitting on the stairs, and Mica had the impression he didn't want to bother the Captain too much. At least he stayed quiet.

"Probably came aboard at Kamere," Mica replied. He laid on his back, his arms up in the guts of the engine, feeling out more of the trouble, so he knew how much to strip out. "The war, Merriweather. The city is in ruins, and I suspect the rats had been in the warehouses and ran for whatever ships they could find."

"Yes, you're probably right." He heard the swish of the air and another startled squeal and gasp. "Another one down."

"You're good with that knife," Grayson commented as Merriweather crossed the room and retrieved it. "Have the men dump them overboard whenever someone comes by."

"Good plan," she said.

Mica pulled himself back out and stood as Grayson left the engine room, leaving he and Merriweather alone for the moment. Mica grinned. "You have them all properly cowed now."

"And I didn't have to pull the pistol," she said, patting the pack she still carried. "It might help. They're a worried group, and I don't want them to think we might be easy to push. Besides, I hate the damned rats."

"I'd just as soon not have them around," Mica agreed. He sat down on the floor and took one of the wrenches and began pounding on a rather large gear.

Merriweather killed another rat.

The day wore on. The Captain came in more often than the others, and though he never looked pleased, he also didn't argue about anything they were doing. Mice began to think that the engineer, seeing how things were going, had decided to leap into the ocean and chance swimming for the shore rather than face the crew.

"There are too many pieces broken," he finally told Grayson as they ate a quick meal on the steps, Mica in the middle range and Merriweather at the bottom while Grayson sat at the top. "I can't just fix the pieces and put them back in. We don't have a forge, and as far as I can tell, the fool had no more than a couple small replacement parts."

"Must have been skimming the money," Grayson said. Merriweather had suggested the same when Mica and she and discussed the situation earlier. "We did pay him to keep things running properly, you know. Browton had suggested there might be something going on, but we hadn't had a chance to hire someone new before the war began -- and after that, the army grabbed up just about everyone."

Mica nodded and sipped the cider Grayson had brought down from his own supplies. Mica could feel the minutes slipping away and had stopped looking at his watch.

"If you don't have the parts, what are you going to do?" Grayson finally asked.

"Rebuild it into a new configuration." Mica stood, worked his way past Merriweather, and walked around one side of the engine and then back to the other, poking and prying at more things. "Here's the good news: this is an older engine, and the newer ones are far more streamlined. This won't be perfect, but if I can get everything aligned, then we should be able to get to the next port -- providing the damn storm goes away."

The ship had begun dancing around a bit more again. The storm did not die down, and Mica had started to worry that maybe there was more to it than just bad weather, though he didn't say so aloud. He probably should have considered the problems they might face out on the sea, though. He tried to brush that thought away from his mind and focus on just getting the others out of this mess.

Merriweather started holding pieces for Mica so that they didn't leap over and land on his leg. It hadn't stopped her from taking out a few more rats. Mica suspected they wouldn't see many more in this room, though he hated to think where else they might be hiding. Maybe he'd loan Merriweather to the cook for a while.

Grayson stayed and helped as best he could. Hours passed, and Mica wondered, realizing it must be about dawn again, if they shouldn't break and sleep for a while. Something pushed him on, though. He didn't want to leave this unfinished.

The Captain came in not long afterward and seemed to note that there were fewer pieces on the floor and more of the engine looked complete. Mica hadn't stood back and taken note of the progress, so seeing the man's nod made him feel better.

Captain Browton went back out again, stomping up the steps and heading down the short hall. They could hear him throw open the door to the deck as a breeze rushed in --

And then he screamed in fear.

Mica threw down a wrench and rushed out after Merriweather. Grayson caught up with them in the hall and followed up to the deck. The Captain gave another cry, but by the time they reached the stern deck they saw no sign of him --

"There!" Grayson shouted and rushed toward the railing.

For a moment they saw the back of the Captain, a frantic arm waving -- and then something pulled the body down into the water.

"Oh gods," Merriweather whispered. She had her knife in hand again, but even she trembled.

More of the crew appeared. Others had seen the Captain go under and as they crowded round, voices loud, a few shouts that hinted at panic. People wanted to head straight for land, a few wanted to go back to Kamere -- but Grayson said neither were not good choices. People listened, but there was a growing sense of confusion and worry.

Grayson had been watching the ocean as though he hoped Captain Browton would surface and swim back to them. He finally looked away and back at the men. No one had made much notice of the bad weather or that the wind had picked up again.

"I am now Captain of this ship," he said, his voice steady. The men all looked at him, and there were nods and more worry. Grayson, after all, was relatively new to the ship, but at least he'd been there long enough to prove that he knew how ships worked. "And this is my first order -- no one is to go out on the deck alone."

Mica gave a nod of appreciation as the others agreed. Grayson showed a logical mind and had given an excellent first order. The others seemed to realize as well.

"You all know your jobs. Let's do them and find our way to a safe port," Grayson continued. "Once we're there, we can decide what to do next. This is not the time or the place to make any rash decisions. Besides, the storm is blowing in again."

"Yes, sir -- Captain sir," one of the men said, and no one

else argued. They moved off, and Merriweather took Mica by the arm and dragged him back inside and out of the weather -- or away from whatever had grabbed the Captain.

He didn't argue.

Grayson followed them. The man looked steady until they were down in the engine room and he settled on the bench, his face gone pale and his hands shaking.

"You did well," Mica told him.

"Well enough for now, but this is a hellish situation," he said. "What took the Captain? And the Engineer, I suspect. What's out there?"

"Something bad, I suspect," Merriweather said and looked at Mica with open worry.

Oh hell. This might have to do with the problems they'd had back closer to the tower. Mica didn't think Atric was back, but could there be something else that had worked with him?

Should he say something?

No. It would only muddy the waters. Better that he put his full attention to the work of getting the ship out of here.

"You are doing well, Captain Grayson," Merriweather told him. "And you are right -- we all know what we need to do. Even Lord Raventower and I know our work. We'll get this ship running again and head for a port. And no, you are not going up there alone, Captain Grayson. You're going to obey that order, too. I'll be back in a moment, Lord Raventower."

"Make certain she has a couple guards so that they can go back out together," Mica said -- and yes, it was an order, and Captain Grayson did not mistake it. Merriweather said nothing.

Merriweather wasn't gone long, either. Mica had begun to put another housing together and tried not to curse that things did not quite fit correctly. All it had to do was to hold together. Once the engine started, they wouldn't go fast. Just get to the port --

"The next time we have to leave the city, we are going by airship," Merriweather announced as she sat on the steps again. "The worse that could happen is that we would crash, but at least it would be on land. I looked around. I didn't see the shore at all, not in this weather. We have to be miles out to sea, my lord."

"Airship," Mica agreed. "Especially one with an engine that I have built."

Merriweather gave an enthusiastic nod of agreement, and then they went back to work. They slept for a few hours there in the engine room. Grayson had bedding brought down for them. Mica couldn't tell if it was better than what they'd had in their tiny room or not, and he really didn't care. Mica slept. Afterward, Merriweather did as well while he tried to quietly put more pieces together and not curse.

Hadn't he wanted to just sit and play with gears in his workshop? This was fate stepping in his path.

"I still don't know what you are doing on the ship," Grayson said later that day. He'd rolled up his own sleeves and helped Mica get a few of the larger pieces into place. They were much the same build, but Grayson had lighter hair and eyes. "You can't tell me it was because you were afraid.:

Mica looked at Merriweather, and she nodded. There was no way to secretly go to the next port anyway. Word would get out.

"The King asked Merriweather and me to go south on a special mission," he said softly, and still not letting out the worst of the news. "Leaving without others knowing was the best plan."

"And you are going all the way to Argine, aren't you?"

"Yes. But I cannot say more."

Captain Grayson didn't ask. He helped until some of the crew sent for him to work elsewhere. The sailor who had come with Grayson had been half asleep by the steps leading out of the room and went back with him.

Mica could tell from the movement of the ship that the storm grew worse and imagined they were preparing as best they could for another round of the weather. Grayson was not gone for long, though.

"They're nervous, but they're handling things well enough," Grayson said. "And if I can be of help here to get us moving at the first chance, then this is where I should be. Besides, it means they will always know where to find me."

"Yes," Mica agreed. Grayson had been good at following orders, and Merriweather was good at fitting pieces together. Under other circumstances, Mica would even have considered this enjoyable. "Normally, I would have experimented, tried one system and another to see what works best, but we don't have the time or the resources to risk breaking more pieces just in trials. In this case, we're going to have to trust my judgment."

"I've seen what you can do," Merriweather reminded him. "You are not throwing pieces together and hoping for the best, my lord. You are making these adjustments based on your expertise."

"And if this doesn't work?" he asked.

"Then you try something different."

Even Grayson nodded. "I've seen what you have to work with here. I watched some of those pieces fall apart in your hands. If this doesn't work, it isn't your fault."

Mica gave a half-hearted nod of agreement. He knew the Captain and Merriweather were right, but that didn't help when he had several lives in his hands. He continued to work while the damned storm grew worse again. Grayson left and came back, looking at the continuing mess on the engine room floor.

"I recently learned that the Captain didn't like to replace parts -- saving money. The Engineer fit in with his plan since he was lazy. They were both fools."

"It's just as well neither of them is with us right now," Merriweather mumbled as she slid out from a particularly small place Mica couldn't reach. She handed over a cog and broken gear. "I might have been inclined to have words with them."

Mica grunted agreement and went to work filing down parts of the cog.

"We searched Belsa's room -- he was the engineer. We found two good sized bags of gold. Given the circumstances, those should go to you, Lord Raventower."

"No," he replied with a smile. "No, I really don't need the gold. Find a more worthy home for it."

Grayson looked startled. People rarely understood that Mica really didn't need money.

"Captain Merriweather --"

"No," she said as well.

"But a Captain surely can't have so much gold that she can --"

"We are to be married."

"Married?"

"Lord Raventower and I," she said as he looked from one to the other. "I am here because it is in my best interest to keep him alive."

Mica laughed. "Don't let her fool you. She's here because she wants the adventure."

"Is that what this is?" Grayson asked, though he still looked stunned.

"It will be once we're all safely on land," Merriweather replied. She even patted Grayson on the arm, uncommon friendliness for her. "This is a mess, there's no doubt about it. However, Mica really does know his work. If I didn't know better, I would think the gods themselves directed him to be here when you needed him most."

"Merriweather --"

"You don't think so?" she said and looked into Mica's face.

"I don't want to consider it. Let's get the engine together and get to port -- what now?"

All three of them could hear loud voices heading their way. They were not frantic voices this time, but they were not happy, either. Grayson sighed, put down a tool, and stepped toward the stairway as they appeared at the open door above. The five men had someone in hand, dragging the uncooperative person to the stairs and down, all bunched around to keep him from running.

"We caught us a stowaway trying to break into the food, sir," one of the men said. They dragged the man down the last steps and deposited him at their new Captain's feet. He looked upward, his face white --

"Oh, for the love of the gods!" Merriweather said and stalked forward. She caught the man by his hair and jerked his head up. "What in hell are you doing here, Burnis?"

Mica had not clearly seen his face until now and felt the same surge of surprise, though not the anger, that Merriweather obviously felt. Burnis, seeing his sister, seemed to lose some of his fear -- which only proved the man was more of a fool than even Mica had expected. Burnis pulled away and settled on his knees, staring up at her with a glare and disdain that Mica so remembered.

"I was told to keep watch on you," Burnis said. Merriweather frowned. "It was obvious things were going on, Jewel --"

He pulled back in haste when she almost kicked him, and that looked like an automatic reaction from both.

"Have you gone insane?" Merriweather demanded as she leaned down closer, a hand on a knife hilt at her waist. He didn't like that much, especially since the sailors seemed to be enjoying the show and had even backed off to get out of range. Grayson gave one quick glance at Mica who only nodded and even dared a little smile.

"Are you going to tell me there are things you haven't been hiding?" Burnis continued. Mica imagined such disagreements between them down through the years. "I've been watching! You were called to the palace. You took off quickly, but your *beloved* here left under twelve guards, delivered to his tower where other guards still watched him. You both slipped out and went to Admiral Rose, but she clearly wouldn't help you escape. You almost lost me there, but I was waiting for the storm to ease and was in one of the nearby buildings. So, you came to this ship in the dead of night and were going to sail away -- obviously in trouble and something his brother couldn't even get you out of this time."

Mica found himself looking at Merriweather in surprise. It almost sounded logical.

"The note said to find out what you were doing and let the King know --"

"You don't know who sent you on this chase?" Merriweather asked, more stunned rather than angry now.

"No. I've had notes before." He looked from one to the other and then at the sailors and back to Merriweather. "I pick them up in an alley near home, deliver my reports back there when I learn something. The minute I realized you were heading south, I knew something serious was going on, given the news about the clockwork creatures down there."

"Clockwork?" Mica repeated and looked at Merriweather again. She gave a slight shrug.

"With all of that adding up --"

"If the King and Gregorian didn't know about clockwork creatures," Mica said and finally came closer. He must have looked intimidating because Burnis appeared worried again. Maybe it was the wrench in his hand? "If they didn't know about this, how do you?"

"I was at the dock to take delivery of lace for father this afternoon, not long before you left. You are in league with the trouble, right?"

"You are an idiot," Merriweather replied and all but threw her hands up in disgust. "Did it never occur to you that we are here for the King?"

"But all the guards --"

"*Assassins*, Burnis," Merriweather remind him with what must have been an annoying tap on the top of his head. Burnis snarled up at her. "Assassins after Lord Raventower. I suppose you forgot that part."

"Why would they still be after him? The war is over."

"Then why is the enemy still burning down parts of Kamere?"

Burnis blinked a few times.

"You clearly know this man," Grayson said with an uncertain nod at Burnis.

"My brother. Get off your knees," Merriweather said with another snarl.

He took that as a good sign. Mica wasn't so sure. Merriweather now had a better chance to just pummel him.

"What did you think you were going to do after you slipped on the ship?" Mica asked.

"Find out what I could -- but you were always in that room until the storm, and then I couldn't get anywhere close. The storm messed me up. I figured in a day I'd slip off again at the port and then ride back to Kamere with the news. I knew I had to be right about you when the two men went overboard."

"I happen to know they were both here when the Captain died," Grayson said. Those last words seemed to have pushed Grayson back into a reasonable stage, instead of listening to Burnis.

"Where were you?" Merriweather asked with a jab at her

brother -- even though she knew the truth about what had happened to the engineer and the Captain.

Burnis went red. Then so enraged that he couldn't speak at all. She'd done that on purpose.

The rest of his story was troubling in another way, though. Who had set Burnis as a watchdog against him? Not that it would have taken much to convince Burnis not to trust his sister or future brother-in-law. Mica wanted to see those notes, but he'd leave all that to Merriweather, and probably they wouldn't deal with it until they went back home.

"I can lock him up," Grayson said and signaled his men to take hold of Burnis.

"I don't think that's a good idea," Mica admitted and won a snarl from Merriweather. He lifted a hand as though placating her. "Not in this weather. We could still go down, and you don't want him locked away with no chance of reaching a rowboat. No, put him to work on something --"

"Rat catcher," Merriweather suggested with a bright smile that clearly worried Burnis. "Everyone is working on this ship, Burnis. We'll find you a net and a cage. I don't expect you to do it the hard way with a knife."

CHAPTER NINE

T hey passed through another day of storms, and everyone grew even more anxious to get moving. Mica and Merriweather had spent a night of restless sleep in the engine room. Mica awoke several times, played with a few of the pieces of gears and snarled at the walls. They could not remain here much longer. The boat was taking too much of a battering, and if this storm grew worse again --

Mica needed to get the engine repaired. At least they hadn't lost any more of the crew since no one, even Burnis, went up on deck without a companion.

They were not supplied for a long journey, and even with a few more fish -- most of which had landed on the deck in the high winds -- Mica knew the food would soon run short. Grayson did not try to push Mica to work faster, but the worry showed in the man's eyes every time he came down to help. Mica also noted that Grayson had begun skipping meals, as did he and Merriweather, for all the good it would do.

The big surprise was that Burnis turned out to be good at catching rats -- and at helping the others with grunt work. They called him Stowaway still, but the anger disappeared from their faces over that first full day. Even Merriweather talked to him sometimes when he came down to catch rats.

Mica did not intrude since he had trouble enough with his own family. Mica knew she would not mention that Kistrin was missing.

That thought made him worry again. Too many days had passed while they remained trapped here. Maybe they'd get lucky and find the Prince had made it back home once they got out of this mess?

Thinking about other things almost led to a mistake in his work. Mica had to shove the problem with Prince Kistrin aside and concentrate on this engine. Mica was, he knew, creating a miracle here, and one that would save the others. The storm still raged, but they would have the power to move once it dissipated. Mica was determined to be ready.

He had no sea metal which would have helped. He could have started this engine, and it would have run forever with the right amount of sea metal at the heart. However, knowing sea metal had once been part of a statue haunted by a god made him a little leery of using any these days, especially on something that would be out of his hands.

Mica had to work with regular metal, broken parts, and a plan he kept only in his mind. The huge winding springs of the clockwork heart of the engine had remained intact, and he'd seen on crack on either of them -- so once they got the first going, the mechanisms should set the second one under tensions -- back and forth as long as the engine ran, and then restarted by cranking the first down tight again. It took relatively little steam to run this sort of machine once it started.

Under most circumstances, this would have been a joy for him, rebuilding something so sub-par to a lovely new engine that Captain Grayson, or whoever took over the post, would appreciate. Mica just didn't like having so many lives at stake there with him, though.

And Merriweather.

Logically, Mica knew he couldn't have stopped Merriweather from going on this journey. It was more likely she would have gone without him. He counted it good that they were both here because he knew he could trust her.

Then in the late afternoon he stepped back from the engine. "Get Grayson. I think this is it."

As if the storm had heard him, the wind howled so loudly over the upper reaches of *Grayrun* that he could hear them clearly and feel their pull down here. The ship swept up and down over another swell. The weather had probably been this bad all day, but Mica kept so focused on the work that he had stopped noticing. It happened. It was why he needed a keeper.

Merriweather went to the top of the stairs and yelled for someone to get Captain Grayson. Mica walked around again while he waited, peering and prodding at things until the man showed up. Grayson looked harried, worried, and wet.

"The engine won't work?" he asked softly.

"What? Oh, no, nothing like that. I was going to start it up and thought you ought to be here. That's not saying it will work, you understand."

Grayson looked hopeful. So did Merriweather. They let the coals beneath the smaller of the water tanks, enough to get things moving. Mica took the captain through the steps of starting the new engine. All the time, he worried about what would go wrong, but at last, Mica checked the steam pressure and finally gave the crank several quick turns.

The engine coughed once and then came to life with a purr. No clanks and bangs, though Mica thought he could hear a little click where something didn't quite match up right --

"Well, damn," Grayson said with a bright smile. "I don't think it ever sounded that good!"

Others began to gather by the stairs, and there were shouts of appreciation that took Mica by surprise.

"I haven't hooked in the rudder yet," Mica explained as he

waved toward that section of the room. "I'll do that now that we know it works, and then we can start moving as soon as you feel the time is right."

Grayson's eyes narrowed as he looked toward the stairs. "We think there might be some clearing toward the east," he admitted. "If the storm lessens, we could be heading for a port within a couple hours. Can you be done by then?"

"Yes," Mica agreed. The idea of getting back to land cheered him up quite a bit, and he'd work diligently to make certain it happened soon. "That should not be a problem. I've already looked the couplers over, and they'll be an easy fit."

"All right then. Let's prepare to sail --"

Sudden shouts came from the deck -- fear, surprise, worry. This time they all rushed upward, and Mica feared they had lost someone again.

No one had gone in the water this time, but they could see what had happened to the others. A creature had begun to swarm up onto the starboard edge, almost to the stern. At first, Mica thought it was a gigantic octopus, but then he saw the hands -- human hands -- at the end of each tentacle. A moment later the thing heaved its body upward and regarded them with a baleful stare, the hands reaching as though to grab any of them it could.

Payton Honorgate's head sat on that grotesque body. The creature turned to Mica, eyes of sea blue glaring as the mouth opened into a predatory grin that showed shark-like teeth.

"Ra-ven-tow-er," the creature snarled. Then it howled in anger and surged upward again.

Payton had survived the fall of his god. Mica had been right; this had been his fault. He took a step forward as the thing swung toward him, some hands holding to the railing, but the teeth snapping in his direction as Payton leaned toward Mica.

Mica knew enough to keep this unnatural thing's

attention while Merriweather maneuvered to her chance at him. She made a little hiss of sound when he took another step closer to the creature, though. Others helped as well. They had gathered up some of their fishing equipment, and spears flew; Payton knocked them aside with supernatural speed. When it looked as though the sailors would charge, Merriweather ordered them back.

They had distracted the creature though, and just long enough for Mica to reach into his pocket and pull out a handful of clockwork insects. He tossed them straight into Payton's wet, fishy face.

Merriweather leapt forward, jabbing at the body, and then slicing off a hand when the thing tried to grab her. Payton screamed in pain and threw himself backward, the hand falling into the water with him. The creature thrashed in the water, blood staining the sea -- and then it disappeared.

"That was too easy," Mica said. The others looked at him in surprise, no doubt at his calm.

Merriweather only nodded.

"What the hell was that?" Grayson demanded. "What is going on?"

"That was Payton, wasn't it?" Burnis asked quietly. He stood behind his sister and looked over her shoulder, his face pale -- but he wasn't the only one who appeared unsettled, and all of them with good cause.

"It was something that had been Payton Honorgate once," Merriweather replied and never looked away from the sea. "We thought he was gone. Mica --"

"I have no idea. There he is."

They all turned back to the sea, all but ignoring the howling wind, pouring rain, and pitching deck. The head had surfaced, but the creature did not come close to the ship this time. His voice, though, carried through the sound of the sea and the storm.

"I will find him! You have not won!"

And then it disappeared again.

Merriweather shook her head. "Not what I wanted to hear right now," she mumbled. Then she straightened. "How soon can we get out of this area?"

"I'll get everything hooked up immediately," Mica said and stuffed the last of the insects back into his pocket. "Captain Grayson, keep an eye on the weather, and as soon as you think we're clear to go, let me know. Don't rush. We aren't going to dare go fast, and if the seas are too rough, it will just make it more likely we'll break down again."

Grayson nodded, looked out at sea, and began ordering the men to their work, including leaving some on duty to watch for the creature again. None of them, though, would stand alone.

Merriweather moved closer to Mica as the others left. She frowned this time. "Payson knows what we did with his god," she said softly.

"He has a lot of ocean to search," Mica reminded her. "And the fact that he's still around here makes me think he's not going to have much luck."

"Excellent point." She let a spray of water rush up over the knife she still held and clean off the last of the blood. "Let's get out of the open."

"The others -- he was after me, you know," Mica said.

"Maybe. But if that were so, Payson didn't have to kill the others," she replied and began herding Mica toward the door that led back down to the engine room. "In fact, it was stupid for him to do so. Sooner or later, we would have shown up on deck and without any warning of trouble."

That was true, but it didn't make Mica feel any better about the deaths, even if the two men would have annoyed the hell out of him by now, given the other problems with the ship.

Put all those feelings aside. Get back to work.

Mica happened to get a glimpse of Burnis before he and Merriweather went down to work. He was part of the crew guarding the rails, watching for any sign of Payton. Burnis looked pale and trembling, and Mica didn't think it had anything to do with the weather.

"Burnis has seemed a lot more reasonable than I had expected," he said as he went back to work with the engine.

Merriweather handed him tools again. "True. He's the last person I ever expected to trust," she admitted and shook her head. "I still can't believe he slipped aboard to watch us. It would have worked, too, if we hadn't gotten held up by this storm."

"Someone put him up to it. Someone he knows, though whoever that is, he's kept it a secret from Burnis."

"You think he's telling the truth about the notes."

"Yes. I hope he's held on to them. I want to see the handwriting."

"After we save the ship, go to Argine, do our other work --"

"Yes, things do seem to be piling up a bit, don't they?" Mica shook his head and began adjusting the link to the rudder. "Get to dry land. That's our first step."

"Considering these storms that we've had, I don't think actual dry land will be possible. There will be floods everywhere by now."

"True."

Soon they could feel the storm easing, though. Mica wasn't certain if he trusted such a fortuitous break in the weather, though. However, by the time Grayson was ready to go, he had everything in place.

"North or south?" Grayson asked as he came down to watch Mica prepare to start the engine up again. "We could sail west about another day and hit the northern current and head back to Kamere."

"The storm has been pushing us southward," Merriweather replied. "I vote for that direction. I think the port will be closer than Kamere."

Mica nodded agreement. "But it is up to you, Captain Grayson. Right now, I don't care if we sail to the Middle Islands or lands unknown, as long as we are going somewhere."

Grayson gave a grunt of agreement. "Let's get it --"

"Something coming," Mica said. He lifted a hand. "Airship. *Flash*."

"Admiral Rose's ship?" Grayson said with a shake of his head. "I hear one but how can you --"

"My engine," he replied and started up the stairs, Merriweather, as always, a step behind him. Grayson followed.

Crew lined the deck and were watching the sea, though some of them did look up at the sky now and then. The airship wasn't long in arriving, the craft circling downward out of the thinning clouds.

Mica wasn't particularly surprised to have an anchor drop down, and he helped secure it to the ship's railing, though Grayson looked dubious at this arrangement.

"Trust me," Mica said with a slap on his shoulder.

"I suppose I ought to by now," Grayson said. "But you do have odd people dropping in."

Mica couldn't argue with that observation, especially since he could see Admiral Rose herself starting down the ladder, which was dangerous given the amount of wind. Grayson and Mica caught hold of the moving rope ladder and held tight while first Admiral Rose and then her second, Greenwood, came down. Greenwood did not look steady on the deck which almost amused Mica, except he could tell something more must have gone wrong.

"I'm glad we located you so easily," Rose said with a slap

on Mica's shoulder. They went into the Captain's deck, where they were a bit out of the weather.

"We had engine trouble," Mica said, waving Grayson in with them. He looked reluctant. "And I had to work on it --"

"You rebuilt it, didn't you?" Greenwood said with a bit of a smirk. "Someone really needs to warn people not to let Lord Raventower travel with them."

"To be fair, they didn't know who I was when I came aboard," Mica replied. Then he sighed. "So, are you here just to insult me? Aren't you supposed to be in the Middle Islands?"

"We saw that monster of a storm blowing in and turned back," Rose said.

"We were already too far out to go back," Mica explained. "And then we lost the Captain and the engineer."

"Lost?" she said, looking startled.

"Payton took them," Merriweather explained. Greenwood gave her a worried glance.

"Payton Honorgate who is dead," Rose replied.

"Not dead enough," Merriweather replied with a sigh. "He's now an octopus creature with a human head, and he has hands on the end of his tentacles."

Silence for a moment. Then Admiral Rose shrugged. "I'm not surprised. And you had engine problems."

"There would have been problems anyway, though maybe not while I was on the ship. That was just luck. Now, why are you here?" Mica asked.

"We went out searching for ships in trouble since the storm took so many by surprise. We've had a couple crews rescued. But mostly we were looking for you."

"Not surprised by that one," Grayson said.

"Once we had made it back to port, we learned from Gregorian that several of the priests and priestesses were saying this storm system was not natural -- that it was something magical, and they feared it might be aimed at you," Rose said, poking Mica in the chest. "They began working on taming the storms, and when they finally got a handle on the magic, we went back out to look for you."

"I appreciate it," Mica said and meant those words.

"There is more," Greenwood added. "Just hours after you left, news spread of something odd going on in Argine."

"Clockwork stuff," Mica said, and the other two nodded. "We heard the news from Merriweather's brother -- who stowed away on the ship, thinking the two of us were sneaking out of town and escaping justice or something."

"Idiot," Rose mumbled, and Merriweather nodded agreement.

"To be fair, he's done all right since he was found out," Mica replied, and Merriweather gave a reluctant nod of agreement. "But the clockwork news is all the more reason for me to go south, you know."

"Yes," Rose said. "Just not by sea. You endanger others as long as you are out here with these poor people."

"I agree, and not just because of the storms."

"Pardon, Admiral Rose," Grayson said with a frown. "If he's a danger at sea, isn't he more so on your airship?"

"Maybe so," she admitted. "But we are at least forewarned, having traveled with our fine Lord Raventower several times in the past. Thank you for your concern though, young man."

"Slight problem, Admiral," Mica said with a lift of his hand. "We haven't fully tested out the engine yet, and I can't just fly away without knowing if it works."

"Good point," she agreed which surprised Grayson. "We could take the crew and abandon the ship -- but that might not be wise since we won't be taking you back to Kamere, and the Captain here has pointed out that you are not safe company. Okay, we'll cut loose of the ship. You get your engine running and then signal, and I'll drop the ladder down on the next pass."

"Yes, good," he said. Grayson still looked stunned that they worried over the ship and crew. "We'll need our trunk, too -- at least if we hope to go on with our original job."

"We can hook it and pull it up, too," she said.

Grayson agreed though he didn't look so happy to be rid of the two. Mica suspected he might still be worried about the engine.

Rose and Greenwood climbed back up. Mica and Merriweather went to Burnis, Mica casting one worried glance out at the water.

"We will be going with Admiral Rose," Merriweather said. "You --"

"I'll stay here if Captain Grayson doesn't mind," Burnis said. "I'm pretty sure I've made some mistakes here, Jewel."

"Don't use that name," she snarled.

Burnis lifted a hand in a gesture to ward off her anger. "I don't want to do anything else stupid. I'll sail with them to the port and then figure out what to do from there."

"I don't mind having you aboard," Grayson said. "You do good work."

Mica wondered if anyone had ever said those words to Burnis before because the man had an odd look. Merriweather seemed relieved though, and she said nothing more as they went down to the engine and did one last check before they called the word up to the captain that they were ready.

The engine started again, and the coupler worked without a problem. With the anchor up, they soon began to move southeastward. Mica was glad to be there for it. He would have worried.

"There's still a little something off," he admitted as he and Merriweather started up the stairs. "But I don't think it will cause them a problem before they make port."

"Once we're done with everything else, you can hunt the ship down and fix it," Merriweather said with a bit of a smile. "But let's take on the first job we were supposed to do."

"Find him," he said softly and without much conviction.

They moved to the end of the deck, away from any obstacles that they could hit, or the ladder entangle with on the ship. *Flash* had circled back around, and he could see the ladder dropping. They were going to have to grab it, first him -- he knew better than to ask Merriweather to go first -- and then her.

"No swordfight this time, Burnis," he said as he waited with him. "I think our relationship is improving."

He heard Burnis laugh as he caught the ladder and started up fast while *Flash* made a quick curve outward over the ocean -- not pleasant thinking about Payson out there.

He kept heading upward and felt when Merriweather grabbed hold as well, and that kept him moving as fast as he dared. He did not want to drop, especially not in that water with the Payton creature probably far too close.

He made it up and let Greenwood pull him to the deck. Then he grabbed Merriweather and hauled her up as well, both hooking into the life line while Greenwood and another pulled the trunk up that the crew had managed to snag onto a dangling hook. Mica watched the crew below get back to work. Mica finally stepped out of the way, Merriweather at his side, and looked at the doorway where he found someone he had not expected to see at all.

"Shipley?" he said.

Merriweather turned and looked just as surprised.

"Hello, me lord," Shipley said. He did not leave the doorway or look downward toward the ocean or at clouds that were starting to obscure the view as they went upward. "Captain Merriweather."

"What are you doing here?" Merriweather asked and

moved to block the view, seeing that the boy was having trouble with the heights.

"We were reporting to the admiral," Shipley said and backed up so they could all enter the hall to the cabins. Mica realized he and Merriweather dripped seawater everywhere. He couldn't remember the last time they'd been dry. "Bear and me both -- he's in the room. I couldn't leave him behind, alone there at the airfield, right?"

"Right," Admiral Rose replied decisively as she stepped in with them. "While the boy was talking with me, Priest Seldon arrived."

"Seldon," Mica repeated with a sigh. Not a big surprise there, at least. Less so than finding the boy on *Flash*.

"He gave us the news about the storm being unnatural and that there would be a clearing for us to get to you."

Merriweather just sighed and nodded.

"The priest, he said I should go with them," Shipley added with a look of disbelief. "He even said I should tell you that I will be of help. It was odd, you know, but he didn't seem like the kind of person you should argue with."

"So, we got the dog on board, and off we went," Rose replied.

Mica didn't tell Shipley that they had been dealing with a god. Why complicate matters for him?

"Come on to the control deck," Rose said. "You as well, Shipley."

The boy nodded. Shipley held tight to the rail despite the life line and looked at Mica with a shake of his head as they stepped out into the open. He was dressed for the cold, at least. "I never left the city before. The airfield was farther than I'd ever gone."

"And now you're on an adventure," Merriweather said and helped him make the transition into the control deck's life lines.

"I like my adventures on the ground, Captain."

"I kind of agree," she said. "But we never get a choice with Lord Raventower. Do not ever go on a sailing ship with him."

Shipley glanced down at the tumultuous sea below and then back at her. "No, ma'am."

"Before we go too far, are you certain about leaving your brother behind, Captain Merriweather?" Admiral Rose asked. She had moved over to the glass covered map that showed the shoreline. "We can still pick him up."

"I would rather not have him with us," Merriweather said. "Being on the ship will keep Burnis out of trouble for a while longer. Besides ... I think he's gotten a bit more reasonable since this whole mess began. I hope that holds until he gets back home."

"I believe they'll get to Stravil before the storms break loose again," Greenwood said, tapping a spot on the glass covered map. "They're only a few hours out."

"Seldon said that they could hold back the weather for a while, but it was going to break out again," Rose warned. "They're not sure what is fueling it, and they think in a couple more days the weather will die out anyway, but it's going to be rough still for a while. We think most of the ships, if not all, have gotten to port -- except for yours. Greenwood, head us back toward Kamere."

"Yes, Admiral," he said and took over for the pilot.

"We should --" Mica began.

"We should put on a show of heading for home," Admiral Rose said. "There is no telling who might be keeping watch on you. Besides, if anyone asks the crew, we don't want them to say you headed straight south, right?"

"Right," Mica agreed.

"We won't be going far," she offered and watched Greenwood as though she expected a mistake. "We'll just get out of range of everyone."

"Ah. Of course," Merriweather said. She sounded as though she couldn't decide if they should be relieved not to be going back to Kamere or if he really wanted to go some place safe and rest. Get dry.

"You'll be heading south again soon, Mica. And we'll get you there fast. Very fast. You should have had me take you from the start."

"It seems so," he agreed. "But on the other hand, I helped with that ship."

"And Burnis maybe learned a little truth," Merriweather added. "So perhaps that was where we should have been. Besides finding out about Payton."

"Payton Honorgate?" Shipley asked with a frown.

"He's taken on a new form," Mica offered and stopped there. "But we don't have to worry about him right now."

Shipley looked unsettled. Mica wondered why Seldon sent the boy. Seldon could have provided a few more instructions -- but probably he was trying to skirt around whatever problem he was having with other gods. Mica really didn't want to think too much about that part, either.

Mica took a seat toward the back of the deck and Merriweather, and Shipley sat with him. He felt worn. They'd already been at this work for at least four days -- maybe longer, he'd lost track -- and they'd gotten nowhere at all. Mica wanted a long sleep, and almost suggested Rose arrange a little more time --

No. It would not help. When she looked his way about an hour later, he gave a nod. They had already turned farther out at sea.

"We're going to put you inland, a bit northwest of the border in the wildlands. Greenwood, get our headings aligned and kick in the second engine when you're ready," Rose ordered. "Is everyone secure?"

"Secure?" Shipley asked, and looked at Mica with both eyebrows up and a touch of panic --

And then began to really move.

The second engine, which his father had built but Mica had installed in *Flash*, was powered by sea metal. It was powerful and fast. The sky blurred and clouds streamed by like a river flowing over rock.

"I -- I used to think that going very fast meant people traveling by horse," Shipley said. He stared ahead where land already showed through the clouds. "Then I come on this ship, and we travel out over the sea, sailing with the winds. And now -- now -- we travel faster than the winds. I think maybe this is faster than humans ought to go."

Mica thought he might be right. "Maybe so, Shipley, but I'm grateful to have this at hand. And we won't be going this fast for long."

"Not long," Greenwood agreed. "Shutting back in seven minutes. We'll be in the foothills by then."

"And we'll be back on the ground soon," Merriweather said and even managed a smile for Shipley. "Are you sure you want to come with us?"

"We can take you back to the city. You do realize you can't tell anyone about the extra speed and jaunt down south, right?" Rose asked looking at him.

"Oh, I guessed that right enough," Shipley said and nodded several times. "But then there's Priest Seldon, you see. He says you will need me, so I ought to be there, right?"

"I am going to have words with Seldon," Mica said aloud and won a worried glance from both Merriweather and Rose. One did not, he supposed 'have words' with a god. "But yes, I suspect you are right, Shipley."

Merriweather didn't argue. She had the look of someone with several worries on her mind.

They anchored a little later over a wild looking an area of

wild, but open land with trees all around and not a village anywhere close enough for people to see the airship letting off a few passengers. Merriweather went down the rope ladder first, then Mica. The grass turned out to be almost knee high and smelled like fresh hay. Shipley followed, and then the crew lowered first Bear and the trunk.

Rose and Greenwood followed down into the late afternoon world of a brisk wind and strange sounds. Mica realized he hadn't been warm in days and that his clothing wasn't quite dry. This was not going to be pleasant. He wasn't surprised.

Greenwood handed over a couple large packs he'd carried down. "Supplies. This should help."

"Thank you," Merriweather said with more than a little relief in her voice.

"The boy doesn't know what you're doing, does he?" Rose asked.

Shipley shook his head, frowning.

"Prince Kistrin went on a mission to Argine and disappeared," Mica said. The boy looked at him, shocked. "He and his personal guard. They were traveling as merchants. We're going to try and find out where they've gone."

"Ah. Yes." He just nodded, but Mica knew there was a lot of thought going on in that head. Bear just dropped to the ground as though he hugged the grass and never intended to fly again.

"Gregorian sent me a few more pieces of information for you. He says that there is trouble at the border and rumors about large clockwork men -- and lots of people seem to be disappearing. He said to be sure I told you that so far there have not been many bodies found, so he takes that as a good sign."

"Yes," Mica agreed but still frowned at the news. "We should have stayed around a little longer, I suspect. But still --

saved ship, found out about Payton, and all of that. Finding out about Payton could be crucial -- even in the way we come back to the city. I would not want to put Kistrin in that danger."

"Excellent point," Merriweather said with a whole new frown.

"Good luck, Mica. Good luck to all of you. We're heading back out to sea and then back home. I'll see you when you get back." Admiral Rose frowned for a moment. "Gregorian did say that you might be contacted in Taginta by those you trust. Oh, and the nearest village and trail south is that way."

She gave a wave of her hand and then stopped to pet Bear. Greenwood climbed back up, and she followed.

Mica and his friends watched the ship start to move away -- and then saw it disappear in a flash of light.

"Never saw the ship go like that from the ground," Merriweather said. "We'll have to warn her about the flash of light -- appropriate to the name, though. That was pretty impressive."

"Do we make camp here?" Mica asked. "Fair warning -- I've never camped anywhere before."

"Good thing he has you and me to take care of him, right Shipley?"

"Ha. This is *woods*. I never seen big trees before. What do I know about surviving out here?"

"What you know about surviving on the street. We get firewood, we get as comfortable as we can --" Merriweather stopped and looked around. "But not right here. Someone might have seen that light when the ship left, and we don't know if there are people in the woods --"

"Why would people be in the woods?" Shipley asked. He sounded upset by the idea.

"Hunting, maybe. Some animals are good to hunt in the dark -- especially if this happens to be someone's land who doesn't want people hunting here. I don't want to take any chance about being tagged with something odd happening here. And worse if anyone caught sight of the airship, you know, and guessed we came from it."

Mica sighed. "Let's get the trunk up --"

"No," Shipley replied and looked around. "We need to make a sled so Bear can help pull the trunk along, and me to help him. We have to look like we work for you, me Lord --"

"Mica," he corrected. "No lord out here. And no Captain Merriweather. Call her Hope -- or Mistress Hope."

They both nodded though they didn't look any more comfortable with this situation than he felt just then. He had never intended for either to take on the role of servants, though the occupation made sense for this job. He did wish Shipley had remained in Kamere, but the boy had been right about one crucial fact -- Seldon was not a person to ignore.

CHAPTER TEN

They left the weed-covered knoll, Merriweather finding a path at the southeast corner which took them into the shadows of the trees. Merriweather went first, with Shipley and Bear pulling the trunk tied to a set of branches, just behind her. Mica came last. He wasn't sure being last was such a good idea, really. He'd never been out in the woods, either -- and as the day grew darker, Mica felt increasingly uneasy.

Merriweather, though, identified the few odd sounds that came close to them -- deer, fox, a hawk in one tree, and an owl in another. Bear was curious about every sound, and Shipley remained close to the dog. He'd do fine. Mica hoped to stop jumping at every peculiar sound himself.

Mica mostly wanted to rest; just stop for some rest, even right here amid these wild trees. Merriweather kept going for some reason. Mica didn't ask because he didn't want to sound as though he complained. After all, she'd also had very little rest over the last few days.

When Merriweather finally stopped, the sun had gone down, and the foggy night felt cold.

"There is a farm field beyond the line of trees," she said softly. "We're near a farm and maybe a village. Let's go back about half a mile, and we'll camp there. We should be good for the night."

Mica didn't want to walk back. However, what she said made sense. Merriweather knew best how to handle the situation -- and besides, she promised a camp and rest. He wouldn't argue with her if it meant stopping soon.

They didn't take long to retrace their steps. Merriweather led them to the right of the deer trail and down a small incline until Mica found a little brook at their feet. There they settled, all of them silent, even the dog.

"Some of the cloth in the trunk is heavy and will double for blankets," she said as she opened it up. "We'll just have to try and keep it as clean as possible. Here. Wrap up and put your cloaks on the outside. I'll find us some firewood, and we can have a little warmth at least. Do you want food before we sleep?"

"After for me," Mica said and Shipley nodded agreement. "I can't stay awake."

"Sleep then."

"Merriweather --"

"Don't worry. Just rest."

Mica decided that sounded like a good idea since his eyes had started to close the moment he sat down. The cloth Merriweather gave him felt nice. The ground was hardly less comfortable than sleeping on the floor of the *Grayrun's* engine room -- and how odd that the ship felt days behind them already. They were in a different world now. New rules applied, and ones he didn't fully understand. New....

Mica awoke the next morning to the smell of tea and warmed bread. His body ached, but at least the mind-numbing exhaustion had disappeared from his brain. He sat up. Fog swirled low around the camp, and the smoke from their fire disappeared as it rose. Shipley still slept, curled up with Bear, but Merriweather was at the fire with a small metal pan and pot. Cooking. Ham, he thought. Some bread heating with cheese --

The heavenly scent woke even Shipley before Mica could move.

"We'll be going on soon," Merriweather warned a little later as they ate. Mica had washed the pans and himself in the icy water of the brook, and he suspected his days on the ocean had dulled the shock a bit. The food had been excellent, too. There had been nothing warm -- and very little that hadn't been somewhat soggy -- since they went to sea.

"Go today?" he asked finally. "I'm not entirely opposed to napping."

She gave a slight laugh. "We aren't going to rush off, so don't worry. You two need to learn some about the cloth trade -- and for us to get our story right before we run into anyone."

"Good point," Mica agreed, not at all opposed to sitting and listening to Merriweather.

They stayed until nearly noon, working out details, learning about the cloth they carried, and creating a believable story about coming south and heading for Argine in hopes of getting clear of the war. The bit about the missing cousin was tougher, though.

"We can't be certain what he called himself," Mica pointed out. "And we can't go around asking for cousin Kistrin before someone maybe starts putting things together."

"We can ask about other merchants, though. It would be natural that we want to know who was through and where they went since we don't want to follow where they've already sold cloth," Merriweather said. "And if we find one that sounds likely, we latch onto that name for future questions."

Mica agreed. It wasn't going to be easy, but there was no turning back. Not yet, at least.

They wandered into one village that afternoon. The place was too small to do any real trading, and they drew some attention, but no real surprise. That helped settle nerves. So, did meeting a few people on the road, none of them shocked to learn they were escaping toward Argine. Bear drew a lot of notice, of course, but that took attention away from the others, too.

When they reached the next village at sunset, all three of them were far more at ease. Merriweather bargained for a room and food. Mica had feared they might have to stay in the common room -- and it turned out Shipley and Bear would stay there with the others that night.

"It's fine, Master Mica," Shipley said, though softly, after they'd carried the trunk up into the single room. "It suits me, you know. Wouldn't be the first time for Bear and me, and we'll be safe enough."

Mica supposed that was true, and this choice did add authenticity to their show. He nodded and watched the boy and dog head back down the short hall to the stairs.

Merriweather had a cot of her own in the room, the perfect servant, and the locals could snicker all they wanted about the two of them sharing the room. They put the trunk in place, carefully locked, and headed back downstairs. The quick meal tasted good. Mica and his companions ate in the common room with the others. Mica stayed clear of anything stronger than a weak cider; he didn't need to be muddled.

"Wha' ha' bring such as ye clear ta' here?" one of the local men asked.

"We heard you hadn't many traders come through this area," Merriweather answered. That brought nods. "And we wanted to stay clear of the trouble that they've had in Kamere and probably along the main road."

"Ha, yes -- bad that in Kamere. And now in Argine, we hear -- but you head for the border, yes?"

"Yes," Mica replied. "I hope the trouble in Argine and Taginta isn't as bad as north in Kamere."

Grumbles and nods, but no one seemed to know. By the time Mica and Merriweather were leaving the room, Shipley and Bear had already staked out a place by the door -- a cool spot for the huge dog -- and it looked as though Bear had been given a good-sized bone as well. Mica thought they would tip the innkeeper on their way out. It wouldn't hurt.

Then he went upstairs, stripped down to his pants, and crawled into bed --

A real bed. One with a feather mattress, even if it was a bit lumpy. If Merriweather said anything to him at all, he never heard it. He slept so well that he didn't even have nightmares, which -- given the situation and the trouble before now -- seemed odd the next morning. Merriweather was already up, of course, but not by much. She sat by an open window and brushed her hair.

He hadn't realized it was so long and he watched, enthralled.

"It's just hair, my -- Mica," Merriweather said with a bit of a laugh as she began to braid it and wrap the braids up around her head.

"Lovely hair," Mica replied. Did she blush? He loved how her hair seemed to change color with every twist and turn. "Can we stay here and just send others out to do the hunting? I want to sleep for another week."

"That was nice," she admitted, glancing back at her cot. "But the sooner we move on, the sooner we can go back home."

He wanted to ask if she meant back to Kamere in general, or back to his tower. He said nothing, though. He would not be demanding or needy. The uselessness of this journey weighed on him, though, and threatened to make him surly. *Going home* was becoming more and more of a distant quest.

Shipley and Bear already waited when they got downstairs.

"Bread that's not as fresh as I would want," the

Innkeeper's wife said when Mica asked about buying a bit of travel food. "And some Cheese about to turn. I have some bones for Bear there. An' he earned it all for you. Better ratter than the two cats I got, he is. Cleared out a whole nest a' them for us. Sit down. I'll get you a bit a' breakfast."

Mica patted the dog on the head as he went past and headed for the privy. He thought Bear looked inordinately proud of himself.

Breakfast came on a platter: cakes, eggs, syrup, and even some nicely smoked ham. Mica made a mental note of the village and thought he might do some trading with them, once all the rest of this trouble got cleared up.

And as they started to leave, he pulled out a silver coin and handed it to the woman.

"You paid --you paid enough --" she said, startled.

"We have not often had such wonderful care on this journey," he said with a smile. She still looked stunned. "Thank you."

"Probably a bit out of character," Merriweather said when they were out on the road and nearing the end of the village. "But I approve."

They left the village of Bethon in a better mood. The road, at least this early in the day, proved not so crowded that they couldn't discuss the situation and what they thought they might do.

"We're heading straight toward the sea," Merriweather said. "As if you couldn't tell by the weather."

The clouds had piled up over the last hour, and a fine mist of rain had begun to fall, though nothing like the storms they'd face out on the ocean.

"We should connect with the main road from Kamere to Taginta before too long," Mica said and peered ahead into the glades of trees as though he could see the crossroads. "And at the crossroad is the village of Nov. That's the last place where

Kistrin sent a note home."

"Ah," Shipley said. "And it's not far from the southern border?"

"A few hours good walk," Merriweather said.

The sun moved slowly across the sky behind the spitting clouds. Not a horrible walk, but to Mica it seemed a waste of precious time. They were already five days away from home and only now at a spot they should have reached that first day.

More people began to show up and the road grew wider, but more given to ruts. They fell quiet. A group of men rode by, probably conscripts for the border from the way they looked. Someone herding cattle followed them. Bear didn't much like the animals, and they kept to their side of the road.

It was a sign, Mica knew, that they were near Nov. The road rose, and a sturdy stone bridge spanned a full stream that he suspected was usually shallow, but now raged with runoff from all the storms.

They paid a toll to get across -- only a copper a piece and one for the dog and trunk. The man who took the coin was a squat, older man missing a few too many teeth -- but it was the two burly young men who enforced the collection. Mica made a study of their faces. The man with the cattle cursed as he tried to find enough coin -- Mica guessed this was a new toll -- and illegal, of course. Mica made a note of it, as well -- and slipped the man with the cattle a few coins to get his herd across. Then Mica moved quickly on over to join his own people and get out of the way of the cattle.

"I don't like people preying on others at times of trouble," he explained and walked on, though none of his companions had questioned his actions.

"That toll keeper is not going to be unhappy once we're back to Kamere," Merriweather said with a snarl over her shoulder toward the burly men still harassing others.

"Or sooner, if we get a chance," Mica replied. "There's the

village."

They could see the scattering of buildings in a lower valley not far away, a misty view through the slight rain. The main road showed clearly as a path cut through the trees and bushes, and there was far more traffic there then they'd seen so far, all of it heading toward the border --

"Show time," Mica said.

The other two nodded.

"My guess, from the looks of those wagons, is that they're calling in supplies for the border guard," Merriweather pointed out. "That sounds as though they're digging in and expecting trouble. The border may be closed."

"Not good," Mica replied and shook his head with worry. "I would hate to think we'd come all this way and can't get through."

"Might be we don't want to," Shipley said, but he gave a smile afterward. "I know, I know. But seems to me that wise people would be heading away from the border."

"And when did you get the idea that Mica and I were ever wise?"

That set Shipley laughing. He also did not argue the point.

The man with the cattle caught up with them a mile or so later and slapped Mica on the shoulder as though they were old friends -- a move which almost got an adverse reaction from Merriweather. Bear seemed a little more amiable to the cattle now, so Shipley took over pulling the trunk and let the dog help herd dozen or so animals. The farmer soon realized no harm would come of it, and the dog seemed born for herding.

"Good animal, despite that limp. I don't guess ye would part with him?"

"Never," Mica replied and won a bright smile from Shipley.

"Didna' think so," he said. "I'll pay you back, wha' ye did

back there. Damn the Champlyns anyway. Never used to charge us to cross they bridge."

"Not theirs," Merriweather said and sounded surly. Maybe she was at this point. "That was built by the army."

"Well, yes," he said and looked at her, frowning.

"We travel a lot," Mica said, drawing his attention back. "Seen a lot of bridges and know the looks of them. That's a military bridge without a doubt. Which means these Champlyns don't own it."

"On their land though," the man pointed out.

"It's a law though, you see," Mica said and tried to sound less like Lord Raventower. "The military comes through and builds a bridge. They pay the local farmer for that bridge and the right to run a road through, and then they use it in emergencies -- and everyone else uses it all the time. It's not right legal what they're doing. It might be some local military officer would like to know."

"Huh," he looked back and scowled. "I was delivering these to the army, you know. Charging a good price, just what it cost me to bring them up -- I want the military holding things here, given what we hear from over the border."

"Oh?"

"Civil war and scary things," he said, and his wrinkled face creased with true worry. "I hope ye aren't heading that way. Already lost one merchant an' his group."

"What?" Mica said, startled. "Heading for Argine?"

"That they were. Never made it to the crossing from what we can tell. Found a few a' their things on the road. The only way we'd ha' known they didn't get there. No bodies mine. They were a good strong group, those five. Wouldn't be easy to just take them."

Mica gave a pensive nod, wondering if he dared ask more. Merriweather took over, though, sounding worried about the possibility that they might have trouble. She got a few more facts, and Mica suspected that they'd found their first real sign of Kistrin ... and it wasn't good.

The man moved on, but not without another promise to pay them back if they ever crossed paths again. He reminded Mica of the people on his own country estate, a place he did not visit nearly often enough. It might be helpful to go there for a long rest after all of this was done.

There were no rooms to be had in Nov, but several travelers had set up a small camp just the other side of town in a far too muddy field. Not the best place to spend the night and Mica again regretted leaving Bethon and those lovely beds behind.

Mica wondered if Kistrin had managed a room that last night. He could not imagine the crown Prince sitting out here - - ah, but the man wasn't entirely unused to being away from luxury. While he had never gone into a major battle with the army, he had been out with the men on field trainings a few times. Kistrin had probably been far better prepared for this type of setting than Mica.

The travelers all shared food around a fire and spoke about the trouble. Mica and his friends heard tales, including some about clockwork men that attacked others -- but no one had seen the unnatural creatures. Just as well, Mica supposed. Someone would have gotten suspicious if he had started asking specific questions.

"Sounds like the clockwork is real," Mica said a little later when he and Merriweather went back to where Shipley and Bear waited. Merriweather had taken the boy some food already with one sharp look at Mica that warned him to stay out of trouble. He hadn't even asked questions while she'd been gone.

"Sounds true," Merriweather agreed and looked worried. "But maybe not so crazy as some of them say. I don't think they could be like --" She stopped and looked around, but they'd moved to the very edge of the field, away from all the others and even most of the light but feeling safe enough with Bear to guard them. "I don't think they're like yours, though."

With souls, she meant.

"I hope not."

Merriweather gave a grim nod of agreement. Then they settled into sleep as best they could while Bear kept the watch. He chased off a coyote once, and something smaller later. The night was filled with fog and sometimes rain -- a damp, uncomfortable night on the muddy ground, and Mica was glad to see the dawn.

They started out ahead of the others -- and didn't get far at all.

"No one is going through, merchant," one of the soldier's said. They'd felled trees and blocked the road completely. Mica thought he could see the same roadblock about a mile ahead -- probably the other side of the border. They were very close!

They also knew better than to argue. Instead, the four headed back toward the village -- and let others come and go around them, Mica and his companions moving as though they were uncertain what they would do. Mica knew where they were headed and slowed when the small deer path came into view.

They were a mile back from the guard post and down a slight hill. Nov still sat a couple miles ahead. This deer path was their only hope.

"Now," Merriweather whispered when no one was in sight again.

Mica and Merriweather grabbed the trunk while Shipley unhooked the sled and lifted it up, staggering under the weight as he followed them. They hurried into the brush a few yards away from the road and knelt, silent while more people headed toward the border. Hadn't they'd heard it was blocked by now? Maybe some of them thought they could buy their way through, but Mica had seen the look in the officer's eyes. He was panicked. He was not going to let anyone through because something out there scared him.

They didn't move far from the road for a couple hours. The rain had stopped, but it was still cool. Mica prayed to the gods that none of them got ill from this journey. Bear and Shipley napped, the boy with his head on the dog's side. He seemed to be doing well enough out here in the wilds. Mica realized he was as well, and Merriweather did well wherever she went.

"They're going to be looking for us back in Nov," Merriweather finally said as she stood. Shipley and Bear rose as well, the dog shaking dirt and leaves from his fur. Mica rose last, not in a hurry to go again.

"And this trail is going to be the most obvious place we took off," Mica added. "So, should we go back to Nov?"

"I don't think so," Merriweather replied as she looked around. "Let's at least see if there's a chance of getting across somewhere nearby without being stopped again. There must be some other game trails through here. We just need to find them before dark."

"I can't say I like the idea of sneaking around in the trees between two nervous armies," Mica admitted.

"There is that problem," she agreed. Shipley looked a bit more worried. "Just move as quietly as we can, and if I give the signal, turn around and head back. Otherwise, I fear we'll have to find a port and take a ship in -- if even any of those are getting through."

"If we're right, Kistrin disappeared somewhere around there," Mica reminded her. "We'd have to hike all the way back from the other side, and from what I saw, they look a bit wary on that side, too."

"True on all accounts. Here is the good news, though. All the tales about the missing merchant -- none of them even hinted that bodies had been found. There has even been talk about others disappearing -- but again, no bodies."

"True. Good. And better still -- if they weren't killed, they were taken somewhere away from this area."

"Right. We need to get clear of here, and then start looking for other signs. We might make a guess at what is going on, too."

That improved Mica's mood as they went into the wild country, leaving the deer trail for something more challenging to traverse, the sled catching now and then on weeds and vines.

Then Bear, who had gone a little ahead of Merriweather, suddenly stopped and dropped to the ground. They all froze.

Mica heard a loud voice and then more sounds of people, all of them speaking quietly now. Merriweather crept forward, Mica at her shoulder, while Shipley and Bear held back, silently waiting.

They had found an encampment of some type.

"Hiding," Merriweather whispered. "No campfires and far from the road. They should have been quieter, but they don't look like they're well-trained."

"Two tents," Mica whispered as they knelt by the edge of the trees. A guard went past but never even glanced at the shadows. *Very* badly trained. "The tent to the right looks like it must be command -- people going in and out of it. But look at the one behind it. Look at the man out front."

"He's working with weapons --" She stopped and stared. "Not weapons. Those are huge gears, aren't they?"

"I think we've stumbled on real trouble," Mica said and leaned forward a little.

The man with the gears stood and gave a nod to someone in the tent. Another man came out, this one carting a metal casing with what looked like a square head on the top. They began to fit the gear inside.

Merriweather signaled Mica to get back. He wanted to watch a while longer, but she was right. All of them slowly retreated through the brush and weeds until they were at least a quarter of a mile from the site.

"So, the tale of the clockwork men is true, to some degree," Mica said and won a look of worry from Shipley who had not seen them. "I wonder how they move."

"I suspect we'll find out," Merriweather replied with a worried glance over her shoulder. "While you were watching, I was listening, though. They're preparing to pack up and attack -- the post on the Argine side from what I heard. And I caught the implication that there are also explosives, and that seemed to be linked to the clockwork devices as well."

"That's a dark thought," Mica said and looked back over his shoulder. "I don't know how they move, or how they might be directed. I sensed and saw nothing out of the ordinary in that one, but it wasn't completed, either. Damn. I really hadn't expected this despite what we'd heard."

Merriweather nodded agreement and led them away, but a while later she stopped at another trail. "I think this one will lead us closer to the Argine post rather than the Sedina one. Since that is where the attack is going to head --"

"Yes, go there," Mica agreed. "It won't be long before that group is on the move."

They abandoned the trunk and the sled, shoving as much of what they might need into their packs. Mica suspected their disguise as merchants wouldn't be much use now anyway. No one was going to be looking to buy cloth any time soon in this area.

They found one of the Argine Guards patrolling away from the post itself, and he took them straight to the Captain.

"They say they saw people, sir," the guard said and sounded as though he didn't quite believe them.

"We were on the deer trails and saw a group about five

miles northeast of here," Merriweather said. She even dared tap a spot on the map the man had on the table in his tent. "They were hiding, but we heard them -- they said they were heading this way to attack you. And they had some sort of metallic thing they were putting together."

The last got the Captain's attention. He looked at the guard. "Good work. Get a few scouts and go check -- fast like, boy. There and back. We might have time to prepare for them."

"Yes sir," he said and gave the group another disbelieving look.

"So, you were just out in the woods?" the Captain asked while others headed out almost immediately.

"We were trying to find our way into Argine," Mica replied. "We were in Kamere during the battle and decided going south seemed wise, you know?"

"Only not so wise. Taginta has problems, too -- though so far not as bad as up north," the captain replied.

"We hadn't heard anything until we were too close to turn back," Merriweather said with a frown. "More fighting?"

"Looks like highlanders thinking the Sedina war would make Argine weak. They've been held off so far. But the clockwork men -- they're a different problem. From what I hear, they explode as soon as they hit something. They've been used in attacks far from the mountains and the other battles, including not far from here."

"Damn," Mica said and felt shaken by the news.

"They've been used in a couple villages. We get the feeling maybe they're getting ready for something bigger." The man looked them over again. "You stay here, under guard, until I saw otherwise."

None of them argued. Bear was on his best behavior.

It didn't take too long for the scouts to return and confirm the story. The Captain rushed back to the tent. "You didn't have to come and tell us, and I appreciate that you did. My men found your trunk and sled. It's out there ready. Go while you can -- yes, toward Taginta, but I'd not go to the city if I were you. It's full of crazy people right now -- refugees all panicked by what is going on. Go. You won't have much time to get out."

They didn't argue. Shipley got Bear hooked to the sled, and they were soon heading down the trail with a group of soldiers, though the soldiers headed into the woods within half a mile. Mica looked back, but the soldiers had disappeared into the shadows. There would be an ambush waiting for the enemy somewhere in those woods.

"We could stay close," Merriweather said as they trotted along the deserted road. A mist clung to everything again. "We might learn more about the clockwork designs and this war."

"And I think the Captain wouldn't be quite as happy if he found us again," Mica said. "No. Get clear of this one. He said other villages had been attacked. I get the feeling I might find out more there. I wish we could have asked about Kistrin, though."

Merriweather nodded as they kept moving. When the battle was finally enjoined, they could barely hear the shouts. One explosion did shake the trees all the way to where they had traveled, though.

Merriweather looked back, but she didn't turn around to help. Mica decided he didn't want to go where so many people might be dying. Not safe for him. Better to head for the villages.

They continued through the night, following the empty road that led up and down through the southern hill country. With nothing coming from the border, the road seemed totally abandoned, though the lights of a few cottages showed now and then. People in Argine must have realized they could not get through the other way -- and probably didn't want to head from the Argine war to the Sedina one.

A smaller trail headed west. Merriweather stopped and stared at it in the faltering moonlight as more rain clouds swept in from the sea.

"I don't think we want to continue on this road," Merriweather suggested, though she sounded exhausted. "I'm surprised we haven't had anyone along yet, to be honest. We don't want to draw attention, either -- so let's head west and find another path toward Taginta. One that the locals are taking.

"At least it's not snowing," Shipley offered, though he didn't sound happy about the mud.

"Not here," Mica agreed. "We don't want to go too far west, which leads into the higher mountains. We're in the foothills of the range that circles Sedina and comes very close to the shore here, and the western highlands in this area get snow quite often in the winter.

"We are not going to hike that high," she said. "I refuse."

"Best news I've had on this trip," Mica replied and gave a little bow for her to lead the way.

They passed a farmhouse, dark and quiet, but with chickens in the yard and a couple dogs who put up a racket. They hurried on and heard the man cursing the dogs for barking at rabbits again. Before midnight they'd found a wide path heading southward once more and it looked more travelled by the recent ruts and muddy prints. Merriweather admitted she didn't know if it would lead where they wanted, but it did get them away from the border and the tales of trouble that were soon going to overtake them.

They camped by a stream not long before dawn, only a few yards off the trail, and started again at mid-morning. A few people had gone by, along with a couple horse-drawn wagons, so they were no longer the only ones moving when they started on their way again.

The first village they found was more extensive than Mica had expected, with two inns and a market. An old-fashioned place, without a sign of any steam-driven vehicles and not even a clock in the square. They might have stepped back a hundred years. The place had a peaceful feel, and Merriweather looked pleased.

"I can trade some of the cloth in the market," she said. "Get us a few supplies while we can because I get the feeling that we'll have less luck the closer we get to the city."

"Should I go with you?"

"No," she answered. "You are going to set up in an inn and do what you do best."

"Which is?"

"Be charming and polite and get people to talk to you. I'll take Bear, and you take Shipley. That way if either of us gets in trouble, we can send the other to get help."

That sounded wise. They'd already worked out a tale of coming from farther north. They set up in the less popular of the two inns, too. Calderville on the market day turned out to be a boon for both of them. Mica talked with some local farmers and knowledge from his estate stood him well there. Merriweather struck up conversations with several merchants, some of whom would have gone on to the city under better circumstances.

Over dinner, they compared notes.

"Everything looks bad for Taginta," Merriweather admitted after they'd laid out what they'd learned, their voices quiet though their conversation was little different from the others around them. "The western tribes have been gathering for an attack and the city is preparing for siege. They are moving as many people out as they can, and they're not letting anyone else within the walls."

"I heard the same," Mica agreed. "And I heard a number of local people have disappeared."

Merriweather nodded. "The traveling merchants at the market are anxious." She bowed her head toward a table to their right where three men and two women had gathered, murmuring and looking worried. "Some of them think they should band together for travel."

"Sounds wise. We can't join the group, though. We'd either give ourselves away as not being what we claim, or else we'd find something we need to investigate."

Shipley and Merriweather nodded. It looked like Bear nodded as well. Mica almost laughed.

Their story about having been north and escaping Sedina seemed to have held up well. They were not, it turned out, the only ones hiding out on this side of the border.

"Most of them think it's too early to assume the war is over, wise people," Merriweather said a little later. The food had been rather bland and undercooked, but they didn't complain. She stabbed at a scrawny piece of carrot. "The problem is that some are also running out of goods for trade."

"The world has gone mad," Mica replied and toyed with his bread.

"Was it ever not mad?" Merriweather asked. Then she lifted a hand. "I know. This isn't normal. Let's hope we can do something. If we can't find ... someone, maybe we can help in other ways."

Mica nodded though he didn't want to think that they'd already given up on Kistrin. That night they managed to take two rooms, side-by-side, despite the cost. Mica and Shipley took one and Bear went to help guard Merriweather in her own room. She even had a bath and Mica could hear the water splashing the other side of the wall. Shipley went straight to sleep, but Mica sat braced against the wall at the head of his bed and played with clockwork insects while he tried to sort out what they should do.

They could go back home. There was no way to track the

Prince.

However, there were also the clockwork devices and ones that apparently exploded. Mica didn't like the thought of such things turned loose -- not here or in Sedina. He and his companions would have to go on for a while yet and see if they could learn a few more things.

Mica slept well past the sunrise, but he awoke refreshed. He'd come to appreciate beds. He would never take his own for granted again.

They went downstairs to find soldiers at the doors to the inn and several others lining the other guests up, going through their belongings and asking questions. This, Mica feared, would prove difficult for them. However, they didn't argue when they were told to stand by the wall and say nothing to each other.

Mica wondered what these men searched for today. Had something happened? A couple of soldiers headed up the stairs to check the rooms as well. They'd been careful though --

Except for the clockwork insects in his pocket, along with a few more bits and pieces. If they found those, he suspected there might be trouble. A casual glance around showed nowhere easy to deposit them, either. And if he had found a spot, wouldn't that just make the soldiers more inclined to keep everyone and maybe lock them all up?

Damn. How could he --

The man in charge of the soldiers came out of the kitchen area, still talking to the innkeeper. "We won't be here long. We're just looking for anyone with dangerous materials, sir. This won't take long. We haven't found anything --"

The soldier glanced their way and stopped talking. Merriweather gave a slight smile.

"You three travel fast," he said as he crossed to them. "You did us a good turn back there at the border. We had no idea those people were so close."

Mica realized he was the guard who had first spotted them in the woods by the guard post. It felt like seeing an old friend from home, especially when he signaled them away from the wall and to the table with him. No check of Mica's clothing.

"We wanted away from the border as fast as we could," Mica admitted. "So, we walked and walked, and got clear of the area. From what we heard the battle didn't sound good."

"No, not good," the soldier agreed. "But we got lucky, both with you and with the soldiers on the Sedina side who came to our aid. The Captain plans to write a note of honor to King Abertus."

"Good. I'm glad they helped," Merriweather said and felt pleased. "We heard at least one explosion --"

"That was the worst," he said, his face going pale. Mica hadn't noticed until now, but he could see bandages underneath the young man's tunic. "I guess they were clockwork men like we'd heard about, and they must have had explosives for guts. Four of them, and they exploded when they hit something. We think they were supposed to stay to the trail, but it was too rough for them and one sort of lost its footing -- it was like they had sets of wheels that moved up and down with the terrain."

"And one fell?" Merriweather asked, frowning.

"Yeah. Right at the edge of the trail and close to our camp. He blew up, and that seemed to unsettle the other three. They all hit trees, almost all of them at the same time, and they all exploded. The people who were fighting us hand-to-hand saw what happened and just took off into the woods. We never got any of them alive. So now we're out looking for people with explosives or clockwork pieces."

Mica managed not to squirm. Merriweather didn't even glance his way, but he was aware that she realized the trouble they had barely avoided. They had also learned all they were going to from the soldier. To ask more questions would have drawn attention, but he probably didn't know much more anyway -- except for one thing Mica wanted to know.

"Did they sound like they were locals?" Mica asked as the soldier started to stand.

"Mostly. A few from the mountains, probably. Not from Sedina, if that's what you are worried about."

"I was thinking of Atria, actually," he admitted and smiled. "I try to think kindly toward home, even though it's not where I want to be right now."

Mica had put the man back in a good mood. "No, not from there unless they didn't speak at all. Seems like there is too much going on in the world, and none of it good. I suppose you haven't heard about the trouble out at sea. Ships going down, and huge octopus-like creatures. I suggest you don't go near the sea."

"No, we won't," Mica agreed.

"Have a good breakfast. Looks like everyone is clear here. You're all free to go. Sorry for the worry we cause."

And with that, the soldiers left the building and moved on.

CHAPTER ELEVEN

"They said nothing about the human head and hands for the octopus," Merriweather offered once they were out of the building and mostly alone on the road out of town. "But even so, it sounds like Payton is on the move."

"Or...." Mica stopped speaking as they passed a group of women gossiping on a corner. He kept himself from scowling in their direction. "Or the *Grayrun* made port, and this is just the tale they told. They were bound to speak about the trouble. As for ships going down, that might just be an addition to the tale told by other people in taverns."

"Yes, maybe so," Merriweather agreed. "But he was right: there is too much going on in the world. And we got damned lucky back there."

"Should I get rid of them?" he asked, holding out his palm with a couple of the insects on it.

"Not now. I doubt we'll have that problem again."

"If you ever needs to get rid of something fast, just tell Bear to bury it," Shipley said.

"Will he? That's good to know," Mica said and patted the dog on the head.

Mica shoved the insects back into his pocket but planned

to transfer them into a pouch that Bear could take away. That would be a good plan.

The road proved to be busy with troops heading toward the border. There were several little villages and hamlets, each crowded with more people than Mica had expected --

"They're clearing people out of the capital, remember?" Merriweather reminded him in mid-afternoon. She'd been listening carefully to everyone they passed, and as long as the three of them didn't stop, no one paid any attention, except sometimes to note Bear. Bear pulled the trunk though, which helped to make him seem less dangerous than a huge dog on the loose.

"More of the same," Merriweather said after they passed through a third village. "Soldiers won't let people back into Taginta, though they don't feel safe here, especially after a couple villages were attacked. Normally, they'd be heading for the city and getting behind the walls -- but the explosives have everyone spooked. And we're starting to draw notice heading in the wrong direction."

"Yes, I thought so," Mica agreed. They'd slipped a couple yards beyond the village's last building. People traveled the road, but only a few headed the same direction they did, and Mica suspected they were local farmers heading for homes nearby. "How far to the next village?"

"Queton. Not far," Merriweather said. "Just about four miles from what I could guess, and we're in luck -- it's one that has been attacked."

That caught Mica's attention. He started to move faster but slowed again for the sake of his companions, including Bear who appeared to be wearing down and annoyed by the layers of mud that had matted his fur. Shipley went to help the dog, and the two pulled the sled along the mostly smooth road. Merriweather said nothing more, and Mica wondered what she thought. This still was not a safe place to talk, though.

What were they supposed to do now? Mica needed to learn more about the clockwork men. He wanted to hunt for Kistrin, but they were far from where the Prince had -- maybe -- disappeared. They would have to circle back around to that area -- but for now finding out about the clockwork men seemed important. He was, after all, an expert in that field, and these creations appeared to be dangerous.

Maybe they could send a report back to Gregorian about the finds, and then continue looking for the Prince. Mica had known they really hadn't much of a chance to find Kistrin; however, he couldn't give up so easily. This line of inquiry wouldn't last much longer and then they would have to try to do more. Maybe traversing the land and hearing what is going on might even help, especially since they'd heard more tales about people disappearing. If he learned more about what happened to those people, he might have a link to Kistrin.

The clockwork men? That information seemed to be falling into his lap anyway. He need not give up one for the other.

About halfway to the next town, Bear gladly took a quick bath in a shallow brook and rolled in leaves -- not dirt -- afterward. They all sat in the sunlight afterward, a rare break in the cloud cover, though it didn't last more than an hour.

They reached Queton and found half of it in ruins with those buildings no more than piles of debris and the signs of massive fires everywhere. They passed through that section of the town to the area where people still moved. An old steam car, blackened by the flames, had been abandoned in one of the ruins where it must have been stored. That was the most modern thing he had seen in Argine, a country which seemed to exist in a past century.

Signs had been posted to keep out of the debris. Mica couldn't go in during the day then, which meant wandering around in the dark. He saw the glitter of metal pieces in one of the buildings, but he didn't even dare stop to check it out. Merriweather trapped him on the arm when he slowed, and she kept him going. He would have to go back. She knew it.

The first inn didn't have a room on the ground floor. "For the dog, you see," Merriweather said, as though the dog and boy didn't usually stay in the common room, but tonight they needed a room to share. She repeated the tale at the next spot, and they got luckier.

"The boy what took care of the stables has disappeared," the older woman said as she led them down a narrow hall that seemed to be mostly old beams holding up the second floor. "Run off with the army, I suppose -- happened just after we was attacked. Been a lot of young ones going since the attack. Suppose it's right. This was his room. Not much, but -- maybe it will work."

Merriweather peeked I and looked around. "It will be fine. Thank you."

"You pay good coin," the woman replied and sounded grateful for the few coins. "We take in the army for free, but it's starting to wear on us all."

The woman turned and walked away.

Mica stepped in and found only one bed in the small room, but he supposed they could fit in another cot and take turns sleeping. Bear had settled down, flopping across the entryway to the door. They'd left the sled in the empty corral and carried the trunk in, Mica and Merriweather putting it down by the wall. Shipley sat down on the floor by Bear.

"Never done thought the world was so big," Shipley admitted softly. He rubbed at his right ankle. "We walked too far. And we have a long way to walk back home again."

"I don't intend to walk back," Mica said. Then he shrugged. "But who knows how we'll get there otherwise."

Merriweather poked around at things and turned back to

him with a frown.

"The boy who left -- he didn't take any of his things," she said with a shake of her head. "There's clean clothing in the bag there. Some coin, too. I don't think the boy went to the army."

"Another who disappeared."

She nodded.

Shipley looked bothered by that idea, as though the words had called a ghost into the room. That didn't stop him from settling his head on Bear's shoulder and going to sleep, though. Shipley, Mica had noticed, had that ability to sleep whenever he got the chance.

Merriweather didn't bother with another cot. She sat down in a corner, pulled her pack around to make a pillow and curled up there like a cat in the small shaft of sunlight from a tiny window. Mica took the blanket from the cot and tossed over her. She started to protest, but he shook his head, and she went right back to sleep.

They were going to be out after dark, so sleeping now seemed like a good plan. No one would get close with Bear and Shipley in the doorway, even with the door open. If nothing else, this might make them look more trustworthy, that they didn't go around asking questions. Mica laid down on the cot -- and slept easily as well.

Bear and Shipley were up first, but Mica had heard the increase in noise out in the other part of the inn. The evening crowd must have arrived, and Mica could smell food, too. That would help since his stomach rumbled in protest. The four of them wandered back out and found a table.

"Must ha' been tired, you were," the woman said as she brought bread and a weak stew, though it smelled fine. "I looked down the hall there, and I could tell you must all be asleep. Even that huge dog. Take it you walked far, eh?"

"We came down from the highlands, hoping things were

better here," Mica said. "Didn't seem safe, heading back for Kamere just yet. But now ... now -- what happened here?"

"Bad things," the woman said, her face gone bleak. She shoved pale blond hair back from her face which had gone pale again. "Bad things what scared off most the town, except for us what can't leave behind everything we have with any chance of another life somewhere else. Metal men, they was. No eyes nor faces, and they moved like they rolled on the ground. Just comin' straight down the street and then, suddenly, they turn, left and right and go to the buildings -- and the moment they touch a wall, they explode. People died. Many people -- exploded or burned. It were horrible."

"I'm sorry," Mica said.

"People died," she said again and gave a sigh. "And they just laughed --"

"The metal men laughed?" Merriweather asked, looking shocked and afraid.

"Oh no, not they. About a dozen men and one tall woman with dark hair and a hawkish face -- they all came with them. Won't never forget her. They each had a kind of box they held, and I think that directed the metal men. They never said nothin' aloud, you see. But they laughed when people died. Seven days past now, but it stays too clear."

Mica nodded and silently blessed the woman's ability to remember the details of the scene. He asked nothing more, but he was getting far more anxious to get out and look at the sites. Too bad he couldn't have come in as some sort of expert -- which, in fact, he supposed he was after all.

They'd been friendly for a while, talked with the few locals who still came around, and retired once more, this time with the door shut. They even slept for a while again. Mica was aware of the innkeeper -- Marly -- going by to her own room. Then he slept again, with the vague worry that they would sleep through the night and need to find a reason to stay through the next day.

Merriweather, though, woke him late in the night. Bear and Shipley were just standing and stretching, too. Mica had thought to leave them behind in the room, but he supposed that it would hardly matter if he and Merriweather were caught.

"Midnight," he whispered, glad for a watch powered by sea metal and that he never had to worry about winding it. The metal gave off a slight glow, too, so he could easily see the time. "We'll take the outhouse door."

Merriweather nodded and moved the door open a slight inch and then more. She went to the right and looked in on the common room. Mica could hear the snores and rustling of sleeping people. Nervous people, he would guess -- they did not want to get caught in this act of slipping from the building. In a moment Merriweather nodded and signaled them to head out of the building. Mika was the last out of the room and closed the door. Then they were out into the inevitably damp night. A fog lay low across the yard, and a couple rats, cats, or rabbits took off at a run.

The gate had a lock. Shipley had that open before Mica got close enough to look at it. They went out into an alcove between the fence, another building, and the quiet street.

"Nowhere to go but out in the street," Merriweather whispered as she looked carefully around the corner. "No one I can see, but if you hear sounds, drop to the ground and cover your face. Bear -- well, let's just hope we don't see anyone."

Shipley nodded, but he didn't look worried.

They scurried along the edge of silent buildings like mice running from one hole to another. By the time they had reached the first of the destroyed walls, Mica was ready to go back to their room. He didn't like this risk, though he did want to see the structures more closely.

The constant rain had washed down the ash and soot, but they still had to be careful not to brush against anything. Mica took the lead now, leading them behind the partially standing wall of one building and out of immediate sight. They dropped on their heels there, and Mica stared into the darkness before them.

"Try not to get too much soot on you," he said. "It'll be hard enough not to track it into the inn. Shipley, you and Bear look around the edge and see if you can find anything at all. Merriweather and I will look at the debris, but we don't dare move much. I just want to see what the place looks like."

What Mica found was troubling, and he visualized most of what had happened without doing more than nudge a few pieces of burnt wood aside. The burn marks spread out in spirals, and he found small pieces of metal were embedded in some of the timber and melted to slag in other places.

Mica lost track of what he was doing and realized he only survived because Merriweather watched over him and kept watch for anyone wandering the streets. Soon they went back out of one building and into another, but it was much the same.

"I don't need to see more," he said when they came back out of the few pieces of wood still standing.

"Good. Let's clean up and get back in. You can tell me what you found tomorrow on the road unless there's something you think we should know?"

"No, nothing that will make a difference," Mica admitted and looked back again as they walked away.

"Bear and me found these," Shipley said and held out something in his hand. "We saw more, but they was embedded in the trees."

Gears. Cogs, bits of metal.

"Oh, excellent work!" Mica praised. He took them and began to look them over.

"Later, Mica. We don't want to be out here much longer," Merriweather reminded him. "There will be people up early soon."

He nodded and reluctantly shoved the pieces into his pouch, though the larger one didn't want to fit. Merriweather took it and slid it into what must have been a large pocket in her skirt. He nodded appreciation.

They had no trouble getting back to the inn, but just as Mica opened the door, they could hear footsteps in the hall.

Shipley shoved Mica back and signaled Bear forward.

"Oh, ma'am," Shipley said as Mica and Merriweather flattened themselves against the outer wall. "I hope we didn't wake you none."

"I didn't hear you," Marly said, her voice a little gruff. "What are you doing?"

"Bear needed to go out, ma'am," he said and kept his voice soft. He even managed a yawn. "Best to go out with him, so he don't start barking at the wind and wake everyone, you know."

"Oh, yes. Well done. I'm going to start the bread."

"I'm going back to sleep," he said. He even went inside and let the door shut.

They waited, though not long before the boy reappeared at the door and waved them in. Bear stood at the open door to their room, and the moment the three were past him, he laid down. Shipley settled in as well. They could hear Marly in the kitchen.

That had been far too close. Mica curled up in the corner this time, waving Merriweather to the bed, which she took reluctantly, but soon fell asleep. So did Bear and Shipley. Mica examined a couple pieces of metal, but the light was poor. He pushed the metal away in his pouch and thought instead about what he'd seen inside the building.

Mica wished he knew what was in those boxes that the

others had been using to direct the clockwork men. That was a piece he really needed, but short of tracking them down -- no, that didn't sound wise at all. But how many did they have that they could waste a few on an inconsequential village?

Mica and his friends were closer to the sea than he liked as well. He had felt it in the wind, and the taste of the salt sea that almost overcame the smell of fire and decay. He rethought the situation; Atria didn't have much in metals, though that might have changed with a few finds. However, getting those large pieces of metal into Argine would have drawn attention since there were so few ports this far south. Airships, especially the large clumsy ones the Atrians used, would have been noticed. Maybe the fact they'd had encounters closer to sea was only chance -- or design. If someone in the west -- where there was already trouble -- had created the clockwork men, then they might not want the truth traced back in that direction.

No way to tell, really -- but it did make more sense. The western mountains were close, and a lot of the mining groups up there used explosives to open new mines. The western curve of the Tilday Range seemed the best answer, and probably the most dangerous. The locals could stop ships at sea, but could they even find people moving along unmarked trails?

If these people did severe damage to Argine, what would stop them from going on into Sedina? That thought gave him more of a chill, though being here was bad enough. No one had said anything about a tall woman before this. That might be a help if they ever saw a suspicious group.

Mica didn't sleep well at all.

They took their leave not long after sunrise. The path remained nearly empty, though within a few minutes a group of soldiers rode by in some haste. Their horses looked as though the group might have been on the road most of the night. That didn't look good, either.

"Have you figured anything out?" Merriweather asked once they were clear of the buildings.

"Not enough," Mica admitted and almost asked for the larger piece of metal. No, he wanted to study that in more private surroundings. "The metal men must be directed in some way. The metal boxes -- the ones Marly said the people carried -- seem most likely, but I have no clue how it might be done. I do know that they are made to explode and purposely inflict the most damage possible. It's not just explosives, but also some flammable material that is ejected at the same time. I think it might be some sort of resin mixture. It sticks, and it burns; no one would have a chance to get it off."

"That's terrible," Shipley said with a shudder. He walked with a hand on Bear's shoulder as the dog pulled the trunk. "Why do people do awful things like that to others?"

"Because there is evil in the world. If you see these metal men, you and Bear head the opposite direction," Merriweather said. "Promise me you'll do that and get you both out of range."

Shipley gave a silent nod, his hand clutching the dog's fur as though he thought to pull Bear away right now. Mica trusted that the boy would never put Bear in danger -- and that Bear would not leave Shipley in danger, either.

Mica explained a little bit more about the metal men as they walked along. He had seen the tracks where wheels rolled one after another.

"The tracks were not like anything else I've seen, so I can assume that's where they came from, especially since the tracks went to the buildings at odd angles to the road. Once they hit a wall, though, they created an inferno."

Shipley and Bear had moved a little ahead. The discussion obviously bothered the boy. He had grown up rough enough that not a lot would surprise him about evil, but Mica thought he understood this problem. These things were not human, even if they had humans controlling them. They could not be reasoned with. Even a wild animal might back off if it thought it wise, but these metallic creatures had no such sense.

Mica fell silent, and Merriweather didn't pursue the conversation. According to Marly, they were no more than ten miles from the outskirts of Taginta, for all the good that would do them. They had been told by many people that no one got inside the city, and even a few of them heading back along this road -- a road that should have been very busy -- repeated the tale of guards, weapons, and closed gates.

Mica hinted that they had a little business with an army officer concerning cloth -- more than they carried. Marly didn't ask questions. The woman had looked worn and dispirited, and Mica suspected that she would soon give up all she owned and take to the road as well.

He had left her some extra coins.

They walked in silence for some distance. Mica began to see more steam vehicles, all of them older models and abandoned. It would be hard to get coal out here, and all the horses would have been bought up by anyone with enough coin -- the rich who had owned the machines they left behind and taken to the road on foot like so many other refugees. They'd probably buried treasures in the woodlands nearby.

In the final miles to Taginta, they began to see increasingly ornate country houses on hillsides not far from the road. Some of them looked empty, but more had guards patrolling the grounds. Even the four of them drew attention and they didn't argue when two different groups looked inside the trunk. Worried people -- Mica did not want to give them reason to mistrust him.

The land began to fall off in craggy steps, the road cut through in a gentle, downward curve. They'd seen no houses for the last two miles, only stands of pines and ash, and a few tumultuous streams and small waterfalls that might have been dry in less rainy weather.

Shipley moved on ahead along the curve, but before long he returned and met them with a shake of his head.

"They got the road blocked ahead," Shipley said, pushing hair back from his face and looking bothered. "Lots of soldiers this time and none of them too friendly like. I can't see we could get through there without no trouble."

Merriweather gave a nod without questioning his report. "Turn back. We'll take the deer trails again."

"Oh, because that worked so well the last time," Mica mumbled, but they all followed her.

They had seen very few people during the long day, and the road stood empty now. They had no trouble finding a place to slip off, and Merriweather even covered the trail with some dead weeds. The path turned and twisted through the rocky hills, not heading directly toward the city, but Mica knew Taginta couldn't be far away.

"Let's leave the trunk here," Mica suggested as they climbed up another slight incline. "We can cover it with weeds and branches, and if anyone does happen on it, they'll just think someone fleeing the city left it behind and hopes to come back for it."

"Yes," Merriweather agreed. She'd just shoved the sled and trunk a few feet upward and sounded more than pleased to be rid of it.

They unhooked Bear who stepped aside and shook all over, dislodging leaves, twigs, and bits of mud. He looked happy to leave the sled and trunk behind, too. They retrieved anything they might need from inside and once again stuffed that into the smaller packs they carried. Afterward, they covered the trunk and left it behind.

Mica noticed far too few wild animals in the area. Everything had seemed to leave, not just humans. He also knew, from what he'd seen, that there would still be a lot of people in Taginta. Some of them would be essential for the army and the guard, and others probably had nowhere else to go. Unless the military carted them out and deposited them beyond the gates, those poor people were going to remain, for good or bad.

And did Mica want to go into a city in that sort of state?

They found their way to a steep cliff that looked down at the town and the wide harbor -- mostly empty -- that curved back from the canals that lead out from the tamed Vintino River. From here, things appeared mostly calm, and entirely too quiet.

Soldiers were camped directly before the gates, and they even had a couple good-sized cannons on mounts pulled out to guard the road. He saw the first working steam engines, too -- those cannons had not been pulled by horses, and the vehicles stood too either side of them, ready to retreat to safety. Mica expected such groups guarded the other three gates as well. The camp still looked new; if Mica and his friends had arrived a few days earlier, he suspected they could have walked right in.

"They're set to retreat into the city walls as soon as trouble shows up," Merriweather pointed out as she studied the situation. "And maybe hope that this show of force would keep the trouble away. Oh, and wise -- looks like they're digging trenches. The metal men won't be able to get close to those walls."

"The gates though," Mica said with a shake of his head. "Those will be vulnerable once the army retreats inside."

"Guard posts above both sides of the gates," she said with a small wave of her hand. "If they have learned much about the devices, they'll know that they just need to stop them and they'll explode -- but yes, that would be close to the gate, too. I don't think there are easy answers."

"And no way in that I can see," Mica added.

"Port," Shipley said and pointed down at the docks, mostly bereft of any craft, though two were moving down canals toward the center river. The wide delta area here had been tamed for hundreds of years. "Soldiers patrol there, but they don't guard like -- not posts set up. Somewhere there's a secret way from the port to the city proper. How else could thieves move things?"

That was a kind of logic Mica had not considered -- he thought suddenly of Seldon sending Shipley along to help.

The city spanned two sides of the river, but most of the port sat on this side, along with the more significant part of Taginta. Across the river sat the massive, white-walled castle complex and several ornate temples, some of them pushed right up against another tall, craggy outcrop. A vast stone bridge spanned the river and wetlands from one side to the other, but Mica couldn't see many people even there. He imagined that in the dark of night, though, small craft might float from one side to the other if they were careful. Black market goods from the incoming ships would likely stay on this side -- and that made Shipley correct. There would be secret ways past the toll keepers and the tax collectors.

"We need to go in," Merriweather said. She sounded more assured than he had expected. "There are still people within those walls, some of them refugees who came here after they'd faced trouble. That means more answers here, Mica. It's going to be dangerous, but if we can find a way --"

"Let's get closer to the port," Shipley said.

They made their way back into the trees and down the steep hillside. Guard patrolled below, but they never saw the group, even Bear moving carefully from one bush to another. They kept to the deer path when they could and carefully through the brush at other times. Mica realized that he was learning all sorts of new skills.

Night had fallen by the time they reached the cleared area near the docks. Shipley and Bear sat there for a little while and then the boy gave a faintly seen nod to the other two.

"Go back to the trees then," Shipley said. "We'll be back by midnight if all goes well. Don't worry none unless we're not back by sunset tomorrow."

"Shipley --"

"It's not like we haven't done this before, you know. Not here, but this ain't that much different than home, is it? I feel better now, seein' something I understand. Go."

Mica gave Shipley a pat on his arm and scratched Bear's ears, winning a sloppy dog kiss of appreciation. Then the boy and dog moved out into the dark and disappeared.

"Gods keep them safe," Mica whispered. He had stopped asking the gods for things of late, but this time....

Mica and Merriweather moved away from the area and back to the last line of trees and cover there. Guards walked past within a hundred yards. Gregorian would have been appalled, but Mica appreciated how lax these soldiers acted. Mica wished he could have heard more of their random conversations, especially when he heard the word clockwork mentioned.

Neither he nor Merriweather spoke much or slept. The night wore on, the unnatural quiet of the city weighing on him. They watched the city walls and counted the guards. They watched one boat come in and how the soldiers boarded and searched it -- well done in that, at least.

Time went slowly.

When the moon rose, Mica spent some time studying the bits and pieces of gears again. There were still secrets to be found.

"These are mass-produced," he whispered holding up the larger piece that Merriweather had been carrying and then one of the smaller ones. "That's not how Nyle and I do it. We have some molds, but they're delicate and small. These things are rather crude, and no one has even filled down the cogs to fit things together properly as far as I can tell."

"If they're just going to blow up, it's probably not worth pending the time on them."

"True."

"Quiet. Guards."

Another two soldiers went past. The Taginta soldiers were starting to look tired, having been pacing the area for a few hours already. Mica hadn't been able to tell if there had been any change in guards during the long night.

"Still better than in the city," one of them said. "Out here we have a chance to run. And I don't much trust some of them what's left behind --"

And they went on, down a slight incline and up again, disappearing into the shadows.

"Anything more?" Merriweather asked with a nod back to the gears he held.

"The amount of metal flying through the air would be horrible," Mica admitted and tried not to imagine it. "And there would be no easy way to stop these things. I doubt a bullet would penetrate the shell, though one might just cause it to explode. Remember that, Merriweather. You don't want to be close."

She nodded, a slight movement in the darkness. "I hate to think about the people who might be trying to deal with them and have less information than even we do."

"I know. I'm trying to find answers. We don't want them to win in Argine, Merriweather. If they did, they'd turn on Sedina, and by then I suspect they'd be well past the testing phase."

"Kistrin --"

"I haven't given up on him. But this isn't something we can ignore, either. These things are not like the spiders. There's no sign of sea metal or a taint of it in these gears. Granted, I've not found many of the parts, but as far as I can tell, they seem to be nothing more than clockwork windup device."

"No reasoning with them," she replied softly. "We'd have to deal with their creators, and anyone who created these monsters is not going to be reasonable."

"I fear not."

They fell silent again. Mica continued to study the pieces while a bit of fog rose on the river but never lifted high into the hills. It partially obscured the city, though.

They waited.

"There," Merriweather finally said. She pointed to the dark. He saw nothing at first, and then movement that came and stopped came and stopped. "Stay here."

Merriweather crawled out into the weeds and past the path the guards had paced along the edge of the forest. From there she could see the guards' movement better and able to direct Shipley to move at the right times. Soon, Merriweather and Shipley came back, crossing the guards' path on their hands and knees while Bear crawled on his belly behind them -- an amusing sight now that Mica could see the boy and dog were safe.

"Took a bit, it did," Shipley said as he accepted some bread and cheese from Merriweather. He instinctively broke off half and handed it to Bear. "Found the way in, just where I expected it, down on the bank just a little distance beyond the dock. It's an old tunnel but been redone recently, it has. Good and solid. We went all the way inside the city walls and out. Didn't see no one used it the last week or so, but we best be careful. Did a little exploring of the city, too. Not far, but thought we ought to have a feel for the area afore we go in. People are nervous and I heard talk about riots, palace locked down, lack of supplies. No telling when an attack might come. Many seen the metal men and they had one attack what didn't get through at the south gate, but it was enough to scare them."

Mica gave a nod of appreciation at the information. The boy had learned well in Kamere. Merriweather asked a few more questions, but it was plain they were going to leave soon.

"Better to go in at night," Shipley advised. "And I think there might be more ships coming in soon from how busy people at the docks got since I went in. Best to go now afore others start using the tunnel, too."

"Besides, I don't want to be sitting here in the daylight, not anywhere near this path -- and I don't want to retreat so far that we have to hike back in. Let's go," Merriweather said.

They headed down into the fog, which provided a good cover now. With luck, Mica thought they might learn something helpful in Taginta -- thought lately, they'd not had that kind of luck.

CHAPTER TWELVE

M ica had thought to leave the few bits of clockwork material behind, but if they were going to bypass the guards, then there was no reason to fear the gears and such being found on him. If they were caught, he suspected the clockwork material might at least intrigue them. All Mica would need to do then was to find someone who knew him, which wouldn't be difficult in the capital city -- he hoped. He had no idea who might have remained during this crisis.

Mica hoped they would be able to work without notice and he wouldn't need to find someone who could identify him.

Shipley led them upstream along the bank for a few hundred feet, moving silently through cattails and mud. Mica never would have found the opening, but Shipley led them straight to a little dark spot, mostly covered by more weeds. It looked like some animal's den, and the bits of bone and skin strewn close by and just inside did help with the disguise.

Dark inside. Mica could hear Shipley and Bear ahead of him and Merriweather behind. He would not give into fear here as they took one turn and another.

"Going to light a candle," Shipley advised. "I found them here, just like I expected."

The sparks of a flint briefly flashed before him, but then a light steadied. The candle sat in a glass ball and looked easy to carry. Several more sat on a shelf beside Shipley. None of them looked very dusty.

"This is set up well," Merriweather said as she joined them and looked around the area.

Shelves, all of them empty now, covered the right. Mica imagined that good would be brought there, easy to smuggle out to a waiting ship. "Not abandoned, is it?"

"Just not used lately. A week and maybe longer. Not sure with all the strange weather they have here, but I seen no sign anyone's been through since the start of the rains."

The tunnel was well-made and reinforced with braces of sturdy wood. They could stand now that they had moved away from the opening, though Mica had to stoop a bit. Still, he liked it better than crawling as they had at the opening. The world had opened back up a bit, and he found he could breathe easier.

"Definitely a smuggler's passage," Merriweather agreed and patted Shipley on the shoulder. "And I would have thought they'd be using it more now, instead of less."

"Harder to get things in what with the guards out there. Imagine if we'd been trying to lug the trunk in here." Shipley started forward; his voice stayed soft but steady. The place didn't bother him much, it seemed. "And this here is old work. Kept well of late, and a few spots where they shored up the walls right well, but old. I think it might ha' been abandoned for long enough that everyone forgot."

Mica noted the spots where Shipley pointed out more recent work, and he agreed with the assessment. Another thought had occurred to him, though, and one he didn't like much.

"This might be a way to slip the clockwork men into the city," he said.

The other two looked back at him. Merriweather shook her head. "They couldn't bring one of them in where it would have to crawl, right?"

"They could bring them through in pieces," Mica said. "We saw they were assembling them at that tent out by the border. They wouldn't want them full of explosives anyway."

"Good point," Merriweather said. "We'll have to get the local guard watching the spot."

"Seems a shame, don't it?" Shipley said with a rueful shake of his head. "All this time when it been here, and now it's a problem."

"It was always a problem," Merriweather corrected.

"Why? Because people got to buy things without the King's taxes and such? Do they even have a King?"

"King Dynis," Mica supplied and ducked his head at another low spot, though his hair brushed against the dirt which cascaded across his face and down his neck. "The local king is about fifteen years younger than King Abertus, and rather more inclined to take his position seriously and to believe he knows everything."

"You don't like him much," Merriweather said.

"He lectured me on clockwork creation once. If he'd even known half of what he pretended, it might have been an interesting two hours."

Merriweather gave a little laugh. Shipley said no more, except to point out where they passed below the thick walls of the city. This area had been reinforced several times, and Mica hurried past that hundred feet that crossed below the towering stone walls. He stopped and looked back. Mica could see the discoloring of the ground that lay below the wall, but none of the actual stonework, for which he was very happy.

"An explosion here, and this part of the city wall would collapse. A regular army wouldn't have a lot of trouble fighting their way through, especially if it were unexpected," Mica pointed out.

"More warning to give," Merriweather agreed. "Sorry, Shipley."

"Just sayin' it be a shame, that's all. This is fine work."

"I agree," Mica said.

They kept going and finally took a set of steps up to small stone-carved covering that pushed aside, so they had to crawl out and into an alley filled with debris. The lid had a covering of brick on this side and they came out under a broad set of stairs that ran up the side of a windowless building. Across the alley stood another building that looked much the same.

Past midnight by now. Silent. They were in Taginta, and Mica wasn't so sure this was a good idea. He probably should have scouted around to find the enemy army -- though he suspected the local soldiers had already tried. If they could have learned more, turned the information over to someone in charge here, and...

And not gone straight back home. Mica still had to find out about Kistrin.

Maybe the Prince had turned up back at home by now. Maybe this was useless?

All those missing people....

Taginta was older than Kamere, the south having been settled before the colder north. The age showed in the layout of the city and the slow decay of older buildings. The streets and alleys had no set pattern. Even Shadow Walk, with all its hovels, was better laid out than the path they had to take away from the smuggler's tunnel and toward the sound of voices.

An old city, clinging to old ways; Mica didn't see many signs of newer technology here. The streets still showed the ruts of wagons and carriages, and no sign of the smoother tracks where steam vehicles traveled best. Horse troughs and hitching posts dotted the wider streets. The army had at least a couple engines to pull cannons, but all Mica saw here was a broken steam bike, left behind by someone who had probably abandoned he city. Mica hadn't seen much of the city when he'd been here with Gregorian, but he remembered how even his brother had mumbled about it being old-fashioned and conservative. They didn't like change, Gregorian had explained, and hinted that it was the fault of their rulers who feared anything that might upset their rule.

The royalty lived in the castle far up an escarpment on the opposite side of the river, in a place without a personal link to those who crowded in the city where Mica and his friends walked. Even now, Mica hardly considered King Dynis as a part of the situation.

It turned out there were still many refugees in the city. They had taken over the city's two fountain-filled squares which stood within half a mile of each other. People also crowded the streets and alleys between. Mica and his companions didn't go too near any of them yet. The last thing he wanted was to draw attention as a newcomer.

Even in the dead of night, birds circled overhead, their caws and yells mostly lost in the noise of the city. Mica saw one sweep down and grab up food, sometimes to the dismay of someone nearby.

"The two squares," Merriweather said and drew his attention. She nodded left and right. That means Merchant Street must be off to the right, there at the edge of the square. This way."

Mica was surprised that she knew so much about the city's layout. There was nothing about Merchant Street that he knew, but then he wasn't the daughter of an important Kamere cloth merchant, either. Had Mica asked if she had ever been here? He watched her and thought that was a stupid thing to have overlooked.

They drew some notice, but people didn't come near after Bear growled a couple times. Mica had never heard the sound from the huge dog before, and he wasn't surprised to see people rush away in haste. It was more notice, but at least they didn't look like easy prey.

The guards who were patrolling the area glanced their way but didn't look interested in anyone not creating trouble. Shipley kept Bear mostly to the shadows and out of notice when he could. They walked along the edge of the square, skirting people who were curled up and asleep, despite the noise. Mica felt sorry for the younger children and wondered why these people had not left. He suspected they must be refugees who had come here for safety. Some discussions with them might give him some insights into what was happening with the war.

Merriweather was leading them somewhere, but when he moved up beside her, she shook her head, and he knew to be silent, especially in this crowd of people. She found Merchant Street; the name carved into the side of the building at the corner. There were people here, too, but not as many as Mica had expected. Someone who was not a city guard tried to stop them. Merriweather whispered to the man, making certain that no one nearby could hear what she said. Unfortunately, Mica couldn't hear either. He was glad he trusted her.

The man let Merriweather and her companions go through into the street beyond. People had gathered here, but they all looked tougher than the refugees out in the squares. Merriweather led them straight to a rather loud tavern, the shingle showing a crossed dagger and short sword. So, not going to see a friendly cloth merchant apparently.

The building stood two stories tall and looked to be full with loud people and flickering lights, making it a beacon in the coming dark, but he couldn't say he thought this a welcoming place, especially not with the glares the men standing on the stairs by the door.

So why was Merriweather bringing them here?

No one stopped them at the door, so they went on into the crowded interior. Mica didn't like the notice of all these scowling men and women. Most had hands on weapons and clearly didn't want strangers in their place.

Then a tall, broad-shouldered man with curly black hair stood from a table and crossed to her.

"I'll be damned. Have you finally come to join us, Merriweather?"

Mica was not even amazed that someone knew her. Merriweather seemed to know people in a lot of places.

"Not exactly, Storm." She gave a smile to Mica and looked so relaxed in this den of predators that he began to suspect she might be a changeling. "General Storm and I served together on the Middle Isles during the war."

"Tried to steal her away from the army then, but she wouldn't have any of it," the man said with an exaggerated sigh. Some of the people began to smile. "You've come a long way to see me, and not an easy journey from the look of it. Come and sit down, you and your friends and the horse that follows the boy. Bring us some food!"

"Storm --" Merriweather began.

"Sit down. We can pretend that we're all civilized while we talk, right?"

Mica liked him, and he was glad to sit at a table near the corner of the building and with a window just a foot or so away, high up and open to let in a bit of a breeze. The food arrived soon: rabbit, bread, potatoes, and ale. Someone found a bone for Bear. The dog was probably putting on weight while the rest of them lost it.

"I wasn't sure I'd find you here, given how things are going down in this part of the world," Merriweather said. Mica could hear a little surprise in her voice, in fact. "Storm, has anyone from Sedina showed up trying to hire mercenaries in the last few weeks?"

Mica had already guessed they were mercenaries. The man sipped his ale and frowned at the question. "No one has come to us, but there had been a rumor about someone coming our way and going to offer big money. That was about the time the war broke out in your part of the world."

Mica sighed. The food didn't seem so good now.

Storm tilted his head and looked at Merriweather again, no doubt noting both her frown and her silence on the rest of the matter. He also glanced at Mica but didn't ask any questions.

"No one else hired you," Merriweather said with a look around. "What are you doing here, sitting in the middle of all this trouble and not out working?"

"The city hasn't met our price yet," Storm replied and waved away someone with more ale. The woman snarled and backed off. A couple of Storm's men came in closer, though, circling the table and cutting them off from escape.

"It's not like you to let things go to hell just for pay," Merriweather said, her voice soft but clear.

Storm frowned and then leaned forward. "We are already in the city's employ. That's not for common knowledge. We hope to get an offer from the other side and track down who is really behind the trouble. They've been elusive little bastards, Merriweather. We know they're tied to some of the western hill tribes, but there is something more going on out there, and even my people can't hunt it down."

"Do you know anything about the clockwork men?" Mica asked.

Storm frowned as though he had expected the questions to come only from Merriweather, but a glance at her settled his mind. Storm sipped his ale and looked back at Mica as though he really noticed him for the first time. "We have heard about more of the attacks outside the city. I think they're doing testing before they go against Taginta again. They seem to be getting better at directing the damned things, and the explosions are worse. Now you tell me what you are doing here."

Mica looked at Merriweather. This had to be done on her judgment since he had no real idea of what they were into here. He wasn't surprised when she gave a quick nod.

"Trust them," she said. "With everything."

So, he did.

"King Abertus sent us to Argine to find the person who came to hire mercenaries. That person is Crown Prince Kistrin, and there has been no sign of him, except a possible tale about a group of merchants who disappeared like so many other people out in the countryside."

"Crown Prince," Storm repeated so softly that Mica barely heard him. His face did not change, except for the movement of his eyes. The man was good at hiding shock. "So many people have disappeared --"

"And no bodies," Merriweather added. "Or have you found them?"

"No, at least not very many," he said with a significant shake of his head. His hand wrapped around his ale cup again and he looked troubled. "We have tracked some of those taken into the mountains, but we lost them in bad weather and back trails, and we haven't found another trace."

"That's something, at least."

"Sedina has enough problems already," Storm said and looked troubled. "The loss of the Crown Prince could put the country into a panic."

"Exactly," Mica replied.

"And you are?" Storm finally asked.

Mica looked around the room and then back as he smiled. "I am Lord Mica Raventower -- and if these people are interested in clockwork creations, I can help you get their attention."

Mica held up his hand, and one of his ravens flew from the window and landed on the table, metallic head turning from side-to-side as he surveyed the group. Merriweather looked surprised and pleased. Shipley and Bear looked intrigued, but not surprised. Storm just stared.

"Well, damn," Storm said at last. "Welcome to the mercenaries."

CHAPTER THIRTEEN

They quickly ate their meal and then Storm took them to a room upstairs. Dawn wasn't far away.

"We do a lot of work at night and rest through part of the day. Just come down when you are ready. No hurry. Merriweather, does this suit you?"

"Fine," she said with a nod. "Thank you."

"There will be a guard for now," Storm added as he turned to Merriweather.

"Of course. You're not a fool."

Storm nodded again and left them at the door, which opened to a large room with five beds. Even Bear wouldn't have to sleep on the floor if he didn't want to. The single window looked out onto the street where the first gray of the day started to outline the nearby buildings. There was far less activity out there now than there had been during the dark night.

Mica put the raven on the nightstand.

"How did he get here?" Merriweather asked though she looked pleased.

"I saw one flying with the rest of the flock in the square-- or at least I thought so," Mica replied. "I suspect Gregorian sent them to hunt for me. Rose had even said I might find help when we arrived. I assume they were not to show themselves to anyone but me -- and not speak except to me, of course," Mica said. The bird nodded and looked around at the others. "You can speak to them."

"Yes," the bird squawked. The clockwork birds had never learned to be quiet. "Gregorian sent us. Let him know when you arrive in Taginta. One of us flew back tonight. Two still here. We keep out of sight."

"We have to be careful. We don't want people to realize Lord Raventower is here."

"True," Merriweather said and sat down on a bed. She looked worn. "Storm won't say anything, and we can talk to him again later. I want to sleep first, though. This isn't someone you want to have a verbal fencing match with when you're half asleep."

"I had that feeling."

"I was with the army on the Middle Islands during that war," she said and starred at her hands for a moment. Shipley had settled on another bed, Bear on the rug at his feet. "The mercenaries were working with us. We ran into some hellish trouble, and I ended up with them instead of my team. It was five days before I got back to my command, and by then I'd learned that Storm was a man I could trust, as were his hand-picked people. He'd told me where to find him if I ever got here to town. Since no one was talking about mercenaries involved with anything, I thought we might get lucky."

Mica nodded agreement and sat down on the bed by the window. Another raven sat on the building across from them. He felt safer knowing they watched.

"Watch Lord Raventower," the raven cackled. "Find and watch."

Shipley gave the raven a worried glance, but then he threw himself down on the bed and fell asleep. Merriweather hadn't bothered to change either, which was probably wise. Mica had to believe that people hadn't recognized him, but he knew they might have to leave in a hurry.

Mica kicked off his boots and laid back while the raven moved slighly up to the window ledge. It felt more like home at that moment.

By the end of the fourth day staying at the tavern, Mica had customized the room they shared for his own work. They'd moved out two beds, and Storm had secured a large table that had been brought up in pieces and now sat in the middle of the floor. Mica had made a makeshift lamp on a hook above to give light to work. Odd pieces of metal, mostly battered bronze, sat everywhere in the room, and both Merriweather and Shipley had stopped complaining about having to clear off their beds.

No one had found any sign of the Prince, though Storm's people had taken up the hunt in ways that Mica couldn't have managed even with Merriweather and Shipley. The mercenary leader had sent out two long term scouting parties already, and his people had begun to ask more questions in town, too. They were discreet and only said they'd been hired by relatives to find any word on the poor, lost merchant. They were reasonably liberal with their coins, too.

Storm had come to believe that Mica might be the answer to his own dilemma, so he was happy to put his people to Mica's work. This allowed Mica to sit in the room and work on clockwork items, which was as close to feeling normal as he'd had in a while.

This rest would not last, though. If the other side did not show interest in Mica-- and if Storm didn't find any news about the Prince -- he, Merriweather, Shipley, and Bear would have to move on to some other plan. As much as he wanted to stop the clockwork men, Mica could not abandon the King's request to search for his son.

Besides, making purposely flawed clockwork items proved

to be an unpleasant pastime. Too often, Mica would let his mind wander and then he would put together something too good and have to rip it apart again. It was good that he spent most of his time alone. The others didn't hear him curse and snarl.

The plan might work, though. If Mica could infiltrate the other side -- western mountain people was the current thought -- then the ravens could lead the Merriweather and the others to them. He knew it would not be that easy, but this could be a start. All he had to do was draw the right attention and get them to take him away.

Shipley and Bear came back in the late afternoon of another drizzly day. The boy had begun spending more time out on the street, learning the ins and outs of the town. The day after they'd arrived, Storm took advantage of three ships coming into port to set up a story for the boy. Some of his men pretended to be sailors from one of the vessels, looking for a boy and dog who had jumped ship. They said they didn't have much time, and the ships did sail within a few hours. Since there was no money offered, Shipley and Bear just became two more refugees in a city full of them. Shipley, with his northern accent, fit in better once the story spread that he had left a ship, and he soon made friends. No one tried to take Bear after the first day, and since Shipley made it a habit of helping the city guard when he could, he soon gained a sort of immunity to trouble.

Merriweather usually went off with the mercenaries as they wandered the streets of the town. She had abandoned the despised skirt and blouse she'd worn and dressed in plain pants, warm shirt, and a tunic that probably hid more than a few knives. It was vital that she be seen as a regular member of the mercenaries and not as someone new and an outsider. Some of Storm's people knew her from their fighting days during the war, and apparently that counted for a lot with them. Mica tried not to worry.

He always listened for her coming back, though.

Merriweather hadn't told Storm that she and Mica would be married. They both agreed that it seemed an unnecessary complication to a situation already rife with odd problems. Mica suspected Storm had an idea that something more was going on between them, though. Maybe he thought it only an infatuation on Mica's part and didn't want to embarrass either of them. Perhaps he'd seen something more in Merriweather, as well. The man did seem to be perceptive.

Mica and Merriweather had fought together during more recent battles. The head of the mercenaries might not have heard about what they'd done in the north and he might not realize that Mica -- Lord Raventower -- could take care of himself if in the face of danger.

Shipley came in and took the chair to his right and began to sort the piles of items there -- little bits and pieces of metal and glass. The boy's hands quickly moved things from one collection to another; he was a quick learner. He also was excellent at observation.

"Not so good today, huh?" Shipley finally asked. He had begun to sound more like the locals, something the boy worked on to fit in better.

"I made a wonderful little cat," Mica offered. "Then I took her apart again and made a spider that had trouble with its legs."

"That's better then," Shipley said with a nod.

"This is not easy. Tell me things you heard today."

"Not much. There might be a ship coming with supplies from the north. People aren't sure. They think it unlikely that our people would send supplies to them when they just got through the war."

"Depends on the supplies." Mica pushed aside the pieces of metal he'd been working with in disgust. "Our hinterlands were virtually untouched, except for the refugees who headed inland from the coast. We lost a good part of the capital and goods there, but Sedina has supplies still."

Shipley looked around. "I still have trouble realizing the wideness of things, you know? Even after all our journey, I still see the world as just the streets of cities. Why does Sedina have food and such to give away, and Taginta don't? Oh. It's them hills, right?"

"Exactly. Less arable -- not good farmland. Under other circumstances, we'd be trading for Argine metal, which they have more of than we do. Right now, it might be that the King sees it is wise to support the people here and not have to deal with a new set of rulers."

Shipley nodded and sorted more of the pieces in silence. Shipley had gathered up an extensive education on his own, including putting clockwork pieces together. It was good to have him around because Mica missed Merriweather and her good judgment. She went off with the others most days, proving that she trusted the mercenaries. He did the same.

Besides, Shipley had begun teaching Mica how to not sound like Lord Raventower. Mica learned the slang and practiced the accent. He'd also started letting his hair grow out, cultivated a small beard and mustache, and wore plain glass spectacles. Mica tried to remember to squint a lot when he took them off. A rock embedded in the heal of his shoe also created a decided limp and a grimace when he walked, which also helped hide his change in identity.

Mica was learning to be someone else. He had to be if he dealt with these other clockwork people. Mica knew Merriweather didn't like that part at all, but this was far too dangerous of a situation to ignore, and there wasn't going to be anyone else the mercenaries could bring in for this role. Even Storm had agreed, though he had reservations about an important lord from Sedina going into any danger. They talked it out and with Merriweather's help, convinced him that Mica was not some wilting flower that would crumble under the first sign of trouble.

Mica sat at the table and created flawed creations. The most important one was the three-foot long centipede -- a poor choice since he had forgotten Merriweather's dislike of the creatures. It was showy and moved well on open ground, which he hoped would be a lure. They'd taken it outside to crawl up the building twice, just to get it out in the open. It had failed that part of the test, of course, but did well enough to draw a few crowds and get the word spreading through the town.

"They will have people in the city," Storm said as he sat at the table that night. He'd had dinner brought up, and Mica cleared work. Storm came up every few days to keep them informed on their two projects. "We've planted a few rumors so we can track some of them, but we haven't been able to pin down any specific group."

"Annoying," Merriweather said between bites of rabbit stew. They did eat well. "Mica, we heard that they did two more tests in villages nearby. It sounds as though they might be getting better with the devices."

"Damn." He stopped and sipped the cider and then frowned. "Have you decided on a target for the real test of the centipede?"

"Copper Merchant's holding house," he said with a wave toward the window. "Rumor has it that they haven't moved out all their gold yet."

"A rumor that your people started," Mica said.

Storm grinned. They were getting along better. "Yes, that's true. I want as much control over this show we put on as possible. I have to hope they won't just kill you as a potential rival."

"They won't," Merriweather said, and that reassured them

both. "They're still doing tests, Storm. They're working out the kinks in their own system, and someone with Mica's amount of knowledge is going to draw them straight to him, especially if they think he's involved in something illegal already. We just have to be ready."

"The ravens will help," Mica reminded them both with a nod toward the metal bird that sat on the windowsill. "We're damned lucky to have them here."

"They aren't normal," Storm said and looked at him.

"No, they aren't." Mica looked as well. He'd sent a bird north with word of the plan and what little they'd learned about Kistrin. "But they are clockwork, and they are mine. These people are likely to take me out of the city, and the ravens will be able to track me."

Storm stared at the bird but then looked back at him and nodded. "I want the clockwork men stopped."

"The tall woman was with them for the tests, Mica," Merriweather said. "And they had those boxes again. Someone said they saw dials on them, and they held them with straps over their shoulders."

He nodded. "Some way to control the metal men. No new changes to the clockwork devices?"

"None in how they appeared to work," Merriweather replied.

"Good. These people are locked into a single design for some reason. I suspect they don't have anyone who can plan another system. And that, Storm, is why they're going to want me. The centipede will look like a way to get into smaller areas or over walls, and maybe move better on solid ground."

"As long as they don't actually get it to work, we're fine," Storm replied. He'd finished his food but didn't look in a hurry to leave.

"The design is flawed," Mica reassured him with a wave at the centipede. "And since they don't have anyone making other than clockwork men, I have to think they are not going to do better without me. I am not really going to help them, you know. You are going to track me and put an end to all of this."

Storm nodded and might even have looked a little more assured. Merriweather frowned, but then she'd done that every step of the way so far.

"I have a report back from one set of scouts today," Storm said, leaning back in his chair. "There is definitely something going on west of the city and far up in the hills. And yes, that is where it seems they've been taking people, most likely to help them with work. They're hidden in the back country somewhere, but it's a land filled with hills and valleys, and it could take months to track them -- maybe even a year or more with winter setting in. They do get snow and lots of it back there. That means they are either going to actually attack soon or wait for spring."

"I don't have that feeling they're willing to wait," Merriweather said. "The tests indicate they are moving closer."

"Yes," Storm agreed. "And we can even hope that the weather will force them to move sooner than they want. Winter is coming early this year. I have not found any specific sign of your Prince, but if they are grabbing people for work -- "

"They won't know they have him," Mica said and dared hold a little hope at that thought. "Kistrin is smart enough to keep his identity a secret, he and his guards. Let's hope I am taken to wherever they are building these things. That would be where they need people."

"At least we don't have to worry about the war in Sedina," Storm said. "Word came with supplies today. There has been no sign of Atrians coming back, and the ocean appears to be clear all the way to the Middle Islands."

"Good," Merriweather replied.

"I would have thought a war would have suited mercenaries better, though," Mica replied.

"I like border conflicts, small battles," Storm admitted. "That's how we've done so well. Outright wars are too bloody and destructive."

That was an interesting take on it.

Shipley, Bear, and Merriweather went down to spend time in the common room, but Storm paused at the door for a long moment while the three walked away. Then he turned back to Mica and gave a sudden smile.

"She calls you Mica. What do you call her when you are alone?" he suddenly asked.

"Merriweather -- because I am not going to be stupid enough to use any other part of her name. You won't get it from me."

Storm laughed and left.

Mica considered the news for the rest of the evening while he toyed with the centipede. He weakened one leg and set the opposite to move faster than the others. He tightened the springs and turned the dial, bringing it to life. The thing limped across the floor and startled Merriweather when she came back through the door.

"I may not forgive you for this one, Mica," she said, but she laughed. "How do you make it limp like that?"

"By doing stupid things with the settings," he replied, not happy that he had to do it. "This would be a fine little machine for some work, you know. Make it smaller, and it could climb apple trees and vibrate, bringing ripe fruit down --"

"Hadn't thought of anything useful." She dropped into a chair. "It looks as though things are starting to move, Mica. I don't think we'll have much more time. I want this over with, but I want you to be careful."

CHAPTER FOURTEEN

A second clockwork raven sat on the windowsill the next morning, and the third kept watch across the street.

"News back from Gregorian," Mica said, waking the other two. He wondered why Merriweather didn't have her own room, but he supposed she still took the work of protecting him seriously. Good. He felt safer with her around, knowing his mind wandered too often.

The raven carried a pouch around its neck -- the raven clutched it in metal claws and handed it to him. Mica had mentioned in his last letter that talking ravens could cause trouble here. The message was in Gregorian's hand and didn't reference anyone, but Mica understood the allusions. He read while Merriweather went to get Storm. He began to think the man never slept.

"The King is glad we're working on the clockwork men trouble," Mica told them. "He also hopes we're right, and the Prince was taken by these people."

"And they're both not happy with your idea of going with them," Merriweather added with a tap of the paper she had taken in hand.

"Gregorian doesn't like it when I go riding by myself and

on my own estate," Mica reminded her.

"I can understand that feeling," Merriweather replied and sat the paper aside. It would go in the fire after Mica read it again. "You are given to doing odd things, Lord Raventower."

"And you aren't?" he asked.

"You two work well together," Shipley offered.

Even Storm laughed. Good.

"He sent an odd bit of news," Mica said. "Down at the bottom, the postscript. "Priest Seldon says to look to the west, and he fears we'll be cold soon."

"I'm not really surprised," Merriweather said. "But I hope that he means some people are behind this, and not some gods."

Storm didn't take the words too seriously, and probably had no real use for Priests. He was a lucky man who didn't deal so closely with them and the gods they served. Shipley headed for the door to take Bear out, and only gave them a quick frown. He was here because of Seldon and must have started wondering at the power the priest had over others.

"There you have it," Mica said, waving the paper before he crumpled it up and tossed it on the brazier where it flared and burnt. "The King, and even General Gregorian, have approved of this matter."

"It sounded as though they had reservations," Storm protested.

"Gregorian didn't order me to stay here, and there are no troops on the way," Mica replied. "Though we could probably get some if we wanted."

"Not yet," Storm said. "Not here in the capital. The Sedinans have built up a larger force at the border, but since that group has helped fight against the clockwork men and the barbarians from the mountains, no one is complaining."

"Has there been another attack in that area?" Merriweather asked.

"Not on the soldiers, but at a couple of the villages nearby."

"I want a map showing where all the attacks took place."

Storm nodded. "I have one in my room. I'll bring it."

Storm headed out, leaving the door open which meant he'd be back in a moment. Mica and Merriweather were alone for only moments. There really wasn't anything to say, though. She just patted his shoulder, a sign that she was both worried and pleased that things were moving forward.

They studied the map for a while. Merriweather tapped spots on the paper. "Everything has been either to the west of Taginta or south of the border to Sedina -- even though going over the border would not be that difficult."

"They don't want to stir up that sleeping beast," Storm suggested.

"Probably true. If Seldon is right --" Mica began.

"Has he ever been wrong?" Merriweather asked.

"Not that I've seen. So, we can assume there we are right about the trouble in the mountains. Honorgates would be my first guess about who is behind it, but then I might be fixated on them." Mica stopped and shoved back his scraggly hair.

Storm might have been ready to ask something, but someone downstairs called to him, and he left.

"Looks like a lot of damage out there," Mica said, his fingers tracing the lines between the villages. "I wish I was doing more to stop this."

"We can't push them into grabbing you." Merriweather leaned closer over the map, studying it intently. "They aren't using any of the marked trails, or else they'd have been spotted. They'd be seen with all the people on the move --"

"Would they? Or could they look like just more refugees heading one way or another?"

"Maybe. Pieces of their creatures spread out -- but I don't get that feeling, Mica. I think they're on unmarked trails, and that means they would need to have guides --"

"You guessed that right," Storm said as he came to the door again. "Just got another scout group back. Whomever this is, they are getting help from tribes in the mountains. My people ran into a group of them and had a short battle before my scouts retreated in haste. They were harried for a few miles, but as long as they didn't head into this area -- his finger circled a wide swath of land on the map -- they didn't have any trouble."

"There are a couple villages back there," Mica said noting the spots. "Any word on them?"

"Nothing I have heard," Storm said. "I'll ask around. No one really heads up into the mountains this time of year except for a few trappers, and they wouldn't be back to the city this early unless they were run out."

"Or they could be captured," Merriweather reminded him.

Storm nodded and gathered up his map. "I get the feeling we're going to be moving on this soon," he said and looked at the two of them. "A bit of coincidence, I think; we had a ship come into port today saying they had trouble with some strange octopus creature that tried to take them down. From what I heard, they're pretty shaken."

Mica and Merriweather both nodded.

"You know about this thing, don't you?"

"We started out by sailing to Argine," Mica said. "We soon gave up the sea."

Storm gave a grim nod and left. He pulled the door closed this time, and they could hear his heavy steps all the way down the stairs.

"He didn't ask us what we knew about it," Mica pointed out.

"One battle at a time," Merriweather explained. "And as long as Payton stays in the ocean, we concentrate on this."

"He's attacking others."

"Probably to try and draw you back out to where he can get hold of you. Not yet, Mica. We've invested too much in this problem to abandon it and start something else. Winter is going to strike here soon, and the clockwork men will move before the snow is too deep; that's my guess. If I'm wrong, we will know when there are no winter attacks. We don't have the resources for both -- and Payton, as far as we can tell -- is alone. He's also attacking, but letting the ships go so that he has your attention. Let's do this right."

Mica agreed. "Besides, if Payton is still here along the coast, he's not out looking for his lost god."

"Good point. We'll deal with him soon enough."

Mica knew she was right. He spent the afternoon working on the centipede and trying hard not to make it better. By evening the weather had turned damp and cold, and Mica didn't need the barometer he kept back at Raventower to tell that the weather was about to change.

By dawn, they had high winds, snow, and ice everywhere. Mica and his friends were all glad to huddle into the room, staying close to the brazier. They had coal for warmth, and Mica wondered if it came from the coal fields in the northern corner of Sedina. He suspected so and worried about the supply in the city since the war had slowed down production. And what about the people out on the streets, all those refugees they'd seen on their way into town?

Not his city, Mica told himself.

Like that would make a difference to him.

"I get the feeling the storm might not be natural," Mica told Merriweather and Shipley. "There's just a feel to it that I don't much like."

"At least the ships will stay at port." Merriweather stood by the window and seemed to watch the ice building up against the already pitted glass.

"I'd like to know what the local priests think," Mica said.

"I'll find out," Shipley said as he stood. He lifted both hands when they started to speak. "I have to take Bear out anyway, and it's not like the two of us never seen worse than this in Kamere. The temple districts not far. I know people there."

He left.

"That boy is too good at this work," Merriweather said with a shake of her head. "Good thing he's smart."

Mica agreed, but he shivered at the sound of the wind at the window. Something told him they'd be going out in the weather soon as well.

"There he goes," Merriweather said and suddenly laughed. "Bear looks like he's really having a good time, too."

"Good. I suppose it's not so bad out there, really. I had come to like the southern winter before this, though in the spring. I'm glad the snow comes so much later in this area, unlike Kamere."

"I haven't minded myself." She came and sat at the table. "But I still want to go home -- even in winter. We're going to finish this up, Lord Raventower. Then we'll get back to Kamere, take the pod out, and deal with Payton."

"Ah, good plan! I hadn't considered the pod in a while. That might take him by surprise."

Maybe that trouble would be ended soon, too. Mica liked the idea. Then they could spend the rest of the winter at Raventower and perhaps a few weeks in the spring out at the estate. He wondered if Merriweather liked kittens. They needed a cat or two in the tower to keep the rodents down. They should work on remodeling more of the building.

Such odd, domestic thoughts.

Shipley came back about midmorning. Bear sat by the heat dripping ice crystals and snow around him and looked infinitely more pleased than the humans. Merriweather pushed a rug his way, and the dog flopped down on it, looking both tired and happy.

"You guessed right about the storm," Shipley said. He'd brought up a tray with tea and wrapped his cold fingers around a mug. "More than one priest is saying there's magic in the air. Storm wants to hire me, and he doesn't seem to know that more money isn't going to change my mind."

Merriweather slapped the boy on the shoulder which was like getting a hug from her. Mica felt an odd surge or relief. He had known Storm had taken notice of the boy's abilities, just as Gregorian, Rose, the King -- and probably even Seldon by this point. In fact, he suspected that might have been the reason Seldon sent the boy to them. Shipley knew what information they needed and how to get it.

Storm came up a little later. "I have news. There is a group in town that looks like they might be our people, sans their metal friends. They've been asking about you, Mica. About the man with the centipede."

"Showtime," Mica said with a glance at the centipede. He frowned at the weather. "I don't know if the storm helps or not, but they set the stage, not us. You know where they are?"

"Not too far from where we planned to do our show," Storm said. "Not so close it won't take them a bit to get there, though, so it won't look like a setup. It'll just look like we're taking advantage of the weather."

Storm agreed. Mica had the feeling he was going through the list of every protest he'd made so far, but he didn't bring any of them up, especially when Merriweather said nothing. They took the pieces of centipede down the steps. Shipley and Bear came with them since the boy had his own part in the setup. Spreading news of what was going on would be tricky. They let Shipley out first, and he hurried off. Mica gathered what he needed and went out more slowly.

Mica found that he didn't mind the weather so much after all. The brisk, cool wind, though it came up the river from the distant bay, still felt like a winter wind off the sea. The faint scent of sea water helped as well. Even the snow was not so bad. This was almost like home and he lifted his head into the feel.

"Northerners," Storm grumbled as he pulled his cloak tighter. "Stop looking so happy. You'll give yourselves away."

"Alas, he's right Merriweather," Mica said. He hunched into his cloak and pulled the hood up. The stone embedded in the shoe still helped with the limp, but he had gotten somewhat used to it, which made it look more natural. The glasses wanted to slip down, and he pushed them back again. They came around the corner and found that most everyone who had been living in the squares had found what cover they could. Even better since he didn't want any real trouble starting when they did the show.

Mica caught Merriweather by the arm and shoved her into a pile of snow and ice.

She came back up sputtering, and not gaining her feet as fast as she usually would have.

"All for the show," Mica said and managed not to even grin.

Storm had begun coughing as he fought back the urge to laugh aloud. Mica suspected they were both in a lot of trouble.

A half dozen of Storm's men followed them, all carrying the various pieces of the centipede rather prominently on display. The ravens fluttered from building to building. They were not alone up there, either, so they hid amid the other birds. He hoped no one looked too closely. Best just to get this business done and to make it possible for people to go back home again.

The refugees did have tents now, though, he noted. Bonfires, too. While this couldn't be pleasant, it might have been worse. The people in the north had survived in much the same sort of covering, and with even colder weather.

Unlike in Kamere, the King and Queen of Argine had not opened their grounds to people in need. Mica had barely even thought of the ruling family, and probably because he had known how ineffectual they had been even when he visited with Gregorian. They were symbols, but the real power rested with the merchants. Mica wasn't sure if that was bad or not, except he would have liked to see better care for these poor people.

Then he wondered who had gotten them the tents.

They found the Copper Exchange, a building with decorative ribbons of pounded copper and solid copper doors. Mica had been inside. The ostentatious interior had won a smirk even from him back then, who was not ever the most discerning of people. He played along with Gregorian, though, who had absolutely agreed that they had no building like this in Kamere.

He almost wished they were really going to rob the place.

They began to draw a crowd. Part of that was Shipley's work, but many were mercenaries dressed and acting like locals -- loud and belligerent demanding what was going on and carefully keeping the real locals away from any trouble. Storm, though, was well known and drew the attention as he stood just a few steps from Mica who knelt in the icy street and put his creature together. Merriweather didn't stay near him for fear that someone would recognize the two of them if they were together. There could be some people from Kamere who had gone south to escape that war.

Some of the local guards did come around. Storm's people handled them, drawing them off in a bit of an argument and away from Mica. Mica put the creature together, snarling and cursing the whole time. Storm stalked over to him.

"Make it good. We appear to have someone watching from the roof across the street. Lucky that your raven flew off before they arrived. We think they have others nearby. And I like this less and less."

"Let's just get it done."

Mica stood and all but threw the centipede against the wall. These were not his creatures, not like the butterflies and ravens. Just a tool.

The centipede's clawed feet caught in the uneven grooves of the stone surface and started up, slipped halfway up the first floor, and tumbled back down. Mica made a quick adjustment.

"Let's do this right," he said softly and put it back on the wall.

The clockwork centipede stared up, began to slip -- there was ice after all, but not much on this side of the building. It caught and kept going up. It was, in fact, doing better than Mica had expected, which might be a problem.

Then, at the second-floor window, the centipede started to fail. It reached a window, but only one of the legs caught hold. The rope deployed but snarled.

"You told me --" Storm thundered.

Mica spun on the man. "I tells you it needs work!" he whined. "You want everything now. Clockwork isn't that easy! I'll take it back. I'll work on it."

"You said you could do this," Storm said. He caught Mica by the collar and almost lifted him off the ground. There was a glint of humor in his eyes. "If this thing can't even move properly, how can it help us?"

"Give me a chance," Mica begged. His voice had gone up a few octaves and grown louder. "You know I can do better."

"I don't know anything of the sort about you," Storm said and let him go with a little shove. "Get the damn thing. I'm going back."

Storm stalked away along with some of his men, though a couple stayed close as though to make sure he didn't run. Merriweather was not one of those left behind. Better not to be seen close, he reminded himself, though he knew she wouldn't be far.

Mica knelt on the cold ground and began taking apart pieces of the centipede, muttering curses and taking the time to fit a few of them together again, as though to prove that it would work. He suspected they would have to do this show again before anyone really took notice. He was too anxious to be done with the entire project --

And this was just the start of it, Mica reminded himself. He still had to get to that woman and put an end to whatever she had planned. He especially wanted to know how she controlled the metal men with those boxes. That was something he had never tried because he had a particular tie to some of his creations. Mica had not wanted to use sea metal again after learning it had come from a statue long haunted by a man who had become part of a god. It seemed too dangerous to play with now that he knew the truth.

The sound of a dog barking almost made him smile. Shipley and Bear were letting him know they were watching too. When the dog barked again, he knew to be ready. The two had seen trouble coming this way, even if his guards had not.

"Trouble coming," he warned softly. "Don't fight too hard."

"We have to make a good show for Merriweather," one of them said. "We don't want to annoy her."

"Or make the people wonder why we gave up so easily," the other added. "But yeah, mostly we don't want to annoy Merriweather."

They almost made him laugh.

The people coming down the street looked like priests heading for a temple. That annoyed Mica, maybe because he was a High Priest, though he had never acted in that capacity. If the people of Kamere knew that a god walked among them

--

Focus on here and now. Deal with this problem.

The attack was swift and over quickly because Mica let himself fall into their hands by trying to run away and proved that he was not a fighter. Storm's men only made one feint and pulled back. One ordered the other to run and get help.

"You come with us," a man said as he grabbed Mica by the arm and hauled him along. They kept their hoods down. Afraid of being recognized? "You come with no fight."

"No fight. Yes, no fight."

A couple others had grabbed the centipede. They headed quickly down a side street and another, all of them empty in this weather, though Mica feared he saw one dead body, so they had probably killed anyone who might have seen them. Somewhere behind them, Mica could hear shouts and Storm's loud voice above the others. A dog barked again, but this time he couldn't be certain if that indicated Bear and Shipley or not.

Remembering the body, he hoped the boy stayed back this time.

Birds took flight on the building beside them, and he heard a couple odd caws as they wheeled around in the air. That would be his ravens moving in and keeping him under watch. Unsettling other birds made it less likely they would be noticed. They, in turn, would show the way to Merriweather and whoever came with her.

She would be back there. Mica had no doubt of that part and didn't worry so much that she might fall into a trap. He hadn't seen any more than these six, and no sign of guards they'd passed along the way. They seemed just anxious to get out of the area and to get him away.

Mica didn't argue. He mumbled and cursed and asked -- but they told him to shut up, so he did. They took his meekness for granted before too long. A slight shove would get him rushing faster, and a glare would quail him before he said anything more than a whispered curse. He limped and they had to slow or carry him. He shoved his glasses into place then let them slide down and peered over the frame while he tried to keep a mental map of the twists and turns they took.

Tall buildings filled this part of town and few had windows on the ground floors. If there were people anywhere in the buildings themselves, they made no show of seeing the odd group rushing through the streets below. Mica glanced up once or twice and realized this was a factory district, much like part of Kamere. The buildings had the feeling of being shut down, too. He supposed that with everything going on, getting supplies to make whatever they made here might be difficult.

Maybe the workers were the people who were sent out of the city in case of trouble -- trained factory workers who would be needed more than the poor, he supposed. Maybe he should have tried to see the King and Queen after all. Could he have talked them into a little better care of their poor? The royalty he had seen years ago had been afraid of their people, he realized now.

Fools.

Mica and his new companions had gone a long way already, and he thought he ought to complain again, though he did so softly and with a bit of a gasping breath. The man in charge -- a scar across his chin, his gray eyes glaring -- slowed a bit again, but not much. That told Mica they still had some distance to go.

He hoped his friends were still following, although not too closely. He didn't think this group had lost them, no matter how often they changed direction. The ones who had grabbed him were also not the people in charge, he realized. They were following orders. In fact, he had no way to know if they were involved with the clockwork men or not.

Merriweather and the others didn't dare act too quickly though. Mica had hoped that they might be going to some secret house in one of the buildings, one where he would meet

people sufficiently in power to make it worth a raid. Otherwise
--

"I don't know Janeh's going to like him much," one finally muttered. They were heading into an alley that didn't appear to have a way out. Maybe the place was close?

"No matter. He's her toy now."

Not a building. Someone pulled open a part of a wall, to steps downward. How the hell many secret passages were there under this town?

They went in quickly and pulled the covering back in place. Had his ravens been close enough to see? The others would figure it out eventually, but he could already tell this was a maze of passages, and all of them looked well used. More thieves? With his luck, he'd just fallen in with a Thieves' Guild and not the enemy army.

They kept him under guard, a single candle lighting the way. He couldn't even leave a scrap of cloth or paper with men spread out all around him. He made no protest, though he did sniff and cough now and then, and start at any sudden sound. He and Shipley had worked out the show, and he mumbled and cursed -- and hoped that this was not going to go on too long.

Maybe he would be home soon....

CHAPTER FIFTEEN

Four days later, they were still on a desolate trail heading west.

Mica had not expected the men to take him straight out of the city, and certainly not bundled up, shoved on a horse -- which gave him trouble all the way -- and led off into the dark of night. They'd been hours in the tunnels until he had no idea where they'd finally come out. It was not at the same spot where his group and come into the city, but somewhere to the west and already into some hills.

Mica had found no sign of the ravens, either. Hell.

His friends would have guessed the group had slipped out of the city. Merriweather would be out looking for their path and Mica had a firm belief that she would not give up. Mica and his surly companions were not moving quickly, either. Each night they slept on the ground and ate mediocre food while huddled around small fires. The land rose and fell, and the paths were little more than deer trails the farther they went. His bad-tempered horse balked at anything out of the ordinary and slowed them down a bit each day. Mica didn't even have to encourage the bad behavior very often and the horse was willing to play along with the game. He loved the animal that was his unintentional ally and slipped the creature some of the coarse bread now and then since he didn't much like it.

The others wore the clothing of the western tribe, mostly leathers and fur, their light hair long and wild. They spoke the language of some western tribe sometimes. Mica didn't understand much of it, but that gave him something to work on and kept his mind occupied during the ride. Better that rather than to think the others might not find him again.

Well, he'd just have to make sure he could get back out on his own, then. Understanding more of what the people said would help. He kept his head down, mumbled and cursed now and then, and just listened.

They spoke of Janeh often, and not in tones of pleasure or even respect. Janeh, he suspected, must be the tall woman seen with the clockwork men. They did not speak much of the devices themselves. In fact, he had the feeling they thought the clockwork men were taboo in some way -- evil demons, perhaps. He filed that thought into his hold of useful information for the future.

And they rode on.

The landscape grew rougher. The party followed the edge of a half-frozen stream as they climbed higher in the towering mountains where snow glinted on the high peaks, but each day it appeared to slide farther down the terrain. The trail showed signs of wagon travel now and then, but those were older prints, and Mica thought they had not had anything of that size up here since maybe last spring since the ruts had been dug in the mud and then trampled over by horses.

By midday, he found snow on the ground, mostly in the shadowed spots. Mica scowled at it and pulled the blanket he used as a cloak all the closer.

They camped again that night, but he had the feeling they were very close to their destination. The men had been sullen for days and now actually smiled sometimes. They had not mistreated him, but he had hoped for better. Janeh wanted him, though. They took him to her.

He began to suspect that they didn't expect him to survive the meeting with their leader, and so they didn't want to make friends. That was a chilling thought, but he'd just have to win Janeh over. So far, he thought maybe she was mostly more than a little egotistical. She had command. What did she offer these men, who did not seem entirely bad, that they would join with her?

Did she rule them through the fear of those demon metal men?

Things to find out.

It snowed that night. Mica huddled under his blanket, unhappy with everything and tried to remember why he thought this was a good idea. He wanted to stop the war -- Mica knew that without a doubt -- but there must be better ways then traipsing through the cold western mountains, riding a bad-tempered horse and being snowed upon.

They were getting closer to the destination. Good. Be done with this.

Go home.

That night, as Mica laid down with the blanket tight around him, a creature crept closer to the fire for warmth, and he almost kicked at it away in annoyance. Maybe he was getting too deep into his act. He couldn't blame some poor animal for wanting warmth, or maybe stealing a bit of the food still sitting on plates by the fire.

The creature came closer, slow steps.

The sound of metal feathers fluttering slightly. Oh yes, he knew that sound. When he lifted the edge of his blanket, the raven rushed forward. Someone moved and coughed. Mica stayed still, and the raven did not move.

Not alone out here. Mica knew it even before the raven moved close to his head and whispered. "Merriweather nearby."

"Wait for my sign," he said in return. "Let's find out what is going on."

Someone moved again. A little later the raven walked away back into the woods. The falling snow soon covered the tracks.

Mica had to work hard the next morning not to smile for no apparent reason. They loaded up and rode away again, the day turning cold and the wind bitter and filled with snow. Mica tried to look worried, and he did not watch the trees nearby or look up when he heard a bird go past. They were near the end of the journey, and then if all went well, it would just be a matter of taking care of what they found.

The nebulousness of that idea did suddenly bother him, but they did have mercenaries to handle that sort of work.

Didn't they? The raven had said Merriweather was near, not that --

Mica chided himself for inventing more trouble. After all, he'd put Merriweather by herself up against any group of rebels and invaders. They rode on, but with a little more speed, and Mica knew they wanted to reach a specific destination. Once he thought he saw Bear standing by some rocks in the distance, but it might have been a wolf or even an actual, but young, bear. Mica didn't want Shipley and the dog to be close by. This was not a situation he could fit into this time, but the sight had reminded Mica of not being alone again.

Mica had done too much traveling of late. It was time to get done with this trouble and settle in for the rest of the winter. That thought pleased him again, though he kept a snarl on his face. Ada and the others at the tower had to be worried by now, though he supposed Gregorian would keep them as informed as he could. His brother considered such odd things like the feelings of Mica's servants.

Or maybe he realized that they were Mica's family. His brother was wise in that way sometimes.

Mica wanted this madness done, so he gobbled his food, mumbled and snarled, and stayed in character knowing now was a more crucial time than the rest of the journey. Mica dared not do anything that would make them wonder, so he was careful when he gave the horse his bread, and he sat hunched and cursing in the saddle the whole morning. That part really wasn't so difficult. The ride had been uncomfortable from the start.

Mica had not had his hands on any sort of clockwork material since they left the city. Playing with such things might have calmed him, but that was such a Raventower trait that he even had to fight to keep his hands still.

He did have the parts for a few insects scattered through his clothing and one bag he'd had when they left Taginta which was full of things that he could have used on the clockwork centipede. He had hoped that if he needed to run, having his insects might prove helpful.

They passed a spot where there had been a battle, the sign of a mass grave not far off the main road, and not old. The dirt that showed through the layer of snow held no summer grass, and it had not worn down at all. He thought he could see where wolves and probably dug in as well.

The grave was a sober reminder that this was more than a game of clockwork toys. Mica pulled his makeshift cloak closer and bent lower over the saddle again.

They finally met with a guard -- and one who was not a tribesman, so they had to speak words Mica fully understood.

"This is him?" the man snarled. He shook some snow from his hair as he came forward -- someone used to the weather, at least. "Doesn't look like much."

"No care," one of the men who had brought him said with a snarl. "Got him for Janeh, him and his machine. Collect bounty. Then hers."

The guard nodded and waved them on and didn't pay any

more attention to Mica. Good. He did notice more guards in the woods and began to recognize the bird calls they used as warning systems. The others would not get too near yet unless they intended to attack before Mica went into the enemy camp. After all, they must know where it is by now, right? He could almost hope for a last moment rescue before this got worse.

But no. While Mica knew his friends might be near, that didn't mean Mica knew any more than he had in the city. He had a name -- Janeh -- whom he thought would be the woman. The tribesmen had also hinted sometimes at a northerner. Mica could be wrong, but he had the feeling that there might be someone from Sedina involved in this. If that were so --

Mica did not give his own signal to be taken out, not yet. If Merriweather decided to get him without that signal to the ravens, then that was her choice, but Mica had finally gotten close enough to the people involved in all those murders that the journey might have been worth it.

Since Mica had not attempted to escape during the long ride to this winter land, they did not try to restrain him more than making certain there were other guards near. That meant he had a clear view of the enemy camp when they finally came to it.

The path had been hewn through rock with cliffs around them and a scattering of trees. He had started to notice a strange scent to the air. Metallic? The cold had become bitter in the last day as they climbed upward, and it was not just his horse that complained now. Guards moved on the trail itself, but they were screened by rocks and trees, and not even one of his ravens would have dared to get this close. Then Mica heard a different set of sounds as they topped a rise and he saw the camp at last.

Not a camp -- a small village, and it looked quite normal from where he sat on his recalcitrant horse as they came over the last pass and started down the hill. Soon, though, they were recognized -- and the normality disappeared. Guards moved out from beside buildings, herding people who did not appear to be clothed appropriately for the weather, toward some work. The houses were supplemented with a row of shacks, and Mica could see, a bit higher on the hill, what must be a mine and the area where they smelted iron ore. From what he could see, the ore production looked primitive -- but probably effective.

The locals were herded about by guards and must have lost their battle against the invasion. Probably, if anyone came this way, they saw normality until they were either sent away or captured and put to work. Up by the mine stood a set of shacks that looked as though they might fall over at any moment. That would be the people who dug the mines and the ones that worked the metal. It must have been a hellishly good iron strike here and probably what drew the enemy from the start.

They kept the village intact for show. If someone noticed how things were out of place, they would likely become part of the workforce. People had been disappearing to this place for some time, and no one had caught on yet, nor would they with the hard winter settling in and all the passes soon closed off.

Did they intend to winter here and attack in the spring?

Mica still didn't think so, but it was something more to find out.

Once they were down in the village, they ordered him to dismount, and someone took the horse. Mica gave the creature one last surreptitious pat and silently wished the animal luck. He hoped they kept the poor thing fed. Probably it would do better than him, though. They'd want the horses when they began their attack.

The guards took him into the best of the houses -- a place with rugs, wall hangings, and odds and ends of the family that must have lived there before these enemies moved in. He shivered a little, a real one this time, and wondered where the family had gone, and if their ghosts watched.

A warm place. After all the days out in the cold, it almost felt too hot.

A tall, hard-faced woman came from another room. The guard who had brought him in -- not one of the people who had transported him to this winter world -- gave her a quick bow of his head and salute of hand to shoulder. Mica mimicked the bow and watched her through the fall of his long and dirty hair.

"This is it?" the woman demanded.

Odd accent. Not a local and not from Sedina, either. He had only heard that harsh and guttural inflection a couple times in his life and he thought she might have come from over the mountains, and those lands to the far west. They rarely got even trading parties from there in Sedina because the mountain crossings were so difficult to traverse. What had brought this woman? She would have to be a strong person to come this far and set up to conquer a different land with, at best, a handful of her followers. Did she have more of an army nearby?

"Look at me," she ordered.

Mica looked up, down, and then up again as though he fought against his own usual tendency. She walked around him, sniffing disdainfully. He shuffled his feet and then went still at a snarl from the guard.

"You make clockwork devices," she said.

He looked up more steadily now, as though surprised and perhaps a little proud.

"I do."

"But I hear they do not work well."

So, someone had gone ahead, probably while they were still in the tunnels under the city.

"The bastard, Storm, he wants everything now, *now*. Never gives me time, you see. Won't let me do the work proper and then yells and threatens. He --"

"Silence, you stupid little man," she ordered, staring him full in the face.

Mica did fall silent; he would have stopped even if he weren't playing the part of a sniveling little coward. He had seen her eyes this time and knew this was not a woman to cross, even in so much as talking. Madness lurked in that hard, bright stare from her brown eyes. She wanted him to argue. He also saw her hand form into a fist and move -- but she stopped herself.

"I am Janeh," she said and leaned closer. "And now I own you, man. You understand? You are going to do what I order and nothing more."

"I -- I came here without a fight. I am not -- not a slave. I --"

He had started to sound panicked, and she did what he expected. She slapped him hard enough that he fell back against the guard who grunted and started to shove him away until he realized Mica might fall against Janeh, so he grabbed him instead.

Mica sniffed and cowered away from her, though not too much. She wouldn't have any use for a true mouse, he thought. He could be someone very much worried about his own survival. That she would understand.

"I'll do the best I can," he finally whispered.

"Well, let's hope that's good enough or else you'll be down in the mines. I don't suspect that you would last long there."

Mica would probably surprise her, but that was still not a future he wanted.

"Who are you? How did you learn to make clockwork devices?"

"Nikeh," he said with a lift of his head, as though the name should mean something to her. "I learned from my grandda. He would make little things that wound up played music, danced -- useless. Gave them away. But I wanted to do better. I can see -- they can do jobs. They can do things humans can't."

He laid out his history in those words. If Janeh asked more, he would tell her he was from a border village, just over into Sedina. She didn't seem to care, though. He'd given her a tale that showed he had learned just enough to teach himself more, but no formal training, so he might make stupid little mistakes. She could teach him better.

Mica wondered where she had learned and glanced her way -- and knew better than to ask. Instead, he let his eyes drift quickly around the area, like a nervous gesture of someone who expected trouble to come at him at any time. Mica saw mostly what the people had left behind, but on the table were maps and notes. He couldn't see them clearly, though.

Janeh grabbed a cloak hanging on the wall by the door, and then she and the guard took him out of the house and marched him, limping still from the rock in the boot, through the village. She would not expect him to try and run, given that limp. It gave him a secret he might use, if need be.

Mica had not noticed that the town upward on the smaller hills, and from the spot where they had ridden in, he had not seen the little box canyon that probably held livestock in better times. Now falling down shacks stood there, and outside one he could see the pieces of the clockwork men.

"So, it is you," he said looking back at Janeh and giving a nod, trusting he looked hopeful than disgusted. "I heard of these metal men in the city. I wondered."

She nodded and seemed pleased. Mica played it up a bit, asking how the pieces hooked together and how the explosives were placed, so they didn't explode too soon --

"You'll learn all that if you prove yourself," Janeh replied, cutting off his questions. That told him a great deal about why he was here. She really did need help. He could make himself indispensable, at least for a few days, and learn all he could about any other forces she might have hidden away in the mountains. A word with a raven would hold the others back for a little while. Merriweather would even understand the need for more information and would hold back, as long as he was not in too much danger.

Mica took in all he could of the camp -- including the spot far off to the left where a group of children handed out bread and water to a line of men who must be getting ready to work the mines. He even saw how some of the men gave pieces of food back to the children.

If he'd had a weapon in hand, Janeh might not have survived the walk -- which probably would have been bad for him, but momentarily pleasing.

A man stood outside a long building and gave Janeh the same bow and salute. Mica decided he would have to start practicing that as well and win her over by little shows.

"Is Marst ready for him?" Janeh asked.

The man nodded.

"Go in. Make yourself useful."

CHAPTER SIXTEEN

Mica stepped into the somewhat dark building and paused while his eyes adjusted. He even took a moment to try and wipe his glasses while he looked around. A dozen people stood at a long table, all of them glancing his way with worry, and then going right back to their work. From what he had seen in the village, this was probably the kind of job you didn't want to mess up because there were far worse. Men and women here, all of them thin and ragged, but determined.

Pieces of metal men lined up on a long table around which they worked. A few people put pieces of them together, some pounding things into place while others screwed a few other parts together. They were not actually building the metal men, but they were putting pieces of them together, probably for more accessible transport. Mica saw no sign of the explosives. The way some of these people worked, they would have blown everything up by now.

Might have wanted to, he supposed.

"You go there," Marst said and pointed to a spot across from him. "You pound that piece to that piece and then screw it in, there."

Seemed easy enough, though a rather stupid use of his

skills. Mica picked up one piece and fit it together with a bit less pounding than he saw, and the put in the bolt. It fell back out. He found a washer and nut for the back, but they were loose.

"This won't work," he said aloud, despite himself. "And this is a stupid way to do this work. Drill the holes after they're put together, not before. Find something that works better, too. This falls apart before I put it down."

Marst grunted but didn't seem upset to have complained about how things were done. Then he looked at some of the others, and growled out a few more changes --

Janeh came back in; she must have remained close.

"They do things wrong!" he said with a wave of his hand. "This is bad, and this. You want something that will move and not fall apart?"

She smiled, which was not a pleasant look, but it did show him the truth about the situation, which he had already guessed. She had just tested him, at least in some small way.

"Marst, give him Andel's place, along with the tools and the designs. Assign Andel's former helper, the idiot, to him." She stopped and stared at Mica. "I expect you to do well. If you do, you will be rewarded."

She didn't need to say what would happen if he didn't do well. Mica bowed his head and even attempted the salute. She smiled brightly and went off, leaving the guard and Marst to deal with him.

Marst had gone to a trunk at the side of the room, unlocked it, and pulled out papers all folded into a bundle and tied with a bit of string. He shoved them at Mica.

"You study this. You fix them," Marst said with the same grunt of words. He had an accent like Janeh's but not quite the same. "Come with me."

The guard stayed with the other people who continued to work, though a little more carefully now. They had to be captives, Mica thought, and that made them little more than slaves. He could see resignation and desperation in those faces.

Mica stepped back out into the cold with Marst, both silent and scowling as they headed away from the box canyon and to a hut that Mica had hardly noticed. It sat alone and across from the door stood the mine entrance up a hillside and some distance away. Mica could see two men being carried out, obviously dead.

Marst kicked open the door and all but shoved Mica inside before he closed the door and stomped away.

The hut had a small window with no glass covering, but a couple layers of cloth could be tied in place against the weather. However, the window also gave the only light, and in truth, Mica had gotten used to the cold so closing it off wasn't so important. Having it open might even show some trust.

Guards paced past the window even while he stood there. They must be patrolling the opening to the box canyon and guarding against escapes. That put Mica's hut where it would always be in sight of the guards. Not good -- but if Mica made no show, it might be better than some other place. The guards might stop looking at him.

That might take time. Mica didn't want to be here that long.

The hut turned out to be small and filthy. Mica chased a rat out with a curse. A rickety cot sat on the wall beneath the window and he almost started to move it. The placement might be wise -- the wind would blow over him, he supposed. He could feel the cold mountain breeze, laced with the scent of iron smelting.

Mica put the papers on the small worktable and untied the string, letting the papers unfold. He found pencils, a quill and dried ink, and some second-rate tools along with a pile of small metal pieces. A set of cogs and gears had been put together and left to gather dust. From the looks of the notes, this Andel appeared to have been working on a better knee joint for the clockwork men.

Mica spotted a brazier on the far side of the table, which he had not expected. Beside it sat a few pieces of wood, though mostly fast-burning pine. Still better than nothing at all, and he got the fire going with the flint provided. Good. A rusty pipe took the smoke out the roof.

The spitting pine resin did leave a more pleasant scent to the little room. It helped Mica relax a little, though he worried there was a limit to what he could burn each day. It might be wiser to light the fire at night when it was cold. The blanket on the cot did not look promising against the bitter nights -- but he'd already survived a few in the blanket he still wore like a cloak, which meant he had two coverings. He might be doing better than a lot of the people here.

A high-legged chair sat on the other side of the table, and he settled there and finally studied the papers. This was at least part of the plans to the clockwork men, with a few spots circled to show problems, including the new joint. Nothing proved detailed enough to show him what he needed, though. He studied the problem and then began to think about what he would put in there as Mica -- and from that, what Nikeh would put into place instead.

Mica realized that he couldn't come up with any plan too quickly, and whatever he decided couldn't be too good. He needed to do enough work to keep Janeh hopeful about his presence, but not do anything that would give her any real edge. Mica began to clean the tools. He'd have to think this through. He needed to be wise and hope that he could get to a raven soon.

A little later Marst arrived dragging a hunched over, grunting man who kept trying to pull free. Marst slapped him before he shoved him past the open door.

"You are going to work with this man now, you

understand idiot? You do what he says, or you will be whipped. You do the work, and you get food."

Marst yanked the door closed with a bang and then stalked away.

This was going to complicate things.

Or not. The two men looked into each other's face.

"Glad we found you, Prince Kistrin," Mica said softly. "This saves all kinds of additional work."

Kistrin stared at him, eyes blinking, and for a heart-pounding moment he feared something really had happened to the Prince --

"Damn, Raventower," he whispered. "What the hell --"

And silent at the sound of a guard going past. Kistrin had been here before, Mica reminded himself. He had worked with this Andel, so that was going to be considerable help in all of this.

"Sit. Just sit. There." He pointed toward the wall by the brazier. "Sit until I figure out what to do with you. Understand?"

Kistrin grunted and moved over by the heat. He gave Mica a grateful smile, but they said nothing more. Mica let Kistrin choose the time to speak, realizing he had the feel of the place already.

"What the hell are you doing here, Micalus?" he finally whispered again. He held his hands to the warmth and Mica could see that they were bruised and cut. He'd lost considerable weight which wasn't disguised by the couple layers ragged clothing. The wild hair and beard helped hide his face, though. Neither Janeh, nor any of her people, had recognized him.

Mica told Kistrin the story in bits and pieces, starting with how they had begun by looking for him before they found themselves caught up in the clockwork trouble -- which they had already guessed included the missing people and might lead to him.

Kistrin nodded several times. Grunted now and then when a guard came by, and finally helped to clean the tools, which seemed better than leaving him just sitting with nothing to do. Mica realized that he needed to be sure Janeh realized he wanted *the idiot's* help.

Maybe he could just play up the idea of having a slave of his own making him important. If he read her right, she might be amused.

"Can't say much now," Kistrin whispered finally. His voice sounded rough as though he hadn't spoken much of late. "I grunt and pretend not to understand even simple commands sometimes. It was amazing what she said in front of me when she talked to Andel."

And silent again. Mica was starting to get annoyed by the guards who always slowed as they went past his window and door.

"What is this village?" he whispered.

"It's only called Janeh's place," Kistrin replied. "Even the locals don't say the old name. She's been here about a year, killing or capturing traders who happened along."

"I trust not many outsiders come this way."

"Especially not since there is trouble with the mountain tribes," Kistrin said, reminding him of that problem. "She's had her hand in that trouble, of course. Mica, they're worried about you showing up. Be careful."

"And you as well. I want to get you home and please your father -- not to mention your mother."

"Heard there was trouble in Kamere," he said, and his eyes looked at Mica full of worry this time. "Heard there was a major battle."

Mica nodded, fell silent again, and then told the Prince much of what had happened -- without reference to the help of gods -- and reassured him that they had come through it rather well.

"Janeh isn't the top person," Kistrin whispered. He looked worried. "Not sure who -- but I think there is someone from Sedina."

"Damn. Maybe an Honorgate or one of their followers," Mica mumbled. He picked up a cog, looked it over, and began filing down a rough spot, mostly to give his hands something to do.

"Be careful," Kistrin said again. "The last man in this position was not happy. I don't know if he killed himself or if Janeh finally had him killed. Or maybe the fever took him -- been a lot of that in the village. You are just what Janeh needs right now, but she doesn't trust such luck."

"I have Merriweather and some mercenaries not far away," Mica said. The Prince looked at him with open surprise. "We'll get you out --"

"My guards are working the mines," he said.

"We'll get everyone we can," Mica answered.

Then they fell silent in truth, with nothing more Mica could think to say right now. They worked after that, cleaning, filing. Mica yelled a couple times when the guard was near enough to hear, and he thought they had done well with the act.

Kistrin had given him a good amount of information. Mica had also traced some rough designs for a new joint. He based it somewhat on the centipede, which Janeh would be taking apart by now, but with a few small improvements, as though he had been working toward that change already.

At sunset, the guard stepped in and took Kistrin away. Mica knew better than to argue. Janeh came in a little later, looked at the room -- which they'd cleaned up -- and then at the drawings he'd made. She said nothing, but he had the impression she was pleased with what she saw.

Food arrived not long after she left, too. It was better

than Mica had expected -- better than he'd had since he left the tavern in Taginta. Then he remembered the mediocre fare that seemed to be what she fed the others, and the food didn't make him so happy.

He saved some of the bread and meat for Kistrin, a small salve for how badly he felt just then. He worked on drawings until the darkness came and then put a bit more wood on the brazier, pulled the ragged curtain into place and tied it down against the night cold. He took off his boots and crawled under the blankets.

He didn't sleep. Mica listened to the sounds of the camp. The guards marching past continued, though not as often as during the daylight. The sound of their feet crunching against the frozen ground and weeds made it obvious no one would get far in the dead of night when all else was silent.

Mica could hear the distant work of people in the mine. The blacksmiths continued for a while, but finally their hammers fell silent as well. Janeh had everything she needed right here. The mine could not hold out forever, though. Was this supposed to be a long-term project?

A sound on the roof.

Mica carefully moved out of his bed and climbed up on the table. He tapped lightly on the wood.

The tap was returned.

The ceiling was not high. Mica stood close to a spot where he could feel a hint of cold air seeping through. He listened. No sound of anyone breathing, and besides, he could tell the roof wouldn't support much weight.

"Tell Merriweather I found the Prince," he whispered. "More going on here, though. Pull back. Don't get caught."

Another two taps.

"Thank you. Go."

The bird flapped wings that did not sound entirely normal as it swept away in the night.

"What was that?" one of the guards asked, only a few yards away.

Mica climbed down quickly and slipped into bed.

"That?" someone else asked, also close by. "Just another damn bird. The dead draw them."

A grunt of agreement. The guards went on with their work.

Mica slept.

CHAPTER SEVENTEEN

Three more days.

Time kept passing too quickly for Mica. He had gotten back into the habit of losing himself in the clockwork, even if he did constantly remind himself not to do too well. It helped though. Even Kistrin agreed that this was not a job to rush.

They talked little these days, even with no one else listening. The guard gradually stopped slowing by the window. Janeh no longer checked on them several times a day, but Mica had the feeling that might be because she planned something else.

That couldn't be good.

The small improvements he'd made in the designs did please her, though. Janeh took the drawings away with her each visit, and the smiles she gave seemed almost genuine. By the third day, Mica had started planning ways that he could build in a failsafe to stop the creations, though he still hadn't learned how they were controlled. He had made one guess, though, and had it confirmed in an odd way.

"No magnets," she said when he had suggested something for the movement of the legs. "It interferes with ... things."

He only shrugged and showed her another drawing. She

took them all and left again, leaving the guard to close the door behind her. Mica sat back down at the table and grabbed at papers before they flew off. Kistrin giggled and grabbed at them as well.

"Give it back, fool."

The guard yanked the door closed. The weather had turned bitterly cold out there, and in many ways, he and Kistrin had it better than the guards. They had a little warmth and were out of the direct wind, though the hut was far from weatherproof. Breezes kicked up dust inside and even sometimes left a layer of powdery snow around the window frame and the door. Mica had silently thanked the gods that they were not here in the rainy season, though a bit more warmth would have been welcome.

When the guard had walked sufficiently far away, Kistrin moved closer.

"Magnets," Kistrin mumbled and Mica nodded agreement, glad the prince had caught that implication, too.

Janeh had brought him all the pieces for one of the leg joints. He laid the gears and casing out on the table, and in his mind, he could see that she had based this one on his design from a couple days ago. Good. He started to put things together and then stopped and took some of it apart again while Kistrin looked surprised.

"Can't do this too well or too fast," he quietly told Kistrin. Then, realizing someone moved closer to the hut, "I said to put the wood on the fire. Don't play with it!"

Kistrin grinned and obeyed, though he did build a little house out of a few pieces. Mica went back to work.

Another day. It took him two to put the piece together, but Janeh apparently hadn't expected anything faster. He had better food again and kept enough to share with Kistrin who was always grateful.

"A question occurred to me," Mica said quietly. The wind

howled outside today, giving them a few more chances to talk, especially since they sat on the cot by the window, sharing both blankets, and listening for any approach. "Did the last person in my position have any idea you were acting?"

"No," he said with a bright smile. "It was Ovete's idea when we were brought here. By then no one knew where we'd been captured and we'd certainly lost any trace of being upper class, let alone royalty. Ovete told me to stay quiet and play stupid, and just do whatever they said, and be of use."

"Wise man, Ovete," Mica said, remembering the tall guard who had always been one of those at Kistrin's side.

"Yes. My guards started it by ordering me around. I tended the fires, did what work I could. Janeh heard, of course. She watched me for a few days -- and then she took me away from them. I don't think that was part of Ovete's plan, but it still worked. If I don't do much more than grunt and shuffle through my work, I remain safe."

Mica nodded. Kistrin didn't seem much like the Crown Prince he'd known back in Kamere. Mica suspected Kistrin thought the same of Lord Raventower. He could see the Prince watch him sometimes, even when he was playing with clockwork pieces, just as he would have at home.

Every night they took the Prince back to wherever he slept, and Mica worried that he would not come back the next day. Why he didn't just call in the troops and be done with this?

Janeh kept saying things. She was on a tight schedule now. They would be packing up soon. He might even be rewarded for the help he'd provided, at which Nikeh grinned brightly and saluted her, while Mica wondered if the reward wasn't going to be a knife in the back.

Sometimes when he looked out the window, he could see birds in the trees along the edge of the canyon and suspected his ravens were there with the real ones. They all stayed in shadows, and only Mica paid them much attention.

On some nights a clockwork raven would come to his roof, and he would relate what information he could. The raven never spoke at all, and he was left wondering if the others were even out there or if the ravens alone had tracked him this far. He didn't dare ask for fear of what the truth might do to his state of mind.

On the seventh night, an explosion shook the camp, and he rushed out the door to see a bright fire rising upward into the snowy night. He wasn't sure what had been destroyed, but as the guards shoved him back inside, he heard one of them say that Janeh was not going to be happy to have the project set back.

Good.

When she came by the next day, her eyes flashed with rage, and he carefully kept out of her reach, all the time babbling about how worried he was about evil people trying to kill them.

She left.

"I don't know who did it," Kistrin admitted softly. "It was the place where she often worked though. Too bad she wasn't there at the time. They did damage a good many of the clockwork creatures, though."

Mica grunted agreement and went back to work on another leg joint. He carefully filed down one cog on a gear so that eventually it would break off and the device would no longer be able to move.

Late that afternoon, Janeh had five severely damaged clockwork men dragged to his little hut and laid out by the door. He looked out and frowned. They looked like soldiers brought back from a battle to be given a proper burial.

"I need them fixed," Janeh said with a snarl. She even kicked one. "I need them fixed and moving. You do that, or I swear to all the gods of your people and mine, that you will suffer for it."

She stalked away. Mica dropped on his heels by the nearest one and shook his head. "Never seen a whole one. What am I supposed to do?"

"Fix it," the guard said with a kick at him. "Fix it, or you're no use to her."

That didn't sound like a good option. The two guards had to help him get the first one inside the hut and laid out on the table. Kistrin cowered back in the corner. The guards left when Mica scowled and told them to get out of the way.

He finally had one of the full creatures in his hands. The guard was still close by the door and would probably stay there to watch the other two. Mica could only give Kistrin a few sharp orders, but even the Prince smiled when they began removing the chest piece. That was easy, in fact. There were latches, which he had expected since that was where the explosives would have to go.

He dared not spend much time looking, though. Just grunted a few things and mumbled about nothing to fix there. Behind covering was a cavity, and it was apparent something had been there and yanked out -- he could see where metal had scratched metal, and where a couple magnets were secured to the sides.

He put the chest piece back in and began working on the legs and wheels which had been badly twisted. When Janeh came back again a little later, he was fitting the new knee joint in and cursing his assistant for getting his fingers in the way.

"You're too slow!"

"I had to build it," Mica said, waving the pick he was using at the open area. "I need more parts. You want this done, then give me what I need."

Mica realized he had maybe pushed too far and not sounded nearly enough like Nikeh that time. If she noted that part, she said nothing, but he saw the anger in her eyes as she turned and stalked away again.

"Dangerous," Kistrin mumbled.

He nodded agreement and went back to work. He fixed the broken pieces on two of the devices, and then purposely created a problem with a part of the third that he should not have even been looking at deep in the hip area that had enough metal shielding that nothing had been so much as shifted.

Janeh came back again at sunset just after Kistrin had been taken away. She snarled at all his answers, and he did his best to play subservient, sniveling Nikeh, but he knew it wasn't going to do any good. She had not liked his attitude.

Kistrin found him the next morning, still on the floor where the guard had left him after the beating. The Prince made a hissing of sound in surprise, and the guard gave a little laugh and pulled the door closed. Kistrin got him up on the bed and dragged the blanket over him. Mica lifted one hand -- bruised and the fingers swollen but indicated that he was all right. Kistrin did not look as though he believed it.

Mica couldn't be certain himself. His ribs hurt, his hands ached, and his head pounded. He'd had no food and suspected none would come today as well. Worse, if Janeh was done with the project, then she might not need him in the future.

Could he get the ravens to go for help? Do it without drawing attention? He needed to get the Prince out of here. This game had gone too far.

"Clearing an area of huts," Kistrin mumbled as he looked out the window. "Moving the prisoners up with the miners. Flattening it out."

"Airship," Mica said, worried for new reasons.

He nodded. Then he went to work cleaning tools, picking stuff up, making soft keening sounds whenever a guard came by. Some opened the door and looked in, but they never seemed to find anything out of place.

Mica slept through most of the day. There was no food that night, and he really didn't care. Kistrin went off with the guards, and Mica simply closed his eyes again and went back to sleep. Feverish, he thought and didn't care about that either.

By the next morning, he could move better. The latrine was not far, and he limped there and back with his guard, shying away whenever the man came too close. He could see the landing field, though the snow had started to fall. Maybe they'd get lucky, and the ship would crash.

Janeh checked on them that afternoon. Mica cowered away from her, but she said nothing. She left more items to be built and stalked away again.

"Not a happy woman," Kistrin whispered.

Mica nodded and went to work with the pieces. Kistrin stayed quiet most of the day, listening as the winter storm grew worse, the wind howling past their window. They'd run out of firewood, and Mica had begun to think they would freeze or starve now --

But some wood arrived a little later. He built up a little fire, and Kistrin nodded his thanks.

"No airship in this," Mica whispered. "I don't know if I should be happy or not."

The guards took the Prince away, dragging him off into the storm. Janeh sent him food though, and Mica shoved some of it under the bed again. If Janeh ever found the bread and meat, he could claim he feared not being fed again. Cower a lot.

That night he happened to hear some horsemen ride in, despite the weather. By the next day, Janeh was in a much better mood. He got a distinct impression that she'd learned she had more time.

Maybe more than time. A day later new prisoners arrived. The guards spoke briefly about having grabbed them from a village to the south, and they'd be put right to work. Mica did his best to look at them out the window. He feared to see Shipley or even Merriweather, knowing both were apt to throw themselves into danger when following him.

He saw neither of them, but he did see four mercenaries he recognized. He grinned at Kistrin and told him what he'd seen, and then went back to work. They had some help at hand. It might mean the others were preparing to come in, but they might be waiting for that airship, too. They'd have seen the cleared area, or at least the ravens would and would tell Merriweather about it.

As Mica had pointed out, Janeh expected more people to join her soon. He didn't want to strike before they arrived.

Do this wisely. Get them all at once and end this nightmare.

Then things changed.

The next day, Janeh brought him someone new to work with instead of the Prince. Mica glared at him once Janeh had gone, but he put the man to work. The problem was that the man -- obviously a spy and one of her own people, not a prisoner -- was so incompetent that he broke two tools just trying to clean them.

"Sit there. On the cot," Mica ordered with a snarl. "Just sit there and do nothing. You make it worse!"

The guard who had been passing by looked in smirked a little and moved on. The spy glowered from where he sat. Mica went on about his work and tried very hard not to think the Prince might have died, and they put this person in his place. If that were true, he thought Janeh would have said so -- unless she never considered that it would matter.

When Janeh came by a few hours later and found the man on the cot, she looked more confused than annoyed.

"Why isn't he helping?" she asked.

Mica swallowed, bowed his head, and then forced himself to stand up a little straighter. "He broke tools. He's impossible.

I'll do it myself. At least the idiot could obey orders, you know."

"I thought someone with brains might help the work go faster."

Mica held up the broken tools.

"Huh. You, go," Janeh said with a wave of her hand toward the man.

The man scurried away like a whipped dog and probably expected to be punished for his failure. Mica didn't care. Janeh stayed for a little longer than usual, checked over his work, and then left again.

New tools arrived with his food that night.

Prince Kistrin was back the next day, and he looked more than a little relieved.

"One day back in the mines," he said softly. "Not the work I want to do, the gods forgive me. I feel sorry for the others trapped there. Got to see my people, talk with the mercenaries and say you are doing well -- but I don't want to go back there."

Mica nodded. They were more careful that day, too. It seemed that one guard stayed close to the hut now, which proved annoying. They wrote notes in bits of dust, but neither really knew anything more, except one thing Kistrin had learned from the mercenaries: they had more soldiers coming and would make their move when they arrived. Storm was nearby in the woods, though. So was Merriweather. They were not going to take chances. Slow movements of people, just a couple at a time, and staying off the main trails. It would take some time for them all to get here.

The next day the people of the camp rioted.

Kistrin had just arrived and was nibbling on the bread, and meat Mica had saved him, warming it in his hands as he sat on the floor by the heat. He looked troubled and finally met Mica's look.

"There is going to be trouble," he said softly. "A ten-year-old girl died last night. She might have been in the hands of one of the guards. The villagers have had more than enough."

"They can't win," he said softly.

Kistrin nodded agreement.

The trouble began within the hour. Mica had expected it to be handled quickly, but the people seemed to explode outward and spread across the village, up into the mining camp -- and toward the hut.

"Oh hell," Mica whispered. "This could be a real problem --"

Yells came from just outside the small building, and then a cry of pain.

Mica moved back to the corner, and Kistrin looked at him, stunned by what appeared to be a real show of cowardice. It wasn't -- it was outright fear of what he knew was going to happen.

"The guard has moved on," Kistrin said, his voice soft. "You don't have to worry --"

"The man out there hasn't died yet. Gods, please don't let him die so close -- damn!"

Mica felt the release of life, and a moment later the tiny life lights began to stream in around the door and rush at him. Mica held up his hands and tried to push them away.

"No! Go to where you belong! Go in peace!"

He caught sight of Kistrin's surprised face. Not afraid, just stunned at what he saw. Mica had nothing he could do, though. He had no creature with sea metal where he could put the soul if it did not merely go away. He'd had some cling to him for hours, and that would only get him killed in this place. Janeh would not deal with anything so unusual.

"Go," Mica said more softly. He had managed to gather everything into a ball that glowed with twinkling lights. "Go I peace. We will do what we can."

Maybe the essence of the man understood. Mica felt something lessen in its rush toward him and the lights began to fade, one at a time. He felt some of the man's life then, but mostly it was the utter despair of what had happened, and the fear that no one would ever come to help them.

"I am here. I'm sorry I failed you."

The last light faded. Mica fell back against the wall and almost toppled into the fire. Kistrin caught hold of him and would have pulled him to the cot, but they heard more of a battle coming closer.

A second person died. This one let go faster, but by then Mica could hardly think straight, and his head pounded so hard that he curled up in the corner --

The trouble died down. Cries and despair rose through the village, but if others died, it was not near to their hut. Mica didn't move. Kistrin sat beside him.

"I don't know what the hell that was," Kistrin finally whispered. Mica blinked trying to focus on him. "But I think we need to get you out of here soon, my friend. I suddenly think you might be in more danger -- she's coming."

Kistrin dropped onto the floor beside him, half crawling under the table. They could hear Janeh's voice as she ordered bodies carted off. Mica wondered why no one had managed to kill her. Everything would have fallen apart if she had died.

Could he do it?

Janeh kicked the door open and stepped in. Snow dotted her cloak, and her hair had come free and moved in the breeze like something alive.

"You -- are you hurt?"

"Are they gone?" Mica whispered. He had to fight the words out. "I could hear them fighting. Just outside. Are they gone? Are they going to kill me?"

"He's fine," Janeh said as she left the hut, the door closing behind her. She hadn't even glanced at the Idiot. "Useless little coward."

"Useless? She came rushing to make certain you were alive," Kistrin pointed out with a soft whisper of a laugh.

Mica nodded and tried to move. Everything ached. It took Kistrin to help get him onto the cot and covered. He slipped away, perhaps more unconscious than asleep, but it helped. He woke late in the afternoon and worked a bit, Kistrin silent today. He knew that the Prince was bothered by what he'd seen, but he asked no questions. This was probably wise. They would discuss it later, back in Kamere. Over an ale or one of Ada's excellent meals --

Yes, *time to get home.*

CHAPTER EIGHTEEN

"Pack what you can for work in the field," Janeh said from the door. "We'll be gone for several days. We have a test to make. No, don't bother me with questions. The guard will take you to the wagons."

She left again.

Mica shook his head. Kistrin said nothing.

Mica was ready to go a few minutes later. He was the only prisoner, and twenty guards went with them. So did three of the clockwork men, leaving more than twenty behind as far as he could tell. That meant she was telling the truth; this was a test of some kind and not a full-fledged battle. Mica had no way to reach Merriweather and the others. He had to trust they'd figure things out.

Janeh was manic. She seemed to think this was some sort of game and laughed as the others loaded supplies.

Going to *destroy* something, Mica thought. Janeh couldn't wait to blow things up. He had no idea where they were going, except that they appeared to be heading south, at least at the start. Not Taginta, he thought. She'd have taken more than three clockwork men, even for a test.

"We'll be gone a few days," Janeh said, which made Mica think they were not going too far. "We will have all the tests done by the time the airship arrives. Yes, do you want something Nikeh?"

Nothing more than what he had already gathered. He bowed and shuffled. "Where do I ride?" he asked as though he feared Janeh would say that he walked.

The thought obviously occurred to her as she smiled. Not a pleasant look because her smiles never meant anything good.

"You'll ride in the wagon with the explosives."

"But -- but --" He fell silent at her next look which dared him to say more. One of the guards took him to the wagon and shoved him up on the seat with the driver. He did a quick glance at the bed of the wagon behind him, apparently worried, but the explosives were packed in separate packages as he had expected, and it was unlikely anything would happen on the way to Setton, which apparently wasn't too far away.

Mica also saw some ragged clothing tossed into the other wagon along with a few more supplies and the clockwork devices themselves, which were quickly covered over. He guessed that they would appear as more refugees on the road, something he suspected must be familiar enough of late.

Mica caught sight of one of his ravens in a tree near the wagons. Someone still watched. He thought of a way to get more information to Merriweather. Mica put his little pouch of tools on the edge of the seat and tapped it once.

The raven swept in and grabbed the bag so quickly that it even took Mica by surprise. He gave a yelp of shock, hoping the raven had stayed in the shadows enough to look real. Then he leapt down and chased after it, limping past two trees and a high boulder.

The raven waited. Mica took back the pouch.

"Setton, a quick last test. Airship arriving soon. Go."

The raven took off, and he started back around the trees before the guards had caught up with him.

"Got it!" he said and held the pouch up.

Even Janeh only nodded, too anxious to start the travel to complain. Besides, getting the tools back probably saved them time since she didn't have to hunt down more of them for him.

Mica still made a show of being nervous in the wagon, but the driver mumbled to him that they were safe, nothing set to explode. He slumped down on the seat beside the man and gave a nod of thanks. Soon they were on their way.

Snow lay everywhere along the trail, but he could see that wagons had come this way not too long before yesterday's storm. They must bring in supplies from somewhere. Raided villages? He suspected most of them were abandoned by now -- and that made him think Janeh couldn't remain here for much longer because this site of habitation would become too obvious.

Things were going to happen soon.

The journey, though, proved to be boringly dull and cold. Mica stayed wrapped in his blanket, gobbled down the food they gave him -- not as good as he usually got -- and curled up near the fire until someone came along and kicked him out of the spot to somewhere a bit colder. He'd suffered through worse of late and only whined a bit. Mica worried about Kistrin back at the village. He didn't even know the town's name, all of it lost to Janeh's evil.

Mica worried that Merriweather and Storm would not get to Setton in time to do anything helpful, but then he realized that Janeh, for all her excitement, was not rushing forward, but keeping to the pace the wagons could make without breaking down on the rocky path. Wagons, he soon realized, were more precious than workers.

The wagon with the three heavy clockwork men moved just ahead of the one that Mica rode, and that gave him some chance to look the devices over again. They were uniform in size and shape. Whoever did the metalwork of the bodies had to be a single person since the design remained too uniform, even to the edge cuts and mallet marks. Mica had never seen that man and didn't think he was with them, either. If the hard shells failed, there was nothing they could do, but Janeh had brought Mica along to make sure of their ability to move.

The boxes that seemed to control them sat at the bottom edge of that same wagon. They did have dials of some sort and straps that must go around the neck. Not too heavy, Mica thought, or else they would have made the straps wider and maybe spread some of the weight to the chest.

Then luck came his way. On the second night, Janeh had the boxes taken out to her tent because it looked like it might snow, and she didn't want them getting wet. Mica got to carry one.

Light. Hardly more than the metal case, about two feet square. Whatever was inside did not rattle at all. He gave the three a curious look -- she had to expect at least that much from him -- but rushed away at the start of a snarl.

He'd had the pouch with his tools strung around his neck and the metal there had felt the pull of a powerful magnet. That confirmed something, at least, but he had no idea how it might work.

The ravens did not come near him on this journey, leaving Mica to wonder if the others had gotten his message or not. The trees were sparse along the high trail, though, and any glint of metal feathers would have drawn attention.

Mica worried about Prince Kistrin. He had started to think of him as just another prisoner in this madness, but he began to wonder why Kistrin had not insisted on being rescued before now. Someone might have gotten him away and maybe left Janeh none the wiser if he went with a group of prisoners.

Kistrin had not suggested such a plan. Kistrin had played his part, and they worked together to learn Janeh's secrets ...

and over those long days, Mica had forgotten the Prince's actual role in life. He would succeed his father at the rule of Sedina -- unless something unfortunate happened to him.

Mica also remembered how the King had talked about keeping his son out of the army and out of harm's way as much as possible. Mica had done just the opposite --

No. Kistrin had been there long before Mica arrived. They'd been lucky to fall in together. Luck? Maybe he ought to send a prayer of thanks to Seldon and whatever other gods had put them both on this path. If Janeh succeed in this war, she'd gain the strength to build more of her clockwork men. With the wealth she'd gain, Janeh could build an army of them that she -- and whoever was coming in that airship -- could use to rule this part of the world.

Better to take the time to find the rest of the enemies and root this trouble out completely. Gods grant that no one else died while they played this as far as they dared. This --

This was not all in his hands, Mica reminded himself. The mercenaries would make up their minds on when to attack. He was not in charge of them. They were waiting for others to arrive because this would not be a case of just killing everyone in an enemy encampment. They'd have to save the prisoners, too. Besides, it wasn't as though the rest of the mercenary band could just march into the area. They were discreet in their approaches.

On the morning of the second day, Mica found Janeh sitting by the fire while they took down her tent. It had not snowed much after all. A man sat with her, someone who had not been with them when they started the journey, and whom he had not seen in the camp, either. Janeh studied a map and had a packet of letters in her hand that the man had probably brought.

Mica feared a change of plan, but the party went on down the trail, and the man rode away later in the afternoon, heading back toward the lowlands and the sea that was so distant that they couldn't see it from here. Mica counted that good. There was still that trouble with Payton.

They passed two deserted villages that day and only a handful of refugees, but they rushed off at the sight of his group. Neither of the villages showed any sign of destruction, so the locals must have merely panicked at what was happening in the area. Smart people, he thought. Janeh had probably grabbed a few, and that might have scared the others off. She didn't send her guards after the few people they'd seen, though. She wasn't interested in more prisoners, at least not now.

Why didn't she use these places for tests? Was it that no one was around to see the glory of her work? That seemed the most likely. Janeh craved attention. Mica supposed that witnesses would be a good part of the test, to spread the terror of the creatures to other areas, as they'd done already. The people of Taginta had been cowering in fear, the capital filled with refugees from everywhere else, though many had been turned aside once the King ordered the gates closed. Mica would have disliked that idea more, but he realized it was possible that the people were safer outside the city at this point. He had the feeling that Janeh was nearly done with her tests and that she would soon make the real attack.

Mica knew they were near their destination when some of the men finally dressed in the ragged clothing that they'd brought -- it did make them look like refugees. They returned before nightfall. Scouts then, and not people who would infiltrate ahead of the attack. He wanted to hear what they said, but he was never invited to their camp. There was a downside to acting like a sniveling coward; Janeh didn't trust him with any more information than what he needed to make the clockwork men move.

They reached Setton the next day, and Mica understood why Janeh had come all this way. Not only was the village still inhabited, but it also had tall, though ancient, walls. Janeh still needed to see how well her clockwork men would do up against that sort of construction since there had been changes since the last small attack on Taginta. Mica remembered the massive walls of the capital, and how he had thought the next of these attacks would concentrate on the gates.

Janeh had stopped the wagons barely half a mile from the gate ahead of them, a massive ancient barbican that looked like it had been built at the beginning of time. Guards stood on the wall and watched without coming out to ask questions. They would have already guessed, even if Mica's friends had not gotten here.

Janeh had Mica help implant the explosives in the machines. Maybe this was a final test of his nerve. His hands shook at first, but he focused on connecting one piece and another and knowing it could all blow up if he did something wrong made him extra careful.

If one blew up now, it would take the others, too. And Janeh.

And him.

"Once you put it in, don't move it," Janeh said. She even smiled. "Don't open it back up. It will explode. No one gets my secrets."

The lure of blowing them all to the ten hells had a draw at this point, and if Mica hadn't looked up on the wall and seen Merriweather watching him, he might have been tempted to a quick end of everything. She, though, reminded him that he had a future and a home still and that there was more to this than just what happened at the camp.

Mica finished his work. Merriweather's presence meant they knew the attack had been planned and he need not worry.

Mica stepped away from the metal man he had armed and gave a quick nod to Janeh.

She and two of her usual guards took up the square boxes and put them around their necks. Mica watched as carefully as he dared, though he quickly retreated now that they were prepared to start the devices moving. He didn't have to entirely pretend to be worried, either. Mica had finally seen more of the explosives. It was material often used in mines, and he had heard it was extremely volatile once the mix of the two parts was made. What he had seen was one open section and a second with some sort of trigger.

Mica watched Janeh. She pushed a button he had not seen on the box and heard a low rumble of sound that seemed to shake the air itself. A moment later, he could hear the whirl of clockwork gears begin to move. The initial rumble of sound must have triggered one of the magnets that pulled back a crank to set the creature in motion.

The clockwork men made their way down the well-traveled road toward the gate. Shouts of fear and worry came from above, and soldiers began to fire arrows at the devices.

Janeh laughed with delight. She began to move forward as well, though her two companions kept a little farther back. Apparently, the control from the boxes only reached about 150 yards. That made no sense, though. It was far too close to the explosion area.

Ah. All Janeh and her people had to do was get the clockwork men aligned with the wall and in an area that no longer needed careful navigation, and then they could just let the devices move forward until they hit something. Mica had always assumed that there was a way to trigger the explosive without hitting a target, but now he thought not.

Bad. Mica would have liked a way to simply blow them up without having them destroy a target.

The first of Janeh's machines hit the gate. The explosion sent metal and rock flying so far that even Janeh backed up in haste. Before the dust had settled, the second clockwork man had gone inside the opening. Another explosion rocked the walls, and part of the guard post fell.

The third went on through.

By the time the last explosion had happened, Janeh had signaled the rest of them forward. She wanted a closer look at how much destruction they'd made. Mica moved along with the others, staying well out of the way, and far more interested in the people who were retreating in haste from the gate rather than the fallen debris. Merriweather moved with those people, and so did Storm. They did no more than glance his way as they herded townspeople back away from the little square inside the town.

It was a pretty little town. Mica was glad they were not going to be doing more damage. Janeh didn't even go far beyond the gate, though half of her people went to gather a few supplies.

A few dead were scattered by the gate, and Mica felt his heart leap in fear -- but they must have been dead before the attack and put out to stage the scene. There were no life lights. Ah -- most of them were not even real bodies, just manikins that must have been on the walls.

Janeh noticed.

"Put up on the walls to make us think there were more guards," one of her men said. "Look how few there are here."

Janeh nodded. She did not go near the bodies, and at first, he suspected her of being a bit squeamish after all -- but then he changed his mind. She simply didn't care about people, living or dead, except when she could use them or when they moved against her.

Arrows flew their way, but they were careful of Mica. A couple of Janeh's men fell. Mica wanted her dead, but it was not going to happen here.

"One more arrow and I'll turn this village into dust!" she shouted at the people she thought were town guards. They believed her. "Do not try to stop or follow us. I'll blow this place up if you cross me."

Mica realized that she'd brought far more explosives than she had used with her devices. He gave a quick nod to Storm and hoped he realized that meant they needed to stay away. Mica would be riding with the explosives, and he wouldn't be surprised to see Janeh rig something up to quickly prime them.

"This was well done," Janeh said as they started back out of the opening. Mica kept hoping for arrows at least. If they took down Janeh --

But she had surrounded herself with her guards, and they moved quickly back out of range and to the wagons. The drivers had already turned them, and they started away, considerably faster without the weight of the clockwork men.

Half a mile later, they blew up a bridge. That would slow anyone coming after the wagons, though Merriweather and Storm would not be held back for long. Besides, they already knew where to go and didn't need to track Janeh's location. Janeh took what precautions she could, though, including sending one wagon down a side trail.

Janeh remained happy, though that didn't make her any more pleasant. Everything had worked well. Should he have tried to sabotage the test? He didn't think he would have had the chance to do so, but the thought plagued him for the first day and night. Then he thought better of it. If the test had gone badly, this might have dragged out longer. Instead, everything moved forward, and they need only wait for the last person and his airship to step onto stage now.

They hit a winter storm the next afternoon and had to hold up for an entire day. Mica cowered under a wagon with a couple guards. Janeh did not invite anyone into her tent, which was just as well since it caught fire and she barely escaped. He even wondered if one of the others hadn't set the fire in spite. It was clear that no one really liked the woman much.

How did someone like Janeh get in charge of this project? What did these people want? She was not the only one from the other side of the western mountains, but most of the people in her group seemed to be from the mountain tribes. He'd never heard that they were interested in wars between the larger nations. Such a change in attitude would be something to study when he got back home.

The horses had trouble dragging the wagons through the snow the next afternoon and Janeh finally abandoned the wagons and they rode the horses, bareback, the rest of the way, trading off from one rider to another -- except for Janeh, of course. Mica limped along with the other soldiers. He was not slowing them down -- not in this weather.

Just before sunset, they were attacked. This was not Merriweather and the mercenaries. The group had the look and sound of desperate locals. Mica doubted they even realized the importance of the group when they sprang out of the bushes with swords and began attacking anyone they could reach.

They didn't know Mica was on their side -- he realized that fast enough when one sword cut his right arm while he threw himself off the left side of the horse and rolled into the bushes. It may have been a Niken move to run from danger, but it was also wise in this case. He had the feeling the dozen attackers would not last long, and he did not want to be in the middle of the slaughter. Mica could see a little through the screen of weeds while he tried to tie a bandage around his bleeding arm. He saw Janeh and one of her people moving toward the battle. The man had something in his hands, and he didn't look happy --

Mica would have called out a warning. He tried to stand, but pushing up on his arm shot pain all the way up through his shoulder, and he fell again --

And then the world moved.

Dirt, rock, and parts of trees flew everywhere. So did parts of bodies, though he was lucky to have been far enough back to avoid being splattered with them and blood.

Mica feared the life lights from such carnage, and he scurried back farther into the woods, away from the trail and he hoped out of their reach. Mica had learned from other experiences, that so many living people passing through would disrupt the power that fueled the life lights. Gregorian was the only one who knew to keep others away from the dead if he hoped Mica could find some answers. Mica supposed he ought to tell Merriweather as well.

Mica only had to stay far enough away that the dying wouldn't sense him. Mica thought a few lights might have glittered nearby as he rushed through the woods, but they never got as far as him, and apparently, no one saw them. Mica could barely see the trail from his new position, and he stayed by some tall trees, listening as Janeh shouted for her people to take care of things.

The attackers had not survived. Neither had some of her own people and a couple horses. One of the tribesmen at least went through and made certain everyone had died and didn't remain there, suffering. The man did not do it to make sure the rest of them were safe. No, not from the look he gave Janeh. The tribesmen were known for their honor. The use of the explosives had not been an honorable act.

Mica suspected Janeh was going to lose some of her allies. Would it matter to her? Mica grew more and more assured that her plan was nearing completion, but that a final piece had still not arrived.

The weather had been too bad for airships to come over the mountains.

"Where is that fool!" she shouted suddenly. Had she been calling Nikeh's name? He had fallen out of character, but now he forced himself to stand and stumble out of the weeds. "Hiding. Of course. Someone check his arm. Get the rest of the horses. Let's go."

No one looked too closely at the area of the explosion. The men had trouble leading the horses past the destruction and death. Mica lowered his head, but that didn't help. A hand sat in the path, and he thought the fingers still twitched, which made him fear someone newly dead and life lights. One of the guards caught hold of him and got him past, whether out of kindness or because he didn't want Janeh upset again didn't matter. Mica saw a last twinkling of lights back at the battle site, but they were already moving on.

The tribesmen remained silent and angry. Mica watched them gather up one of their own from the dead. Janeh didn't bother with the rest of her people who had died.

Mica rode with one of her people the rest of the way back. He wanted the mercenaries to ride in and get him out of this nightmare, but then he feared what would happen to them if they tried. Time to go back into her lair. This was going to end soon. He was not going to let it end well for Janeh.

CHAPTER NINETEEN

They came back to the village along the same trail. Mica had dreamed each night that Merriweather and her friends had taken the place over while they were gone, but this was not so. He couldn't say he was glad to be back, but at least it was a destination after that horrible journey. A guard took him to his hut, and Mica threw himself back on his cot and pulled the blanket over him. The arm wound hurt and bled still, but he didn't care. He just needed rest.

He awoke with a start to find Janeh standing over him. He scrambled up, pulling the blanket over his shoulders, hoping he had not said anything in his sleep. She stared in his face and said nothing. He felt a chill at the look in those wild eyes -- but then she turned and left again.

He looked out the window. Sunset. The village seemed unsettled, and he prayed that no one started trouble now. He wanted others to survive. He wanted Kistrin to come back and help him with whatever new work Janeh needed, just to hold the calm for a while longer. Everything had changed in that last explosion and the killing of even her own people. Mica realized that she had done it simply to clear the way so she could get home faster. Something was going to happen here, and soon.

Mica curled up and slept. The guard came in and lit the fire, and he whispered a thank you but said nothing more. Mica did not go right back to sleep this time. Instead, he listened to the whispers of the camp. The guards took their path, sometimes meeting beside his door.

"She shouldn't have," one of them said. "The tribesmen are going to pull out."

"I think she's done here," the other said. They both grunted and moved on.

Done because the tribesmen were pulling out and leaving her without enough guards? Or done here because her work was finished? Mica suspected the second answer. She'd given the impression of someone who was about to move on and didn't really care what the others thought.

He remembered waking up to find her staring at him. Had that been a nightmare? He hoped so.

Then he slept fitfully through the rest of the night.

Kistrin showed up the next morning. He'd already lost weight again in those few days since Mica had been gone and not sharing his food. The day maintained a dull gray light, the wind cold, and the trees stark. No snow fell, and they had an almost comfortable day in the room. There were still some clockwork bits and pieces sitting around, and Mica went to work with them as though this was just the return to normality.

He was able to tell Kistrin what had happened since only one guard patrolled today, and he never lingered by the hut.

"The rest of the clockwork men are ready for the attack," he said after he'd told Kistrin the tale. "And there's nothing I can see that will stop them from working. The best that anyone could do would be to put something in their way and get clear of the area. They don't seem to turn quickly, and as soon as they hit any solid object, they explode. I heard the tribesmen have gone?"

"I saw them hike out," Kistrin replied with a glance toward the window. "They were carrying a body, too, on a travois. I don't think this is good for us."

"Neither do I," Mica agreed.

Janeh came by at mid-day and seemed amused that he had taken it upon himself to get back to work. She had brought a few more joints to be put together.

"We're almost done here," Janeh said, unfortunately confirming what Mica feared. "Get these finished."

Mica gave a bow of his head and a salute which won a bit of a smirk from her. Kistrin just cowered in the corner with his arms around his head -- he was good at making certain no one looked too closely at him, even now with his wild hair and scraggly beard.

Janeh glanced around the hut as though she had never been here before and Mica thought she might be searching for something, though he could not imagine what it might be. If she suspected him of anything that bothered her, she'd simply have him dragged away, and the hut stripped down to pieces. Not finding anything, she would probably have Mica and Kistrin rebuild it and complain about the time wasted.

Not a pleasant thought.

However, Janeh said nothing more and walked away again.

"I don't like the looks of that," Kistrin whispered long after she'd gone.

"Neither do I, but I think she's sidetracked by her final plans."

Kistrin nodded and polished tools, frowning slightly. "She let the tribesmen go. Didn't even try to stop them. I get the feeling it won't be long now."

"I'd take that as good news if I had any idea of what she really plans. I think more and more that the attack is not aimed at Taginta."

"Which makes Kamere the most likely target," Kistrin said, having put that much together.

"Or maybe somewhere across the mountains in her own lands -- no. She wouldn't be moving in winter, not across the mountains."

Kistrin nodded. "It could be Atria, of course. Rumor is that she's waiting for an airship, and we both know that's why they cleared that landing area."

"There would be the worst irony," Mica mused. "That we are working unwillingly with someone who might actually have been an ally at a better time."

"Never," Kistrin said, and for once Mica thought he sounded like the Prince again. "Not that woman."

Mica gave a nod of agreement and went back to work. At least it passed the time.

"What has held her back from attacking before now?" Mica suddenly asked. Kistrin looked at him, startled at first and then looked more contemplative. "I can tell that she's anxious to go, but something is holding her back. The airship is part of it, but I still get the feeling of someone more involved."

"I'd like to know who is funding this project. Who helped Janeh get set up here? She doesn't have riches of her own; you can tell just by the way she acts -- unless she's more like you than like me."

"Me?" Mica said, startled.

Kistrin gave a little cough of a laugh. "You have never acted rich."

Mica supposed that was right and considered that fact while he played with more clockwork pieces. Not acting rich probably made him better at this job than he would have been if he'd ever acted like the other Lords of Sedina. Mica found himself amused, really, that being odd in so many ways had finally worked in his favor.

Janeh came by the next day, too. She said nothing as she stared into his face again, as though looking for some answer that he'd never provided. If he had known what she wanted, he might have been tempted to play along, and maybe get closer to the center of this mess.

Or maybe not. Mica didn't trust the woman, and he didn't feel up to the kind of concentration it would take to remain in the Nikeh persona for every moment of the day. He'd gotten lazy with Kistrin as his only real companion, but it hadn't mattered. This madness was almost over with anyway.

And then the weather turned bad again. He could almost believe this was the help of the gods since it made an airship landing impossible. The storm swept down along the mountains from the north to south, the winds howling and the snow so deep by nightfall that the guards did not keep their usual watch, and no one brought Kistrin the next day. He thought that was alright. Kistrin had said they had blankets back at the hut where he slept. No food arrived, but he'd saved a little for Kistrin and ate it himself, trying not to feel guilty. He had firewood still, and he'd burn the damned table and chair if he had to.

While he missed Kistrin, Mica was glad enough not to have to deal with Janeh for the day. Despite it being cold enough to form ice inside the cloth covering and around the door, he didn't feel so very cold. He must have gotten used to the weather, though he still longed for an evening by the hearth in the Raventower kitchen.

By that evening he had begun to sweat and realized a fever, rather than adaptation, had kept him somewhat comfortable through the day. He had chills before the sun went down and shoved everything away from the small fire so that he could pull the cot closer and pretend to be warmer.

Mica suffered through a long, miserable night. He was ill several times, barely managing to make it to the door and around the corner, despite the knee-deep snow. Mica wasn't sure how he made it back to the bed the third time because he remembered falling in the snow.

Another day. His arm ached. Infection from the wound? He'd checked it several times before now, and it had seemed to be healing fine.

The next day they'd managed to make a path to his hut. Janeh came again, looked him over, and frowned.

"No, we can't lose you now," she said and turned to the guard. "Get the idiot and make sure he understands that his own survival depends on our fine friend here. I'll send broth."

Mica watched her go, frowning because he knew she really didn't need him. Her reaction made no sense.

However, Kistrin arrived, listened to the orders with eager nods, and then turned, showing real worry for the first time as he crossed to where Mica sat curled up in the blanket. Mica's throat hurt. He tried to speak, but only a slight caw of sound came out.

"It's going around the camp," Kistrin said softly. "Almost everyone recovers. Just keep warm."

Mica nodded, relieved to know this was probably not an infection from the wound, but no happier with how miserable he felt. Food arrived, along with two more blankets. The guard dumped them on the table, and another brought in more wood.

"Well," Kistrin said after they were alone again. "You must be more important to her than we thought."

"Can't be," he croaked and shook his head.

He sipped the broth, which helped. They curled up in the blankets and relished both the warmth and the fact that they did not need to work.

The guards didn't take Kistrin away that night, either. He curled up with his blanket by the heat and refused to take the cot.

"I have slept on the floor since I arrived in this winter paradise," Kistrin replied softly. "And not often this close to any warmth. Besides, we don't want someone checking on you in the middle of the night and finding me there."

Mica had to agree. Besides, he was too tired to fight about it.

A guard did check, too.

Just before dawn the next day, a raven turned up at the window, trying to pull aside the cloth. Mica sat up with a start and got the metallic bird inside while Kistrin watched with a new show of surprise.

"Merriweather must have been watching and knows something is going on," Mica whispered. His throat felt a little better. A small piece of paper had been secured to the leg -- she wasn't taking any chance with talking ravens, at least.

"That's not natural, you know," Kistrin said. "That clockwork ravens can be sent to you."

"I know. And we'll talk about it someday in your favorite pub."

Kistrin looked startled and then shook his head. "I'm not that person anymore, you know."

"I know. We've both changed." Mica held the paper to the light of the fire before he gave a short laugh that turned into a cough.

"What?"

"Merriweather's note," he said and waved it a bit. "She says if I die here and ruin our wedding, she'll kill me. And you know, I take that far more seriously than I probably should."

Kistrin stared and blinked a few times. Then he shook his head. "You and Merriweather. Wedding."

"Ah, there's a tale I haven't yet told," Mica said and tossed the slip of paper into the fire. He put the raven back at the window. "Tell her I'm better. Tell her things are happening soon."

The raven gave one nod, a red-eyed stare at Kistrin, and then took off into the night.

"The raven will tell her."

"Yes."

"What in the name of the gods is going on?"

"Do you want to know about the raven or Merriweather?"

Kistrin stared at the window for a moment. "Merriweather."

So, Mica told the Prince the story about how they came to be engaged, including the trouble with Merriweather's father that prompted the sudden decision. He amused Kistrin, but he saw him look at the window now and then, as though he might still dare to ask about the raven.

"You are not what I always thought," Kistrin suddenly said. The first gray of dawn highlighted the ice around the cloth-covered window. "I always thought you were not well connected to the world --"

"And that's true most of the time," Mica admitted. He could even wish for that distance again. "I would much rather be in my workshop making clockwork butterflies right now than anywhere else -- especially if Merriweather had her chair by the stairwell and kept guard."

"Hell, I'd rather be there right now myself," Kistrin said.

"Roaring fire. Ada's food --"

"You are trying to torture us both, aren't you?"

"Just reminding us both that there is a better world out there, and we're doing what we can to save it from people like Janeh."

Kistrin gave a sudden nod of agreement. It helped that Kistrin didn't ask the more difficult questions. He'd managed to skirt around tales of gods and gifts, and battles that he feared were not quite as finished as he had believed. That was not a pleasant thought. Mica wanted the battles done. He'd had more than enough adventure. It was time to go back to his real place and live a quiet, unpretentious life -- and hope that the King never had reason to call on him again.

They worked some more in the muted daylight, but just to pass the time. They listened carefully to the guards who liked to take a little cover by the hut's wall and out of the never-ending wind. There was not much news, except what Mica had expected -- Janeh was re-checking all her clockwork men and preparing them and the explosives to be taken somewhere.

That confirmed what they'd both thought. Mica had hoped to say more to Kistrin about it, but the guards took him back to his own place that night. They left the extra blanket. Mica felt sorry for Kistrin, but he wrapped up in the extra covering and slept better.

The next day had turned gray and dull, the wind sharp and snow hitting with sudden intensity and dying away again. Kistrin had not been brought back, so he was more than happy to see one of the ravens suddenly arrive, even in the light of day

The note said that the rest of the mercenaries had finally arrived, and they had numbers now that made an attack feasible. They were in an abandoned mine no more than four miles away. They had to be careful, Merriweather said, but they were close and ready to move.

Mica sent word back to watch for the airship. He hoped they would wait, but that decision had to be in Storm and Merriweather's hands. He had barely put the raven back out the window when Janeh arrived, despite the weather. He heard her voice before he heard her movement.

"What was that?" she demanded.

"Another damned bird," one of the guards replied. "Been more of them lately."

"Yes," she replied, but Mica wasn't confident she sounded assured.

He had thrown himself into the chair, and quickly pulled apart a piece of delicate work he'd done that morning and was holding it gently in his hand and putting it back together when the door banged open.

"Damn!" he yelped and caught the piece he had started to drop. "What -- oh. Your pardon."

He sat the work down, bowed his head, and saluted.

She looked at the window and back at him, but he'd pulled it tight and disturbed as little as possible of the snow and ice. If she suspected something, she didn't say so. Which, he thought suddenly, was rather odd. She'd been quick to jump at anything else before now. Whatever was going on, it held much of her attention.

"You have done well enough," she said looking him over again.

"I am glad to serve you," he said and offered a bit of a tight-lipped smile. No one could really want to work with Janeh so she wouldn't expect him to be sincere.

"See that it stays that way," Janeh said.

And then she left again.

Janeh had not come for a friendly visit, and yet that was what it had amounted to by the time she left. He couldn't imagine what drew her to this hut. Was she just bored? Mica suspected he was the only other person who knew anything about clockwork devices. Maybe she came to see his work and to have that little connection. Perhaps, if she'd been at all sane, she might have stayed and talked -- but the moment they confronted each other, her paranoia probably kicked in. Janeh would not discuss her secrets with him.

Didn't matter. Mica knew most of them anyway. All he really needed was one of the boxes to see how she made those connections. With the mercenaries this close, it wouldn't be long now.

Should he call them in? Could they get the last information out of Janeh? Or should they wait for that airship and catch all of them at once? He liked that idea best, even though there was some chance of trouble. There had been trouble all along, though, and he could last through a little bit more.

Kistrin came the next day again, and Mica could tell he was bothered. He went to work silently for a while -- the guards remained outside the hut and didn't seem likely to move on any time soon. Mica had to focus on his work to keep from snarling, and he took his frustration out by giving Kistrin a series of contradictory orders that almost won a laugh from the Prince. That helped.

The men finally moved on, and Kistrin came closer.

"Someone slipped into the camp last night, came to the rest of the miners. Found some of his own. Told us all to be ready. I think your mercenaries are going to move despite what you want."

"Maybe wise," Mica admitted. "Maybe just as well to get this all done."

Kistrin nodded.

But the mercenaries didn't move fast enough.

CHAPTER TWENTY

J aneh came to see him twice the next day. Mica couldn't imagine what kept drawing her there so often, and the visits were beginning to tell on his nerves. Kistrin had not been brought to the hut, and he dared not ask, either.

The next time she delivered his food. What had gone wrong? What did she need so badly? There was nothing good in the look she gave him. Had she detected some of the small *corrections* he'd made that would interfere with the clockwork men? No -- she'd just have killed him for that sabotage.

"The idiot is working in the mines now," she said as she stopped by the door. "You won't need him anymore."

Janeh smiled as she left. It did not make him feel better. Mica ate the food. If Kistrin wasn't coming back -- and he had no doubt she meant those words -- then there was no reason to save any of it.

The mercenaries, as well as his own guards, would take care of Kistrin. He would be safer with them when the real trouble started, which would be soon. Mica sent a message to Merriweather as soon as he could, along with news about Janeh's odd behavior.

Mica felt miserably ill before the sun had gone down. He'd rested on the cot and tried to get up -- but his body refused to obey him. Every part of his body ached, the thoughts seemed muddled, though Mica fought to focus better.

Poisoned. The food.

Why? Why would she kill him?

Except Mica wasn't dead. Miserable and his body didn't want to obey him, but he didn't have the impression that he wouldn't survive. Mica could only lie there on the bed and wait for a raven so someone could save him. At least he'd pulled the blanket up when he had first started feeling weaker.

Mica thought about being home again. Why in the name of all the gods had he kept dragging this out? To find one more person? If they shut down the operation, would that final person matter? Mica couldn't even be certain that this was a threat -- even a distant one -- to Sedina.

Mica was not going to die in this damned hut. He refused to.

Sometime in the late of the night, Janeh came to him again.

"He's ready," she said to the outline of guards behind her. "Carry him to the house."

The two guards took Mica out in the darkness and dragged him across the ice and snow-covered terrain. The moon sat obscured behind a veil of clouds, but no storm would come of it. Had Janeh seen the same thing? Did she know enough to realize that the airship would be coming in soon? He suspected so.

His mind worked, even if his body would not.

Mica also knew Merriweather would have the camp watched, even if by nothing more than his ravens. They would know Janeh took him from the hut. In fact, he could hear a distant call of birds in the trees somewhere up the canyon wall.

"I hate those birds," Janeh mumbled. "Well, I won't have to listen to them much longer."

Everything falling into place, including, apparently, him. Mica wondered if he should have done anything differently. He couldn't decide what Janeh planed now. Maybe she had always intended to make him weak and unable to fight when the time came to leave. Perhaps they would go in the airship, and she feared him being a fool once they were in the air.

The guards took him to that first house where he'd been brought weeks before. How odd that it hadn't changed much. Mica managed to twitch his head a little the side as they went past the table. The map there showed the city of Kamere and quite detailed with distinct points of attack marked, including his tower. He only took it in with one quick glance, but the symbols seemed to burn into his mind, and he closed his eyes to keep them there -- and because he wanted Janeh to think him unconscious.

So, this was the work of the Atrians after all. They had wanted Raventower destroyed so they could rebuild their temple. They must still want to do so.

The house felt uncommonly warm, and it smelled of fresh food. He felt anger growing, and his body twitched, but then he forced calm again. Rage would win him nothing right now. Better to act weak. Better to let her men drag him up the short flight of stairs with Janeh following behind.

They tossed him into a room, and he dared not break the fall except to make certain he didn't land on his face. Janeh followed him into the little room and rolled him over onto his back. She towered over him. The wax from the candle dropped into his beard.

"Well, someone will be happy," she mumbled.

Then she left the room and locked the door behind him.

Mica remained on the floor for a long time. The place grew quiet though the light from the lamp outside the room never dulled. Mica thought he heard when Janeh climbed the stairs and went to a bedroom somewhere down the short hall.

He knew that the guards remained outside his door, not taking any chances.

The room, even though unheated, still felt warmer than the hut. The floor was hard, but Mica's body was mostly numb from whatever drug had been in the food. Gradually he felt his legs, arms, and feet. His fingers still didn't want to move well, but he could at least turn a bit. He didn't attempt to stand, but he did try to get a little bit more comfortable.

Mica slept. No reason not to. It was even somewhat pleasant being this warm for a change.

What did Janeh want?

The morning light came too bright through the window, and he saw the room clearly for the first time. A child's room, he realized as he forced himself to sit upright. Toys -- dolls, so a girl's room -- and books still sat neatly on shelves along one wall, but they were covered in dust. Someone had slept in the bed small bed, but not recently. From the state of the bedding, he didn't think the last person had been a child.

The door opened, and Janeh walked in. She stood over Micah as he faltered and fell, hitting his head loud enough to draw the attention of a guard from the hall. He did not moan. Janeh grabbed him by the arm and yanked him until he was sitting again -- and then she leaned to look closely into his face, much as she had that night when he had found her in his hut. Janeh still said nothing, and he couldn't imagine what she looked for yet again.

Janeh let go of his arm; Mica fell once more and didn't try to get back up. It didn't seem worth the effort. He watched as she left the room and hurried down the stairs. Mica crawled to the window, but found the frame nailed shut, though he could see out. Later, the guard took him to the outhouse and back into the building. Janeh sat at the table working on sketches of something new. She didn't even bother to look up. Mica said nothing, pretending to be cowed still, but ... what did it matter if she didn't look at him?

Once back to the upstairs room, Mica stumbled across and sat on the bed. He'd had no food, of course, since he clearly was not a guest here. Janeh kept him locked in this room rather than in the hut -- but why? Why the change?

The next day a guard brought him a couple pieces of bread and some water. He nibbled as he sat on the bed and watched the world beyond the window. What had the child watched, back in the day when this had been a home and not a prison? What had interested her?

Where was she now?

Mica watched what he could and mapped out the streets and houses, the new huts and the paths the guards walked. He could see steam still rising from the distant forges. Did she make more of her clockwork men?

Map.

He remembered the map he had seen when they dragged him in here. Mica closed his eyes and called back the lines and the marks, including the places where the person had put an x on one area and another. Those spots had been annotated with a single word: ruins.

This was a very *new* map. It had been made -- or at least updated -- since the war. Mica knew that Janeh sometimes got messages from others, and he supposed that someone might have made a check of the city and brought the information on to her. It bothered him, though, that someone in the Kamere might have been collaborating with her.

Well, why not? There had been people working with the Atrians, too. His first thoughts went again to the Honorgates. Where was the Lady Honorgate? Where were the other members of the family? He knew where Payton had last been seen -- at least in part -- which had indicated that he still had some power, too.

Damn mess. Mica longed to go home. He wanted to tell Gregorian everything he'd learned, hand the Prince over to his father, and then lock himself in his workshop.

Mica couldn't get to a raven. The ceiling was solid, and he suspected an attic above it. The floor was solid, and even if Mica could pry up some of the boards, at best he'd only drop down to the dining room. Sometimes he laid with his head against the floor and tried to hear what Janeh said to her men.

"Tell them they'll be warmer in the mines, then," she said, her voice a little louder, a hint of exasperation there. "Take the kettles of soup early."

Uncommonly kind. Mica didn't trust it, but he watched from the window as the guards went to a building where most of the cooking must be done. They loaded food on a sled and had a horse drag it up the hillside to the huts and then on to the mine. Soon the people were being herded toward the mine as well. He thought he saw Kistrin once and felt better for it.

He wandered around the room for a little bit, searching for anything that might help and finding precious little at all. Then he went to the small bed, curled up, and slept for a little while.

And woke to a sound he had anticipated for the last few days.

Airship. Two and maybe more, though it was hard to tell with the way the sounds echoed around the mountains. He crossed to the window and craned his neck to see one craft anchor itself to a building, and the other settled close to the ground over the open area.

This was it. Janeh would come for him soon, and they'd head for Kamere. He would be going home, and he damned well knew he'd do something to make sure that the clockwork men never did any damage or killed people there.

Janeh and her companions would not attack his tower.

Mica watched the airships. Only a few people came off, but many were going back on, and he saw some carrying the pieces of metal men that were hoisted up to the decks of the craft and stored away. They were heavy, and they were being spread out between both airships.

Someone came down the ladder, a tall man, he thought, wrapped in a fur collared cloak and scarf and walking quickly despite the snow and ice. He kept his head bowed and a cadre of guards surrounded him as he crossed the open ground. Paranoid. Mica watched him; the guard brought him straight to this house, but there was never a clear view.

Janeh had been up and down the steps already, packing her own belongings, ordering the guards to take her trunks out to the airship. Then someone cooked -- Mica was sure it wasn't Janeh -- and he could smell the food too well. The meal was doubtless a show for the man who had already reached the door.

He put his ear to the floor and tried to listen, but they spoke softly. Didn't trust the guards, Mica thought -- and wondered if she would drug this stranger as well.

They laughed.

A guard arrived not much later and dragged Mica down to the dining room. He kept his head bowed and hoped he would only be introduced, ready to go on to the next step. He would find a way to stop them. He would --

"Oh yes, we were both right. It is Lord Raventower."

Mayor Corinth.

Mica didn't pause on the last of the steps. He did stand up straighter and shook back the hair that had partly covered his eyes. He thought Janeh looked shocked at the change in his demeanor, but he was not going to act in front of this fool and there was no reason to play games with Janeh any longer.

"Sit him in that chair," Corinth ordered with an imperious wave of his hand.

"I can sit myself," Mica replied and dropped into the chair. His legs felt weak, but that was because he hadn't eaten much in the last couple of days. Corinth didn't frighten him; in fact, in some ways, he found it a relief to know this was the other person involved in this trouble.

Corinth leaned across the table. "Speak again without my permission, and I'll have you whipped."

Mica started to answer and thought better of it.

Corinth laughed. "Well, and here you are without your guard, without your brother, and without even the King to stand between us. Just the table. You look rather a mess, my lord. What would your brother say?"

Mica stated to speak and changed his mind again. Even if it had been a sincere invitation to speak, Mica knew there was nothing good that would come of the conversation. He could see the joy in Corinth's face. Mica could tell this was a chance the man had never expected to be handed to him.

"Have you done what I said, Janeh?"

"Yes sir," she answered. The *'sir'* came with a little grimace, but Corinth never turned her way. "The moment you said you suspected my new helper and gave me a description, I knew you had to be right. I went back over everything he'd ever worked on. Clever boy, really. Some of the problems were quite small and hard to find, but they would have stopped my devices from fully functioning. They're fixed now."

Mica had to hope that was not entirely true. He had the feeling he would never know, though. Merriweather -- the thought of her almost won through his mask. He hoped she realized this was not her fault. He hoped --

Corinth stood. Mica did not, and neither did Janeh, but Mica's skin crawled when the man stepped behind him. He grabbed Mica by the hair and jerked his head back.

"Put your hands on the table where I can see them. I don't trust you, boy. You have shown yourself far too clever with your hands. That surprised me."

Well then, the man was an idiot because Mica was better known in Kamere for his clockwork creations than he was for being Lord Raventower. Of course, he was good with his hands.

He did put his hands on the table. Corinth released his hair and moved away, but not back in sight. Mica had to fight not to look back at the man. He stared at Janeh instead, though that wasn't entirely pleasant, either. She didn't like that she had been tricked, even if she'd figured it out. The rage in her eyes was not much better than looking at Corinth --

The mayor moved closer. Something flashed to his right, and Mica started to turn.

A knife plunged into the back of his right hand, a burning pain that ran from hand to shoulder, to brain and heart. A guard moved up and caught hold of him, holding his arms in place by brute force. Corinth moved slightly to the side an pulled the blade back and jabbed again, twisting this time, the feel of things severing, of all control lost. Mica heard the hiss of pain he made, but he did not speak. Not even when Corinth moved to the other side and plunged the blade several times into his left hand. The right flopped against the table, beyond control now, reacting to the pain he could not fight. Blood splattered and flowed, his breathing coming in gasps, his head swimming --

But he did not cry out. He did not speak.

"Oh no, I am not going to kill you, you little bastard. No. I am taking you back to Kamere where I will execute you before your brother. You aren't going to die that easily, not after all the humiliation you've caused me."

Mica closed his eyes, started to slip from the chair.

He came back awake. A servant had been wrapping bandages around his hands. When he almost cried out, she shook her head and put a hand to his lips. The older woman worked as quickly and gently as she dared, and he gave her a silent nod of thanks when she finished. Shock, though, had set him shivering. His fingers did not move. His hands were bands of fire at the end of his arms, and the pain and loss of blood had left him weaker still.

"Get the last of my things on the airship," Janeh ordered when the girl had backed away. "Mayor?"

"We'll haul him up like the rest of the baggage. Is everything else set?"

"Yes," Janeh said. Her eyes brightened, and she smiled.

This would not be good.

Two guards caught him under the shoulders and marched him out of the building and toward the airship. Every step made his hands hurt worse, and he momentarily lost consciousness as they neared the craft. When he came to, again, they'd tied him by the legs and were hoisting him up to the deck, no more than fifty feet from the ground. Corinth laughed with delight.

Birds called out in the trees. Did his ravens see him? Birds circled, came closer -- but they were not his birds, although his ravens might be in the flock. Mica couldn't tell.

Hit his head on the side of the craft. His hands pounded with pain and blood dripped downward. He could not, he realized, move his fingers at all. Were his hands ruined? Would he never sit in that workshop and create things just for the joy of it again?

Despair took him before they finished yanking him over the railing and dropped him on the deck.

Everything he'd done, all the clever work, had been for nothing. He'd failed, and he only hoped that the Prince survived, and the others would save him. Corinth had not seen the idiot. He also didn't seem to realize Merriweather was so close, or that the mercenaries were only a few miles away. Some chance, then, to save some of this disaster.

Merriweather and the others had not come to help him. Mica had never considered that Janeh might simply pack up and leave so quickly. How far away were his friends? Had Janeh and Corinth figured that out as well and settled the trouble with the mercenaries?

No. These two would have said something by now. Janeh and Corinth would not overlook a chance to gloat.

Mica sat on the deck with his hands in his lap, too weak to stand, his eyes closed.

"Oh no, Lord Raventower, you need to see this."

Corinth yanked him back to his feet. The airship had started to lift, a slow movement -- overweight, poorly tuned engine. Maybe they'd crash. The other ship had already brought up the anchor and turned northward toward Sedina. Their craft appeared to be making a full circle of the village.

Janeh moved up beside him. She had one of her control boxes in hand.

Going to blow up --

No!

He tried to move to stop her, but Corinth laughed and yanked him back. They went low over the mine, and she jabbed at one of the buttons.

They moved away, but the explosion almost took them down before the pilot surged upward and to the right. Janeh slipped, and he tried to push her off the craft. Corinth grabbed her and then threw Mica against the wall. Dirt and debris billowed up from the mine, obscuring the area below

Even the Prince had died. Mica had failed in everything.

CHAPTER TWENTY-ONE

The dust still billowed up behind them as they moved away, a dreadful gray in a white world. As the airship gained speed, the wind it made whipped in around them, cold as death. Mica stared, trying to make his mind go blank, trying not to see Kistrin or the mercenaries who had come to the camp to help them. Tried not to think about those women and children who had also been herded up to the mine.

Dead and dying. Corinth and Janeh stood there at the stern of the airship and smiled in delight at the destruction.

"Oh yes," Corinth said. "That sort of explosion will take down everything we want, including this bastard's tower."

Before they had gone more than a mile, another explosion shook the world, and even the airship trembled slightly as the impact as the displaced air reached that far. More rock and dust rose upward in another cloud and settled. A bright flash of flame shot into the air and died away into a haze of darker smoke

"Well, that was more spectacular than I had expected," Janeh said as she pulled her jacket a little closer. "They had reported gases, though, but it hardly mattered. Just as well we don't need the mines any longer -- or the people. It's cold. Let's get in. The army is ready?"

Corinth still had hold of Mica's arm. The man started toward the door, anxious to get in now that they were climbing in altitude. The fools didn't use the life lines that dangled from the rail. Mica looked around and realized these were old Sedina ships, sold off when decommissioned from the fleet. Corinth had wanted a newer one, Mica remembered. More powerful transport -- that was what he had wanted, and not just for show.

Even the King had said he planned to investigate the man's work as soon as things settled. Had Corinth gotten word of that possibility, or was he just taking advantage of the Atrian attack and the chaos afterward? Despite how long Mica had been gone from Kamere, he had no doubt they weren't ready for another major attack so soon, and especially one from an enemy they had never realized. They'd be looking to the sea, not to the west and the air. If they moved quickly and at night, staying south of Kamere in the less settled lands --yes, they might pull off a surprise attack.

Merriweather would have sent messages back to Kamere if she had a chance, likely by a raven. However, Mica and the others had assumed that the attack would turn against Taginta first, and then move on --

Mica hadn't been paying attention. A guard had arrived with chains that clamped around his wrist -- heavy and painful he as dragged Mica to the edge of the deck. He wrapped the chain several times around the rail and secured his other wrist in another cuff.

"Rest while you can," Corinth chortled and kicked him in the chest.

The man almost fell and probably would have fallen off the edge of the deck. No luck there, though. The three walked away.

"We'll be at the other camp in a few hours," Corinth said as they reached the door. "And two more airships will be ready in no more than four days. We have to be sure of the weather before we --"

They went inside the control deck.

Maybe they thought he would suffer sitting out here in the open air, but it wasn't so bad. Mica didn't mind the cold, and they had placed him in a position where the bulk of the airship blocked the wind created by the craft's forward movement. Mica didn't think he would survive for long -- but probably long enough to get to the other camp.

No, no. Mica was not going to let Corinth control him, even in this situation. He tried not to think about his bandaged hands. Where were his ravens? Would they come to him?

He suspected that only one had been watching the camp of late, hiding in the flocks of other birds as best it could. That one would have seen him being taken from the house and to the airship -- and would have gone to tell Merriweather. He had hoped they'd seen the airship and had already been moving in.

They hadn't moved fast enough to save him from this trip. No raven had come near once Corinth and Janeh had left him alone on the deck. He was, he guessed, on his own.

Did it matter? He'd failed in everything already.

The airships were heading more inland than north, so the other camp must have been close to the Sedina border. They wouldn't be going far which was why Janeh got so many messages, even in winter. It even explained the first time they'd seen the clockwork men being used, so far from Janeh's camp.

He could not entirely ignore the cold. Mica tried to think about anything but the failure he'd made of this trouble that he'd hoped to end. He tried not to think about Prince Kistrin, or about how Gregorian would watch him die. No, he would not do that to his brother.

The chains were well secured to the rail, his hands held up so maybe he wouldn't bleed to death. They did not hurt so much now, and he suspected that came from the cold.

They had not left a guard.

And they had not searched him. Mica had spent two days in that little girl's room, and he had found at least a few small things. One was a long nail that he'd worked out of the wall and hooked into his pocket.

He tested one hand and the other. The left had a little more movement. The chain was just looped around the rail, and he was able to work it up and down until more reached the left side than the right. His fingers could barely reach the pocket, and they were almost too numb to feel the nail. His hand bled more, as well, and Mica feared he would drop the nail --

But he didn't. Mica felt the rough, old metal in his fingers, and he could see what the fingers did. The clamp around the wrist slid upward slightly -- just enough to bend the hand and fingers over the lock.

Mica knew how locks worked. He concentrated on this one, focusing on where the nail worked in, where it turned and a slight jab. He had to work without any mistakes. Mica feared the others would come out and find him, and this last chance gone.

Last chance for what? He couldn't take over the craft.

Get free first. Focus.

The careful work took a long time before the lock clicked open and the chain fell away. Mica grasped the other end and pulled it free from the rail. That side of the chain wasn't nearly so difficult to unlock.

Wait for Janeh and Corinth? What if they didn't come back out until they were at the other camp? What if guards came out and overpowered him again?

Could he get to the engine and take the ship down?

He didn't know how many guards were aboard and where they might be. Mica knew he wasn't strong enough to take on others. Failed had in everything else. He couldn't even guarantee the deaths of Janeh and Corinth in a crash since they were not far up. The weight of the clockwork men weighed the airship down, and the pilot didn't take many chances. Besides, since Janeh and Corinth were on this ship, the explosives would be in the other craft.

Mica's eyes watered so much he could barely see the railing as he stood. Everything appeared to be gray from air to clouds to land. He held up his arm, hoping for a raven, but none came.

Trees passed not far below them, and he heard the engine laboring to go higher. The trees gave way to silver again --

A door opened behind Mica, and he heard a shout of surprise and anger. Mica had no chance to do anything else, except that he would not make this worse for others. Mica would not let them use him to torture Gregorian or Merriweather.

The guard rushed toward him, but Mica swung the chain and tossed it at him -- and then he threw himself over the rail and out into the endless gray.

For a moment he felt like one of his ravens, and he wished he could truly fly. He and Merriweather had once, off the roof Raventower. It had been glorious.

Merriweather.

He hit water.

Lake, Mica realized with a shock. The silver had been a lake below him. He sunk into the frigid depths, shocked and cold, the world turning murky and dull. Something swam away.

Sinking.

Mica had already been prepared to give up and die. This was no different --

Except Merriweather would be annoyed if she ever realized he'd had a chance to survive and had not even tried to save himself. His feet hit the rocky bottom of the lake -- not far -- and he used that to push off and upward. No air -- but the surface wasn't far. Up and --

The lake had not iced over, but it was damned cold. Mica came up gasping and stared upward thinking he could see the edge of the airship as it disappeared over the line of trees. Would it circle back? They had nowhere to land and collect him again. He grinned even while his teeth chattered.

The shore seemed far away, though. Mica watched the disappearing airship, and then turned around toward the water's edge in the opposite direction. That was the way they had come, and not gone far, either. Could he somehow reach the shore, hike back to the village, and find enough there to survive?

Did he want to survive?

Mica almost stopped fighting the pull of the water -- and then he heard the damned airship coming back. He should have known that Corinth would not give up that easily, not with the years of frustration behind his temporary win. And now he would see him --

Floating on the surface?

This was not going to be easy, but he stretched out, draped his hair around his head and face, and laid his hands on the water surface. He held his neck at an odd angle, but one he hoped they could not see clearly from the ship, especially with his long scraggly hair over his face. He had not tried to swim yet, so there were not much in ripples.

Just hold still. Mica's neck already ached, but given what he'd been through of late, it wasn't hard to ignore. Just hold still.

He thought he could hear Corinth shouting above the uneven roar of the airship engine. A flintlock fired -- once, twice, the water rippling near him -- and then the shadow of the ship moved on.

Mica let his head rest a little, looking down in the water where fish swam and darted. Then the ship circled back around, and he lifted his chin just above the water so that he could breathe.

The airship went over. No one shot. Mica feared they might use the anchor to try and grab his body, and if they did, he'd have to swim away and hope to escape --

The ship went on. The sound grew fainter. He waited.

And then he swam toward the shore.

Then what?

Mica thought he would avenge the people who had already been killed at the village and maybe save those who would die soon if he didn't move quickly. The guards had gone on the airship. Had they left the horses? He hadn't seen the animals herded into the mines as well.

That gave him hope.

He tried not to think about his hands. They hardly hurt at all, but he realized it was because they were nearly frozen, not much blood getting to the fingers which he noticed were turning blue. He'd need to get his hands warm if he hoped to save them at all. Would he ever be able to do clockwork again?

Something to worry about later. Instead, Mica concentrated on moving toward the shore, one stroke and another, his feet kicking as though they knew what to do without him considering the motions. The worn boots were heavy, and he shoved them off, one foot against the other. That helped, though he'd probably miss them on the hike. At least he wouldn't have that rock digging into his heel any longer.

Keep moving.

Mica thought that if he got to the village, he might find a horse, food -- and clothing. There had to be some clothing left behind. Don't go near the mine. He had no time to measure that loss and to grieve. He'd come back later.

He would think about the deaths at the village after he saved Kamere and his tower, along with Merriweather, his brother, the King -- even Honoria. Save people who still had lives. They could deal with Janeh and Corinth. Who was working with them? Was it the Atrians still? Had Corinth skimmed off enough coin to buy the airships and troops?

Swim, swim. Don't rest. Don't let the cold lure you into thinking you should sleep here. No. Keep thinking. Keep moving. The shore looked closer. Think about that damned Corinth and what he was doing to the land and people that Mica loved.

Could Corinth have enough money to fund this war?

That seemed unlikely, Mica realized. The King and council would have noticed that much in funds missing from the taxes. Corinth had a small estate -- something he'd bought quite a few years ago --

Purchased from the *Honorgates*. Bordering on their land.

That realization annoyed Mica even more. He couldn't seem to be rid of any of them, including Payton. At least Payton wouldn't be in this body of water, though.

He hoped.

Keep moving.

Corinth targeted Raventower for all his own reasons. Childish resentment seemed to be at the bottom of all he was doing, as far as Mica could tell.

Swim, swim. Rest for just a moment. Just a moment more. Just --

No. Swim.

Corinth. Dangerous. The others would not realize they harbored a viper who had access to the King as well as Gregorian. The Mayor would have a reason for not being in the city right now, but Mica suspected he would be back before the attack came. Back in place with the others so that he could stab them --

Stabbed Mica's hands. The memory of that moment, so intensely real, got past his defenses. Mica cried out this time and tried to pull his hands closer to him. His legs went numb and dropped. He was going to drown --

His feet touched the lakebed. Mica almost slipped, but when he stood, the water reached only a little over his waist. He hadn't noticed the change in the lake, but to the left a jut of land looked far closer than the shore he'd been trying to reach. Was it just an island? He pushed himself that way, wanting to get out of the water. He might have to swim again, but if he could find some cover, dry out a little. Rest --

He would freeze, though, soaked as he was already. Mica knew it. He had no fire and no way to get warm or dry.

At least he was mostly out of the water. Mica took the last few difficult steps, pressing against the water in a stumbling rush and fell forward, his hands hitting weeds and rocks. They didn't hurt. Everything numb.

Snow laid in spots along the shore and strands of ice hung from plants bent low over the surface. Mica knew he would be like them if he didn't get away from the shore and somewhere out of the breeze. Oh, and look, it had started to snow again. Mica couldn't even feel a surge of anger or acceptance. Just move, on his hands and knees now -- leaving a trail of blood -- from the shore and up the incline --

Someone sat there.

Mica gave a cry of surprise and started to scramble back before his mind caught up with reality. A tribesman sat against a tree, a few baskets before him, a blanket over his head and body, though the covering flapped in the wind and he made no move to catch hold of it.

Made no move at all.

Did not breathe.

It was hard to tell how long the man might have been dead -- or at least Mica thought so until he saw the stump of the right hand the signs of burns. This was the dead man that the mountain tribesmen had taken back to the camp and then departed the with the next day. Janeh had not tried to stop them knowing she was both going to be gone from the area soon, and also because she wouldn't want to risk more of their displeasure for fear they'd come after her before she got away. The woman had always been careful of her own safety.

Mica looked into the face. Calm. Accepting. The baskets held bread, cheese -- how was it the wolves had not been around yet?

The gods were with them, here in this place -- with both of them.

Mica carefully removed the blanket and wrapped himself up in it. Wool. He took a little of the cheese from a basket -- that was all he could manage. Then he curled up and slept.

CHAPTER TWENTY-TWO

Mica slept -- or more likely fell unconscious -- long into the night. When he woke the bright moon hung over the lake, the light reflected like a silver arrow. Geese swept through the illumination, floating on the water, wings sometimes fluttering against the ice and cold. Deer stood by the water several yards away, nibbling on grass and weeds that sometimes crunched slightly with ice. Snow lay unbroken across most of the landscape.

Mica shivered, though the blanket helped. He suspected that he ought to be dead by now. Wet, freezing, injured -- but Mica still breathed. It wasn't always pleasant since he seemed to have bruised ribs somewhere along the way, but he could see the slight mist of his breath every time he exhaled. Ice had gathered in his mustache and beard, and he could hear it like pieces of glass.

Quiet. Lord Raventower hadn't spent much time out in the wilds, and certainly never alone. The silence was broken only by the movement of the deer, a slight breeze through the trees, and the sound of owls crying one to another.

He went back to sleep.

Dawn arrived with a mist up from the lake, like all the ghosts of everyone who had died because of him. Mica buried his head in the blanket and wept, surprised to find himself alive and yet to have failed at so much. He prayed to the gods that the others all found peace. Should Mica ask the same for himself? Mica had been ready to die in the lake, hadn't he? Why fight on now? Why not just throw off the blanket, walk down to the lake, and take his place among the rest of those ghosts?

Mica hadn't the strength to move on or to go back. He began to think that maybe he didn't care if he lived or died. All his work with Janeh had proved useless, except that he might have inadvertently taught her how to do a few things better. Oh, so brilliant, the wise Lord Raventower playing his little games. Had he so wanted to be the one to save the Prince and catch the enemy? Had he played along and ruined this chance for everyone? It had not seemed so at the time ... but if he'd told Merriweather to move in sooner, the others would still be alive.

Time to let Merriweather, Storm, and his people take up the battle that he had never been prepared to fight. Time to close his eyes and sleep again.

The soft fall of snow woke Mica in the afternoon again. He sat up for a moment, ate a little more cheese and even considered standing, but his legs wouldn't hold him. He had managed to get slightly out of the wind. This was a huge of ancient pine with a trunk so wide four people would not have easily embraced it. The scent of pine needles where he settled proved to be a pleasant smell. He leaned back and watched the woods rather than the lake.

And slept again.

Mica dreamed about his beloved home which was not much of a surprise. Pleasant dreams, where he was with all his friends, including Merriweather. The food tasted wonderful, the kitchen felt warm, and clockwork butterflies fluttered through the air around them. People laughed. He couldn't quite make out what they said, though, as if he were not really part of them.

Wasn't that how he had felt most of his life? Hadn't he felt as though he would never fully connect to the world of other humans? He all but panicked in crowds, and too many bright colors and noises distracted him so much he couldn't focus --

In his dream, Merriweather took his hand.

She pulled Mica into the real world with all the others, but at the same time, she protected him from the worst of the input. They went to a ball and danced again. Mica delighted in the connection that no one else had ever made for him. Merriweather shared her world with him.

They danced. Mica never wanted that dance to end, while the world spun and moved around them as he and Merriweather held on to each other and ignored everything else. Were they at Raventower? He didn't know, but it didn't matter, as long as they danced together. What music? Something bright and cheerful, he thought. Even in this dark time, something bright and joyful that would see them through this trouble.

I love you, Merriweather. Had he said that to her? Even once? That thought drove a sword into the dream; Merriweather moved away from him again, and left Mica there, sitting in a swirl of color, alone in the world.

Mica opened his eyes to another dawn. A hawk flew overhead. He had hoped for one of his ravens, but if they hadn't found him yet, they wouldn't. Mica watched the world for a while. And tried not to feel so cold with the snow falling more heavily on him. Mica thought he should give the blanket back now. It hardly mattered to him, and he did not want to upset the spirits of this place.

For the first time, he looked at other trees. More dead sat there, all facing the lake. Some, he could tell, were no more than bones and scraps of cloth. This was a funeral land for the tribes. Well, at least he wouldn't be alone.

How strange a place to end his already unusual life.

Mica closed his eyes again. For a little while, the sun came through the clouds, and he felt almost warm sitting with the light against his face. He rested ... slipped away to dreams about his brother, mostly, this time. Remembering how utterly insane Gregorian had become when his children were being born. Half scared out his mind for his wife and the child -- but also so full of joy at the idea of each new child that Mica had always envied him, thinking he would never have that same experience.

And then Mica's life had changed.

Only now ... now he would lose it all. The desire to fight to save his life rose up once more, but his body would not obey. He struggled for a few minutes, got all the way to his feet -- and fell again before he could step away from the tree. He laid there for a long time, and then finally moved to lean against the tree once more and rested just because it was more comfortable.

Mica thought he would try again later. Just rest for now. Dream of better times because that seemed to give him strength.

Later in the afternoon, a loud howl startled him fully awake; the wolves did come around. He could have accepted going to sleep to die, but not to be attacked and too weak to fight back. Mica wondered if he could get back to the lake and drown. Would that be better? He was tired of being cold and wet.

The howl did not come again, though. The sun began to go down, dark shadows spreading everywhere. He'd already survived longer than he had expected. The ravens had not found him so there could be no hope now. Mica realized that all he had left was to decide how he wanted to die.

Cold again.

He closed his eyes and thought he heard Merriweather calling to him and smiled, drifting back into sleep.

Didn't stay there this time. Something called Mica back to the darkening dusk. Mica moved a little to look back at the lake where he could see a bear shuffling along the shore, sniffing at the ground as it went. Just as dangerous as a wolf, Mica realized, and hoped that it did not --

But the creature suddenly turned from the shore and charged straight toward his tree. Mica tried to stand. He tried to find a weapon. This was not --

"Bear found him!" a voice called out.

The creature came around the side of the tree and slammed into him. They both tumbled, and the beast shoved his head into Mica's chest making soft huffing noises that did not sound like death coming at any moment.

Not a bear -- *Bear* himself, a huge furry mass of warmth that Mica finally threw himself into, holding on as though he feared the dog would pull away and disappear. Mica heard voices, and horse hooves as well, but they were not close, and he couldn't decide if they were a dream or not. He didn't look, though he was aware of Shipley close by, babbling on about hunting him and how none of them would give up --

"Mica."

A hand rested gently on his shoulder, and Mica finally lifted his head from the warm fur and looked at Merriweather, staring into her startled face as though she hadn't believed it could really be him after all.

"I haven't said that *I love you,*" Mica told her.

Merriweather didn't move. She didn't even seem to breathe, and Mica wondered if maybe this was a dream after all. He didn't mind if it was. He got this chance to study her face --

Merriweather dropped to her knees and grabbed him into her arms. "Blankets!" she yelled. "Get a fire going --"

"Not here," Storm said, dropping down on his knees as well. "Not here with their dead. We don't want to provoke trouble now. I'll get him back to the woods. It's not even a mile away. Come on, Merriweather."

Storm practically pried Mica out of her hands. Mica put a hand on her arm when they got him to his feet. She put her hand over it and then looked at his hand, startled.

"What happened --"

"He can barely stand, Merriweather," Storm said and took tighter hold of him. "Let's get him somewhere better before you start asking --"

She looked ready to argue, but Mica thought that was more a reaction to fear than anything else. He pulled the blanket off his shoulders and gave it to her. She looked startled.

"I borrowed it. Please -- please give it back." He gestured to the other side of the tree. "And an offering, if you can. I ate his cheese."

Merriweather took the blanket and stepped back to look. "Oh. Yes, I'll handle this, Lord Raventower."

"Thank you."

Almost ... almost normal.

Storm started to lead him away, then gave a curse and just picked Mica up. Mica felt appalled -- but grateful they made such good time. The rest of the mercenaries had stayed back at the edge of the area, but at Storm's shout, they leapt from their horses and prepared to make a camp. The noise and movement seemed half wild. Some laughed while others rushed off to find wood for a fire, and the last cleared an area just off to the side of the road, but well away from the dead.

Storm helped him stand again. Mica looked back at the lake. He thought a few ghosts might still be watching them, their fog-like bodies drifting on the water. Mica felt as though this sacred place had a soul of its own, too -- and that something was pleased to find he had survived. Had he touched something holy there and not even realized?

"Don't hunt here," Mica said to Storm.

"No, we won't," Storm replied with a quick look back at the lake and the dead settled by trees. "I had heard about these sites before, but never found one. They bring their dead to sit beside someplace lovely, to help them find peace and move on."

"I found peace," Mica admitted. "And I am ready to move on in my own way."

"Get him warm," Storm ordered as he handed Mica over to others.

Blankets quickly made a nest around him, and the others got a fire going, almost at his feet. He heard the order not to hunt, and no one argued. It turned out they had snared a brace of rabbits earlier that day anyway, and a couple of them went to work on them.

Storm got Mica to drink a sip of ale from his flask, but Mica shook his head at a second offer.

"No food except for a little cheese for days," he warned. The warmth down through his body had felt good, but the wave of dizziness afterward wasn't pleasant. "I don't think that's such a good idea."

"Clear-headed though," Storm said and seemed impressed.

"How -- did you find me?"

Merriweather settled beside him, so close that he could lean against her if he needed to. Bear and Shipley settled on the other side. The boy looked worried

"When the airships arrived, the raven came to let us know. We were getting ready -- but they moved faster than any of us anticipated. A raven saw you taken on the airship,"

Merriweather explained. She had a blanket, too, and she looked as though she had not slept in days. "It tried to follow but didn't have time to catch up after the people left the deck and you leapt into the water. He came back and got us and led us to the lake."

Mica dared a glance at Storm.

"The raven is a bit odd," Storm admitted. "And that's as far as I'm willing to go with it. And thank you for saving my people in the mines."

Mica went suddenly cold. This wasn't real after all. Tears started to form in the corner of his eyes. "I did nothing -- I watched the explosions -- I wasn't there. This isn't --"

Storm dropped on his heels again. "You weren't there, but --"

"But you told me what to do if I ever faced one," Kistrin said as he sat -- just sat -- on the ground across the fire from Mica. "You said to get something in front of it and get the hell away. That's what we did. We were all far back in the mine when the explosion came. Then we took all the blasting powder we could get out of the supplies and went to the area the others knew was close to the outside and blew a hole out."

"They'd been digging that way on purpose, as much as they dared," Storm said. "The miners were planning to break out and take over."

"That -- that was the second explosion?" Mica asked. He wanted it to make sense.

"And we saw the airships sailing away," Kistrin said. He still looked wild-haired and bearded. "The guards were gone, the tribesmen already left -- so we found what we could. Merriweather showed up, found out you were on the airship, and we were all heading after it."

"You just don't argue with Merriweather," Storm added as he brushed a hand through his hair. "And especially since your raven had shown up and told us that you were in the lake. It was a big lake, though, and we didn't know where you might have gotten back to shore. Bear, though, he tracked you down without a problem."

Was that why Seldon had sent the boy and his dog? Mica reached out and patted the animal and won a smile from Shipley.

"They didn't throw you in the lake, did they?" Storm asked.

"He wanted to kill me in front of Gregorian. I couldn't let that happen -- and I thought I had failed at everything. Everyone dead."

"The villagers are taking back their little town," Kistrin said. He sounded worn and did not look like the Prince from Sedina. He'd changed. "A few of them took horses and headed out to find supplies for the winter. I think they'll do well."

"We'll get supplies to them," Storm promised.

"Good," Kistrin said. He sounded pleased and relieved.

The others continued to move around still. Mica saw the raven in the tree above him, keeping watch. Good. He needed to pull his thoughts together. If this was real --

Storm spoke to him, but Mica couldn't quite drag his thoughts back to listen or answer. The warmth of the fire lured him into a stupor where he wasn't sure he could move at all. The warmth also brought aches and pains out from the numbing cold, but Mica welcomed them this time. He had sat frozen and on the edge of death for too long, and now even the aches were welcome. Shadows moved around him and a light snow fizzled into the fire, and leaving a scent of damp warmth. He had rarely considered the beauty of a fire, the flames dancing in orange and yellow spires. He stared for a long time.

He could feel his hands again, but he did not look. His toes burned with the heat that slowly spread upward through his legs. The beard dripped water into his lap while the ice melted. It seemed even his eyes cleared of misty ice.

Survived.

Merriweather took a mug from one of the men and held it out to Mica. It steamed and smelled of herbs. He tried to take it, but it almost slipped through his bandaged hand and Merriweather held on and got it to his lips. He sipped his thanks.

"What happened to your hands, Mica?" she asked softly. The others had gone silent.

"He stabbed them," Mica said and could not entirely hide the shudder as he remembered the scene.

"Who?" she asked, the anger barely masked in her voice. Mica knew that rage was not directed at him, at least.

"Corinth."

Merriweather hissed in shock and anger. He could feel her body tense and saw how her eyes went hooded.

Kistrin had said nothing. Now he leaned closer to Mica, and his eyes showed rage as well. "Mayor Corinth?" he asked, the words cold and hard, but making certain of the identification.

"Yes."

Kistrin looked at Merriweather as though waiting for some kind of confirmation.

"It makes sense. I'm sure we'll find the mayor has been out of the city a great deal lately --"

"Corinth said he was trying to find needed supplies for the city -- even before the war. My father found it odd to see him so worried about such things. We actually thought he was going to his estate to make certain he was supplied there."

"His estate is next to one of the Honorgate lands," Mica reminded them. "Bought it from them."

Kistrin nodded. Merriweather helped him sip more of the warm tisane. She paled a little when she saw his hands again, but then the rage returned in the next breath. Mica wondered if he wanted to be there when she caught up with Corinth.

"Drink a little more," she said. "We'll have food soon. No, don't even think about arguing with me, Lord Raventower. Let me remind you that I am still tasked with keeping your alive -- and while you were out of my sight, you threw yourself off an airship and into a frozen lake. You cannot be trusted."

"I suppose you're right. Tired, Merriweather. I am really just tired."

"Sleep then," she said. She even pulled Mica closer so that he could rest his head on her shoulder. "We'll wake you for the food. We're camping here for the rest of the night, but you must be ready to ride tomorrow, Mica. We dare not wait any longer."

"We must get the word to the King," Mica said. He looked up at the raven, and it came down to settle by the fire as well.

"Snow coming," the raven said, which still seemed to startle and worry Storm. "Can't go."

Mica nodded. "We have a little time," Mica replied, some of the thoughts coming back. He had not failed after all -- not yet. "They still had things to do at the other camp. Rest for now, but we dare not stay too long."

No one argued.

CHAPTER TWENTY-THREE

"We should go at least a few miles," Storm said. He'd been arguing with Merriweather, Mica realized. "If the raven is right; this is not where we want to be with bad weather heading in."

"Lord Raventower is not --"

"I'm ready to go," Mica interrupted and drew both their looks from across the fire. "Let's go, Merriweather. Let's not mess this up now. I want out of this area before we do something unforgivable, and I want to get word to Kamere."

Merriweather looked at him with a frown, the dying firelight flickering across her face. The morning light showed as only a line of gray against the trees and a touch of snow had started to fall. They needed to go. "He'll ride with me," she finally said

The others prepared to leave with a whisper of voices and protesting horses. Mica managed to hold a cup in his right hand and steady it with the left, sipping herbal tea spiked with honey and cider. The taste made him think of spring and hope. His mind still wandered, but more and more often it came back to the realization that they had survived against all the odds. This had to be real.

The others packed up the camp, though they left him and the fire until last. Mica felt more like a much-abused piece of luggage right now, but one that he was glad they didn't simply leave behind. Mica forced himself to stand on his own, just to prove he could, though he didn't think he'd be on his feet for long.

A horse came up and pushed at the back of his head.

"That damn horse again," one of the mercenaries said. "I have never seen such a badly trained --"

Mica looked back at the animal and grinned. "You again. So, we both survived, did we? If you have an extra piece of bread, this horse will do anything for you."

Merriweather was the one who found a crust of bread and held it out. The horse all but danced to her and won laughter all around.

"We'll take this mount, Enker," Merriweather said and patted the animal on the nose. "No, really. It appears to have formed a bond with Lord Raventower. Maybe he can keep it in line with better luck than the rest of us have had."

"Do we have more bread?" Mica asked.

They mounted a little later. Mica managed not to moan as Storm helped him up behind Merriweather. The horse behaved, too, which surprised even Mica.

This was not going to be a pleasant ride.

"Okay, Merriweather -- now is the time to decide," Storm said as he pulled his horse up beside theirs and with everyone else falling in behind them. Mica had two blankets around him again, and he tried not to think how he already felt cold. His fingers had turned stiff and unresponsive, so he had trouble holding to Merriweather. Storm had changed the bandages and put something that burnt a little in the wounds, but they'd both seen the fingers moved a little still. Storm had looked almost as pleased as Mica felt in that moment.

It gave him hope. He moved them now, just a little. He didn't want the wounds to start bleeding again --

"Lord Raventower?" Merriweather said.

"Ah. Sorry. I was not paying attention. Is there a problem?" His voice sounded scratchy, and he knew he would be sneezing and coughing soon.

"What do we do now?" Merriweather asked.

"You want me to decide?" he said, shocked. "I have messed up everything I did on this journey. I don't know what to do, Merriweather. I don't think I ever really did."

"None of us did," Storm reminded him. "But you somehow managed to save the others in your own way. And you survived. What do we do now?"

The question had caught his attention. He looked around, bowed his head once to the spirit of the lake, and then looked up and down the trail.

"We'll never find Janeh's other camp in time," Mica said with a nod toward the wilds. His mind suddenly seemed to clear as he considered the possibilities. "As much as I would like to find them and charge in -- even if we could find it, we are not enough to take them on. Back to the village? And do what? Sit out the winter? We could head to Taginta, but that's not where they plan to attack, you know. I saw the map. They're going for Kamere, and we'll have to ride quickly if we hope to get there with a warning. Janeh and Corinth were not quite ready to move. If the weather turns against them, we have a little more time -- as long as we can move faster than the storm."

"Yes," Merriweather said, and Storm nodded agreement though he looked at the sky. " I know. We could find ourselves out on the trail with no cover at all and no way to survive -- but I still think it's our best chance. The truth is, though, that you and your men don't need to come with Lord

Raventower and me. Prince Kistrin, you should stay with you -
-"

"We're all going together," Storm said. "There is no telling what trouble you might face out there. Let's go. There was a trail heading southeast just a few miles back."

"Storm -- you are in charge," Merriweather said and surprised the man. "I might make suggestions, but I think you know this area far better than me, right?"

"Yes. We've worked near here a couple times," he said. He didn't say the one thing Mica guessed -- that they had fought against the local tribe and might need to get away before trouble came. "We'll do our best to get all of us out of here. The border in this area isn't as well marked as on the roads, too. We should be across into Sedina soon -- as long as we don't run into trouble."

Mica looked the group over. There were fifteen others besides him, Merriweather, Shipley, and Kistrin. Three of them were Prince Kistrin's former guard, and they kept close to him now. There had been four -- Mica didn't ask what had happened to Dak. None of them had cleaned up yet, and that reminded Mica of how he must look. He hoped they found some reasonable place to rest soon.

The raven glided down from the tree and landed on his shoulder, startling Merriweather and the others.

"Where are the other ravens?" he asked it.

"Scattered," the raven said with a click and grind of gears. "Only three came to you here. Messages back to Gregorian."

"But he doesn't know about Corinth for that Janeh is on the move."

"No."

"You should go --"

"Snow coming," the raven said, and his wings flapped a bit, metal feathers almost tangling in Mica's wild hair. "Too strong of wind. Ride."

So, they took the raven's advice and headed out on the trail. Mica was starting to think that everyone was going a bit crazy by now.

They soon found that trail heading southeast, and it took them into a wooded area that seemed somehow safer than the open ground. Bear played scout and sometimes without Shipley who rode with one mercenary for another. The dog never went very far ahead. The dog limped a bit more than usual, probably from all the walking and from the cold. Bear and Mica would both be happier to reach home. Mica relaxed enough to sleep, though he suspected he was also unconscious some of the time. That night they camped around a couple small fires while winds shook the trees and branches fell, but not on them. By the next morning snow fell, too -- but the boughs of the trees kept a lot of the area clear.

Not long into the midmorning, they met tribesmen. The warriors stood in the middle of the road, long hair of gold on some and brown on the others, flew outward in the wind, giving the impression of wings. They wore long tunics trimmed in fur and wide, embroidered belts that held weapons that ranged from blades to guns. However, they had no weapons drawn, and Mica didn't have a feeling of threat from them. Neither, apparently, did Storm. He signaled his own people to stay back and rode just a little ahead of Mica and Merriweather.

"We wish only to ride through and get back to our own place," Storm said.

A tall man with gray eyes and scars on face stepped forward. They had horses but had dismounted already. The tribesman looked the group over and then back to Storm. "You did not desecrate the sacred land,"

"No, we did not. Our friend arrived there by accident, and we came to take him away."

"You think such a thing is an *accident*?" the man said with a look of disbelief. He walked past Storm to the place where Mica rode with Merriweather. "Do you think this an accident?"

"No. I think the gods saw me to that safe place and the spirit of the lake accepted me and helped me reach the shore. How do I repay the borrowing of the blanket and eating some of the food?"

The man stared at him and then grinned brightly. "You are not what you seem. A holy man, yes?"

"Of a sort," he admitted.

"And you found peace there, even with the spirits of the place around you."

"Especially with the spirits of the place around me."

"Ha!" He slapped Mica on the leg and then walked back to his own people with a nod at Storm as he passed. "Give them the supplies."

The tribesmen went to the side of the trail and pulled out several baskets and bags. Then they mounted their own horses and rode past. They were still carrying more supplies, too.

Storm stared for a long time as though he expected an attack from behind. "What the hell was that?" he finally asked looking back at Mica.

"I just answered a few questions," Mica said.

"Holy man."

Mica winced. "It's another long story, and it has to do with the ravens, my tower -- my whole life. But not now, Storm."

Storm stared for a moment and then went to help distribute the supplies. They had grain for the horses, food for themselves, a few more blankets -- in all, it was enough to see them all the way to Kamere, Mica realized. He hoped that the group took something to the villagers as well, and he had the feeling that was where they were headed, in fact.

Maybe the mountain people needed to make amends for their own mistakes.

Mica even shared a bit of bread with his mount while Storm and his men fed the horses. Soon everyone moved on. They rode in silence for a few miles, Storm glancing their way often, though he never asked any questions.

"You know what we have to do," Merriweather said at last. "Or at least the choices we have, right?"

"Go by ship back to Kamere," he admitted, but with a shake of his head. "Or try to go by land. Or send the others by ship -- but what if something happens to it?"

"Exactly," Merriweather replied. She shook her head, looking around the area as though she expected either trouble or an answer to leap out at them. "It's not safe for us to go by ship, but anything slower --"

"Maybe there will be an airship," Mica suggested.

"I'd like that," she admitted. "But I don't see it happening."

He nodded agreement.

And they rode on.

They rode a long way into the night before they made a quick camp, and then got back up at dawn, and rode again. Oddly, Mica didn't mind so much. He wanted back to the world he knew, and that meant doing everything he could to stop Janeh and Corinth, even if it meant going by ship. If Payton showed up -- well, they'd deal with him as well.

Despite everything, they had managed so far, hadn't they?

The fever had come back, of course, and it muddled his mind. The scouts who rode ahead found an abandoned village, though. Most of it had been burnt and destroyed, but they were able to find cover in a couple of the buildings. Mica slept on the floor, covered in a pile of blankets and shivering -- but by the next morning, he felt better again.

"Yes, the fever will likely come back," Mica said and shoved the hair back from his face with a snarl. Then he winced when his fingers caught in the snarls. "It will if I stay or go. Let's get moving, Merriweather."

"Let me braid your hair," Merriweather said and did a quick job of it.

That helped. Mica thought about shaving off the beard if anyone had the tools -- but then he thought about that cold wind on his face and changed his mind.

They left the nameless village behind. The trees had already begun to thin, and they passed by farm fields that had been left unharvested. He hoped the area recovered once they settled this trouble with Janeh and Corinth.

That gave Mica a little more reason to keep going. This wasn't just about his tower and his city, his friends and his enemies. No, this was about putting the world back to right.

Shipley rode with Storm today. He had not expected the leader of the mercenaries to take the boy up as his other people had, but Shipley didn't seem to mind. Mica heard them talking about Kamere sometimes, and he thought Storm was getting a feel for the city. That would help.

When they crossed a broad stream, one of the others even took Bear up on the saddle, much to the horse's amazement. Mica thought the huge dog looked like he could get used to riding on a horse faster than Shipley would.

The thought amused Mica. He hadn't expected to be amused. Everything had been so dark for so long that Mica had thought it would never change. Bear and Shipley gave him hope again.

The weather did as well because it stayed bad. It was not pleasant for them to travel in the harsh winds and sometimes blinding snow, but there were other considerations.

"They'll be grounded with those airships -- unless they're total idiots, in which case they'd crash, and I'd be fine with that answer, too," Mica said as the others gathered around the fire that night. They'd found a slight draw, and the wind blew mostly over the top of them, though the snow sometimes fell straight down between the gusts. "The weather has to be worse for them than for us. We're still moving each day."

"We're maybe two days from Taginta, depending on how bad the trails are. Too much ice and we can double that time, at least," Storm explained. He handed out cups of stew. Bear had a bowl of his own and rabbit bones besides. "Lord Raventower is right on that account. If we can find any ship to sail back north -- yeah, the weather will have helped us so far."

Mica moved his fingers a little, although they felt bruised and swollen. The left hand moved better than the right. Any cold set them aching with a white fire that spread all the way up into his arms.

But they moved.

The storm died down somewhat by the next morning. The group rode faster that day and passed through villages that were not abandoned. In fact, the closer they got, the more the villages were crowded with people. Storm left a couple of his men to find out what was going on since it was clear some of those people had only recently arrived.

The men caught up with them barely an hour later.

"The King ordered virtually everyone but the army and the highest nobles out of the city," Enker said, and the other nodded. "They're worried more about running out of supplies than they are about the safety of the people."

"And *the people* are not happy," Mica said with a shake of his head.

"Not much. They had to abandon just about everything of worth. A lot of this last group were not the poor. And there is worse. The city guard decided if there wasn't anyone left to protect, they were walking out, too. The King is calling for all of them to be hung."

"No protection in the city?" Storm said, startled.

"The entire damned army appears to be there, Storm. He's only after the city guard because they stood up to him and made a show of it."

"Argine is heading for a civil war," Mica predicted.

Storm gave a nod of agreement. "I want nothing to do with it. We're going to avoid the city. We'll head on to Stravil which we can probably get to faster than we could get through the Taginta gates. I don't know if we'll be able to find a ship; I suspect they're hard to come by now -- but there won't be any left in the city anyway under these conditions."

"How do we get across the border?" Merriweather asked.

"I know a secret pass, very close to the sea," Storm explained. "I doubt anyone will be guarding it, but if they are, we'll figure a way through."

Storm did not say they would fight, but the implication was understood. Both Mica and Merriweather nodded agreement. Shipley, who was walking with Bear just then, dropped back beside them, frowning.

"I can't say I like riding through the wilds that much," he admitted. "And the villages all seem odd, so small. Strange places, where they're all apt to know each other, right me lord?"

"Yes," Mica agreed.

"Taginta was like home, almost -- but like a kind of nightmare home. Things didn't match up quite right there, but it were interesting to explore. I was in an airship, too, you know. Flew in the sky, Bear and me. And now we are going to sail? When we get home, I'm going to lock myself in a room in Raventower and hope the world stops bein' so strange before I come out again."

Mica smiled agreement, but that giddy feeling came more because Shipley had not said he would go back to Shadow Walk and hide there. He'd go home to Raventower.

Did the tower influence everyone? Did it call people back home to it? Maybe so, but he thought a good part of it was also because Mica had done his best to make it a good place to live. Gram had stayed, along with Ada and Fern, Roe and Nyle. Hell, he had been having trouble getting rid of the soldiers camped in his courtyard.

Mica had no doubt they were still there, protecting his precious tower, even though neither Gregorian nor the King had that same draw to the place that he and his friends felt. That was fine. The place might get very crowded if too many people followed him home all the time.

Closer.

Before long, Mica realized he could smell the sea. Part of the trail appeared to have been covered by a huge landslide, blocking the way. Merriweather cursed, but Storm rode on, going off the trail, down an incline, and then the horse climbed upward and disappeared into the rock. In a moment, he appeared again.

"It's still clear beyond here, at least as far as I can see. Come ahead. Carefully. Bear, Shipley -- don't climb on the rocks. It's precarious enough."

They went one horse at a time up down the hillside and back up. The way behind the fallen stone was so narrow, and turned so sharply, that Mica would not have thought it a way through. The weather being more wet than snowy didn't help. Ice sat in frozen pools, making the horses' steps uncertain within the narrow passage.

They crossed a windy headland afterwards, horses almost slipping there as well, but once down the other side, the trail passed into a narrow crevice out of the wind and with less ice, though a lot of salt encrustations on the stone. They came out, finally, into a marshy area with the sea in sight. No wonder few came this way.

Storm led them along the edge of the marsh and up on dryer ground again, heading along a deer trail that took them back inland. "We're well over the border," he told them. "Close to Stravil. If we can find a ship, it's going to take funds, but I have held on to some gold."

"It's possible that someone might recognize Lord Raventower -- or Prince Kistrin," Merriweather said with a bow of her head to that man. "We might get funds that way, if we need them."

"I'd rather not draw any notice," Kistrin said and shoved back his own tangled hair. "I'd like to get back to Kamere before I turn up again. Call me superstitious, but I don't want to take the chance of drawing unwanted attention and getting us into more trouble."

That made sense and explained why he had not made an attempt to clean up better. Mica just hadn't cared, but if someone recognizing him could help, he'd was willing. Besides, he didn't think word of his survival could get to Corinth or Janeh in time to stop their plans.

They reached the outskirts of Stravil at sunset; the winds had died down a bit off the ocean, and a bit of a breeze from inland had taken over. Most of the mercenaries set up a small camp just outside of town along with the prince and his men. There didn't seem to be many refugees in the area; they had likely moved inland, out of the cold wet of the sea wind, so it didn't seem quite so crowded here. A fog had started to close in, and he supposed that was a little better than snow or rain -- though dry and still would be a welcome change from the constant dampness.

Mica and Merriweather went into Stravil with Storm and two others, along with Shipley and Bear. If they by chance found a room, Mica would be ensconced there until they found a ship -- which wouldn't be more than two days, Storm hoped.

Mica carried a raven under the shabby cloak one of the others had provided. Mica wondered why they took such good care of him and suspected it was for Merriweather's sake.

They'd left the horses behind, and Mica only hoped he wouldn't have to walk too far in the makeshift shoes of rags. It was good, though, to be strong enough to move on his own, even if Merriweather hovered near him all the time.

"The storm will still be strong inland for at least half a day," Merriweather said as she stared out into the fog, frowning. "We have to hope they wait a bit longer."

"They'll need time to clear ice and snow off the airships. Those were older craft," Mica said. "Not much better than what the Atrians had when they attacked Kamere. Janeh and Corinth won't like any ice weighing the craft down, especially since they're going to be adding the weight of clockwork men and troops. Their camp must also be far enough back in the mountains and south near the border or they'd have drawn attention, even in winter. They won't be at Corinth's little estate or at the Honorgate lands. Gregorian wouldn't have missed them gathering in either of those places or anywhere else close to the city."

"Excellent points," Storm said. They passed a few buildings and headed on toward a loud tavern, people spilling out into the evening light. Storms had rested on his gun, but he made no show of it. "The weather might continue to be bad in the mountains. All we need is a few more days."

The tavern stood close to the docks and as they came closer, Mica could see the shapes of three small ships at the little dock. He could not see them clearly through the mist, but he hoped that one of them would serve their needs.

Mica set the raven flying to keep watch while they went inside. Despite what Mica had already seen, the noise and movement of the crowded place still took him by surprise. Merriweather must have seen that old look in his face because she moved up beside him and put a hand on his arm, squeezing slightly, and drawing his attention from the chaos around them and back to her.

He managed to smile and stumbled across the room with them. Bear took the lead, and for some reason people threw themselves out of the way of the large dog, though he never so much as barked or growled. By the time they'd crossed the room, a table had cleared, and they settled in without a problem. Storm gave the dog a pat on the head.

"He's even more useful in town, I see," Storm said. "I think I'll have to find one of my own."

"There is no other like Bear," Merriweather said.

Storm gave a nod of agreement. By then the barmaid had come to the table and Storm flashed some coin as he ordered a jug of ale and a pitcher of cider.

They'd drawn attention, of course. That had been part of the plan. There was no reason to try and sneak around to find a ship, not in an atmosphere like this. Being secretive would more likely get the entire group hanged before anyone listened to their reasons. No, they needed to be straightforward. They had to be bold. They had to --

They had to have *one more miracle*, and it was walking straight toward them.

"Burnis," Merriweather said as she stood. She looked stunned. He'd come all the way to the table, staring at them in shock and a little dismay.

"What the hell happened to you, Je--"

She caught Burnis by the arm and shook him. "If you call me by that name, I swear I'll rip your tongue out."

Burnis took her seriously. He swallowed twice and still stood by them. "What the hell happened to you? All of you look like hell."

"That's where we were," Mica agreed. Then he gave a slight smile. "Are you here with the *Grayrun*?"

"Yes. We got in last night with some supplies for the town." He gave his sister a bright smile. "I found out I like the sea. Father thinks I'm insane, but then he started saying I was too much like you."

"This is your brother?" Storm finally asked.

"Yes, he is. Burnis Merriweather -- and he is here on the ship that we took most of the way to Taginta before Admiral Rose picked us up and set us inland. Can you get Captain Grayson?"

"Yes," Burnis said and darted away and out of the building.

"We should have asked if he's had any more trouble," Mica said.

"Does it matter? Can you think of a better ship to take us? Or should we go in a craft that has no warning at all?"

"Warning?" Storm said and looked more bothered than worried. "Warning about *what*?"

"We haven't mentioned the octopus with hands and a human head?" Merriweather asked and sounded so sincere and matter of fact that Storm broke out laughing. "I am serious."

"Yes -- yes, I don't doubt the existence of this creature," Storm said and took several gulps of ale and set his mug back down. "It was, my good friend Merriweather, how straightforward you were about the tale -- like this is something not at all out of the ordinary."

Merriweather sat there for a moment, and Mica suspected she was going through a list of things that they'd dealt with of late -- intelligent spiders, haunted clocks, pods that swept through the ocean under the water.

"I have to say that really ... no, not so unusual of late. I'm sorry I hadn't mentioned it before, though. It might have influenced your decision on traveling back north with us. We are not safe companions, Storm -- and I don't mean in the way that mercenaries usually fight. Lord Raventower has a link to magic --"

"I would never have guessed, having not seen anything strange around him, like -- say -- talking clockwork ravens," Storm said and looked her in the face. "Sit down and drink your ale. We've been together in this mess far too long to back out now. It is good to be warned, though."

"We would have thought of it before we sailed," Mica said. "Shipley, do you mind going out to the door and waiting for Burnis to come back with his captain. I want the raven to know it's safe. He'll have noticed Burnis running off."

"Glad to do it," the boy said and started away, though he waved Bear to stay. At least Shipley stopped just inside the open door and watched, so the rest of them had no trouble keeping an eye on him.

They had food coming. Nothing fancy, but Mica felt as though they had finally stepped back into civilization again. The sounds and smells were human, the fire warm, the room crowded. Mica let the sensations wash over him from his safe place back in the corner. He could tell they would probably not take a room here tonight, but he didn't really care so much, especially if they were on the *Grayrun* instead.

Burnis and Grayson came back faster than he expected, and both out of breath. Burnis led the captain to the table as Storm pulled over a couple more chairs.

"When do you want to leave?" Grayson asked.

Storm looked as though he really liked Grayson already -- either that or thought he was just as crazy as the rest of them. Mica thought that might be true.

"Have you had any more trouble with Payson?" Mica asked.

"We saw him twice. He didn't come after us," Burnis said. Odd how he even sounded different, as though he had suddenly grown up. "And we've heard rumors that he's appeared to a few others, too. I think he's looking for you, Lord Raventower --"

"Mica," he said with a wave of his hand. "If you're going to be my brother-in-law --"

"Married," Storm said, though the word was almost a squeak.

"Not yet," Merriweather replied and laughed. "I forgot to mention that one, too, right?"

"That's the problem. Once Merriweather is on the job, she's focused on it," Mica said. "I am lucky that keeping me alive has been her job of late."

"And she's managed it despite a lot of odd things that go on around you," Storm added

"When do we leave?" Grayson asked again. "I need to see if I can buy fuel. The weather has finally broken, at least, and the tide goes out in three hours --"

"We'll be on board," Merriweather said. "I am not sure how many of us will be traveling with you. I think you and your men should go overland, Storm. We shouldn't all go --"

"Some of us will go with you," he countered. "And you know that's wise, considering the kind of trouble you might run into, not even counting this odd Payson creature."

Merriweather started to say something and then paused with a new look of calculation on her face. "Yes. You're right. Shipley, you and Bear can go with either group."

"Out on the ocean -- that's the only part I've not done yet," Shipley reminded her with a bit of a laugh. "And I'd like to get home to gram. I don't think I quite like riding horses enough to choose to spend more time on one."

"It's not safe being with us."

He tilted his head and looked at her. "I've been around for a while now, haven't I? You think I don't know these things? I'll go with you."

"Yes," she said and sighed. "Well, let's go get ready to sail, then."

CHAPTER TWENTY-FOUR

The others came in from the camp since they'd be leaving almost immediately. They ate a nice meal of roasted chicken, spitted fish, and fresh, warm bread while everyone sat in a place out of the weather. Tables, chairs, plates, cider -- it all seemed more civilized than Mica had seen for a while. He felt out of place for a moment and glanced at Kistrin, thinking the Prince might be having much the same feelings.

Mica had trouble cutting his meat; Merriweather took care of that part with no show at all. Mica did notice when Burnis saw his bandaged hands and noted how the man's face suddenly paled. He wouldn't have expected that reaction, and suspected Burnis had made a significant change in life.

Good. Mica didn't want to suggest they leave Burnis behind, although he thought the man expected it. He saw Merriweather turn toward her brother a few times, too -- but she said nothing. Mica trusted her decision more than he trusted his own.

Mica sipped sweet cider. His toes had warmed somewhat finally. One of Storm's men found a half-ruined pair of boots for him and Storm himself helped get them on. He'd left his last pair somewhere in that lake at a time he tried not to remember too clearly. The new boots were too tight, and part of the right heel had the leather burnt off, but Mica could walk in them. He'd be glad to get back home to his own clothing, though.

Lock himself in the tower. Not come out for a year, at least.

The short time in the tavern had been pleasant. The walls were thick, the fire warm, the food filling. Mica almost suggested they stay a night, sleeping in the common room right there in the corner. Maybe even stay for a day or two.

"Time to go," Merriweather said as she stood. She put a hand on his shoulder. "Lord Raventower --"

"You really don't think you're going to sail off without me, do you?" he asked. He stood and caught up his ragged cloak. "Let us go and get this done."

Merriweather nodded agreement, and the others all took that as a sign that matters were settled. Storm threw some coins on the table, and Mica grabbed some bread as he followed Merriweather back out into the cold, breezy night.

A slight fog hung over the area, reminding him yet again of drifting ghosts. He couldn't clearly see the village or the bay and ships now, and it felt as though they stood in a place outside the worlds. He'd been to such a location once and hoped never to have to go back. He could feel the real world beneath his feet here. They were still in the realm of humans.

The mercenaries stood with horses. Storm gave last-minute orders to those who were not taking the ship. Only Prinif and Taegin would go by sea with them since the boat had a full crew and little room. Besides, if something happened to the *Grayrun*, there were still these other people to take up the cause -- and without asking about what they'd be paid, Mica realized. Well, it hardly mattered. They would settle that when he got back to Raventower and his funds.

Mica walked over to the horse that had given people so much trouble but had helped him. He gave the animal the bread he'd brought out. "Be good and good luck, friend."

The horse put his head on Mica's shoulder, nearly knocking him down. He thought he should laugh, but it was like the hug from a friend who never thought to see him again. He noticed that the mercenaries had much the same look when they bade farewell to their leader.

Damn this trouble and this war, and all the horrible things that kept happening.

Merriweather patted Mica on the arm as they walked away. Storm stayed a little longer with his men and then jogged down to join the group just before they reached the ship.

Kistrin and his guards were walking ahead of the rest and went on board without any prompting. Shipley and Bear were only a few steps behind Mica and Merriweather, and Storm came behind the entire group. People watched them pass, but not with much nervousness since it was obvious that they intended to sail away soon. Mica suspected they looked like a wild group from the way everyone stayed out of their way. Good. He didn't want to even try to explain things to anyone.

The ship looked -- and smelled -- better than it had when Grayson first took over. That hadn't been so long ago, had it? He couldn't count the days -- just couldn't bring them all into his head and lay them out in any sort of order. Merriweather hovered near Mica as he went aboard, staring nervously at the water now, and not so worried about anyone who might attack from land. Bear followed quickly and Shipley more slowly. He did not look steady, even here at the dock.

Captain Grayson stood on the deck while the others went to work and prepared to leave the dock. "I have been to Kamere and back again since we parted company. Burnis went ashore to see his family -- I don't know what he told them or anyone else, though."

"Oddly, I trust him these days," Merriweather said.

Captain Grayson nodded agreement. "When he came back and asked to sail with us, he said that if he got to a port and heard that you and Lord Raventower were in trouble, he'd probably go -- but we heard damned little at all."

"We were all too far west," Storm said. "There was no trouble in Taginta once the winter set in. None but what King Dynis has made for them himself."

Prince Kistrin stood with Storm, and no one had introduced him yet. His three guards kept close by, though. They'd been mostly silent men while traveling with the mercenaries, but Mica had the feeling that they feared more of being called out for failing to keep the Prince safe.

"There is trouble heading for Kamere," Mica explained to Grayson. "We hope to beat it because they're in airships and were held down by the storm."

"We have fuel, we have food -- and we have an engine that is working very well, thanks to you, Lord Raventower. We'll pull out within the hour."

"This is Prince Kistrin," Merriweather said, with a nod to the ragged haired, bearded man with the three equally ragged guards at his back. Grayson stared for a moment, blank-faced before he bowed his head. "He's the one we went to find. I told you so that you know he's important to get home."

"I found him by accident amid other trouble," Mica added.

"Not accident," Merriweather said. "We ended up right where we needed to be, didn't we?"

"I don't want to think the gods are paying that much attention, Merriweather."

"Considering we are about to go sailing again, I rather hope at least one or two of them are watching over us."

She had a point. Mica studied the rolling waves of the sea and wondered what might still be out there. Bear and Shipley stood by the rail and stared out toward the fog-shrouded sea as well -- Shipley shaking his head now and then as though he didn't quite know how he got here.

Mica understood that feeling. He almost went to suggest one more time that the boy remain behind -- but no. Shipley had made his own choices in all of this, just as he had, as Merriweather had her choices as well. Even Burnis, working the ropes with the others, had chosen to be on this ship. Kistrin might have been the only one in this mess who hadn't chosen this path, but here he stood with them anyway.

Mica crossed to stand by Shipley and silently stared out at the foggy night. A weak lighthouse cast a yellowish glow in a circle, but the light was mostly caught in the fog and looked more like a flickering fire on the water than a warning of rocks. How long would it take them to sail north? If the weather held, and not much else tried to stop them again, it might only be two or three days.

Going home.

That was the thought that finally warmed him and settled his nerves. They were not running from one problem to another -- though that was true as well -- but rather returning home with at least what they'd set out to do accomplished. Prince Kistrin would go back to the castle and Mica could go home to his tower. All he had to do was settle his last trouble with Janeh and Corinth. If there was anyone else involved, he might have to deal with them as well, but he had to hope that maybe others would take care of any other problems.

"Mica?" Kistrin said as he walked up beside him. The guards were there, of course; it would be a long time before they trusted Kistrin out of their sight -- much like Merriweather with him. "Are you alright?"

"I am getting things straight in my head," he admitted and still stared out at the gray sea. "And what Merriweather said made me think about how all of this fell together so well."

"So well," Kistrin said and looked at Mica's hands resting on the rail.

Mica moved the fingers. They did not move well, and he tried not to wince at the pain -- though Shipley did -- but they moved.

"This could have been much worse, you know. Corinth could have crushed my hands. He could have cut them off. He didn't do either. His rage had taken him, but I think the gods stayed with me as best they could. So now we sail to Kamere, and we still have a chance to finish this and make certain Corinth does not win."

"And I think at least a couple people are going to be surprised," Kistrin said. He shoved back his hair. "I wonder if we can find someone to loan us a blade to shave with. Maybe hack off the hair -- though a braid like yours might work better."

"Merriweather's work. I rather like it," Mica admitted. He watched as a small tugboat maneuvered in close and began to hook up with *Grayrun.* "I might keep it, in fact, since it is far easier to keep out of the way. That will be handy for creating clockwork machines."

"We'll start a whole new fashion," Kistrin said and slapped him on the shoulder. Then his face turned more serious again. "Thank you, Micalus Raventower. Thank you for coming to find me -- you and Merriweather both. Thank you for helping me survive in that damned camp. You kept me alive. You shared what little food you had so I didn't get any weaker. You taught me enough about the clockwork men that I knew the best way to stop the ones Janeh sent after us. You also kept Merriweather and the mercenaries apprised of the situation. Does my father know about the ravens and other things?"

"Of late, yes," he admitted.

"Good. I hate trying to keep secrets from my father. Mica -- you are responsible for my survival. So, thank you."

"I wish it had gone better," he admitted and braced himself as the boat started out of the dock. The tugboat was small and labored even more than the one at Kamere. It occurred to Mica that they'd lost a lot of ships in the port at home and that probably even places like Taginta would feel the pinch for a few years.

"We need to think what can be done if we get back to Kamere in time," Kistrin said. He sounded more assured again. More like the Crown Prince.

"There is always something more to be done," Mica said with a sigh. Then he looked to Kistrin and smiled. "But I do have an idea. We'll have a few days to work it out."

"I'm going to get Shipley and Bear down to the room," Merriweather said as she caught the somewhat wobbly dog by the neck fur. "You'll do better there for a while until you're used to the feel of the sea."

"It's not right, is it?" Shipley asked, one hand still tight to the railing. "Odd, like trying to move with the ground movin' 'neath you."

Mica noted that he looked more interested than anything. Shipley would do fine. "You should go with them, Prince Kistrin, just to see where the room is," Mica suggested.

"And leave you here alone?" Kistrin said. "Do you know what Merriweather threatened us with if that happened?"

"She didn't -- you are --"

"Not going to cross Merriweather," Prince Kistrin said.

Storm had arrived and leaned against the railing as he laughed. "Amazing how all of us live in fear of annoying that woman. I even tried to pry her name out of her brother. It didn't work."

"Burnis is wiser than he used to be," Raventower decided.

"He told you her name?"

"No, she did. However, Burnis was rather loose with it at times. Storm is here, Kistrin. Go ahead on down."

Kistrin looked as though he might argue, which showed more of the Prince returning to his old role. However, Kistrin shook his head as though to banish some thought, and then he and his men followed where Merriweather and the dog were just disappearing.

"Why are you along?" Mica asked.

"To help see this done right," Storm said. "They killed some of my men, you know. A few in battles along the way, two died while working in the mines. These are not people I want to see win, Lord Raventower. Not in the land where I live, and not in your land."

"I suspected you weren't from Argine, but I wasn't sure. You live there, though."

"I came over the ocean a long time ago. From Sactwi, which is a little place rarely visited. You know how I got here? I was fishing, and a storm blew up and tossed me out to sea, so far that I couldn't find my way back. I got picked up by a foreign ship several days later. Eventually, I came here." He stopped and shrugged. "I found a place for myself. I've done well. And I don't have to gut fish anymore."

Mica laughed. Merriweather was just coming back up on deck and looked pleased. Mica couldn't decide if it was because they were going home or if it was because he and Storm were getting along so well.

"I told the men we left on land to ride as fast as they dared to Kamere. They might have trouble at the border, but two of them are to go on ahead and try to get word to the army. I can't say it will do any good, but they'll try."

"I could have sent a note or something --"

"No," Storm said. "As it is, they're just a few men heading away from the trouble in Argine. We don't know what stands between them and the capital, and the less they have to link them with what happened at the mines, the better."

"True. Ah, there you are." The raven sailed in and landed on the railing. "Anything unusual we should know about?"

"Nothing," the raven muttered with a sound of gears and clicks.

"Take a high spot. Keep watch."

"Yes!"

The raven took off again, the sound of metal feathers and a slight caw. It flew up to the tallest mast and settled there. Some of the crew sounded surprised and worried --

"Burnis! Can you let them know the raven is mine?"

"On it!" Burnis shouted from half across the deck and started away.

"They are going to start the engine soon," Mica said. "I'd like to be there."

"No surprise in that one," Merriweather said. "He rebuilt the engine on the way north before we went off with Admiral Rose."

Storm only nodded as though he had expected no less.

They went down. The engine room was cleaner. The former assistant engineer looked nervous about having Mica there, but it was plain he'd done better than the man who had run the engines before this. The engine came on with a purr, though Mica thought he could still hear a little clink out of sync with everything else. He'd have to talk Grayson into letting him work on it -- later.

He moved his fingers. No, not yet.

From there they went to the Captain's deck where Grayson had been doing the work of the pilot, preparing to get them several miles out of the bay and into the Northward Current.

"If the weather looks bad, turn back, Captain," Mica said, wondering if the fog looked worse and if the wind had picked up already.

Grayson laughed. "How much worse? Worse than what we faced bringing you here? You need to get back to Kamere, don't you? Something more is going on."

"Yes."

"Then we'll get you there as fast as we can," Grayson replied. He clearly did not intend to put up with an argument, and now that they were away from the dock, Mica wasn't sure there was anything he could do anyway.

"None of us want more bad things to happen, Lord Raventower," Storm reminded him. "We want this business settled and settled well. This Corinth is mayor of the city?"

"Corinth?" Grayson said with a snarl. "On our last time in port there, he tried to claim my ship. We must have put up too much of a fight -- verbal only -- because Corinth backed off and we sailed away. I talked to a few others since I got here, and they say he did manage to get his hand on at least two ships. They sailed off with new crew, and no one knows where they went. It wasn't close, though. They hadn't come back or been seen in other ports in at least ten days, and maybe longer -- no one had seen them come back last time I was in dock."

"Atria would be my guess," Merriweather said, a snarl in her own voice.

"Or the Atrian ships still out there in the open sea," Captain Grayson replied with a wave of his hand toward the vast ocean. "We've been warned in every port to keep an eye open for them."

Mica nodded. "I still think there is more to this than crazy Janeh and insane Corinth," he said. "Neither of them are stable enough to pull this off. Or, really, rich enough."

"Corinth was never well-liked," Merriweather reminded him. "He was too good at tax collecting, and there wasn't much else he did as Mayor of Kamere for the city, at least not in the last decade. He also only served at the discretion of the King, and I think King Abertus had gotten tired of him. Once the war was over, he was probably going to be sent packing to his estate with a pension and no power at all."

"So, the Atrians probably knew to approach him." Mica carefully leaned against the wall, still not strong enough to stay standing for too long. Merriweather noticed, of course, but she said nothing yet. "There are bound to be some spies in the castle."

"We need to talk to someone who knows Corinth," Merriweather suggested. "That might give us some clues about who else to watch."

"Kistrin?" Mica asked.

"Ha. Kistrin did his best to stay clear of Corinth whenever the man came to the castle. No, there is someone better. I'll go get Burnis."

Merriweather went out and gathered up her brother. He came to the crowded area with a bit of a frown, and he didn't wait to be prompted.

"Yes, I know Corinth pretty well," he said. "I assume he's involved in this?"

"Very much so," Mica said and did not look at his hands.

But Burnis did, and for a moment Mica thought he might be ill. Then he stopped and shook his head. "Corinth -- the great Mayor Corinth -- was convinced his career had been sabotaged somewhere along the line. He blamed the Raventowers since your family had more power in the city than he did. You could have turned anyone against him."

"None of us did, though," Mica replied.

"I know," Burnis said. He sounded embarrassed. "But you were an easy target, Mica. Then ... then my sister decided to marry you, and I knew I'd been wrong because Je-Merriweather is smart. It shocked me. I didn't want to believe that Corinth could have lied to me or that I was that gullible and stupid. I still wanted vindication when I came aboard the *Grayrun*, you know. Yes, I suspected Corinth sent me, but I didn't look too closely, not back then."

"But you've changed your mind," Mica said.

"Corinth convinced me that her being your guard was a ruse by the King to get into the Raventower estate, but once father announced you were getting married, I knew Corinth was wrong -- though I still couldn't fully admit it, even to myself. I also knew that Corinth would be more than angry. He'd been hinting to me that he wanted to marry my only sister and that he'd make sure of it before the year was out."

Merriweather's face reddened. "He intended to marry *me*?"

"That was what he said."

"You never mentioned that to me."

"I didn't want to die for his vanity," Burnis replied and won a grin from both Mica and Storm who knew Merriweather so well. "I did mention it to mother, just to see if maybe I was over-reacting. She warned me that if I told you, she would not be responsible for what happened, and none of the rest of the family would be stupid enough to step in to help him."

Storm nodded, apparently finding this entirely reasonable.

"Corinth sent you to have that sword fight with me," Mica said, recalling that night after the wonderful evening that he spent dancing with Merriweather at the castle.

"Yes." He looked at his feet and shook his head, very much like an adult might act when he thought back on some truly stupid thing he'd done as a child. "He got me more than a little drunk and riled up. I was too easy to manipulate."

"We need to know more about what he did, how he might have contacted Atrians, for instance," Merriweather said. She didn't berate Burnis, and Mica could see no reason to make matters worse, either.

"Probably the time he spent at his estate. I only went once as his guest, but there was a lot of activity for such a small place. We went hunting a couple of times. He's a lousy shot, by the way. I had to purposely miss things not to annoy him by doing too well. This was at least a year before the war, though. I had no reason to think anything was wrong."

Merriweather nodded.

"Was Corinth popular on his estate?" Mica asked.

"Ha. Corinth wasn't popular on his estate or at his townhouse. In fact, he told me a few months ago that he'd replaced everyone in his service...." Burnis stopped and tilted his head. "He said they were specially trained just for him. He was always claiming things like that, though. Now I wonder if it is true in a way that had nothing to do with what servants' normal duties."

"So, we know we need to gather up the people working for him," Mica said. Then he shook his head. "Not working for *him*. Using Corinth to maneuver their way into a position in the city."

"Only I think Corinth is out of their control," Merriweather said. "Think about it. Would you let that man and this Janeh run something as important as this? I wonder if the people in charge -- the Atrians? -- even know what's going on."

"What about the Honorgates?" Burnis asked. "They were the only ones I ever saw at Corinth's townhouse. Lady Honorgate even came alone a couple of times. She was never happy to see me there, and for a while, I even thought the two of them might be having an affair -- but I knew Lady Honorgate wasn't that stupid."

"She was also likely the one who was always in charge of the Honorgate actions," Mica added. The ship hit a high swell, and he looked at Grayson, who had remained silent. "Remember what I said about the weather. And that's not just for us. We have Prince Kistrin on board now. I would hate to see him drown after everything else that he's survived."

"Mica, do you think the gods are still with you?" Merriweather asked.

"Maybe one," he admitted.

"Then we need to press on as best we can. Captain Grayson knows it. If something happens now, it's because trouble would have struck us no matter where we had gone. Let's get home as fast as we can. Maybe we can outrun the trouble."

Mica thought that unlikely, but no one argued.

CHAPTER TWENTY-FIVE

For almost half a day, Mica believed they were going to sail back to Kamere without any trouble. They made it almost to noon of that first full day with calm weather, bright sunlight -- even a touch of warmth in the air. Mica sat on the deck and let the breeze blow over him, pushing the ice of the western mountains back out of his blood. Oh, this wasn't a summer warmth, but it was not the winter cold of the western mountains either. They'd be heading farther north, though. Beyond the lower mountains of the Tilday Range, they would once again reach the winter weather that had already hit Kamere before they left the area.

Mica knew he had to be ready for it. He had to remember that winter itself was not evil. Mica had always welcomed the colder season in the past as that restful time of music and rest. That was what he wanted again. Just sail home, settle the trouble there, and have quiet for a while. A year at least.

Unfortunately, that was not going to happen.

"Mica," Merriweather said softly from where she stood not far away.

"I know. I can feel it." He opened his eyes and looked across the deck to where a line of dark gray had covered quickly part of the sky. Magic tingled in the air. "Better warn the others. Go. I'm safe here."

"You are most certainly *not* safe here," she said and glared out at the ocean. "Prinif! Watch his Lordship for a moment and make certain nothing drags him off into the ocean!"

Prinif, a stocky mercenary, darted over and stood next to him, drawing his dagger.

"I really don't think that's necessary," Mica said with a shake of his head.

"If you were in my place and had to answer to Merriweather if anything went wrong --"

"Excellent point. I'll just sit here and soak up a little more of the sun."

"Thank you."

A few minutes later Shipley and Bear arrived. They'd set up a safe area for Bear -- one that Shipley had no trouble washing down. They'd also managed a life line for the dog, and Mica noted how Shipley held tight to it and the dog. As interested as their young friend seemed to be in the ship and life on the ocean, it looked unlikely that he would do much sailing in the future.

Which was good. Bear certainly was not a ship dog.

Merriweather and Kistrin came back to the deck as well, the prince's guards -- who slept in the hall outside the room -- close behind. Prinif gladly gave the guard duty post back to Merriweather, and she seemed more than a little amused. She also caught Mica by the forearm and pulled him to his feet.

The storm looked worse from there.

"I suppose it was too much to hope for one day of calm," Mica said and sounded a bit more annoyed than he had intended. He sighed and gave Merriweather a worn smile. "I suppose we've faced worse."

"Never assume so," Merriweather replied as they watched the clouds billow upward, already nearly a hand's breadth from the sun, which sat high and bright in the sky.

They'd be in the shadows of those clouds all too soon. Kistrin watched with a shake of his head. The wind had started to press in on them already, the gusts lifting sea water spray into the air. Mica wasn't certain any of them had gotten dry yet.

"Shipley -- you better get Bear down below," Mica warned. "This looks bad! Don't worry -- the waves are going to clean everything on the deck."

"Come on Bear," he said and pulled the dog toward the doorway. "This is no place for city rats like us to be."

The dog took one look back at the sea and seemed to agree. Shipley had trouble holding on to him as he hurried toward safety.

Except Shipley would know it wasn't so safe because ships went down in storms.

Captain Grayson came over to talk to them as well. He looked at the storm with a shake of his head. "It's not as though we didn't expect it. No sign of the other problem?" He looked up at the mast where the raven still sat, glinting a bit too much in the bright light.

"Nothing so far," Mica said. "The storm may be connected with Payson, though. I think there might be magic in it, but that could also just be natural. However, the storm was going strong when he attacked the last time."

"I really don't know how you have stayed sane, Lord Raventower," Kistrin said with a bit of a laugh.

"My brother and Merriweather may have something to tell you about the state of my mind."

"I'd tell you now, but I really don't think we have the time to go into all those problems," Merriweather added.

And they laughed. That helped again. Mica realized the true grandness of this group standing on the deck facing down a storm all of them knew could not be normal, not the way it arrived and moved. Yet, even as the sun went behind the cloud, they laughed.

Not all of them should have survived, Mica supposed. Storm, who had come to join them as well, had lost some of his people and Mica felt as though that had somehow been his fault, even while he knew the illogic of that belief. Mica had also not started the war, nor had he sent the Prince to Argine to where he was captured and harried off to that damned village. He had not --

"Mica?" Merriweather said and touched his arm.

"I want all this madness done," Mica said. Something in his voice drew the attention of the others. "I want this done and to go about rebuilding Kamere and the rest of the country -- the world, if we have to. There is no reason why Payson, the Atrians, Corinth, and Janeh, or the rest of these fools should continue the battle. I'm ready for it to be over. Unfortunately, I expect unusual trouble with the storm."

"We all do," Storm said.

"The rest of the crew have their spears ready," Captain Grayson added. "We've got lookouts along with your friend up there. That creature is not going to get anyone this time."

"No, he will not," Merriweather agreed.

"If he's still around," Kistrin said.

"He is," Mica replied. "The storm is the first sign."

Mica wasn't sure how he knew -- and that made him doubt his own pronouncement. Well, it hardly mattered. They'd keep an eye open for the trouble, and he didn't need to warn them.

Storm and his men went down in the engine room -- they'd been mostly camped out there when they were not on deck. Kistrin, with his three shadows, went to the cabin where

Shipley and Bear stayed. The Prince would stay in the small room, which must be crowded even with only the boy and the dog. His guards stayed in the hall outside.

Mica and Merriweather went with the Captain to the upper deck.

Lightning sparked through the clouds. Mica realized that he should have called the raven down -- but then he saw he didn't need to. The bird settled on the railing ahead of them, holding on with metal-strength.

"We're heavy in the water -- we loaded wood, mostly from downed trees, to take back north for fuel in the city," Captain Grayson said. "We're as stable as I think we'll ever be." The ship made a little jump. "We're also in the current, so even if we cut the engines for some reason, we're going to head northward. However, if things get rough, I plan to take us toward land and anchor again."

"And that's when we can really expect trouble," Mica said. "We understand."

"I plan to be ready for him this time," Merriweather added.

Captain Grayson gave a distracted nod as the wind rushed down on them. The sky disappeared in a wall of gray, and the rain came. Mica looked out at it with a sigh of regret.

"One day in the sunlight," he said. "I don't think that would have been too much."

"But we all knew this was coming," Merriweather replied. She watched the world outside their little glassed-in area and saw the waves wash over the deck and off the other side. "I hope we can sail through this one, but --"

"But if it gets too bad, find a place to drop anchor, and we'll see what happens," Mica finished. "Also, keep in mind that the last time a storm like this came up, we had help in Kamere pushing it back. I would not be entirely surprised if

Rose showed up again, too -- but I would rather she stayed at Kamere because they might need her more than we do."

Merriweather nodded agreement. "I wonder if this storm will blow far enough inland to be a problem for Corinth and Janeh. This storm might be more luck for us than our enemies intended. If they really don't realize what those two are up to, then this might keep Janeh and Corinth down for a few days as well. How long do you think it will take such a storm to reach the western mountains?"

"It could be a day, maybe less depending on how fast the winds blow," Grayson said. "They might not have any of the usual warnings that this one is coming, too."

"They might be in the air already." Merriweather gave them a wicked smile. "Maybe we won't have to worry too much after all."

Mica liked that idea, though they all knew they couldn't count on it.

"I almost forgot," Merriweather said and reached into her pouch. "Burnis gave these to me. He thought they might help you."

Leather gloves. Good ones, too -- Mica suspected Burnis had grabbed them from home when the *Grayrun* had last been in Kamere. Merriweather arranged the bandages a little better and then helped Mica slip the gloves on. The sudden feeling of protection did help.

"Thank Burnis for me."

"I already did," she said. Then she shook her head. "I'm starting to think maybe I was as much to blame for some of my brothers' attitudes as they were. I'll have to think about it."

"Not too much. I would hate for you to change."

"That's not likely to happen." She caught hold of him when the boat pitched again and came down with a thump. "I don't know why you were so eager to take us on, Captain Grayson."

He didn't look at them, concentrating now on the work at hand. "Maybe I just wanted to be part of the good side in this battle."

"How can you be sure we are the good side?" Mica asked. He truly did wonder.

"Because you have done your best to save people, while they --" He waved an arm toward the storm "-- don't care who they destroy. Not to mention that creature that took our captain and engineer. Good people do not work that way, you know."

"I suppose not," Mica said. "I wonder how far a good person can go before it tips the balance, though."

"You'll never know," Merriweather said. He looked at her, startled. "It's not in you to do things that will hurt others, no matter what the cause. You'll find another answer."

Mica smiled. "It's good to be back with you Merriweather. You ground me in the real world."

"We are never again going to do anything as stupid as we did in Argine," she promised so fervently that the gods themselves must have believed her. The ship rose and fell again. "No, you didn't do anything wrong, but I was going crazy. Ask Storm."

"I believe you. Still, even for all the egotistical stupidity on my part, it worked."

"Yes," she agreed. "And it would have been far worse if we hadn't been there, either of us. Just the same, we are not going to do anything like that again."

Mica didn't argue. "I plan to go home and lock myself in my tower when this is done. I plan to make clockwork butterflies and drink tea. I might even let Ada spoil me with her baked goods. I do hope that you'll join me there, Merriweather."

"It sounds wonderful."

Damn this storm, he thought, looking out at the waves, the lighting, and the torrential rain. It was just something else that held him back from that time with Merriweather.

Nothing they could do but ride it out. The storm was trying to push the boat toward shore, but the ship held the course on the current, moving northward, though they went slowly. Progress, though.

"Can the sails help?" he asked.

Grayson looked his way with a shake of his head. "I told you the last time we left dock that the reason I was onboard was because the ship had a high turnover in crew. None of the current people have ever taken up the sails."

Mica nodded.

One day, the next. The storm remained strong, but on the morning of the third day, he could tell that it had grown worse. Mica had been sleeping in hammocks like most of the crew. He even liked it, except for getting in and out. That was made worse when the ship was hit by worse storms. That's what he awoke to, and Merriweather arrived and helped him. She said nothing, just shook her head.

They had to use Bear's life line to get to the Captain's deck. He must have been there for some time because Grayson had stopped dripping all over everything.

"Worse weather," Grayson said with a grimace. "Much worse weather."

"Can we sit it out?" Mica asked. He looked toward the west, but all they could see were walls of rain and billowing waves.

"Move off the current and try not to sink on the rocks?" Grayson asked. He looked at Mica. "I think that's the only hope we have since these waves will take us down if we keep the way we're going."

"Let's do it," Merriweather said.

"It's probably a trap," Grayson reminded her, and even before Mica could say anything. "So be ready for him."

"Let's go talk to Kistrin and tell him what's going on," Mica decided. "And remind everyone that Payton will probably be at the ship and on us before we have a chance to spot him. People should stay away from the rails."

"Spread the word," Grayson said. He began to check his charts, and Mica wondered if the Captain had any real idea where they might be.

Merriweather kept hold of Mica as they went out on the deck, found a couple of the crew, and started spreading the word. The men had all seen Payson the last time and were more than willing to stay back out of the creature's reach. They all carried spears, too, most of them attached to their sides like swords in sheaths. Mica and his friends did not have any, but he trusted the others to come to their aid.

All the group was in the hall when they got there -- Kistrin, his guards, Bear, and Shipley. Mica and Merriweather settled on the floor with the rest of them, though it was a bit bumpy. Still, they'd have been sitting on top of each other in the little room.

"We can expect trouble soon," Mica explained and seemed to take Merriweather by surprise. He realized he hadn't taken the lead very often of late. "I'm going to be up on the deck today -- I am, Merriweather. You know I need to be there -- because if he shows up, we want him to come to me, not grab someone else in a moment when they are trying to keep the ship afloat."

"Yes. True." She frowned again, but he thought that was more deciding best how best to watch over him. "I want this done as much as you do."

"The storm --" Kistrin said and winced when the craft leapt up and down, and they all bounced. "What about the storm?"

"I hope that it is linked to Payton and if we handle him, it will die down."

"And if it doesn't, at least we won't have to worry about Payton as well," Merriweather added.

Mica nodded agreement. The ship turned slightly, the waves pushing against the stern more rather than on the side. They moved far too smoothly off the current and toward the shore. Mica wondered how close they were to home -- the current wove in and out along the shore, sometimes within as few as five miles, but more often out at least fifteen to twenty miles from shore. If the storm cleared, could he see a land that he recognized? Would Raventower itself be a line against the sky in the distance?

The idea that they were close to home gave him a little more strength. He followed Merriweather up to the doorway and out into the hellish weather.

Storm and his men had gathered near the door, all of them with weapons, including spears. Mica thought about asking for one and then realized he would not be able to hold it. Odd -- Mica realized that he hadn't been continuously thinking about his hands, even though they still bothered him. He had moved beyond the trauma and had begun to heal in the full sense of the word. Merriweather would be pleased.

He hated being out in the storm, though. And he suspected Payton -- and whatever worked with him -- had chosen this spot because there would be dangers, like rocky outcrops. They had to hope to avoid them by chance alone, he supposed.

Oh, and with the help of the gods.

"We're back in Sedina's waters," he said suddenly, shouting over the sound of the storm. "I hope that means we have some help."

"Seldon?" she shouted.

"At least him."

The *Grayrun* went past one rock outcrop, so close that he could have reached over the rail and caught hold of the stone.

"Yes," Merriweather said with a frantic nod. "At least him!"

Mica, on the other hand, thought of another whom he had not considered. The fishermen he knew at Kamere served the Goddess they called The Fate of the Sea. He couldn't believe she was happy with this intrusion into her waters. Mica hoped that she might at least sway things a bit to their side --

Like the way the ship turned slightly just then and avoided another rock?

"Thank you, Goddess of the Sea," he said aloud.

Merriweather added her own sudden nod of agreement. The engine cut out. Mica's heart pounded harder for a moment before he realized they were dropping anchor since the others had seen the rocks and knew the seabed must be shallower here.

Mica had gotten too used to the roar of the engine masking some of the sounds of the storm. Now the wind howled like a thousand things come alive, and the ship bounced and turned more often. He could hear the shouts of the others, though, and none of them indicated the sign of fear he had come to expect at a sighting of Payton.

They waited. The day drew on. He took refuge in the Captain's deck a couple times to have tea and warm up next to the steam heater that came up from the engine. He thought he could improve the system....

Back out into the weather, playing cat and mouse games with something he had not yet seen. By late afternoon, Mica thought they must have been wrong, though they still would have taken refuge out of the storm anyway. He couldn't decide if the weather had gotten worse or if having the engine off and sitting at the mercy of the winds made it seem so.

Where was Payton?

The sun descended in an early sunset of brilliant reds and black, marking the bands of the storm more clearly than before. Mica didn't see any sign that the weather might be lessening, though. He didn't look forward to sitting out --

A shape rose in the water a splash hardly heard in the din of the storm. Mica stepped backward, his hand signaling Merriweather. No reason to give warning yet if it was Payton. He couldn't be entirely sure, except there was a feel to the air now that he recognized as a hint of magic.

"Closer to the rail," Merriweather said, surprising him. "But not out of my reach."

Mica nodded agreement. Burnis and Storm headed their way, but Merriweather signaled them to hold back. They both understood and drew their own weapons.

Another splash, and this time Mica saw tentacles. In the next splash, Mica saw hands and gave Merriweather a definite nod. She looked pleased. He wondered why. They didn't have any clear plan on how to kill the creature. He supposed it was just that Merriweather hadn't had a real enemy to face much of late. Time to let her have at it.

He had not expected her to let go of his arm, though. He looked back at her with a start --

And Payton surged up over the railing and grabbed him.

"Damn!" Merriweather shouted.

Mica grabbed the rail and wrapped his aching fingers around it, holding on with one hand while he tried to pry a tentacle off that was starting to wind up to his neck. The fingers at the end of the hand caught hold of his shirt, and another tentacle grabbed his free hand.

Storm and Burnis both came in close enough to stab with their spears, rather than throw. Mica appreciated it since he was not steady, and a spear through his shoulder would probably not be good --

Payton's head came close to his, and for a moment he caught a glimpse of the inhuman face and the shark teeth. Mica reacted instinctively; he jabbed an elbow into the nose, winning a howl, a splatter of blood.

The raven swept down with a cry of attack that sounded almost like a real raven. Metallic claws raked over the head and might have yanked out some of the stringy hair. Payton howled as much in anger as pain -- or fear -- and one of the tentacles swung at the raven which came back around for another attack.

"Out of the way, raven!" Merriweather shouted. "Down, Mica!"

Mica reacted instinctively, though he wasn't certain how to get down with Payton holding so tight to his neck. He just leaned toward the deck and tried to drop --

Merriweather fired.

The tentacles spasmed and released him. Mica fell and started to slide toward the sea before Burnis and Storm caught hold of him. He noticed blood everywhere, but the ocean had suddenly become even more turbulent, and waves washed over him -- and washed him and the deck clean before he could even turn to see the creature sinking into the sea.

"That went better than I had hoped," Merriweather said. She shoved her flintlock back into the holster and pulled some oilcloth over the top. "I wasn't sure the gun would fire."

"Nicely done," Mica said and rubbed at his neck. He watched the sea for a moment. Was everything calming again? Even the storm?

"I had to reload the weapon every few hours and hope it didn't get too wet to fire," Merriweather admitted. She also took tight hold of Mica this time, and he could tell she trembled in the aftermath of what had happened.

"You could have told me the plan," he said as they started back.

"Since I didn't know if it would work, I didn't want to give you any false hope. I certainly didn't want you to depend on it. Good work, raven."

The bird made a decisively bird-like sound and flew off again. Merriweather nodded her thanks to both Storm and Burnis. They both looked pleased. Mica could hear sounds from elsewhere on the ship.

"I suppose we don't have to tell them to still be careful," Mica said. He barely had to shout now, the storm settling so quickly.

"From what they've seen, I doubt they'll forget to be careful for the rest of their lives."

"Good point."

Mica looked back over his shoulder. The sea began to settle to small ripples, the rain disappearing, and the wind only a gentle breeze.

He didn't feel any safer.

CHAPTER TWENTY-SIX

They waited out the night while still at anchor. The crew had time to check the ship and repair a few small problems. If there had been a sign of trouble, they would have moved on at top speed, but even Mica agreed that a few hours of calm would not be such a bad idea.

They were, he realized, only hours away from Kamere. He thought about sending the raven on to scout things out -- but that extra set of eyes on the sea seemed far more critical right now. Mica wanted to reach the city and rush to his tower, but they still had problems, and he dared not be careless.

Where were Janeh and Corinth now? With the weather clearing, he suspected that the enemy would arrive soon.

And then would they be done with this entire fiasco?

Mica slept for a couple hours down in the hall with Kistrin's guards. The crew slept in shifts in the hammocks. At sunrise, everyone gathered on the deck to decide what they would do when they got to Kamere. Mica worried because he feared the others thought he had a plan.

Everything would be guesswork, though. For all any of them knew, Kamere had already been attacked. Or, in a better moment of imagination, the storms had knocked down the airships, and the feared attack would never come.

"We have a few things going for us," Prince Kistrin said as they stood on the bow deck, the cool breeze blowing over the lightly fogged sea. "Janeh and Corinth won't believe that Mica survived that leap from the airship --"

"Leap?" Burnis said, his head swiveling to look at Mica, the amount of shock he felt showed by the fact that he interrupted the Prince.

"Into a lake. The ship was low," Mica explained.

Merriweather jabbed at him. "Tell me you even knew there was a lake below you."

He said nothing. Merriweather sighed. The others stared at him.

"Also," Prince Kistrin said, drawing their attention back. "They never realized who I was, and besides, they thought everyone died in the mine."

"If we can slip quietly into the city, then we can prepare for the trouble without alerting the people Corinth obviously has in Kamere," Mica said. Then he shook his head. "Very carefully. It is possible that Corinth went back to the city to prepare for the attack from the inside. He has new servants, remember. They're all going to be people he can trust."

"Or thinks he can," Merriweather said with a shake of his head. "If I were working with Corinth and Janeh, I would want people watching over *them*. Those servants may be less his to command than Corinth thinks."

"Either way, they will be on the same side," Mica said, and she nodded agreement.

"So, we slip into port like usual." Captain Grayson glanced out at the sea often, watching for more trouble. "That's the easy part. How do you get off the ship?"

"Rowboat," Merriweather said. "If we come in at dusk, we can row in with the fishing fleet."

"I like that idea," Mica said. The fishing village sat just below his tower. "Once we get there --"

"We head straight up to the tower if we can. If not, head across town to the castle and hope to get in there. I doubt we'd be able to do that quietly, though."

"Bear and I should come in with the ship and head into town, secret like. I think we can slip off the ship without much notice, right?"

"We can do it," Burnis said and sounded assured. "At least if the docks are still stacked with crates."

Captain Grayson nodded agreement and didn't mention that Burnis had initially slipped on the *Grayrun* that way. "When the harbor authority comes out with the tugboat, I can ask for a docking spot closer to the shore, too -- we just came through the storm, after all. We might have damage."

"Good plan. Shipley --" Mica started.

"I'll go do what I done best in the past, your lordship. I can find out what's going on and then come to the tower. If Corinth is around and he has people, you will want to know where and how many, right?"

"Yes," Mica agreed, despite himself.

He also saw the way Prince Kistrin eyed the boy. Kistrin was not going to steal Shipley away from Mica, but Shipley might have yet another patron who could use his help sometimes -- one who would be King. Mica approved. He wanted to make certain Shipley had protection in the future.

The day grew later, and they drifted slowly northward. Others prepared the rowboat, even lowering it a few feet down the side of the ship so that no one would notice when Mica and Merriweather took it out. The only problem would be if there were others in the bay along with the fishermen. If so, they'd just have to abandon the idea and try to sneak into the city with Shipley.

They sailed along the current for a few hours, and then angled off into Kamere's wide bay. The people who were going by rowboat sat on the deck, keeping low and out of notice as they reached the end of the journey.

"There it is," Merriweather said and smiled.

Mica craned his neck a little and looked toward the shore until he saw Raventower. The building still stood tall, and he thought the others must have done some repairs to the outer walls that had been damaged during the war.

He saw no smoke in the air over the city. "No battle yet," Mica said with a bright grin.

"Not yet," Merriweather agreed. She looked more anxious than happy, but they were still doing well, and Mica knew it. They had a chance to stop the worst of what was to come. All they had to do was be careful getting to the land and not let the word of his arrival spread. He wanted no one to have a warning and change their plans.

Some of the small boats of the fishing fleet had started heading toward their own little bay that sat at the foot of the Raventower promontory. The larger *Grayrun* moved in closer to them, though not obviously changing course.

The group climbed carefully down into the little rowboat -- Merriweather, Mica, Kistrin and Ovete who was one of Kistrin's guards. The raven stayed in a pouch Mica carried -- a quick way to send for help if they needed it. The others would not let Mica row when they got dropped to the water. He wanted to because he felt the drive to get home now. Mica wanted to return to the tower and immerse himself in everything he understood. They headed straight toward the fishing fleet and pulled in among the smaller boats that were not much larger than their rowboat. Worried faces turned their way --

"Endrid," Mica said softly as they pulled up to the boat he had pointed out. "We need --"

"By the gods," the man almost shouted. "Is that you --"

"Shush, quiet. We need to get quietly back into the city. If you could help --"

But the man already understood and helped without knowing any more of the situation. He'd given quick signals to the others. They caught the small rowboat with a hook, while other craft drifted in around them, all looking natural. Mica and his companions went into Endrid's boat, and some of his men and a few fish went into the other. Then they were moving steadily toward the shore.

"We been worried, me lord," Endrid said, setting close to them. Merriweather helped the others row, making the change in crew less apparent. Storm and his men had stayed with *Grayrun*, and he saw that ship still pulling away. "We been worried what might ha' happened to you. You and Merriweather, and others what were not around like they should be. I expected the boy --"

"He's with the ship, along with a few others," Mica said. "There is trouble heading for Kamere, Endrid --"

"Expected so, when I saw you trying to sneak in. You look right rough, me lord. Had a hard time, I can see."

"I'll be fine now that I'm home," he answered and even cast a quick smile up at Raventower. "We need to get in there --"

"No problem, that. We take fish to the tower most nights, your lordship. You just help us haul a few baskets up that way and in the gate we go."

"Better than I had hoped," Merriweather said and grinned. They were almost home.

Mica felt odd when he finally stepped from the boat and onto land. It wasn't far from the shed where he kept the pod in which he and Merriweather had sailed -- underwater -- from the far north to the city and helped saved it from a different attack. This time he scanned the air, expecting the attack at any moment. Janeh and Corinth wouldn't be long in arriving unless the people of Kamere got lucky and the attack didn't happen at all.

Mica looked across at the more massive dock and could just see *Grayrun* coming into dock. They'd made good time. Storm and his people, along with the other two of the Prince's guards, would go ashore like the regular crew. Shipley and Bear would be moving on their own soon.

Those people were out of his hands. Mica turned his full attention back to getting up to Raventower. It had never seemed such a long walk before. He'd been too long at sea again, he told himself, and ignored that he was still weak from Janeh's care. Being in the shadow of Raventower made him feel stronger, though.

They climbed to the top of the first hill where the road curved one way up to Raventower and turned the other way to the level ground on the right, the road going past Shadow Walk.

Mica stopped and looked around, trying to cover how winded he was from the walk.

"Better than when we left," he admitted. "They've cleared some rubble. And maybe rebuilt a little bit?"

"Looks like it," Prince Kistrin agreed. Mica realized that they had not pointed out who the Prince was -- but why complicate this any worse? "How do we reach the castle?"

"I'll send a raven as soon as we're safely inside the tower," Mica said. They had started to move on again. "I want to make sure we have things secure before we call Gregorian out. And he will come out."

Kistrin nodded agreement. He looked worn as well, but he helped hoist the nets of fish and headed up the curve of the hill that took them to the gate to Raventower. Someday soon these common men from the village would realize the Crown Prince had helped them with the fish. Mica thought it was going to make them like Kistrin better for it.

Mica's heart began to beat harder as they neared the gate. One of the soldiers from inside helped push it open; the clockwork mechanism must still have problems. The group went straight toward the steps to the towering building as the gate closed behind them. The courtyard still held a couple dozen soldiers -- not as many as when Mica had left, but still enough to fill the area with strange voices. They almost distracted him, but Merriweather nudged him toward the ice bank where the others were dumping their fish.

"Looks like you had a good haul today," Roe said as he came across the courtyard.

"An excellent haul," Endrid said with a laugh and a glance at Mica.

Roe didn't notice. "How many this time? Or are you going to make me count them? You know the rules. We pay you for the fish."

"That you then cook and give away to anyone who shows up," Endrid said. "Not today, friend. Today we brought more --"

Roe, though, had looked at Mica. He had frozen for a couple heartbeats and then all but leapt forward and grabbed Mica by both shoulders.

"You're back. You look like hell. Merriweather -- good. You're back. Let's get inside. Endrid?"

The grinning fisherman looked at Roe and then caught a pouch of coins the man tossed him.

"This is more --"

"Thank you," Roe said. His voice sounded odd, but he grinned with delight. "Inside. We need to get inside."

Mica nodded agreement. They went up the steps, and Roe opened the door.

Inside. *Home.*

Mica stopped and leaned against the wall as his legs nearly gave way. The others came in. Roe hadn't recognized the

Prince. Mica pulled off his ragged cloak and dropped it on the floor.

"I haven't been here in years," Kistrin said.

Roe stared at him and then gave a quick bow of his head. "Prince Kistrin. You look like hell, too. And you don't look much better, Merriweather."

"We have been to hell --" Merriweather began.

But Ada, Fern, and Gram came out of the kitchen having heard, he suspected, Merriweather's name. They were swarmed and dragged into the kitchen. Roe went for Nyle. In a couple minutes, the larger man had come into the kitchen and grabbed a chair to sit down, looking around in shock.

"I didn't tell him out there," Roe said as he sat as well. "I didn't want word getting out."

"What happened, me lord?" Nyle said and sounded very upset. "And your hands -- there's something wrong, isn't there?"

"Getting better," Mica assured him. It was overwhelming, having all this attention even from the people he knew and loved best. "We found Kistrin at least."

That had been a purposeful attempt to shift the attention from himself, at least for a moment. It worked. Ada became flustered. Fern looked apt to run. Gram sat, grim-faced --

"Shipley and Bear are down in the city looking around," Mica said suddenly. Gram sank back into her seat with relief. "I'm sorry I didn't say so sooner, Gram. This has been overwhelming."

"That it has," she agreed. "Well, glad to know the boy made it back. Glad you all did. What happen ta' your hands?"

"Not something to talk about now," he said and lifted his hand when the others began to protest. He had taken to wearing the gloves most of the time. They helped. "Really, now is not the time. We're home, but unfortunately, trouble has followed us."

"Not followed," Merriweather corrected. "That trouble was already set to go, and we are the hope to head it off. I am going out to the courtyard to talk to the soldiers and see if they have heard anything that we might find interesting and useful."

"Especially about Mayor Corinth," Mica said aloud. He looked at his friends. "Under no circumstances are you to trust that man or a tall, hawk-faced brown-haired woman with an odd accent."

"In fact, I don't think we should trust anyone at all whom we don't know," Kistrin said. "Not yet."

Mica agreed. Merriweather went outside for a little while -- it made him nervous -- but Ada and Gram had gotten up and started making food. Fern came close enough to touch his arm before she hurried away -- her own way of saying she was glad he was back. Roe and Nyle filled them in on what had happened while he was gone, too. That seemed to be very little, in fact, during the long winter months. The calm had settled over the city, and except for a few odd storms, they'd had peaceful days all the time he'd been gone.

"Worried, us though," Roe admitted. He shook his head. "It were too quick, my lord, from war to peace like that. Made everyone nervous for a while."

"And then Roe and I started wondering if the trouble had followed after you wherever you went instead. We guessed Argine, hearing about some odd problems there," Nyle admitted.

Mica grinned. And then he grimaced. "I am going upstairs to clean up, try to shave -- get on some clean clothing --"

"Not until Merriweather comes back in," Nyle said. "Then I'll come up and help you out, but I'm not going to test her good nature right now. I don't think you want to, either."

"Probably right," he admitted. The idea of being clean appealed to him. "I think I have a few things you can wear, Prince Kistrin. Not as fine as you are used to --"

Kistrin laughed, brushed against the rags he'd been wearing all the way from the camp, and then laughed again. Mica did as well.

When Merriweather returned, she quickly agreed with the idea of getting cleaned up before food or any more work. Mica had to send a raven off as well. It was time to get everyone else in on this madness since he couldn't be certain that the attack might not come at any moment. He almost regretted even the few minutes they'd sat at his table in his kitchen. He took the steps up through the tower more slowly today, but he moved toward the world he had known and hoped never to lose again.

"I'll have to go up and get a raven off," he told Merriweather as he looked up toward his workshop -- a draw almost as powerful as getting cleaned up. He pulled the raven from his pouch. "I'll take you up. Then you fly to Gregorian and tell him I am back and want to see him immediately. No more than that."

"Out the window," the raven said and headed toward the end of the hall. Nyle went and let the clockwork creature out.

Roe took the Prince and Ovete to the second guest room. Merriweather went to her room across the hall from him, and Mica even saw her smile. He carefully opened his door and found the bedroom had not changed. The warmth from the steam heating system seemed almost too much after being so used to the cold.

Mica let Nyle shave him even carefully removed the gloves. He managed a quick shower and pulled on his soft robe. Then he remembered to find clothing for the Prince and passed those items on to the guard who was out in the hall.

Mica came back and looked for something of his own and Nyle helped him dress. Mica would have been embarrassed except he had not expected the soft clean clothing to feel so luxurious after the coarse rags of the last few weeks.

Nyle's face showed little emotion except that his eyes narrowed. "What happened to your hands, Lord Raventower?"

Mica looked at them. The scars were prominent, and the three middle fingers of his right hand still did not move well. He frowned.

"Tell me," Nyle said, his voice steady but the look of anger grew with each breath. "Because it looks to me as though someone held you down and knifed you -- and to do that to your hands makes me think it must be someone you know. Corinth, isn't it?"

"You figured that out easily," Mica said. He began working the gloves back on and waved away Nyle's help. "No, this part I can do."

Nyle nodded, his face grim. "You don't want anyone touching your hands."

"I -- I hadn't thought of it. But you're right. Merriweather is the only one."

"Well good, then," Nyle said and grinned so suddenly that it startled him. "You look much better, Lord Raventower. Your hair, though --"

"Merriweather will braid it for me."

Nyle went to check on her, and she came to his room dressed quite properly in her uniform. It looked loose on her, but she grinned as her hand brushed across the brace of knives in the corset.

"This is much better," she said. "The raven will be there by now."

"Yes," he replied and sat down so she could work the magic with his hair. He had washed it somewhat and wished for more time -- but they still had too much work to do. "It might take the raven a little time to reach Gregorian. He'll be careful, so no one else hears."

She nodded. "I could go --"

"No need," he said. She was tying his hair off already. "The moment Gregorian hears what the raven has to say, he'll head straight here. You'd probably miss him if you don't take the same road. Besides, we need to think about the next step."

Merriweather didn't argue, for which he was glad. Mica didn't want her away from him just yet.

Wind and snow blew past the window when he looked that direction. Had it been snowing from the time they reached the shore? He thought it might have been, though nothing serious. He'd been so fully caught up in being home that he'd never noticed.

Kistrin arrived at the door to his suite. Prince Kistrin -- he looked more the part now. Ovete had trimmed back the hair, and he'd shaved down to a thin mustache and goatee. The clothing fit him well enough, too.

"You talked to the soldiers, Merriweather," Mica said as they all started down the hall. "Corinth is in the city, isn't he?"

"Yes. The Mayor has been active in many places around the town. He even tried to point out that their usual savior, Lord Raventower, didn't appear to be much help these days."

"Trying to build up his reputation. Stupid waste of time," Mica said as they all headed toward the stairs. "With the airships coming, he couldn't possibly believe he was going to be a hero for long."

"I don't think that logic applies to him," Merriweather replied. She looked startled when Nyle pushed past her.

"I'll go down first," Nyle said.

Mica thought he did so to make sure the good Lord Raventower didn't tumble down the steps. Nyle might have been right, too. Mica was glad enough to have that solid block ahead of him since he seemed a bit lightheaded. Nyle might save the Prince as well.

Mica did glance at the steps going up to his workshop. The clockwork dog barked and stood at the top of the stairs, tail wagging.

"I'll be there as soon as I can, Tippet!" Mica said with a laugh.

Kistrin looked startled and maybe a little worried about the creature, but he said nothing. The Prince would be heading back to the castle yet tonight. Mica didn't worry about what he thought, not during all the rest of this trouble.

They knew Ada and Gram were cooking before they got near the kitchen. They could have been gone more than half an hour, but the lower levels of tower already smelled like...

Like home.

He must have looked much better by the time he walked back into the kitchen. Prince Kistrin won quick bows, but they must have seen that he wasn't anywhere ready for more pomp.

"We'll have food right soon," Gram said. She buzzed around the kitchen like someone half her age. Ada seemed to be having trouble keeping up. Whatever they were concocting had Mica's mouth began watering already.

"Sit down and stay out of the way," Ada said and then grinned. "If you don't mind, Prince Kistrin."

"I would be a fool to get in the way of this meal," the Prince replied. He waited until Mica and Merriweather had sat down and then took the spot on the other side of Merriweather. He appeared to be willing to wait patiently and politely for anything to happen. He'd even waved his guard off to stand out of the way. Ovete seemed more concerned with proper behavior than the Prince.

"I need paper," Mica suddenly said. Then he looked at his gloved hands and grimaced for a new reason. "You'll have to help me draw a map, Merriweather. I saw one on the table at the village just before we left, and I think I can recall most of what Janeh had marked here in Kamere. We might as well get to it before Gregorian gets here. Besides, it will give us something to do other than drooling over the food."

Ada laughed again, but he could see the way Gram kept looking toward the stairs to the upper level door, waiting for Shipley and Bear. Mica suspected that the boy would not be long in getting here. He'd know Gram would be worried.

Fern found them paper, ink, and a good quill. She smiled brightly, and her butterfly followed her this time. Kistrin looked intrigued.

They had other things to consider. Merriweather quickly drew a map of the city in broad strokes with the main roads and various areas marked. Roe and Nyle helped point out places that were still in ruins and where the streets were not cleared.

"No clockwork men coming in that way," Mica said.

A bit of noise at the door startled him, along with a brush of cold air -- but Bear came barreling down the stairs, and Shipley followed. Gram dropped her spoon in a pan and rushed to him.

Mica had not expected Gregorian to follow the boy. Nor did he expect him to have much the same reaction as Gram, but he caught Mica by the shoulder and hauled him up into an embrace that left Mica breathless.

"I am never letting you out of my reach again," Gregorian finally said and stepped back. "Oh, Prince Kistrin. I am glad he found you. But just the same -- what happened to your hands, Mica?"

His brother, General Gregorian, was babbling, or as close to it as he was ever likely to get. Then Gregorian shook his head. "Tell me what I need to know."

There was the man Mica had come to depend on. Gregorian stood on the other side of Mica and was already studying the map, though his face looked pale.

"Did you learn anything out there, Shipley?" Merriweather asked.

"Oh yes. He's in town and gathering up his people."

"I thought he would be," Mica said and tried to keep his voice calm.

"Who --" Gregorian began and then lifted his hand. "Corinth, isn't it? We had a meeting at the palace yesterday, and he was there. He made a show of asking about you, Mica -- but he could hardly keep from grinning. I suspected he just knew you were not around."

"Yes, Corinth," Mica agreed. "Sit down. We have a tale to tell."

CHAPTER TWENTY-SEVEN

Gregorian filled in a few more pieces of the tale from the Kamere side after he had heard what the others had done. They had even touched on what happened to Mica's hands, but Mica waved that away.

"We don't have time, Gregorian. We really don't. They are on the move, you know."

"I suppose so," Gregorian admitted and purposely looked away from Mica's hands. "And we have a different problem. We had a rebellion at the coal fields up north. We couldn't afford to lose those fields, especially during winter, so I sent several detachments of the army up there. Not all of them, but enough to weaken the city forces. We still have some troops down at the Argine border, too. I'm going to have to set up our defenses --"

"I think I have a better plan," Mica replied.

By then the meal was ready, and they discussed what to do over an excellent and happy meal. Mica and Gregorian mostly worked out the plan. Even the Prince seemed surprised by Mica's ability to point out potential trouble spots.

"We have to be daring," Mica said. "It's the only way we are going to end this trouble because we do not want them getting loose and working up another plan. They will. They'll continue to plague us because Corinth already wants vengeance and Janeh just wants to destroy things."

"We'll keep your return quiet -- both your returns," Gregorian said with a nod to Kistrin.

"They never knew who I was," Kistrin reminded them. "Which means I can go back to the castle and suddenly appear again without drawing any notice."

"That's a good plan. You can come back with me," Gregorian decided and grinned. "We'll say you landed at the fishing village and sent me word. I've come to escort you home through the dangerous streets. I'll take some of the guards from here, Mica."

"Good. I expect our mercenary friends to arrive soon, so don't worry."

"Mayor Corinth, he didn't have no more than a hundred at his townhouse," Shipley said and tapped the spot on the map. "They wait for some sign, and I don't think they can wait crowded in like that for long without drawing attention."

"So, we can expect the attack today, tonight or tomorrow. I need to get word to Rose and send her out over the ocean in search of Atrian craft," Gregorian said with a nod. "That would seem normal enough now that the weather has changed again. She'll go out at dawn. I don't think we'll have trouble before then."

"They'll want a clear view of the city," Mica agreed.

"And something more," Shipley said and drew their attention. "Not much important, but it seems to me, now that I think about it, the voices what I heard at Corinth's townhouse -- they weren't local. Not like Atrian or Argine, but country people, maybe."

"Not trained," Gregorian said with a bright smile.

"That's my take, General Gregorian," Shipley said with a nod. "They was trying to be quiet, and they couldn't even do that well."

"Good. A handful of soldiers should be able to handle them. Mica --"

"I do not intend to let them destroy my tower," he replied with a lift of his head and a steady stare at his brother.

"For the love of the gods, don't --"

The door to the tower opened, a gust of cold air. Everyone stood and many reached for weapons.

Seldon walked into the room. He smiled brightly. "Welcome home, all of you."

"How did you know --" Kistrin began, but then he stopped. "My father has hinted that there is more going on with you. That you are more than just a priest."

"I am," he said and smiled again. Then he looked at Mica and gave a little nod. "I dared not help you much in Argine except to slightly influence Corinth, who is one of our own. I'm sorry. They have their own gods in the south, and I dared not make a move that might awaken them and draw them into this war as well."

"I understand," Mica said. He did. "We have a plan in place now. We should be able to keep this one fully in human hands. Except for the reappearance of Payton --"

"We'll speak of that later. This problem first. You know that this was the heart of my temple, right here beneath our feet. Mine, not Atric's."

The others were all standing rather still now. Mica had not expected Seldon to be this open about what he was -- but then again, maybe now was the time. Right here and now *in his temple*. The words he had said were an affirmation that he and Atric had split apart in all truth.

"What should we do?" Mica asked.

"I cannot foresee what will happen," Seldon said with a slight tilt of his head. "High Priestess Ledea has hinted to me that your plan is sound, but that does not mean you will win. I can only promise to keep watch over you -- all of you."

"Thank you."

"I am not done," Seldon said. He reached out and took Mica's hands, though he had started to pull back. Magic instantly swept over the gloves and then within. Aches eased; fingers moved. Mica looked down, shocked.

"There are a few more injuries that will take longer to heal, but this will see you through the current mess, Mica," Seldon said. He started away and stopped to pat Bear on the head. The dog looked startled. Seldon looked back. "I can, I think, give you one gift still. Fog will help you rather than them. You have all done well. Thank you."

Then he walked back up the steps and out of the building.

"I am never going to get used to dealing with him," Gregorian admitted. "And wasn't that door latched?"

Mica flexed his fingers. His hands still hurt a little, but nothing like before. He kept the gloves on, though. He felt safer with them.

"I --" Shipley began. He stopped and put both hands on the table as though he feared it was moving. "I don't think he's a priest, is he?"

"He's a priest now, of sorts," Merriweather offered. Then she shrugged. "But since he all but admitted it here, yes -- he is a god."

Shipley yelped and slid down in his chair. Ada and Gram looked more contemplative than worried. Nyle, Roe, Prince Kistrin and his guards appeared to be stunned and maybe concerned. They had good cause, Mica supposed. The tales of times when gods walked the world had always been stories of dire times.

"We have a god working on our side in this?" Kistrin finally asked. "And you didn't mention this part to me, Mica?"

"Not my secret to give out," he replied, and Kistrin even nodded agreement. "Raventower is built over his old temple, though. And apparently, I am his High Priest, though I have no idea what that might mean."

"Is this going to help us?" Nyle asked.

"Seldon is trying hard not to draw the attention of other gods. We had that problem during the Atrian invasion, you know, and it almost went badly for us," Mica explained. He sat down again, and the others did as well, though he knew that Gregorian would leave soon. He had a great deal to prepare and had to do so quietly. "Seldon didn't have to come here tonight. And I can bet no one outside of us saw him, you know. He's given us a gift -- and I think that gift will definitely include just enough fog to keep our own actions under cover tonight and tomorrow."

"That will be enough," Gregorian said. He'd known about Seldon and recovered faster from the visit. Merriweather still looked bothered, but it was changing over to hopeful, Mica thought. Shipley just kept shaking his head. None of them asked what god he might be -- and that was good. Seldon had been Troger, a god associated with war toward the end, but he had been more attuned to protection before a high priest, Atric had perverted his cause.

"If this be his temple, should we do somewhat for it?" Ada finally asked. "That's the symbol beneath the rug, isn't it?"

"Yes. I'll ask Seldon next time I see him. He doesn't seem to be worried over it."

Ada stared at the floor for a moment and then gave a shrug. "Apple tarts are done. A bit of sweet, everyone?"

"Seldon left too soon," Roe suggested.

They laughed. That was unexpected, and it helped, and the dread of the hours before lifted. Mica and his dinner guests went over the plan once more while they nibbled on apple tarts. Mica had not eaten so much in quite a while. He feared he was going to waddle out to battle, or perhaps just nap through the trouble.

His fingers moved. He marveled at it.

"I think I know a way that we can lessen the odds," Mica said. He turned the paper over where they had drawn the map and took up the quill himself. He drew out a few streets and buildings. "But we'll have to move quickly."

Not much later Gregorian prepared to leave with Shipley and Bear who were going to do another run through town.

"And I'll go with you," Kistrin said and stood. "I need to talk to my father. Is mother back?"

"Not yet," Gregorian said. "However, she keeps asking about you. We didn't want to tell her --"

"She always knows," Kistrin said with a grin.

"She does," Gregorian agreed. The group was already heading toward the steps, Kistrin's guards falling in behind him.

The Prince, though, stopped by Mica and put a hand on his shoulder. "You saved my life --"

"You had already --"

"*You saved my life*," he repeated and in the sort of tone one did not argue with coming from a Prince. "I won't forget it."

And off he went.

"We still have work to do," Mica said as he looked at Merriweather. "I want to go over everything again before we set things up."

"It's a good plan," Merriweather said and frowned a little. "What is worrying you?"

"I am trying not to be too optimistic and self-assured this time," he admitted. He gave a little shrug. "I felt that way while I was in Janeh's hold, and I got careless. I will not do that again."

Merriweather started to say something and then stopped. She nodded. "Let's go over everything again."

Gregorian had agreed that it was best to leave Corinth alone, though they would keep him and his people under watch and track him in case he had more people hidden in the city. Shipley would head back to the tower or the castle as soon as trouble began -- that would depend on which one was closer. He would also contact Storm and send them up to the tower.

They just had to wait for the trouble to show itself now. As much as Mica wanted to go to his workshop -- His fingers moved! -- he knew this was not the time to lose himself in the old work. Instead, Mica and Merriweather went out into the courtyard and made sure those people were ready for the attack. He spent a little time with Kandris, though. The clockwork horse danced out to meet him, head up and eyes flashing. He also noted that Nyle had rebuilt the carriage for a single horse to draw now. That hit his heart again that they'd lost Lestian in the war, but the clockwork horse had saved them. He wouldn't be forgotten.

Ravens had taken up places on the wall overlooking the road and the ocean. He realized there were more than a few who were not clockwork birds there. Mica thought that odd and he'd have to talk to his ravens after all the rest of this was done. Had they made new allies? The birds had always been associated with the family, after all. He wanted to ask questions --

Tomorrow? The next day? It wouldn't be long now before this new madness was finished. Were there other problems lurking out there? Maybe. Did Seldon give him more hope? Should he accept it? Should he worry about what might yet go wrong?

Yes -- to all of it.

Gregorian's people had worked through the foggy, dark night. Mica trusted that they would have done their best to set everything up properly. If not, they would have to stop the clockwork men in a more dangerous way.

Shipley and Bear came back before midnight; Storm and his men followed the boy in, moving quickly and silently -- there was, in fact, just enough to fog that Mica suspected they had not been seen.

"Shipley pointed out the places where Corinth's people were gathering," Storm said as they headed back into the tower. "We got some scouting in. They aren't going to move before dawn. We have a few hours to rest, and I think we all ought to take advantage of it."

Just the idea of sleep suddenly overwhelmed Mica, although he still wanted to argue. Then he wanted to argue about going all the way up the stairs. Too far --

Merriweather got him to his bedroom door. She even went in and checked the room, so much like her old self that he smiled. And yawned.

"Sleep for a few hours, Lord Raventower," she said. "I'll get you up when it's time. You can trust me."

Mica knew he could. He nodded his thanks and went in, knowing she stood outside until he put the lock in place. Mica briefly thought about taking a shower. Then he saw the bed -- his bed. Turned down and ready for him. He kicked off his shoes and laid down. Pulled the blankets up and sank down into the luxury of being home.

Mica slept without dreams or nightmares, which he had not expected. Just drifted off to calm, peaceful darkness and slept straight through until Merriweather knocked on the door.

"Yes?" he said, sitting up faster than he had intended.

"Dawn, Lord Raventower," Merriweather said. "Gregorian sent word that people are on the move. We think it's about to start."

"Good," Mica said as he grabbed his boots. "The sooner begun, the sooner we'll be done."

He crossed over and opened the door. Merriweather looked him over and nodded. "Yes, I slept in my clothes, too. Wise. There was no telling when trouble might hit."

"Had nothing to do with being wise," he replied and brushed at the wrinkles in his shirt. "Too tired to care."

"Let me fix your hair. Or I could get someone up here to cut it off --"

"I like it this way. Keeps it out of my way and out of my face," he said. The sleep had sharpened his wits. "I don't think I've been this clear-headed in days," he admitted.

"Probably Seldon's work," Merriweather said with a grin. "Because none of us have really had nearly enough sleep."

He laughed agreement. Laughed? On a day like this?

Why not? Why not believe that they would catch Corinth and Janeh in their plan.

"Rose has taken the fleet off over the ocean," Merriweather said as they started down the steps. "So that step is in motion."

"You've been up for a while."

"Not really. Storm sent me a note, and someone slipped it under my door just a few minutes ago. He added that he and his men were heading out to do what they could from the outside."

"Good. We don't dare be careless now, though I wouldn't expect that from Storm anyway."

Ada was brewing tea and put a plate of sweet cakes and apple tarts on the table. Shipley was the only one sitting there, Bear by the hearth and chewing on a bone.

"I'll be off soon as I'm done," the boy said with a nod.

"Shipley --"

"If things go bad, Bear and me will go to cover -- either the castle or here, or if we can't do either, I expect I can dig into a hole somewhere. I can warn those of Shadow Walk to stay clear of some places this morning, and what to watch for when it comes."

"You are a wonder, Shipley," Mica said.

"I'm just smart enough to know there are people what I don't want to live under, them in charge and all. I'd still be on your side, even if I didn't live in Raventower these days. Only a fool would trust Corinth -- but even not trusting him, there would be many what wouldn't know to avoid him today."

Mica nodded agreement.

"Take care," Merriweather said when Shipley stood.

He nodded and started toward the steps. Bear dropped his bone and rushed out after him, and they went off into the cold morning. Mica sipped his tea, and so did Merriweather. The quiet was wonderful, this little time before chaos would strike again. Mica could almost feel the trouble coming. Somewhere not far away, Janeh moved closer with her airships, army, and metal men.

Janeh and Corinth thought no one would know their plans. The enemy would have come in through the mountains -- a dangerous ploy this time of year, but as soon as the last storm cleared, they had a window of calm weather. Mica imagined the old airships coming in over the hills in the darkness of night, rushing eastward toward the ocean and Kamere. They'd be close now. They might even think the fog a blessing for them.

"Ready?" Mica asked.

Merriweather finished an apple tart and nodded as she stood.

"You two take care," Ada warned as they started away. "You take good care. We just got you both back."

"We will be as careful as we can," Merriweather promised. "But we'll also see this ended."

Ada gave a grim nod. Then she smiled suddenly. "We'll have a feast ready for when you come back."

The two went out. Kandris came from the stall at his call. The soldiers still looked uncomfortable at the site of the enormous clockwork horse crossing the courtyard. It knelt for the Mica and Merriweather to take their place on his back. The metal was cold, but unlike 'real' horses, Kandris had a sort of built in saddle. He also followed complex orders.

Nyle opened the gate for them.

"Be careful up here, Nyle," Mica said as they stepped out into the fog. "This is a target."

"They won't get the tower," Nyle promised.

And then Mica and Merriweather rode down into the fog.

CHAPTER TWENTY-EIGHT

The enemy airships arrived with the dawn, just as Mica had predicted. The one problem Mica had trouble working out was where Janeh would land the airships to unload the clockwork men and the explosives, along with whatever soldiers they brought along. Only five airships, though -- the number of troops would not be too many for the people of Kamere to handle.

The clockwork bombs couldn't be marched in from the far edge of town, or they would blow up long before they reached the targets he'd seen mapped in the heart of the city. Janeh would never get the clockwork men up the incline to the castle, either -- that would be where most of her troops would head for a more conventional battle. Janeh would not land at the airfield because they would never fight their way into the city from there, even with a few ships full of troops.

It wasn't until Janeh's ships began moving in over the city and slowing that Mica realized they would not land at all, not even along the beach. They would simply come in low, anchor to a building, and drop the clockwork men and unprimed explosives out, along with the control boxes.

Janeh and Corinth already had people on the ground, but a few more scurried down the ladders from the ships. Some of them did not make it as some of Gregorian's soldiers rushed into the area took up the fight. One of the five airships crashed as well, but they were so low that Mica assumed most of the people survived.

"You were right," Merriweather told Mica with a nod. "They didn't have to fight their way in."

"I saw no sign of any plans for such a battle," Mica said. Merriweather had been standing on Kandra's back and now settled in front of Mica again, a graceful move across the shiny metal. The clockwork horse was on his best behavior, having been let out at last. "One of the ships is anchoring down by the water, though. They'll be going after my tower."

"Looks like Gregorian's people are moving in on those who landed in town," Merriweather noted. They could hear trouble filling the quiet morning. "I don't think they're going to get many of the clockwork bombs primed."

"Janeh and Corinth will think this is just bad luck," Mica replied, distracted by all the activity. He started the horse moving, and they headed for the heart of the city where the mass of the attack would still take place. If the city fell, it would not matter if he saved Raventower.

Mica headed for the largest mass of clockwork men and what would be the hardest battle. Kandris stayed to the shadows and avoided being spotted as they worked their way quickly to the area where the mass of four ships had unloaded things. When they got nearer, they found people with the control boxes settled in the middle of the clockwork men, one group heading north and the other south, so that the soldiers could not get through the mass of walking bombs to them. The clockwork men were not in lines, either, but spread out just far enough that they didn't risk running into each other. They moved along Kamere's well-made main road, but some would turn toward the temples and others would head for the factory district. Mica knew there were other targets, but he couldn't see if Janeh had already set up to attack them. Even a look back toward the tower didn't show him the trouble there.

Other battles had begun to break out in various spots across the city. Mica could hear gunshots and shouts, most of them distant, but some closer. At least two airships were still in the air, one heading toward the bay. Roe worked the tower's cannons today and Mica hoped the craft got too careless --

Mica had to bring his attention back to here. He had a job to do still.

"They're set up just like you said they would be," Merriweather said. She didn't sound surprised, though they both had known that plans could have changed.

Mica gave a worried nod of agreement. "More of the clockwork devices than I had expected, though. I suppose Janeh had already shipped some to the other camp before I arrived."

"Or brought them with her from the west," Merriweather said. "Do you see her?"

"No. I fear Janeh and Corinth are both at work taking my tower."

"We should --"

"Settle this," he said and did not even look back at his tower. "They're going to start turning toward their targets soon. We don't want the devices to spread out on different roads. I wonder if those people at the controls have any idea the size of the explosions. They seem to be staying close."

Merriweather and Mica both looked up as an enemy airship flew over them. Mica didn't think they were spotted there in the shadows of a tall building. He spotted a few people on the deck, all of them with weapons ready, although Gregorian's soldiers had already pulled back. The airship went on, heading toward the castle.

"This is it," Mica warned.

Merriweather's hand went to her pistol. Their mount

moved forward enough to get a better view and to allow Mica to give one shout and a wave of his arm.

The buildings on the right side of the road exploded, the wooden shells shattering while enormous blocks of stone that had been carted from the temple square flew outward. Mica had done a quick calculation back in the tower and hoped it was good enough -- and yes, most of the debris flew outward toward the road rather than upward and back down. Both clockwork men and the people controlling them were hit.

A heartbeat later the clockwork explosions began -- one after another in the circle of downed metal men. Dust, metal, and debris filled the air, and the sound of the explosions shook the world so violently that several other buildings fell as well. Mica regretted the extra destruction, but all the buildings in the area had been cleared during the night. No one had been killed, at least not on the Kamere side.

The airship still headed for the castle, though. Mica could barely see it through the dusty haze and fog, but it swept toward the walls --

Admiral Rose and *Flash* seemed to appear out of nowhere -- which was almost correct, he supposed, if she had used the newer engine to come back what would have been an impossible distance otherwise. Her guns fired and the enemy airship veered westward over the townhouses of Kamere's more affluent citizens. Something exploded, and then another. They were dropping bombs.

He felt Merriweather tense. "Damn them!"

Her family lived up there.

"We can circle --"

"No," she said. She stood up again on Kandris's back and tried to see better, but it must not have worked since she settled quickly. "No. I can see Gregorian and his men coming from the castle now that it looks like no more of the airships are heading their way. And -- yes -- the airship is going down under *Flash*'s fire. "We have work to do. Mica. We need to get back to the tower. If Janeh and Corinth are there, they're going to do everything in their power to bring it down now that everything else has failed."

"I have something to do here first."

Merriweather didn't argue, though it was stupid for her to go with him when he ordered Kandris to stay back.

A second airship had started across the town, but *Flash* attacked, along with another of the Sedina's fleet. They herded the craft off over the sea and Mica had no doubt they'd be down in the water before too long.

His work was a bit trickier right now --

An explosion behind them took Mica's attention. Something had blown up back by his tower, though he could still see it standing through the lessening fog and growing smoke.

Mica didn't go there. Instead, he headed toward the chaos that he'd created with his trap. Elsewhere, others were still fighting and sometimes a clockwork device exploded. Mica had told Gregorian how best to handle that problem and he passed it on to his own people. The largest mass had been bombarded by Mica's trap, though. He had to hope that Sedina's airships and already prepared troops could handle the rest. Janeh and Corinth had counted on surprise and shock, but they had neither in this battle.

As he neared the area, Mica could see one clockwork man still standing and maybe one more down and not exploded. Mica found himself drawn toward the one standing; he needed to know answers about how the devices worked because everything still pointed to someone else behind this attack.

The worst destruction had been confined to the road, which now showed big holes and piles of debris in chaotic piles. People would have to clear the entire area, rock by rock, and hope there were no more unexploded bombs here. Better, perhaps, to level the area with more explosions of their own first.

Mica walked carefully toward the clockwork man that still stood facing toward the path it would have taken toward a cluster of factory buildings. The humans who had died here were not close -- Mica saw a little whisper of life lights but they disappeared in a jumble of rock several yards away. This single unnatural metal creature stood not far from the edge of the debris and had almost made it out. The blank face and squarish body looked dangerous and daunting. Mica had never stood before one until now, and even though the clockwork man didn't live in any sense, he still had a sense of menace from it.

"We can just toss rocks at them, Mica," Merriweather suggested. "You don't need to --"

"I want one of these monsters more or less intact, though without the explosives. I need the last answers of how they work before we face them again," Mica said softly as though he feared even his voice would set it off. He did not mention the idea that someone else with a box -- like Janeh -- might still have some control. He just didn't know. "Please stay back."

Merriweather didn't argue. Good. Mica had to focus entirely on this device. If he got this one disarmed, then they could blow any others to hell. He'd even enjoy it. Mica walked around the creature twice, careful not to dislodge any of the stones. He had seen the inside of the chest shells, though not with the explosives and triggering device in place. He knew how to open the chest, but he also knew that they blew up on contact --

The wheel-like feet stretched out in front of the metal man by several inches. They would hit something substantial before the body did, and it might be that shock which triggered the explosions. The feet were uncovered. A large wedge of stone had hit the side plate of the knee and caught there in the joint.

A thin line of flexible metal ran along the edge of the foot, up the leg, and to the chest. Mica had seen it before and thought the thin brace provided reinforcement to hold things together when the clockwork mechanisms moved. Now he wasn't so certain.

Mica held up his hands and moved his fingers, testing their movement inside the gloves, though those would have to come off. He would need a very gentle touch, though where could he open the chest? Was the explosive attached to the metal when it was put in? Would moving that chest piece away from the rest --

Janeh had said something about getting things in place properly because there would be no second chance. That had been at Setton. He drew his fingers away from the surface, walked around it once more, and then stopped and stared at the neck joint, wondering if he could remove the head --

Mica heard horses coming down the road, and he looked up to find Gregorian stopping at the far side of the debris field.

"Mica, are you trying to drive me mad? Get the hell out of there!" Gregorian shouted as he dismounted.

"I need one," Mica replied, though he moved very carefully. "And we both know it."

"Get away from that thing!" Gregorian ordered. "Just get away, please. I'll dig out every piece we can find and give it to you later."

Mica had never heard that much worry in Gregorian's voice before. Looking around at the destruction in this area, he supposed there was a good reason. Besides, Mica had found no way to open the casing. He suspected that once the connection was made, it could not be unmade. There was no failsafe on these things, and that would have suited Janeh and her unique brand of insanity.

He stepped back, carefully making his way to Merriweather. She put a hand on his arm, and he realized Merriweather had been trembling. Why had he not considered how other people would feel about what he was doing? She would have watched him die. It was hardly fair to her or his brother.

"I'm sorry," he said. Merriweather gave a bow of her head. "Thank the gods for Gregorian and the voice or reason."

Gregorian spread his men out to guard the area and keep people away. The General worked his way around the edge of the ruined buildings and joined the two of them, far too close to the clockwork man for Mica's liking. They were all ready to ignore the fact that Mica had been crazy.

"How do we trigger them without going closer?" Gregorian said with a quick look at his brother.

The battle at the tower grew louder. How could he have ignored that --

"Mica?"

"Keep everyone away until we can get *Flash* to fire on them -- from a distance. Blow up every bit of the road to make certain nothing dangerous is buried under there."

Gregorian nodded and started giving orders to relay back to the airships. Mica and Merriweather climbed back atop Kandris, and he would have galloped away without Gregorian, but his brother called for his own horse, though the mount was a bit uneasy beside the clockwork one.

"Let's go," Gregorian said. "But don't do anything stupid this time."

Mica said nothing as he turned his attention to Raventower. They could hear the battle -- the shouts of people, the rumble of what seemed to be small explosions in many places. They passed dead along the road; there had been a battle here not long ago, and the life-lights lingered and would have gone for Mica, but the horse moved too quickly.

Gregorian's private guard of six followed, and Mica hoped they saw nothing definite through the fog and dust.

Corinth's army had been split between the castle and the tower -- wise, really, because he would have needed to take both if he hoped to be safe in the city that rested between those two high points.

Corinth hadn't taken the castle. One airship would have landed in the gardens, but *Flash* had shot it down and troops had been everywhere on the walls, ready for more trouble. Corinth would know by now that he couldn't win, but he might still have revenge if he brought down Raventower. And for all the mayor knew, no one realized his connection to the attack, either. He would still count on his involvement staying a secret.

Mica caught up with Storm and his men at the edge of Shadow Walk. They had Shipley and Bear with them and looked as though they'd already had some trouble.

"Bear and me were heading for the tower, but got cut off," Shipley said. He had a cut on his face, but he didn't seem bothered by it.

"Corinth hates me more than he wanted the city," Mica said. He felt his fingers flex again out of instinct. "Corinth will know he can't really win, though he might not admit it. And he's egotistical enough to think he won't be caught on the wrong side anyway. He won't back off from the attack against Raventower."

"What did you ever do to deserve this?" Gregorian asked and looked at his brother in shock.

"People like Lord Raventower," Shipley said. "No one liked the Mayor at all."

"Besides, I was the easiest of the Raventowers to attack," Mica added. "And probably the last straw. He wanted to marry your Jenna, but you did. Then he turned his attention toward Merriweather -- and found out I am to marry her."

"What a mess," Gregorian mumbled. He looked at Storm and nodded. "Can I trust you to try and keep Mica safe? I think it's gone beyond what Merriweather can handle."

"We'll do our best," Storm agreed.

Mica thought to argue about his brother putting others watching over him, but he said nothing. They'd reached the curve of the road that turned down toward the fishing village or up to his tower. An enemy airship had purposely come down by the shore, and Mica could see where small, box-like things were climbing upward along the cliff. One fell and exploded.

"Ah. Well, those are different," Mica said. "I suspect they might be based somewhat on my centipede plan. They can't have too many, can they?"

The exploding boxes had already blown a hole in the outer curtain wall, but the soldiers inside were holding the breach without much trouble. The problem would be if the new clockwork creatures managed more holes than the people inside could manage to defend.

Two more of the clockwork men rolled up the road, and behind them came Janeh. She looked pleased despite the situation, but Mica suspected that look only came because her creatures were destroying things. The reasons for the battle had never mattered to her. She remained focused on her toys -- Mica, and his people were able to pull back out of sight. He didn't want her to see Kandris -- not yet, at least.

"How do we stop this group?" Storm asked.

"Ropes," Mica said. "Get a rope strung across the road -- a long rope because whoever is holding it needs to be behind a good, strong cover. When the devices get within a foot, pull it tight. She kept them too close together -- they'll both go up. It's not safe --"

Storm and Gregorian were already gathering all the rope they could, though they did it out of Janeh's sight. She saw nothing but her creatures moving along the road. Mica's only real fear was that the locals would try to stop her and get themselves killed.

"That's her, then?" Gregorian finally asked.

"Yes," he said and slid off the clockwork horse with Merriweather at his side. He patted the animal on the metal neck, drawing Kandris's notice back to him. "Get her attention. Go past and pause, and then up to the gate and wait there. I'll call you if I need you."

The horse gave a slight nod and moved up the path.

And that did precisely what he had hoped. Janeh finally caught sight of the beautiful clockwork creature, and her attention faltered as she watched Kandris prance across her line of sight. Storm took that moment to dash across the road, trailing the rope in the dust.

The horse disappeared around the curve of the road. A look of grim determination came to Janeh's face this time. Mica didn't like to see the change. Even her creations -- both controlled from one box, he thought -- seemed to slow as though they would stop. Janeh knew she had already been bested in the only way that mattered to her. She started to turn away.

Mica stepped out into the open while Merriweather hissed in anger.

"Janeh," Mica called out. She spun to face him; her face had gone white. He'd just come back from the dead as far as she could tell. "And now you know why you'll never win."

She yelled in rage and sent the walking bombs forward. Mica held his place for a moment, a moment longer --

When they were within inches of the rope, he turned and rushed back toward the cover where Gregorian had a hand on Merriweather as though to stop her from charging out. Janeh laughed --

And the rope came up and caught the clockwork devices.

They tottered --

"No!"

And then fell.

The explosion brought down parts of buildings, rocks, and sent dust and dirt into the air. Mica heard Janeh cry out once as the sound of the more massive explosion rose around them.

"I think they were going for the gate," Mica said with a nod up the hillside. "Good we stopped them --"

Janeh came out of the dust and leapt at him. He hit her aside, but it was Storm and Merriweather who grabbed the woman.

"You can't be here. You can't -- that horse. You aren't --"

Merriweather managed to tear some cloth to make a gag while Storm used pieces of the rope to tie her up. She had a cut on her shoulder and dirt on her face that would probably show bruises before too long. Mica looked her over and saw how her face changed. She still saw Nikeh, not Mica. She couldn't believe his true place in the world, even now. The woman had no connection with the real world --

"Trouble coming," Gregorian warned. Storm put the woman in the hold of two of his men. Maybe she recognized the two mercenaries from the camp too. Janeh looked confused, as though she found that nothing in the world made sense.

Mica looked back toward the city and saw a large gathering around Mayor Corinth. He wasn't here already after all, but he would for his prize. Gregorian began ordering his men to prepare for the battle. This was not a good spot, though. They would do better from the walls --

He looked back at Raventower and saw something that gave him hope again. His ravens were flying, and they dropped rocks where the smaller bombs still attempted to climb upward, knocking many down. Then, in a nicely planned move, people on the walls dropped rocks down everywhere. The bots tumbled and exploded at the same time. They were not going to bring down the walls --

More of the enemy began to stream from the downed airship. This was not the place to get caught between two parts of the enemy army. Neither of the enemy groups numbered more than a hundred, but with them trapped in the middle --

"Up to Raventower!" Merriweather said. "We don't want to fight here!"

Gregorian agreed. "Mica, go up and get the gate open for us."

Mica didn't argue. Gregorian didn't send him to reach safety, after all. A few enemy soldiers were climbing the cliffs, and Mica couldn't see what was going on around the other side of Raventower.

He started up -- and stopped to point out at the bay.

"I suspect those are Atrian ships."

"Damn," Gregorian all but shouted as he spotted the gray shapes coming out of the fog. "Of course, they are. We knew there was more to this."

"Corinth and Janeh were only distractions, you know," Mica said. "Keep an eye open for their airships."

Gregorian nodded.

Mica and Merriweather started up the path. Storm and his people, along with the prisoner, followed. The clockwork horse stood by the gate, prancing one way and another, and then came downward to join Mica, ready for whatever trouble might yet come. The city sky had filled with dust, smoke, and fog making it impossible to judge what might be happening --- but since Gregorian had come here, Mica believed that everything else must be handled.

Too much trouble out there. Too many points of attack. They had stopped the Clockwork men, but he knew that the Atrians -- or the Honorgates, or whomever else might be involved in this -- had only sent those crazy people in as a diversion. They were dangerous enough, but they were not the real war.

Gregorian knew it, and the General was prepared for that trouble just as he had been ready since the war began, back in that last invasion by the Atrians just before Mica had headed south. How odd that it seemed as though this was just the same battle, and none of that long, dreadful journey stood between that day and this one.

Mica and his group reached the gate. Mica glanced around once and saw Corinth's people charging toward the road. Janeh's people -- who had stayed back from the bombs -- had not quite made it up the hillside yet.

"I think we can stop them," Merriweather said. "That wall is going to give out soon, anyway."

She was right.

"Nyle! Roe! Open the gate!"

The clockwork gate began to creak open and stuck; Kandris pushed his way forward and kicked it open far enough for them to get through. Mica slid in first, but the rest of them were quick to follow.

"Shipley, Bear -- into the tower," Mica ordered. The boy looked ready to argue. "Make sure the others know we're safe, and then get up high and keep watch for any trouble we can't see from down here. Some ravens will stand by with you and warn us."

The boy nodded and dashed away. Mica saw him pound on the tower door which meant they'd wisely had it fully sealed shut. Shipley and Bear went in, and the door closed tight again, though he'd caught a glimpse of Ada and waved.

Merriweather and Storm went to work on protecting the outer wall. Mica called in his ravens and learned that the other walls were still safe. The seaward cliffs were too dangerous, and no one had made it up that far.

Rose went overhead with *Flash*, three other airships in close formation. She'd be handling the ships out there, both in the sea and in the air.

Merriweather had lined up many of the men, and with a grunt and a shout, a weakened section of the old curtain wall gave way, massive pieces of stone rolling down the cliff and across the road not far from where the explosions had happened and straight into the mass of Janeh's people. Some had died, but the life-lights didn't reach him this far. They had no dead on the grounds that he could see, either.

Mica and Merriweather climbed up the guard tower close to the gate. Not a safe place with the battle coming up the road to the partially opened gate, but one from which they could direct Gregorian and his men. Corinth saw Gregorian in retreat -- or so he thought. It was really the worst position for Corinth to be in, trying to attack uphill -- and made worse when Prince Kistrin arrived with a large contingent of Palace Guards, already shooting and ordering surrender in the name of the King. The odd words echoed around the sounds of explosions and the cries of the wounded.

Most of Corinth's people ran. He looked around, shocked. Some of the soldiers pursued those who ran, but the mass of mounted men came straight at Corinth and with a cry of dismay, he dropped his pistol and fell to his knees.

A ship exploded out in the bay. Mica feared they would never get those waters cleared of debris.

Kistrin and his guards brought Corinth up the hill and through the gate. Mica and Merriweather remained at the guard post, still trying to find more enemies, but as far as Mica could see, the only ones they had to worry about were those who had run. None of the ships would get close to the shore. No more of the little boxed explosives climbed up his damaged wall.

"Down," Merriweather said and signaled him toward the

stairs. "I think we're done here."

"Yes," Mica agreed. He reached the ladder, but then he turned back to her. "Merriweather?"

She paused and looked his way.

He took her in his arms and kissed her -- a long and passionate kiss that he only reluctantly ended.

"That, I think, was long overdue," Mica said. Merriweather looked stunned as he started down the ladder.

Storm, Gregorian, Nyle and a few others were gathered by the gate, watching as Kistrin and his people brought Corinth up to the tower. Mica didn't want him or Janeh here, but he supposed it was safer than taking them through the city.

"I think this settles the trouble," Kistrin said. He had Corinth by the arm. Janeh, still gagged, gave the Prince an odd look. Did she realize who he had been at the camp? How they had *fooled* her?

"You can't be alive," Corinth said, his voice far from steady as he stared at Mica. His eyes had gone wild. "You can't have survived!"

"You have no idea how lucky you are that he is alive," Merriweather said as she stepped closer. Corinth backed into the Prince who looked amused to see the man so afraid. "You don't know what I had planned for you otherwise."

He paled.

"I think we are done here," Gregorian said.

Done?

Mica could not see any more of the battle. There had been no more explosions for a while, though they still had to deal with a few of the clockwork men. There might be a few smaller bombs, but his ravens were still in the air, guarding them.

The day had passed from dawn to noon. It had been a short but fierce set of battles.

Done?

"I'm going to my workshop," Mica said.

No one argued.

CHAPTER TWENTY-NINE

A few hours in the workshop settled his nerves, especially since he kept the windows closed and didn't look out at the trouble. Airships flew over sometimes, but he and Merriweather -- who sat in her usual place -- both assumed they were the Sedina fleet since nothing dropped on or near the tower.

Dinner that night proved a true joy -- a gathering of all his people and none of the war intruding. Ada and Gram looked as though they intended for Mica to gain back some weight in one meal.

Afterward, Mica slept well in his own bed and appreciating it far more than he had the short night before. Home was his last thought of the night and the first thought of the next day.

When the message arrived -- this time from the King and not from Gregorian, Mica almost tossed it into the fire, unread.

"No," he said. "I will not go out on another quest --"

Merriweather took the paper and broke the seal. It was, after all, also addressed to her.

"The King asks that we come to the castle to attend while he pronounces judgement on Mayor Corinth and his allies."

"Not something I want to see," Mica said. Then he gave a nod. "But it will put an end to this --"

Something exploded in the city. Mica started to his feet, but Merriweather signaled him to sit back down. "*Flash* is bombing the area with the clockwork men like you suggested."

"Good. Let's clean up and settle the last of this trouble."

An hour later, they were riding through the city. The break in the curtain wall didn't look so bad today but they'd have to get to work on fixing it before more trouble came their way. When they got to the location where the largest mass of clockwork men had been, there was little left but several deep holes in the road. True to his promise, Gregorian's people were collecting every bit of metal they could find in the debris. Mica looked at the baskets filled with chunks of metal and nodded with genuine thanks that they probably didn't understand. If they found enough pieces, though, he might put enough together to figure out how they worked.

"Janeh may have designed them, but she had help," Mica said as they rode on. Merriweather nodded. "We need a better way to stop the devices in the future rather than just throwing things at them. I fear they will turn back up again."

"Yes," Merriweather agreed. She still didn't look as though she'd slept well.

"I really hope for at least one almost intact control box," he added and looked back. "Those didn't have explosives in them, so there is still a chance."

Storm and two of his men rode with them, guarding against the people who had run from the last battle. Mica and Merriweather rode regular horses today, but Mica intended to take Kandris out again soon. He just wanted a few days of calm in the world first.

The city had taken considerable new damage, and even some of the places that they'd cleaned up and started to rebuild were back down again. The reasonable weather appeared to be changing, too. A winter storm was on the way, Mica suspected. He was tired of winter weather -- but in truth, he'd missed most of the season here, even if he'd suffered in the mountain cold. Spring was not long in the future.

Some townhouses had been destroyed. Ironically, one of them had been the Honorgate's city home, which had not been in inhabited, except for an old caretaker who had survived. Merriweather's family had only suffered a few broken windows and a cracked fence wall.

Mica and his companions were let in the gate to the castle grounds without any trouble and led up to the building by downright cheerful soldiers.

"Just in time," Kistrin said as he met them just inside the castle door. "My father is about to see Janeh, Corinth -- and someone unexpected we picked up in the enemy soldiers."

"An Atrian?" Mica asked as he handed over his cloak.

"No. Chief Sochen, who is a major leader of the hill tribes to the west."

"Of course," Mica said. "I doubt he knows that some of his followers already abandoned the cause after Janeh's careless killing of at least one of their number."

Merriweather nodded. She looked grim, and he supposed he ought to feel the same way -- but whatever happened here was the aftermath of this set of troubles, both for him and for the city. They still had more trouble coming their way, but they would not face it today.

Kistrin led the two into the throne room just as King Abertus began reading the crimes that the three had committed. Sochen was a tall, stately man in leathers and furs who didn't so much as blink as he listened. Janeh didn't look as though she cared. Corinth trembled already.

The King looked down toward the group who had come in and nodded as an acknowledgment of their arrival. Janeh glanced their way and looked troubled. Corinth had to be held on his feet by the guards.

Sochen had a different look, as though he saw the world clearly for the first time.

"You have no excuses?" Abertus asked though the words were not mocking. "No tales of how you were duped? Good, then. Janeh and Corinth, you will hang."

"No," Corinth cried out. "I served you -- I --"

Even Janeh looked disgusted as she glanced his way. The soldiers shook the mayor and he fell into a gasping silence

"Chief Sochen, why did you join them?"

"Not them," the man said. His voice was deep and steady. "Lord Honorgate came to us. He said that if we joined the Atrians, we would again have access to trade and even to the sea, as my people once had known, ages in the past."

"Why didn't you ask us for that access and trade?" Abertus asked and sounded honestly confused.

"We tried. Lord Honorgate told us that you had refused to deal with barbarians."

"He lied," Abertus said with a snarl and a shake of his head. "And he lied to me, too. When he came back from those meetings, he told me that you would not talk to us at all. He had already begun working with the Atrians, but I didn't know it." He stopped and looked to one of the clerks. "I want a list of all the places Honorgate had gone and the work he did for me -- all of them for at least the last two decades. I suspect we'll find deception everywhere."

Mica felt a little chill at the thought. Honorgate had only been one of many Lords who took such missions or met with foreigners in the city. This was going to be a difficult tangle to un-weave.

"Sochen, you and I will discuss treaties and trade," Abertus decided and won at least a tentative nod from the man. "Then you and your people will go home, with a guard as far as the hills. You can then decide if what I offer is worth an alliance or not."

Mica had the feeling the King had already won the man over.

With a wave of his hand, all three of the prisoners were taken out of the room -- Janeh and Corinth under guard, Sochen with a single guard and a bevy of servants who were already asking after his needs. The man looked amused.

But Janeh pulled her guards to a stop as they started past Mica, Merriweather -- ah, and Kistrin. The Prince smiled.

"We have met, you know."

"You cannot be --" Janeh whispered and must have recognized him.

The guards dragged her and Corinth away, and not toward the upper rooms. Janeh looked back at them, as shocked and confused as the woman had probably ever been in her life.

"There. That's done. I thought you ought to be here for it, Mica," the King said. He settled back on his throne. "The prisoners we're capturing are mostly going to go to the coal fields to work since that's where some of them came from anyway. Airships had come in and grabbed them up, and the rebellion up there made counting those who were missing even more difficult."

"I think you need a full military camp up there, sire," Merriweather advised. The King and Gregorian both looked her way and nodded for her to continue. "When Mica and I rode past that area, I could see it was too vulnerable. And the prisoners need better housing and care. It will stop those on short term sentences from leaping at a chance to get away. We don't want to make rebels of them if they aren't already."

The King gave a tentative nod, but Mica thought she had a good point.

"I suspect we are going to have a new ally before this is done," Mica added with a wave toward the area where Sochen had gone.

"I hope so. I am not going to hang Janeh or Corinth yet. I hope to get some information out of them first. It is possible I will make a deal with Corinth and exile him instead of hanging the man -- but only if he can give us something of worthwhile for his miserable life."

Mica was not entirely happy with the idea, but he said nothing. This was in the King's hands now, and he was just as glad to be done with it.

Prince Kistrin walked them back out. Gregorian had stayed with the King, but he gave Mica nod that hadn't looked at all like the reactions he usually got from his older brother. It had been a nod that came between equals after a job well done.

"That was not an adventure I want to relive," Kistrin said softly. His guards trailed after the two of them while Merriweather walked slightly ahead, as though they all expected trouble, even here. "But thank you for taking such good care of me. I was in over my head, you know."

"You were very wise. You played dumb."

The Prince laughed aloud. He was already more himself after getting back home. Mica was having a little more trouble with the transition, but the time up in his workshop had helped.

"I am glad we both made it home because I didn't think it was going to happen there at the end," Kistrin admitted. His voice had softened. "I know you have secrets, Mica. Father and I discussed them last night. Your secrets are safe with my men and me. Now go home and rest. Make more butterflies. Make people happy again."

Prince Kistrin turned around and walked off, leaving them at the door.

Mica and Merriweather rode back down to the city with Storm and his men as their guards. They passed ruins -- but people were picking up their lives again. Mica would have stopped to help, but he felt so tired that all he could consider was getting home and have the soup that Ada and Gram had been making.

They didn't say much. No one argued when Mica turned to the temple square. It seemed to Mica that the place was almost back to normal already. Seldon waved from the steps of the temple of knowledge. Honoria smiled their way as they passed.

"The world has changed," Merriweather said softly. "I think we'll like it better if we ever get a chance to rest and enjoy it."

Mica agreed with a slight smile of his own.

A little later they found Shipley and Bear waiting at the edge of Shadow Walk.

"Nothing new today," the boy said. "And it's not quite safe yet, but they're rounding up most of those what fought against us. Bear, though, he wanted to go home now. I think he misses his bones."

The dog barked agreement.

"I don't want to ever leave the tower again," Mica said.

"I agree," Merriweather added. "I'll be glad to be hone and safe behind the walls -- and in time for food."

Mica grinned with delight.

Merriweather truly thought of Raventower as home.

The day had brightened, and Mica smiled as they passed Nyle who was working on trying to get the battered gate to properly open and close. He and Mica would have to work on the clockwork controls. Some of the soldiers and few of the people from the fishing village had begun rebuilding the outer wall, too. His home had taken a few hits, but she still looked steady.

There were more mercenaries in the courtyard. The group they'd left behind must have ridden like hell to get this far so quickly, and Storm was glad to see them safe.

"We brought it like you said, Storm," Enker said as he slapped Storm on the shoulder in greeting. He waved a hand toward the right. "And we brought him."

The troublesome, bread-loving horse stood with a few other mounts and looking around with some obvious worry. Mica laughed and leapt from his own mount and crossed to the beast.

Shipley pulled some bread out of his pocket and gave it to him. Mica laughed and thanked him, and then held the bread out to the animal.

He'd never seen a horse so happy. It didn't take long to get him settled into the coral with Kandris, and it looked as though they would get along fine. The clockwork horse looked intrigued. Nyle had come to settle them and even managed to find another piece of bread. Mica suspected the horse and Nyle would be friends before long.

Then Mica turned back to his home. Merriweather moved beside him, and he knew she still carefully watched for assassins. Probably wise. They didn't know how many Atrians, or people who sided with Corinth, might be free in Kamere.

Mica could set it aside for a moment, at least. They could focus on other aspects of life. It wasn't always going to be war and killing.

"We need to think about remodeling the inside of the tower," Mica said, taking Merriweather by surprise as they headed for the door. "We need to make it more into a home. It really wasn't under my parents, you know. I think we can do better, Merriweather. Think about what you want."

"Ah," she said and smiled.

"We'll let Ada and Gram design the kitchen," he said. She nodded agreement. "And the rest -- oh, we'll manage things."

She grinned again. "What about pine wood paneling? I saw some in the buildings down south, and it was gorgeous."

But he had stopped and looked back at the open sea, even with the cold wind in his face.

"Mica?"

"We still have a problem, Merriweather," he said softly. "And I will have to deal with it. Payton isn't dead, you know. There were no life-lights."

"Well, damn," she said. Then she took his arm. "We'll deal with him later."

He nodded and took her inside their home.

The End

PREVIEW: TOUCHED BY THE WILD

Pale mist held tenaciously to the ancient gnarled limbs and bright autumn leaves of chestnut oak and sugar maples along the trail. The dampness occasionally collected into small pools on the leaves, and then dropped an icy cascade of water, splashing down on the weary men and horses. The small party rode on, traversing the quiet woods through the damp morning and into the sodden afternoon.

The inclement autumn weather won quiet curses from the three guards, though Derry SanOsen accepted, and silently delighted, in the ride in the growing fog. This wasn't the first time he'd been wet, and he'd spent far more uncomfortable days since the last time he'd traversed these trails. The quiet ride through the mist-haunted hills of Lynashin was nothing less than a wonder to him.

Derry had never expected to come home again.

Home.

The single word made any hardship bearable today. Derry hadn't minded sleeping on the hard ground the last few days, eating trail food, or even riding in sodden cloaks. In one more day they would reach the golden halls of Tyleen Castle and Derry's four-year nightmare would be over. He'd been lucky to leave the muck-covered stinking cell where he'd been held on the Isles. King Robert, who had mistrusted everyone, had been assassinated by a servant. The new Regent, Olivia, had released Derry and several others, sending them back home as soon as they could travel.

The change had come too quickly. Twenty days ago -- or

maybe more since he'd lost track -- Derry had still been a prisoner and expected King Robert to order him killed, as he had ordered the deaths of so many who had shared that cell with him. Instead, he now rode where he could breathe clean air and watch raindrops collect on the edge of leaves, mirroring the world upside down in their reflections.

A symbol of his life, Derry supposed: upside down and backward. Nothing had gone right the last few years.

"Damn weather," Captain Killough growled as he brushed water off the back of his hand as though that particular drop offended him. Derry's horse shook his head, scattering more water through the mist. The older man gave Derry a quick glance and a bow of his head. "Begging your pardon for the language, your lordship, sir."

Derry shifted uncomfortably and hoped Killough took it as a dislike of the weather. The truth, though, was that he didn't feel much like a Lord of Lynashin. King Robert had stripped him of any such pretentions when he threw Derry into a prison cell with thieves, murderers, and more than a few who had done nothing wrong at all.

Like him.

"Lord Derry?"

"My apologies," he replied with a quick bow of his head. Dark hair fell across his eyes; he brushed it aside with a swift, nervous swipe of his fingers. "The weather doesn't bother me much, Captain Killough. I've always loved the wild places, almost as much as I loved Tyleen Castle."

Those were the most words he'd said at any given time since the Captain and his two men collected him at the docks, five days ago. Killough gave him a quick, startled look. Then the older man bit at his lower lip and gave an odd shrug. "Well, Tyleen hasn't changed much in the last four years, my lord."

A warning came in those polite words, but Derry didn't

want to hear it. He purposely shoved the sudden surge of anxiety aside. *I am going home!* He'd dreamed of returning to Tyleen from the day Queen Alisia had sent him to the northern islands as her envoy. The Queen had known she was sending him to a hostile court. She had known he was going to face trouble --

Derry leaned forward on his horse, huddled into the cloak, and fighting tremors that came at so clear a memory of being thrown in a cell. Captain Killough pulled his mount back, riding with Casey and Bay, the other two guards. Derry hadn't spoken much to any of them and suspected they thought him just another snobbish young lord. He didn't care ... much.

Derry's companions did give him the peace he craved and didn't push him into traveling faster, despite the miserable weather. Derry had peace and quiet, though he knew this wouldn't last for long. They were closer to Tyleen, both the city and the castle of his dreams. He thought he might even recognize this area and the brook. They hadn't stopped at any villages for the four nights, and they had seen very few people. He had washed in books, shaved with water heated in a pot and had Casey trim back his hair to a reasonable length. He wanted to be civilized when he came home, not some animal released from a cage.

Still, Killough hadn't taken him near any settlement. Derry now suspected that had been for a reason, just as Captain Killough had tried to give him some warning about Tyleen.

Damn. Derry didn't want trouble.

They took the stone-lined Old Road, a well-kept path this close to the capital. Soon Derry and his guards would pass through a few small villages and skirt the edges of farmlands closest to the city. His little party went unnoticed across the brook on an ancient stone bridge and then went down the other side past the woodcutter's cottage. The place was closed tight, despite it still being quite sunset. Derry hoped the old man was all right and wished to see that familiar gray-bearded face. He did not ask to stop, though, in case the news there might be unpleasant. He wanted no sorrow to mark these last miles home.

They reached the edge of a village not long afterward. The neat little cottages were locked up tight and the windows barred, even though the sun had barely touched the tips of the trees. A single man rushed towards a stockade, trying to herd a half dozen sheep ahead of him with frantic haste.

One scrawny and ragged young boy darted past Derry's group, startling the horses and winning a quick curse from Bay. Derry watched the boy disappear into the shadows between two buildings. He'd had the look of one of the homeless children who frequented the towns and villages, but they usually came begging of anyone on horseback. Only people of wealth rode, and especially beautiful horses like their mounts. Derry would have given the boy his cloak on such a cold, miserable day as this. He had no coin.

Derry had always hated to hear the tales of beggar children who died of the cold and hunger, abandoned on the streets. If he hadn't been the King's nephew, he would have been one of those children after his parents died.

Captain Killough rode up beside him, a hand on the knife at his belt and a scowl on his face. He carefully kept watch to both sides and clearly didn't like what he saw.

"Isn't this Glendalow?" Derry asked, feeling uncertain now because the town had never been this quiet and the mist hid the details of the place.

The question startled Captain Killough, but he gave a quick nod, focusing on Derry for a heartbeat, and then gave a cottage a glare as someone inside laughed. When the Captain looked back at Derry, he gave a nervous nod. "Yes, we've reached Glendalow," he said.

"This used to be a pleasant place." Derry felt a shiver retake him, and it had nothing to do with the mist and the cold. He wanted nothing good to have changed. "My friends and I used to ride here some days; a pleasant trip to a lovely and friendly village. What's happened?"

"Superstition, sir," Killough said with a sneer, though he seemed to relax a little. "A couple children went missing and maybe a few sheep as well, though I doubt for the same reasons. The locals seem to count the loss of the animals as important as the homeless children what disappeared. King Nevin believes there are bandits about in the woods, though his guards can't seem to track them. The locals insist there is a band of fae wandering about the area."

"Fae?" Derry felt the corners of his mouth pull upward in a brief smile. It felt odd and uncomfortable, making him wonder how long it had been since he last smiled. "I wouldn't think anyone would bring those old tales back out again."

"Maybe they just be looking for a little magic," Killough replied with a sigh. "These be hard times, after all."

"Have things gone that badly?" Derry asked. He immediately regretted the words. He didn't want to hear any tales of woe that might overlay the bright dreams that had kept him alive.

Maybe Killough even understood how Derry felt. Killough looked at Derry with a slight tilt of his head before he spoke. "Not so much as you'd see, your Lordship. There have been peculiar things here and there, like fields failing for no reason, especially in the south. Animals dying in the north as well -- I heard of an entire herd of deer dead in a field. There's been an odd quality to the air, though maybe that's just all this damned mist."

Derry felt another small smile come to him, and he accepted the touch of humor this time. He couldn't say he felt better for it, but he was glad for the slight change in attitude.

What would they do now? They'd be camping soon and have another damp cold night unless they rode on to Tyleen and reached the city about midnight. No, not a good idea. That would leave his group sitting at the gates or taking refuge in a traveler's inn outside the castle walls. Those places were not often safe or quiet. Besides, he wanted to see the High Castle in the light of day when he rode home. He was tired of shadows.

Maybe the time had come to quit acting like an animal hunted through the woods, too. "There is an inn here in town -- or there was," Derry said, looking down the rock-laid road. The mist hid buildings even a few feet away. Derry thought the fog came too quickly, gathering up in the shadows and spreading outward like a veil. He wanted out of the weather for the first time in days. "Do you think we might get rooms there tonight? I'd like a good rest and to cleaned up before I ride into Tyleen tomorrow."

Killough glanced his way and then did another quick check to the right and left. The man hadn't been this nervous before they entered this village. Was it the people who worried him or was it the idea of the fae gathering about in the nearby trees? Why hadn't they avoided Glendalow like all the other places they'd bypassed?

Because the King's guards were in the woods looking for bandits and it might not be wise to be slinking around in the trees? Someone might make a mistake, and this was not the time to take such a chance.

Having that thought and connection to what was happening felt like waking up. Derry wasn't entirely confident he wanted to be so aware, but he couldn't hide in his own gray and misty world forever. He had to prepare to go home to Tyleen, and stop huddling in the cloak, hoping not to be seen. That realization was like a slap in the face. He did not want to bring that cell home with him, so he had better start working at a change.

Derry sat up straighter and glanced around the little village again, wishing for signs of the good people he had known. "Is there a problem with staying here, Captain Killough?"

They rode a couple more paces before the older man spoke. The horses even seemed uneasy now. "Sir, I'm going to bold. We've stayed clear of places where you might be spotted. No use taking chances while getting you back home. Besides, you've disdained even the covering of a tent, your Lordship. Why the change now, to go to some local inn?"

"We'll be in Tyleen tomorrow," Derry said and stared down the Old Road where it went past the village. He remembered the curves, the streams, the sounds of the trees and the call of the birds. "I had better get used to being inside again before I set foot in Tyleen, don't you think?"

"Ah now, there's a bit of truth I hadn't considered. I won't complain of a warm meal and a dry bed for the night."

"And some of the local honeyed mead, I imagine." They were moving slowly forward, and Derry could just pick out the swaying sign, moving enticingly in the breeze. The Glendalow Inn had always been a friendly place, and Derry felt as though this was the first true link back to his former life. "Thank you for your escort, Captain Killough. I suspect that I might have simply wandered off, the state I was in."

"We haven't gotten you home yet, your lordship," Killough said with another nervous look around the area. Was he worried about something specific?

Derry didn't ask. He wanted peace, and he'd leave the worries to the Captain and his men for now. Then he looked around the mist-shrouded village and admitted a different truth aloud. "I seem to be having trouble simply connecting with where I am. Nothing seems real yet."

"I'm sure everything will come back to you, Lord Derry,"

Killough said with a worried glance his way. "I suspect you have not forgotten ... everything about Tyleen."

"You don't need to walk so carefully around what you are trying to say, Captain," Derry replied. "I understand your hints. I grew up in Tyleen castle, and we breathed politics from our first moment. I know enough to be careful of whom I annoy. I truly just hope to retire to some rooms and rest for a long, quiet time."

Killough looked oddly relieved. They'd reached the inn, and the older man swept off his horse and took hold of Derry's bridle. "You've been naught but polite to us, your Lordship. Even when it was plain you weren't clearheaded, you never put on airs nor complained about being uncomfortable."

"I was never as uncomfortable on this journey as I had been in that cell in the Isles," Derry replied and felt a shiver pass through him. He dismounted and let Bay take hold of his horse, listening to a few voices within the building, both a welcome and a frightening sound. Strangers.

"Too many Lords moan and groan if they have to ride out before the sun is halfway up the sky, or if there is dew on the ground to dampen their pretty boots," Killough said with a hardly concealed snarl of disgust. "I feared you were one of them."

Well, that certainly wasn't a very politic thing to say on Killough's part, though Derry appreciated the acceptance that went with those words. Killough's words had kindled a rush of memories about those people and brought a grimace of distaste. The worst of the bunch had been led by his cousin, Prince Egan. He and his friends had made games of escaping from the Prince's view...

"Boys' games," he mumbled aloud. He didn't feel much like a boy anymore.

"Lord Derry, sir?"

Derry had been staring at the door, unmoving while his

mind tried to sort through uncomfortable reflections. He could feel all the aches and pains he'd tried to ignore on the horse. The wet cloak seemed little protection against the cold, damp breeze -- but even so, he couldn't make himself walk forward to the door and take that step back into a world he had left behind.

"I have no coin," Derry remembered again.

"The King sent us with plenty to cover far more expenses than we've had, your lordship. Casey and Bay will take care of the horses," Killough said and signaled for the two to take the mounts away to the stable behind the building. "Let's go in and see if we can arrange for some hot food and soft beds."

Derry nodded, but he still didn't move forward. His heart pounded too hard. The door itself, with the old wooden pull and the half-rusting hinges, seemed a pattern of memory to him. This wasn't what he had dreamed about, though, in that cell. The Inn was neither part of the dreams of Tyleen, nor the nightmare of the cell ... and for a few heartbeats he felt lost.

Derry thought he heard odd, pretty bells, but Killough nudged him forward and up the two steps. Killough even reached past and pushed the heavy door open, and Derry stepped inside rather than be pushed forward again. He still had some control over his life.

The common room felt warm and welcoming after the cold, wet days they'd spent riding. Derry found the interior little changed with the haphazard arrangement of tables and benches. Yes, there on the wall was his own pennant, which he'd given to the owner years ago, a proclamation that put this little place under his care, for all the good that did when he'd been gone. A pot with rabbit stew, by the smell of it, hung over the central pit and the fire gave off the welcome sweet scent of cherry wood.

Derry found more people inside than he had expected since they were relatively quiet. Nervous, worried men, he thought. They didn't all believe the tales about the fae, did they? The patrons gave the two strangers looks of worry, then went back to their own meals and drink. Conversations rose a little, bringing a dull hum of noise to the room.

Derry glanced quickly around, his eyes adjusting to the shadows and smoke-filled light. The table he and his friends had usually taken remained empty, there in the corner under the pennant. Derry didn't cross to sit there. Instead, he hurried to a smaller table in a darker corner, pulling the cloak around him as he moved and wishing he could simply hide. He sat with his back to the corner of the wall, there in the darkest shadow he could find.

Killough settled on the opposite bench and turned slightly so he kept a view of the door, and he eyed the innkeeper with some trepidation as the man neared. Finil stood over six feet tall; a big man with wild gray hair and a matching beard, and a no-nonsense attitude that had kept the place free from most brawls. He allowed no trouble from the commoners, and since Derry and his friends were the only nobility to favor the Inn, he didn't need to worry about their manners. Derry had brought no one here who wasn't a friend. He'd been on a first-name basis with Finil, and his wife Cara, for years.

The man crossed to the table, nervously wiping his hands on the cloth in his belt and giving a polite bow of his head. "What can I serve you, gentlemen?" he asked, cautious as he always had been around strangers.

The words struck Derry like the stab of a knife into his heart. This was a sure sign that he couldn't go back to his old life. Derry had held tightly to the hope of return for all those years in the cell, but now as he faced someone who had known so well, and didn't even recognize him, Derry knew the truth.

"I think we'd like to start with some honeyed mead," Killough said, filling the silence. "And dinner for four. The other two will join us after they've seen to the horses."

Finil nodded ... and kept nodding as though his head had come loose from a spring. He took a sudden deep breath and placed both of his large, scarred hands on the equally disfigured table, bending down to stare straight into Derry's face. His hazel eyes brightened, and he grinned with such delight that a mirroring smile played at the corners of Derry's mouth.

"Holy Gods All!" Finil's gasp drew the attention of people nearby. Finil's sudden laugh put everyone at ease as the big man stood straighter, and the patrons paid no more attention than the occasional glance they gave to all the others. The ambient noise covered most of what anyone said, even at Derry's table. "Not a word of it, just showing up without a bit of warning!"

"I haven't even been back to Tyleen yet, Finil," Derry answered softly, surprised by the emotional outburst which proved more healing than he could have imagined. "But how could I pass by my favorite inn and not stop for some of your fine mead and food?"

"You honor me, Prince Derry." The man rubbed the back of his hand across his eyes. "Not even home yet, but you thought to stop here."

"It's Lord Derry, Finil. You know better," he said softly and with a bit of warning.

"You were born a prince," the man replied with an unexpected conviction and a bit more fire in his dark eyes. "No decree to please the queen can change that --"

"I am Lord Derry SanOsen," Derry said and reached out to put a hand on the man's arm. "That's title enough for me. Don't anger the Queen on my account."

"Yes, of course," the man said, though some old anger lingered in his face for a moment. Then he grinned again. "A fine meal for you, Lord Derry. Will you spend the night?"

"If you have room," Derry replied with a glance around at

the crowd.

"Not to worry. These are common room people, most who would ha' spent the night outside in the fields at other times." He shook his shaggy head but said nothing of the trouble they had here in town. "You'll have the best room, Lord Derry. And a fine meal."

Finil spun on his heel, and Derry swore the man all but danced across the room as he headed back into the kitchen.

"I was right," Killough said, leaning back and looking Derry over as though they'd just met. "You are not like any of the other young lords of Tyleen, who wouldn't have a kind word for a commoner to save their lives."

"You must not know any of my friends then," Derry replied. He felt more at ease. "I know four years won't have changed the likes of Shannon SanSota. We are very much alike."

"It isn't time that changes a man, your lordship," Killough said. He must have seen the worry in Derry's face, and he spread his hand in a gesture Derry couldn't quite read. "I haven't had much contact with Lord Shannon, though. Still, hear me out on this: I came to serve at Tyleen barely ten days after you had sailed. The castle was in an uproar still, with your friends angry long before King Robert sent word that he had locked up the *spy*. Your friends could do nothing, though, and many left the King's court soon afterwards to avoid trouble with ... to avoid trouble. You were the lynchpin for your group at the court with your high rank, whether Prince or Lord -- but mostly because people liked you."

This was not what Derry had wanted to hear, but the news might have been worse, considering the situation he'd left behind. "I hadn't considered any changes that might happen," he admitted and finally put off his wet cloak and settled it on the seat beside him. No reason to stay covered now, though he wasn't certain the others had heard Finil. "I had imagined life went on much the same without me. I -- I imagined a great deal while in the Fairfall prison, waiting through those damned long days."

"I'm sure that now you're back, your friends will be more themselves again."

"I do look forward to seeing them," he said and frowned. "I would have expected Shannon to meet us --"

"King Nevin hasn't announced your return to court yet," Killough said softly. "When he sent the three of us, the King said he wasn't sure he trusted the note that you were going to be sent home on the next ship. He didn't want to create a stir if it weren't true. And besides, he didn't want Queen Alisia to know you were heading back to court."

"Oh, and won't that be a wonderful surprise for her," Derry replied with a sigh. A new worry worked up through his thoughts. "Queen Alisia never cared much for me. Is that why we've kept off the Old Road?"

"Mostly," Killough admitted and appeared pleased that he'd picked up that idea. "By the time I'd first come to serve at court, the Queen was under a great deal of displeasure, shall we say, since she sent you on that ill-fated journey to a place where everyone knew you would not be welcome. Lord Shannon was even blatant about you being sent away because you outshined her boys."

"Gods, Shannon --" The words caught in his throat. Shannon couldn't have been such a fool!

Killough nodded at the unspoken words. "Not a wise thing to say, no. The Queen exiled him, but don't worry. King Nevin and the troops, including me, came ridin' back, having settled the trouble in the south, and saved the young sir. Then the King raised hell over you being sent off to the Isles on the Queen's orders. That was before the news even came of you being locked away. When the King learned your fate, well Queen Alisia retired to the Daria Temple up in the far north for her exile. She's only been back to court for a few months. I can't say living with the acolytes did anything to improve her temper, and she's certainly no humbler for her religious sojourn. Egan chose to go with her. Roe did not."

Derry stared at Killough in shocked dismay as the room seemed to swirl, voices melding into a rush of sound. He took several deeper breaths. Maybe the man joked. Maybe. "You can't seriously mean the queen was exiled from court because of me."

Killough gave him another of those odd looks, his eyes narrowed as though they might not be speaking the same language -- or that Derry was too dense to understand. "You are the only child of the King's late, and much beloved, brother. People call you Lord to appease the Queen, but we all know you are a Prince of the Blood, your Lordship, sir. King Nevin favored you, as well --"

"Favored me?" Derry asked. He began to think he didn't understand anything.

"I heard a great deal about you in the last few years," Killough admitted and drew Derry's startled attention again. "You weren't forgotten, you know. And this is what I realized: The King never let his own sons run wild with their friends, nor come and go as they pleased from court. I heard tales about wild races where you won even against the King -- and when he wouldn't let his own boys join in. I gathered Prince Tevin didn't care much, being Heir and knowing you couldn't steal his glory. Prince Egan and Prince Roe, though, listened too much to their mother, and she told them you were stealing their rightful place before the people. You stole their glory."

Derry stared at the older man and felt utterly dumbfounded. Though he had been nearly twenty when the Queen sent him to assess the state of affairs in the Isles, he had been young in many ways. Derry had been trained for such work and handled a few diplomatic assignments for King

Nevin, though those had been within Lynashin where he'd been well known. Protected -- and that protection disappeared when he had sailed away.

Shannon had advised him to take a ship to anywhere but the Isles and wait this trouble out. The King would be back soon from the trouble in the south, after all. Derry, perhaps unwisely, had refused to be a party to anything that might dishonor his family name, which had been left to him when his parents died.

"Lord Derry, sir?" Killough said softly and looked worried once more.

"I was too happy," Derry said with a rueful shake of his head. How could he have been so blind? "I knew Egan never liked me, but then he was snide to everyone, even those who followed him like puppies behind a cook. I knew the Queen didn't like me, but she didn't much care for the King either, so I didn't take it personally."

"But it was personal," Killough said softly, his head bowed a bit as he leaned closer. "Any time you stood beside Egan people would think you the better choice."

"That would hardly matter, even if it were true. Egan isn't the crown prince --"

"Not yet," Killough replied. Derry didn't like the ominous sound of those words. "The Heir has had an uncommon run of bad luck the last half year, but he's survived it all so far. However, we look to Egan with more worry now."

"Ah. I never saw Egan and Roe as anything but foppish young princes, aping the styles of their foreign mother. She always thought Lynashin backward, you know. She's hated everything about our lovely island from the day she arrived. She instilled that disdain in Egan and Roe, but at least the King took Tevin from her hands."

"She won't be glad to see you back, Lord Derry. Just so you are warned. Until you are in the King's company again, you are in some danger from her."

"Should we worry about someone heading for Tyleen and giving her word?"

"Not from here," Killough replied with a wave of his hand toward the others in the crowded room, and more coming in, a rush from near darkness beyond. "I made certain we arrived at sunset for that reason. Remember that they worry about their fear of the fae, so most everyone has already taken to cover for the night. Besides, the King will be careful these last few days of anyone riding in to see the Queen, her servants, or her sons. We're safe enough still."

"We'll leave early in the morning," Derry added and almost regretted that decision. This would have been a nice place to hide and rest for a while, though he still longed for Tyleen. "With only a day left on our journey, I'm betting we'll be safe enough for the night."

"Good." Killough looked at his rough hands for a moment, staring as though they held answers that he couldn't find anywhere else.

"Egan and Roe really had no choice in how they acted. Their mother always controlled them and got more covetous after Tevin officially went to be his father's son and heir at ten. She had power over the other two, and they had no choice in what they did."

"Well, and neither did you have a choice, except if you had chosen to shun the good King's friendship. That wouldn't ha' been wise, even if you had it in you."

"True." Derry took a deep breath and sat back, letting some of the tension ease from his shoulders. Whispers spread all around them and heads turned their way, but no one appeared hostile. "So, is there anything else blatantly obvious that you want to point out to me before I walk back into Tyleen with all my youthful innocence and lack of tact?"

Killough gave a little laugh but fell silent as Finil and his daughter Mina arrived with plates and platters of food and drink. The table was soon covered in bread, cheeses, thinly sliced venison, bowls of rabbit stew, and cups of honeyed mead. Mina gave him a tentative little bow of her head and scurried away. She'd still been hanging at her mother's skirts the last time Derry had seen her.

The smell of so many foods startled him, and he stared at the food for a moment too long, trying to remember the last time he'd seen such a feast. Then he looked up with a start. "Thank you, Finil. This looks very fine, indeed."

"Lord Derry, sir --" Finil began, then bit at his lip for a moment before he continued, his hands mangling the cleaning cloth he kept at his waist. "I can see you ha' been ill-kept these last years. You're too thin and pale, and I can see scars that were not there the last time you dined here. There will be prayers of thanks in the Temple next Holy Day. Now eat a bit and get some rest. You look weary to the bone, you do."

Finil spun and hurried away before Derry could reply.

"Well, I'd say he's covered the matter pretty well, your lordship," Killough said as he began ladling out food like a servant. "Except for one thing: don't change now. I gave you the warning because the Queen has only been back at the court since late summer, and she's not going to be happy to see you returned already to step on her glory again."

"I was never a threat to Queen Alisia or her sons." Derry felt a flicker of anger try to take him, but he'd learned to tame that emotion in the first weeks in a cell where he kept company with men older and tougher than him. He could feel the chill of those damp, stone walls. He focused back on Killough and buried that memory, though the chill remained. "She was petty to send me away, Killough -- and she sent me to the Isles knowing I wasn't going to return."

"But you have."

Derry blinked.

Killough pushed one of the cups toward him and Derry caught the heady scent of fine mead. "Sip this. Just a bit, since you've had little to eat the last few days." The Captain paused while Derry obeyed, picking up the cup with trembling hands. The mead tasted sweet and warm. He thought it might help spread some warmth through him. "I'll tell you some truths. The Queen is a jealous woman, Lord Derry. People liked you, so she was bound to take notice and turn Egan and Roe against you. Roe has slipped the leash a bit of late. Prince Egan never did. I can't say the time of rough beds, and dawn prayers at the Temple helped the young sir. He's still an ill-mannered braggart with absolutely no good sense of style."

Those words came close to winning a laugh from Derry, an unexpected surge of humor. Egan had always been a pretentious fop. He'd remained in his mother's care, while everyone else at court grew up around him -- and she expected him to be a good king?

No. Queen Alisia expected him to be her puppet. There was a sobering thought. Queen Alisia was a foreigner, and she couldn't rule in her own name. She had always favored her second and Derry had thought she was only being petty. Now, a little older and far wiser, he could see the Queen's manipulations and worried move about Tevin than for himself.

"So, there are two people who are not going to be happy to see me returned to court." Derry played with the soft bread, tearing off pieces, but eating none of it yet. Old memories and new worries bounded through his aching head, but he began to sort them out. He especially remembered Egan who had dressed in velvets and lace, though the style didn't suit the pudgy young man. He'd have grown older in the last four years. Wiser? From Killough's observations that was not the case.

Casey and Bay entered the room and headed toward

them. Their moment of privacy was over. "Thank you for the discussion, Captain Killough. I don't like to think I would have been blind to the trouble when we reached home, but my mind simply has not been making the proper connections. Being here at Glendalow Inn has helped. This was a place I enjoyed."

"With good cause. The food is excellent," Killough replied, sopping up some stew with a bit of bread. His brown eyes narrowed. "You'd do well to try at least some of it, your lordship."

"I will. I'm working up to it." Derry still toyed with the bread that never reached his mouth. "I am glad we had this discussion, Captain. You likely saved me from a rude and rather uncomfortable, awakening at court."

"From all I've heard, you were as fine and kind of a young gentleman as was ever at court," Killough said and grinned at the snort of amusement those words won from Derry. "It would be a shame if ... if some people ruined your homecoming. Forewarned may shield you from falling into a trap."

"Yes, thank you," Derry replied. He finally ate the bit of bread and cheese, chewing slowly as the thought about going home in this new light. It did not dim the joy he felt at returning. If anything, it made arriving home seem more real.

He'd be careful, though Derry wasn't certain taking care would help much.

ABOUT THE AUTHOR:

Hello!

I am an eclectic and prolific author whose has published in a number of genres, including Young Adult Mystery, Contemporary Fantasy, Epic Fantasy, Science Fiction and numerous works on writing. While I started on the outer edges of traditional publication with sales to small press and magazines publishers, I have since moved most of my work to the Indie world, and I am madly in love with the new world of publishing and the direct contact with readers.

I live in Nebraska with my husband, my cats, and a small but entirely useless dog.

Connect with Zette:

Web Site:

http://lazette.net

Facebook:

http://www.facebook.com/lazette.gifford

Joyously Prolific Blog:

http://zette.blogspot.com/

www.ingramcontent.com/pod-product-compliance
Lightning Source LLC
Chambersburg PA
CBHW051438260626
47162CB00001B/151